*By the same author*

The Brinkman
A Square Called Silence
The Girl with the Golden Lion

# A TALK with the ANGELS

## A Thriller by DESMOND MEIRING

St. Martin's Press
New York

Library of Congress Cataloging in Publication Data

Meiring, Desmond.
  A talk with the angels.

  I. Title.
PR9381.9.M44T35   1986        823        85-25052
ISBN 0-312-78476-7

First published in Great Britain by Secker & Warburg Ltd.

First U.S. Edition

10 9 8 7 6 5 4 3 2 1

To Steve Cox

We believe that the provisions of Islam and its teachings are all-inclusive, encompassing all of our people in this world and the hereafter. And those who think that these teachings are concerned only with the spiritual and ritualistic aspects of things are mistaken in this belief. For Islam is a faith and a ritual, a nation and a nationality, a religion and a state, spirit and deed, holy text and a sword . . .

Hassan el Banna, who founded the Muslim Brotherhood in Egypt in 1928.

# Contents

# Contents

# I

# A Talk with the Angels

'He may guess that the Angels want to see him,' said the man in front, Abdallah Hassan, dark and thin and restless.

The Angels were the Angels of the Sword.

'He'll come,' said the big man, Abbas Sidki, who sat behind him and looked forward past him through the windscreen. The taxi stood hard right against the start of the small square in front of El Azhar, whose double-arched entrance rose thirty metres ahead; *Bab el Muzaiyinin*, the Gate of the Barbers, because this is where the students used to have their heads shaved. El Azhar was the oldest university in the Arab world, and still the greatest for Islamic teaching, repository of a thousand years of thought and debate about the Koran and the Sunna, the Prophet's actions and sayings established as legally binding; an austere and meticulously carved cornerstone of Islamic civilization.

'*Shortah!*' said Abdallah in front, in warning. But the policeman, in his white summer uniform and black beret, a black Sam Browne round his waist and over his shoulder, the black holster for a Browning 7.65 mm automatic pistol on his right, evidently had other things on his mind, for he walked straight past the taxi, not accosting it for parking unlawfully.

'Take it quietly,' said Abbas Sidki, and Abdallah jerked a shoulder in irritation, and lit himself another Cleopatra cigarette, King Size, with filter, from his white pack of twenty. The silhouette of his head, one side of his beard, jumped black in the mushroom of flame. For Abdallah, cigarettes were a defence, nails with which to hold back a hostile universe. The men all had huge tasks to do in that universe. Abdallah, *Abd 'Allah*, meant Servant of God. They were all four going to be Servants of God that night, thought Abbas Sidki, he and Abdallah and the two outside.

You could learn about God in there, Abbas Sidki knew, through the Gate of the Barbers. Just inside the forecourt you took off your sandals or shoes. You could carry them yourself, held sole to sole for decency, or give them to the doorman, who would put them in a numbered pigeonhole on the wall. You passed under the minaret of Qaitbai, a slim supple jet of stone ecstatic in the sky, and came out into the great open courtyard. By day the *'Ulama*, the Learned, taught here. Each sat like Socrates, ringed by disciples, throwing out questions to provoke myriad answers. He expanded his pupils' knowledge, correcting it most carefully, always within the frontiers of the unchanging orthodox Islamic universe. Here in the weeks before their examinations you would see the students walking with their Korans held open in front of them, their eyes glazed, lips fluttering like the wings of moths, as they memorized the suras, the chapters. They would be judged strictly by the mirror exactitude with which they recited every syllable and Koranic accent, pause and elision; the meaning could come later. There was a link, thought Abbas Sidki, the bigger of the two who sat in ambush in that taxi, between that dominating ruthless formalism and the mathematics on the walls of El Azhar ahead – or of any mosque – the curves and circles and ellipses and squares and arches and arabesques of Islam, that superb interlaced geometry which allowed no representation of the human face or form, that intricate script as soberly majestic as written Arabic itself. The form was all, or nearly; the vaulting architechtonic magnificence of Allah far transcended anything merely human; it was the welfare of the *'Umma*, the Islamic Community, that mattered, the communal living out of the glorious harmonies of the divine plan, not the life of any one person. That night they would judge a man, Suleiman Talkhan. If Suleiman Talkhan was a traitor,

Abbas Sidki knew the Prophet's precept:

'Whosoever amongst you sees an abomination, he must correct it with his hands; if he is unable, then with his tongue; if he is unable, then with his heart.'

Abbas Sidki glanced quickly out of the left back window of the taxi. He was more on edge than he had let Abdallah Hassan in front see. This was no place to hang about in at that hour. The next policeman to pass might be one of the much harsher special police in their bottle-green uniforms and black jackboots and astronauts' helmets. It was already gone seven. The taxi had come fifteen minutes before from Opera Square up Sharia el Azhar, passing under a light blue metal pedestrian bridge, now seventy metres behind. Painted on it in white was:

MINISTRY OF DEFENCE
ENGINEERS' ADMINISTRATION

It seemed solidly built; hordes passed over it. To the left was Khan el Khalili and the Muski, Cairo's greatest bazaar concentration. Here too by the taxi the street and small square hummed with life. Most were Egyptians, men in long white or striped galabiahs, and skull caps or short turbans, or dressed Western in open-necked shirts and slacks. There were a few Saudis and Kuwaitis, mostly visiting for the fleshpots forbidden in their own countries, in long white robes and white or chequered red-and-white headdresses held down by black-ringed *ogals* – once used for hobbling camels. Women were few, most encased totally in shapeless black abayas. Abbas saw the tourists too, the *khawwaghat*, foreigners. Most were very old or very young. Many young girls bared expanses of flesh at which Abbas Sidki, male but also and more profoundly Muslim, recoiled instinctively. The older group seemed exclusively American. Perhaps old Europeans did not travel. Again the women predominated. They looked dehydrated, their skin parched, their faces heavily wrinkled, mouths often like steel traps. Predatory and formidable, they clearly ruled their men. Probably they ate them too; the men were much fewer. These wore shirts of violent hues over their pants, shrieking against their white skin, and remarkable headgear:

caps, straw hats, Stetsons. It was a cacophonic uniform of innocence. Generally pear-shaped, these men had the dangerous docility of fed sharks. Most wore glasses too. The North American culture, granting its devotees affluence, evidently gouged their sight back from them in return, gradually but inexorably, as it had robbed them of their grace.

These gaunt invaders were now themselves being led off like lambs to the slaughter. The guides from their Hilton or Sheraton or Meridien or Shepheard's hotels were shepherding their charges to those shops in Khalili's Caravanserai or the Muski whose owners had had the sense to offer the best rake-offs to these guides on everything bought there. It was elegant fraud. Stemming off from the Sharia Gohar el Qaid were the Scent, Spices, Goldsmiths' and General Bazaars, myriad small shops in twisting alleys, for ornaments and tables of brass and copper finely inscribed, Bedu coffee-pots and jars and beautiful blue Egyptian glassware, clothes and rich carpets from Isfahan and Afghanistan and shrewd fakes from Egypt, gold in all forms, some sold by weight, leather belts, bags, wallets, poufs, pretty silver anklets from Siwa Oasis for slave-girls or princesses, rings and necklaces of precious and semi-precious stones, red-black amethysts from the Red Sea's coral depths, scarabs of all sizes, miniature sphinxes and pyramids and see-through plates and whole arrays of Pharaonic heads — a huge gaudy rain of glittering bric-à-brac; you were generally a fool here if you finally paid more than two-thirds of the asking price.

But the Khan el Khalili and Muski had no monopoly in deception. A hundred metres half-left from Abbas Sidki, across the pulsing Sharia el Azhar, was a great parking square. Past it was the Mosque of Sayyidna el Hussein, Muhammed's grandson, whose head was allegedly deposited there in 1153. It was Cairo's main congregational mosque, shut to non-Muslims. Here, Abbas Sidki recalled, the dog Anwar es-Sadat (and might God always bless Khalid el Islambouli and his companions who had bravely executed him, paying with their lives to correct *that* abomination!) came often, to be photographed from every angle. Sadat had always shown the most

4

photogenic dust-mark on his brow, from bowing so piously to the ground in this most public place.

Far too public for an abduction, thought Abbas Sidki, but it was the best he could do. Talkhan lectured in philosophy at the University of Ain Shams, The Eye of the Sun. He lived here – up the lane to the right past El Azhar, then left, in a hostel. But people pullulated: Abbas had not dared to try to take him there. Once they could get him out here, the Angels had a safe house a few hundred metres off. There were risks. Talkhan might scream for the police, or struggle, and the police could stop them. The Angels had to rely on the momentum of surprise.

Abbas Sidki switched his eyes to the back of the man in front. Abdallah Hassan was twenty-three, one of Abbas Sidki's cell. He wore a taxi-driver's casual shirt and slacks. He was in fact a qualified pharmacist from Cairo University. His two colleagues by the wall to the right were dressed similarly. Both were clean-shaven. A full beard was no longer basic to an Islamic Militant's uniform. In the mass witch-hunt after Sadat's killing on 6 October 1981 the Militants had learned disguise fast. The men's beards and long white galabiahs and cowls had gone like magic from the universities and public places, with the women's *ziyy el Islami*, that robed their hair, head, forehead, even faces with full veils, and their hands with gloves, in order to separate the sexes physically in public, like curtains or membranes. But the Militants had soon been back, more subtly and dangerously, looking like anyone now, much readier to discuss their austere philosophy and more skilled and painstaking in convincing others of its magnificent and total imperatives. The two men of Abbas Sidki's cell who stood now by the taxi had that dedication. They would risk torture and execution; so to die in Allah's service was a short cut to paradise. They knew their privileges.

The shorter of these two, Fuad Wahbah, was twenty-four and a graduate civil engineer. Heavy-shouldered, he had been a good amateur boxer. The other, Omar el Masri, Omar the Egyptian, was twenty-two, and surprisingly fair and blue-eyed – heritage of some hero from Napoleon's invasion in 1798,

5

perhaps, or from the British troops that ousted him. He was a fourth-year medical student at Cairo University. The revolt was by an élite, who saw they had much to reform. Under Sadat corruption had flourished in Egypt like luxurious weeds, soiling even his family. This society was rotten, and Sadat had not cleansed it. The reformist élite had struck bloodily three times against Sadat's Establishment since April 1974. Sadat could never crush them finally. One Egyptian observer said of them: 'For every group that is liquidated, two or three new organizations spring up spontaneously.' The rebels were like dragons' teeth. Their movement would not die until its root causes were dead, and these were still strongly alive. Islamic Fundamentalism had that inexpugnable vitality.

As Abbas Sidki knew with great pride, this bright and shining youth, these fine young men and women quite unsentimentally disposed to martyrdom, came now increasingly to join *his* group, the *Malaikat es-Sayf*, the Angels of the Sword, a name still so secret that few outside had ever heard of it. These volunteers followed the vision of the Islamic Revolution in Iran. That hung before them mesmeric and constant as a great star, giving hope – for there lay the proof that the thing could be done, and now; so why not in Egypt? And these were the young élite who could do it – no mere ragtail bunch, half mercenary, not even from a downtrodden working class. These were young professionals and the cream of the universities, often from the top and most bitterly competitive four faculties of Medicine, Engineering, Technical Military Science, Pharmacy. They were committed to serving the true Islam at literally any cost. Abbas Sidki had watched Khalid el Islambouli, pressed against the bars inside the cage in the military court with his 23 co-defendants, shouting his contempt back at his judges as they sentenced him to death.

No one could doubt that Abbas Sidki's own commitment to this sublime revolt was any less complete. You could not ignore his impact. Muhammed Abbas Sidki was a big man, 6 foot 1 or 1 metre 85 in height and weighing 190 pounds or 86 kilos, naked save for his short black beard. He was dark-skinned, and his dominant feature was his eyes. They were black and glittering, the eyes of a passionately single-minded man, a leader. This fixed quality made them both compelling and slightly malignant. You would not forget them. Abbas Sidki would lead from the front, always assuming the highest risks for himself, generously arrogant.

He saw Hassan's shoulders in front tighten suddenly.

'What?'

'I have him now in my rear mirror. His taxi's stopped just behind.'

Suleiman Talkhan came home very regularly on Tuesday evenings at this hour, from private lessons he gave near Ain Shams. Abbas Sidki and his cell knew that. Good terrorism required learning a victim's timetables exactly. A man was his patterns of behaviour. The less they varied, the more vulnerable he was.

Abbas Sidki looked back carefully through the rear window. Talkhan was paying off his driver. His taxi moved off. As Talkhan stepped forward, Wahbah and El Masri closed in on each side. Talkhan was a slight man, prematurely bald, quick in speech and manner. He looked swiftly at each man and tried to break at once. El Masri held him. Wahbah, the boxer, stepped in neatly half in front of him and hit him with his right hand, a blow to the solar plexus so crisp that it could not have travelled more than fifteen centimetres. Abbas Sidki would not have seen it had he not been watching closely. Evidently nobody else had. As Talkhan sagged, the two men caught him easily from either side and walked him to the taxi. Abbas Sidki leaned quickly to his right and opened the back door. They pushed Talkhan in, Wahbah on his other side, the door shut. El Masri had got in in front, beside the driver. Abdallah Hassan pulled the taxi away from the kerb easily, in no hurry, showing no alarm. No one walking outside seemed interested.

Talkhan was still leaning forward in the back seat between Wahbah and Abbas Sidki, sucking in air in agony; he was not going to make any lunges for escape just yet. He would do so without doubt if and whenever he could. Abbas Sidki knew that Talkhan had never lacked rapid intelligence, only loyalty.

7

You were what your stars made you. Talkhan had to betray someone, some time – the trait was in him indelibly, like an uneasy smile that he could never quite efface.

In the beginning, Talkhan had been a most devoted Islamic Fundamentalist. He was then an assistant lecturer at Cairo University, under its renowned Professor of Philosophy, Doctor Hassan Hanafi. A phenomenologist, Hassan Hanafi was politically left, but took pride in not permitting his politics to enter his professional teaching. It was said that he sacked Talkhan in mid-1981 for doing just that, for proselytizing for Islamic Fundamentalism in his classes. Talkhan had found an alternative post in Ain Shams easily enough, but clearly he resented no longer being in the very first flight of his profession. That summary dismissal from Cairo, Egypt's and probably the Arab world's top university for the humanities, unhinged something in him. From then on he bore a grudge, against Cairo University, against life, against destiny, and even, for some obscure and deadly need for vengeance at any cost, against Islamic Fundamentalism itself. He began to pick diligently away at it, apparently forgetting that he had sworn his life's allegiance to it with the Angels of the Sword, in a darkened room before a Koran and an unsheathed dagger. So for the last months Abbas Sidki had watched Talkhan like a hawk, sensing the battle in and for his soul as keenly as any fine priest or psychiatrist, swaying it discreetly when he could; as cell leader he was ultimately responsible for it. But a month before, Abbas had begun to feel that he had lost.

The day before, he had known it. Talkhan had started by sometimes not being available when the Angels tried to contact him. Abbas usually had at least one meeting weekly with his cell. Talkhan suddenly ceased to attend them. Ten days before, Abbas had asked his Upper Council to have Talkhan followed by members of another Angels cell whom he would not know. These cells were hermetically sealed off one from the other, only their leaders contacting their commanding Council; if the authorities caught a cell member and worked him over until he talked (which the Angels, being realists, knew could happen) he could tell them little or nothing about the rest of the structure. The news had reached Abbas the day before at 9 pm that at 7.30 that evening a second Angels cell had seen Talkhan in the Groppi's café on the arrowhead where Sharia Kasr el Nil meets Sharia Muhammed Bassiuni at Suleiman Pasha Square, drinking Turkish coffee and one of Groppi's excellent fresh lemon-juices. That in itself was harmless. It could even be seen as demonstrating good social taste.

But the fact that a certain Tarek Daniel Gad, also known to the Angels, had been sitting at the next table could hardly be read in the same way, the less so because scraps of paper were seen to pass surreptitiously between the two men. For Tarek Daniel Gad was a colonel in charge of an anti-terrorist police group which specialized in investigating and hunting down secret political organizations and Militant Islamic groups. Whether the first assignation evidently planned between Talkhan and Gad had actually taken place yet or not, it was obviously imperative to stop Talkhan at once. It had to be shown that a member, honoured in being admitted as a lifetime commitment to this select society of the Angels of the Sword, could logically leave it only in death.

Talkhan's ferret eyes were perking up again, flickering to the man on each side of him, then towards the world outside. But the taxi was moving rapidly now, already well past the last of the Khan el Khalili bazaar area to the left. If Talkhan managed to jump out at this speed he would probably kill himself. Abbas would not have minded that, but not just yet. He wanted a small talk with Talkhan first. He saw Talkhan's thin hands clench and open. It could have been a gesture of supplication. Talkhan would know what they were going to do to him. He would try anything at any moment now –

'Khalli baalak!' said Abbas Sidki gently. 'Watch out for yourself, now!'

He moved his left hand so that Talkhan could see. There was a Browning 9 mm automatic pistol in it, lengthened by the tube of a silencer. Abbas held it resting on his right thigh, nice and easy, and pointing a little towards the back of the taxi, thoughtfully, so that if he had to shoot and the bullet at that point-blank range passed straight through Talkhan's body, it would not enter Wahbah's also, on the other side. That way he could kill Talkhan cleanly, harming no one else, and no one outside the taxi would be any the wiser.

'You're all mad!' said Talkhan loudly. '*Magánin!* What the devil is *that* for? And why this brutal physical attack? I've done nothing!'

But his tone was brittle. Talkhan was not a happy man.

'Then you've nothing to fear. We'll just have a little talk.'

Talkhan's eyes flickered to each side again, like those of a dog caught stealing, assessing the punishment.

'You're going to kill me anyway!'

'Why the guilt, Talkhan?'

They had come to the first crossroads. The second ahead was the great Salah Salem Avenue which led left outside the old city walls to Nasr City and the international airport, and right to the Citadel. The first street due left just here was Sharia el Mansuriya. Abbas Sidki glanced back. The policeman at the crossroads was taking no notice of them. Talkhan had lost a last chance there; he had not screamed out. High up behind that policeman, two or three hundred metres back, was Gohar el Kaid, the barbed wire of an old army camp, still dimly lit; high sand, for the desert pressed in relentlessly and without cease upon the great dustbowl of Cairo. At the right of the Sharia el Mansuriya a wall two and a half metres high ran some forty metres, then stopped abruptly. Here began a row of buildings six to eight stories high, often with shops or garages on the ground floor. The higher stories flourished laundry like the brave flags of a final stand. There were kiosks to sell cigarettes and sweets and newspapers and magazines and instant food in the street. Along its centre was a narrow island bearing twelve-metre pylons, arched lights at their tops. Abdallah Hassan drew the taxi into the kerb to the right. There was a break in the island another forty metres ahead, where the taxi could turn back fast in an emergency. Ahead of that to the left a giant Pepsi sign faced them; America's culture penetrated everywhere. Sharia el Mansuriya boiled with life and colour.

'Talkhan, go in quietly. Remember, there are others we could reach.'

Talkhan had three sisters in Cairo.

The Angels' safe house, or rooms, were in a block of flats immediately to the right. At one side at ground level was a workshop, now shut. An open hall led in to the flats. That night there was no *bawwab*, doorman; Wahbah had paid him to be sick. Wahbah got out of the taxi first, to the right, and El Masri from the seat beside the driver. Talkhan looked at them and followed them. He went in with no struggle, Abbas just behind him, his Browning under the folds of his galabiah. Hassan stayed in the taxi at the wheel. Wahbah had the flat keys out. He opened the ground-floor door to the left quickly and the four men went in.

They went through the short entrance corridor to a room. It was bare, except for a table and six wooden chairs, two made-up beds in the corners, and a big transistor radio on a cabinet against one wall. There was an Arabic calendar on the back door, no pictures on the walls. That back door led to a small kitchen, and a lavatory and shower. A telephone stood beside the radio. The flat was austere and self-contained. It had thick walls and its radio had powerful speakers. Abbas Sidki looked at Wahbah.

'You locked the front door?'

'Of course. And bolted and chained it.'

'Good. Talkhan, sit there.'

Abbas Sidki went to the transistor, selected one of the tapes by it, and set it in the radio's jaws. He switched it on.

'. . . The first thing they do is entangle you in love.
Then they demand patience, obedience . . .
And then, with no warning, they leave you . . .'

It was Umm Kulthum, the most famous of all Arab singers, the lyrics by the poet El Tunisy. She sang in *'Ammiya*, Egyptian colloquial Arabic, to her usual strong orchestra of seven violins, a cello, an *ood* or lute, a *kanoon* or zither, a *nye* or bamboo flute, and a *riq* or tambourine. This was a traditional love song, quite like an American Western folk song. It stated its basics, then came back to them again and again, elaborating them.

Umm Kulthum had died in 1975, aged roughly seventy-five; the small and impoverished Egyptian village where she was born had not recorded births too exactly. She had become a legend in her own lifetime, a symbol. She was truly a voice of the people. At her peak she had flown to give command performances to the courts of Saudi Arabia, Kuwait, Syria. Nasser had met her at Cairo Airport when she returned. One story related that Ghaddafi had even had to put off one of his wars for a day because all his senior officers insisted on hearing Umm Kulthum first at a performance previously set for the evening of Ghaddafi's D-Day. Under cover of that marvellous clarion singing, all the more reverenced now that Umm Kulthum was dead, they could do what they liked to Talkhan.

'Talkhan, we're going to tie you.'

'*Lé kidda?* Why this? Look, you're all madmen! I've done nothing!'

But he did not fight. Perhaps he thought of his three sisters. Wahbah and Masri lashed him to the chair of black wood, the heaviest one. It was like a black throne. They lashed him round the wrists and elbows and ankles, and round his waist. When they stood back, Abbas Sidki pulled a lighter chair near to him.

'Talkhan, where are you to meet Colonel Tarek Daniel Gad? Or have you already talked to him?'

Talkhan jerked at that. Again his hands, bound tightly at the wrists to the horizontal arms of the thick black chair, clenched and opened, then stayed curiously open, like the claws of a crab pricked into self-defence, watchfulness; an utterly still small menace.

'Daniel Gad? What Colonel Daniel Gad?'

'Stop wasting our time, Talkhan. We saw you exchange the paper messages with him at seven-thirty last night in Groppi's.'

Talkhan's eyes flickered over the three men.

'Ah, the Groppi's up near Opera Square, you mean?'

'The Groppi's at Suleiman Pasha Square, where 'Asr el Nil meets Muhammed Bassiuni.'

It was like a litany, the calls, the responses, the variations, each small change bringing some new detail. It was like Umm Kulthum's song:

'The first thing, they entangle you in love, with a single glance.
Then they demand patience and obedience. (Where do I get these?)
And then, with no warning, they leave you, they go. (Tell me, where?)'

The *ood* wailed, the *kanoon*, the zither, plucked at the strings of your heart.

In his heavy black wooden throne, Talkhan writhed quite suddenly at his ropes. He clenched and opened his hands at the three men again and again, clenched and opened them, clenched and opened. The movements pushed outwards like little shrieks of despair. They saw the beads of sweat springing out on his forehead, the spittle at the corners of his lips.

'. . . All a lie! It was nothing! I was thirsty, and I just stopped there for a drink! How did I know who sat next to me?'

'And that exchange of pieces of paper? A lie too? What did those notes say?'

Talkhan, still locked hopelessly in his struggle with his bonds, was moaning deep in his throat. Umm Kulthum's lines, rich in anguish, desolate, cut across him:

'. . . And then, with no warning, they leave you, they go. (Tell me, where, *where* could he have gone?)'

Talkhan stopped fighting suddenly. He panted, his head dropped forward on his chest. Then he raised it and stared at his three gaolers levelly. It was as if he had fallen back consciously to a final defensive position, fitting exactly into his bonds for all time, accepting them stoically, his fate.

'Look in his pockets.'

Wahbah stepped in and pulled out what Talkhan had in the two side pockets of his slacks, and the hip pocket and the small one in front: a wallet, holding about £E40, keys, a pack of Cleopatra cigarettes, a throwaway gas lighter.

'No, nothing.'

'Then get his shirt open. To start with.'

El Masri moved in and ripped the front of Talkhan's shirt. He pulled each side back behind Talkhan's shoulders, leaving them and his chest naked. They were thin shoulders.

'Which of you smokes again?'

'Wahbah.'

'Of course. Would you please get one lit? Then the nipples, the throat, the stomach. Leave the face till after. Oh, and we'd better turn up the radio a bit —'

The blond and blue-eyed El Masri went over to it.

'The tape's just about finished. I'll put on the other side.'

'Sure.'

'It's *Wulidal Hoda*. That's all right?'

*Wulidal Hoda* was 'The Guide was Born', he being the Prophet Muhammed. This *qasida* was deeply religious, far from Umm Kulthum's usual splendid tapestry of passionate earthly love, often unrequited, of the sweet agony of separation from the beloved.

'Sure, that's all right.'

'*Tayyib*, fine.'

'What we're doing is hardly irreligious, after all.'

El Masri turned up the radio, and Umm Kulthum boomed even more heartily through the building, her accents resonant with piety:

'The Guide was born and all Creation was radiant,
And the faces of the ages smiled and glowed,
Gabriel, the angels round him, brought the
Glad tidings for religion and the world . . .'

Under that bell-like voice, that strong and continuing orchestra, no one outside this room would hear Talkhan's screams. Abbas Sidki watched him make them, battered by Umm Kulthum into mere mime. Talkhan talked now with his shuddering hands too. He jerked his head again and again. Abbas got up and walked to him, and leaned down next to his head.

'Something to tell us?'

Talkhan turned his face away from him as far as he could.

14

He was weeping without cease now.

'Get his slacks open.'

El Masri pulled down the zip and tore open the underpants. When Wahbah came in with his second lit cigarette there was a new quality of terror to Talkhan's muted screams: an Arab, an Egyptian, was nothing if his manhood was maimed. But there was still no sign from Talkhan that he would talk.

'The face, then. The left eye. Start at the corner.'

El Masri locked his left forearm round Talkhan's throat and held his head immobile from behind. When the coal of Wahbah's cigarette went into the outer corner of his left eye, Talkhan screamed horribly and his hands flickered like morse and stopped abruptly with the palms pointed straight at Abbas Sidki, beseeching.

'Stop. Let him talk. *If* he'll talk.'

El Masri loosed his arm from round Talkhan's throat and the man sucked in air, shivering. The burn mark just outside his left eye was puffed, like a small crater on the moon, but he seemed still, just, to be seeing with that eye. He was no longer resisting with it, though. He was no longer resisting with anything. All men, very nearly, broke somewhere. Talkhan broke here. He was shaking continuously now, as though he were very cold.

'Tonight –'

'What tonight? You were to meet Gad tonight?'

'His flat –'

The man's teeth were chattering.

'Where is his flat?'

'Flat 40, ninth floor, 1121 Bis Corniche el Nil.'

'That's right. When?'

'Nine o'clock.'

'So you could still in fact make it. All right, leave him.'

The two men stood back. Abbas Sidki looked at Talkhan.

'Why, Talkhan? You would have sold us. You had already betrayed us in your heart. Why?'

'Why?' The man, his nipples, throat, stomach, penis and scrotum pockmarked and boiling with burns, his left eye puffed and closing, stared back at him in utter hatred, his mouth jumping, as though he could not get the words out fast enough. 'Why? Because you were always *right*, damn you, Abbas, can't you see? You and Allah never made any mistakes. You didn't even have the grace to have any *doubts*. Your damned piety. Your *righteousness*. It was like living with a mosque. Or the *Ka'ba* in Mecca. It became intolerable. You and your –' he glanced round at them in contempt, '*disciples! A* terrible *arrogance!* I just wanted freedom. I just wanted to be free of you –'

'You'd betray us for that? You'd betray *Islam* for that? You were once a good fighter for Islam. Islam's eternal. You think you can just shed it like *that*? Now you'll suffer the most terrible punishment of all, to be excluded *forever* from the Islamic Brotherhood –'

'I can stand that. Try me. Why don't you just leave me to it?'

'Your oath to us was for your lifetime, remember?'

'Besides, you were never humiliated like me. You always had it all just too easy. You never suffered that. You just don't know. I wanted no more of your virtuous leading –'

'You know the rules.'

Talkhan looked at him. His hands clenched and writhed and froze open, entreating.

'My sisters?'

'No one will touch your sisters.'

'Then *Toz!*' cried Talkhan stridently. 'Fuck off!' And he stared murderously at Abbas Sidki with his one sound eye, then spat heavily. Abbas took out his handkerchief with his left hand and wiped the spit from his face. He put the handkerchief back. Still seated, he raised the Browning steadily in a double grip, and lined it up on Talkhan's left eye. Talkhan said nothing; perhaps he thought this just yet another test of his courage. Only his locked hands, once, repeated their curious semaphore. Umm Kulthum's voice swelled:

'. . . The throne of God and the court bloomed with pride,
And everything near Him was excellent.'

Under that golden voice, through the silencer, the bullet was almost totally soundless. It snapped Talkhan's head back and

16

its impact slid the heavy black chair a few centimetres along the floor. There was a small mess on the far wall. Talkhan sat still in his seat. His head hung forward to show a small bloody circle at the back. Talkhan would not be seeing Colonel Daniel Gad that evening.

Abbas Sidki got up and went to Umm Kulthum and turned her down to a more human level.

'Let's clean it up.'

'His head?'

'A big sticking-plaster will hold it. There are some in the kitchen. And a pail of water for the wall.'

After the sticking-plaster exercise, Abbas covered the head neatly with a red-and-white chequered *kefiyya* and parked the twin black rings of an *ogal* on it to hold it down. Talkhan looked almost as good as new. With his shirt pulled forward properly and the zip of his slacks done up, he could have been a young Kuwaiti out on the town, dressed half Egyptian as a sop to local custom. The other two men had cleaned the wall. They came and lifted Talkhan between them.

'As agreed?' said Wahbah.

'As agreed. Drop him near the Qaitbai Mosque. Keep your lights off then, so no one sees your number. I'll wait for you here.'

If you drove straight on from where they had kidnapped Talkhan, instead of turning left at the policeman as they had done, and took the road slanting to the right, it dipped under a tunnel and curved left and rose to join the wide Salah Salem Avenue that led to Nasr City and the airport. To the left were the eastern old city walls built by Saladin's successors. To the right was the Northern Cemetery, a dusty sea of small houses and innumerable domes rising between them, and the great stone domes and minarets of the Mausoleum of Barquq, the first Circassian Mameluke sultan, and the gem-like Qaitbai's Tomb with its horizontally striped masonry and delicately curved dome and slim high minaret. Not only great Mamelukes and humbler dead lay here. Many thousands of the living dwelt here too, in this Dead City. Twelve million of Egypt's 48 million – where one new net Egyptian mouth was being born to feed every 22½ seconds – crammed now into the dustbowl of Cairo; the population pressure was intense. So Talkhan would not be so badly off here; the Egyptians had always been on close and easy terms with their dead. On feast-days thousands of Cairenes, particularly women, rolled out in their carts with their food and cooking-pots and blankets, to picnic and commune with the spirits in their family mausoleums. Talkhan would be in good company. Of course someone from among the thousands who lived here in or among the tombs would find Talkhan's body soon enough, which is what Abbas Sidki wanted. It would be a neat small warning to Colonel Tarek Daniel Gad. It would also be a small touch of terror for the people, and salutary; people learned more swiftly through terror.

Abbas Sidki left the flat's front door slightly open and went to alert Hassan in the taxi. When he saw a lull he signalled to Wahbah at the flat door, and Wahbah and El Masri walked Talkhan to the taxi, holding him under his shoulders, and put him in the back. The taxi pulled away, and Abbas watched it turn through the gap in the island and come back past him on the other side, effortlessly, even sedately. He went back into the flat and sat by the transistor and listened to the tape. The *Wulidal Hoda* was traditionally of the kind which ended in an individual supplication. Here now came Umm Kulthum's:

'I do not come to your gate to praise you only,
But, by my praise, to beg you and implore you,
Not for myself alone, but for my poor nation, Egypt . . .'

The hope of all Egypt, all Islam, was in the hands of the Angels. Abbas Sidki knew that. It was a bitterly hard, a most grave and beautiful mission.

# 2

# *Copts and Robbers*

'Well, where *is* he?' said Police General Naguib Abd el Nour tartly. Abd el Nour meant Servant of Light. But the General was not looking light and joyous now.

'God knows, General,' said Police Colonel Tarek Daniel Gad, tactfully dropping his gaze to the smooth surface of the desk between them. It was not quite an apology. Daniel Gad knew his General. Abd el Nour tended to trample all over you in high-heeled boots if you apologized to him too unreservedly.

'Who was it again who insisted that we let him run free?' said the General nastily. 'You wrote those lyrics, I seem to remember?'

'Sir,' said Daniel Gad, shifting onto an alternative buttock in his chair.

'And further, your fluent colloquialisms,' said Abd el Nour, breaking into a very tolerable English himself. 'Your "softly, softly, catchee monkey" for example?'

'*Effendim*,' said Daniel Gad once more, still writhing. He rallied. 'Look, General, we may not have lost him completely yet. He could always still turn up.'

'*Ya Salaam!*' said the General. 'A born optimist into the bargain! A *criminal* optimist, even! Look, if Suleiman Talkhan was to come to see you at nine last night, and did not, then I don't think that you will ever see Suleiman Talkhan again — alive, that is. It's what I always said. We should have pulled him straight in from the start. Lead us to the others, would he, your way? Like hell. My way, he'd have sung in any event, in cells, and we'd have been certain of him. He would have talked in cells all right, there are methods for that. And we'd still have had him alive, just. Instead of a dead pigeon, which is probably what he is now.'

And who loves a dead stool pigeon? thought Daniel Gad gloomily.

But he was by no means as sure as Abd el Nour seemed to be that they would have been able to get Talkhan to sing in cells – unless Talkhan had really wanted to. Most police forces in the world had effective means of making most people talk in cells, sooner or later. But Islamic Fundamentalists were not most people. Their convictions were formidable, their loyalty proverbial. Some of them literally would die before they talked, whatever pressure you put on them. You couldn't brainwash a Fundamentalist as you could a criminal or most of the other more respectable sorts of revolutionaries, then send him craftily back into his gang to work for you as a double agent. That just didn't fly. They either (very seldom) came over to you of their own free will, or you killed them. And that was that. Daniel Gad had a lot of respect for Islamic Fundamentalists, which is why he had not wanted to use force against Talkhan. He had asked Talkhan on his little slip of paper in Groppi's if he would like preventative arrest for his own safety, but Talkhan had written back promptly saying that he would prefer to meet Gad in his flat. Well, that made sense too; Islamic Fundamentalists had been known to kill traitors before now behind bars in top security prisons.

'At least you've *looked* for him?' said the General, now leaving nothing to chance.

'*Ya Bey!*' said Daniel Gad. 'I sent a couple of men to look at his room by El Azhar. And a couple to Ain Shams. He was supposed to give a lecture there this morning at eight-thirty.'

'And?'

'No Suleiman Talkhan.'

The General jerked his shoulders upwards expressively.

'You see? It's just as I said!'

Except for that hatchet delivery, there was nothing strikingly General-like about Abd el Nour at the moment. This was partly because his was a plain-clothes unit. Hosni Mubarak had created it immediately he took the succession in October 1981, after Sadat's assassination. Its job was, simply, to find revolution while still in the bud, and nip it. If the same Fundamentalist movement was going to gun for Mubarak too, at least he was going to make it have to work harder for the privilege. So Mubarak put in the best men he could find, and kept up a close personal interest. The new unit's commander, Abd el Nour, reported direct to Mubarak, not through the Minister of the Interior or the Minister of Defence. It was an élite outfit, Mubarak's brainchild, and consequently the rest of the Egyptian police disliked it heartily.

General Naguib Abd el Nour could take that. Indeed, thought Daniel Gad, he probably rather liked it. Abd el Nour was not a man who minded being singled out. At sixty, he was used to it. He expected it. Abd el Nour was a tall man, slim, with good shoulders. He was hard as a nut, an outstanding squash player in a nation famous for them. He dressed nattily. Today, behind his football field of a desk, he sat elegantly in a light-grey suit, a wide darker grey check over it. His shirt was of pure white Egyptian cotton – he had a strong patriotic side to him – and a narrow dark-red tie. The handkerchief negligent at his breast pocket was only a shade darker. There was a gold Cartier watch on his left wrist, worn facing inwards. As Abd el Nour was happy to tell you, he did not depend for his life style on his official salary. His family had had cotton lands east of Tanta since time immemorial, practically since the Middle Pharaonic Kingdom. Of course Nasser's agrarian reforms – and how could Abd el Nour possibly have opposed those? – had chopped them down somewhat, but the family still survived.

Naguib Abd el Nour had in fact shone for forty-three years. In 1942, as a cavalryman, he had been one of the youngest Free Officers under Sadat, then more closely under Nasser. He had worked with Sadat on the innovative plan of sending excellent photos of the Allied defence positions about Egypt to Rommel, in exchange for Rommel's guarantee of an independent Egypt after his victory, a plan which crashed when Rommel's anti-aircraft gunners, knowing nothing of it, shot down the Gloster Gladiator aircraft bringing the Germans this priceless information. And Naguib Abd el Nour was with Nasser at perhaps his greatest moment, when in 1956 he turned the British-French-Israeli attack into one of the greatest Third World victories of all time.

Abd el Nour had always shown a fine sense of political balance. He was a tightrope walker of the first flight in the Egyptian political circus. He had been so close to the messianic Nasser that he had even advised him on his desert detention camps, that sinister and highly secret concept central to Nasser's whole police state. Yet when Nasser fell dead of his heart attack in September 1970 and Sadat succeeded him and set about dismantling much of what Nasser had constructed, including most of his police state apparatus, it evidently never even crossed Sadat's mind to dismantle Abd el Nour too. He emerged buoyant as a cork. And when Sadat was assassinated Mubarak even promoted him. Naguib Abd el Nour just had the gift of survival. Now nothing would stop him. Abd el Nour was not ambitious. He was ambition itself. Daniel Gad knew that he had his sights lined up next on becoming Minister of the Interior or Minister of Defence. Either of those, with another timely cataclysm or two, could form a sound springboard for the Presidency.

This unremitting drive for self-improvement did not always make Abd el Nour the easiest boss to work for. He constantly needed his staff to deliver him large bones, which he could then gambol off with and lay noisily at the feet of Mubarak. Suleiman Talkhan, properly confessed and shriven, could have made just such a bone. The mere departed shade of him would not. Abd el Nour even *looked* like the classmate most likely to succeed, thought Daniel Gad morbidly. There was something larger than life about him. His hair was snow-white, very thick and with beautiful natural waves. His features were extraordinarily regular, those of a Greek statue, though the mouth was sinuous, and there was a strongly marked vertical crease at each side of it. His skin was a very light olive, and there was a bloom of health in his cheeks. The general – and thoroughly misleading – effect was one of easy benevolence.

'Well, better get out and look for him some more, hadn't you?' said General Abd el Nour. 'I mean, you're not going to get far trying to find him in here, are you now?'

'No, sir.'

'He's got to be out there somewhere, hasn't he?'

The General had jerked his right thumb towards the big window half behind him. It looked down ten floors into Kasr el Nil, the Castle of the Nile. The building was on the corner of that and Sharia Sherif. By now, nine-thirty in the morning, those busy streets were already packed with a cacophony of cars, buses, lorries, the occasional natural hazards of donkey-drawn carts, and people. And heat, plenty of heat, a 40°C day. Up here the General's air-conditioner was mercifully keeping it at bay. Down there it would feel as if all of Cairo's twelve million inhabitants had crowded into those two streets. The thought of having to try to find Suleiman Talkhan out there was not exhilarating.

'You can always appeal to the regular police for help if you feel it's too much for you,' said the General, in final insult. Gad glanced at him. Abd el Nour was really looking quite fierce. That made two of them, for there was a picture of Mubarak up on the wall half right. He too stared out grimly, his pupils following you everywhere in the room, the heavy jaw set and shadowed, the skin dark, the nose beaky, and the crinkled hair African. He looked as implacable as his own thick shoulders. Selected and groomed for stardom by Sadat, and ultimately named his Vice-President, Mubarak had first reacted with endearing modesty. This often took the form in public of a wide and embarrassed smile, so that he soon became known universally as *La Vache Qui Rit*, after the beaming quadruped trademark of the famous processed cheese. The nickname must have reached him; that coy smile was wiped out permanently, from one day to the next. Now Mubarak's rugged face was just another august national symbol, like the Egyptian flag which hung in miniature on its tiny chromium flagpole on Abd el Nour's polished virginal desk, with the gold

Egyptian eagle centred in its middle white band.

'Let me know what you find,' said General Abd el Nour, 'even if it's nothing.'

'Sir.'

Daniel Gad got up, inclined his head, and went out. He passed through the General's secretary's office. Hoda was a dark and vivacious lass of thirty summers from Alexandria. She had a superb figure, but like a true Muslim she had covered her good breasts all the way up to her neck. Thank God for Copts, thought Gad, being one himself.

'*Har?*' said Hoda, meaning Hot? She ducked her pretty head towards the General's door.

'Hot, indeed,' said Daniel Gad. 'Try some ice down his neck.'

In the corridor he turned into the Gents for a quick pee. It was the best immediate comment he could think of on his meeting with the General. Gad was himself most bitterly disappointed that Suleiman Talkhan had not come. But he was still not at all sure that he would have been wiser to arrest him. Gad preferred to avoid the crudities of police work if he could get his results without them. All the same, he felt his failure keenly. He had been up most of the night. He had waited in his flat on the Corniche el Nil for Talkhan until one in the morning, thinking that something minor could always have delayed him. At one he had started the first surreptitious and fruitless searches.

Washing his hands, he looked unwillingly into the mirror. It was a fairly debauched sight. His blue eyes, heritage from his English mother, had that eerie dead shade of crevasses about them. Like pissholes in the snow, he thought morbidly. The rest of the structure looked about as gaunt as usual; the highish forehead, the high cheekbones, the narrow, rather ascetic lips (now *there* was a laugh for you!) and the olive Mediterranean complexion. He supposed that his father (*he* was the Copt) was mainly responsible for those. But the hearty break in the once aquiline nose was directly due to a St Mary's Hospital middleweight in a cheerfully bloody fight in the Paddington

Baths. It took all sorts to make a police force.

He walked on back to his office. It was smaller than the General's and moreover it had no secretary's ante-office. Inscrutably, such were the labyrinths of Egyptian bureaucracy that colonels in specialized units like this did not rate their own individual secretaries, but only the services of a subterranean typing-pool of hideous delays and inefficiencies. So Daniel Gad kept his paperwork down to a minimum. When really pressed, he appealed to Hoda's well-developed feminine instincts, sidling surreptitiously into her office when he was sure that her door to the General's (a man jealous of his privileges) was securely shut.

He heard the phone as he neared his office door, and got to it before it stopped ringing.

'*Iwa?* Daniel Gad here. *Min?*'

'It's Raafat, *Effendim*. We have a report from the civil police –'

'Go on. Go on.'

'It fits our description. Up by the Qaitbai Mosque in the Northern Cemetery. He's small, slight, dark, balding, about thirty. No identification. Pretty badly burnt, cigarettes or a small poker, I'd say. And –'

'And?'

'Shot through the left eye.'

Standing by his desk, Daniel Gad stared down at his right hand, hooked rigid in front of his stomach. Gad held the telephone in his left hand. On that dreadful desert retreat in the Six Days War, an Israeli shell had air-burst just to his right. The wide scythe of shrapnel had missed him miraculously, but the blast had not. His right eardrum had never totally recovered.

This could be it. The Fundamentalist group, *Takfir wal Hijra* – Atonement and Holy Flight – was one of the three such groups that had tried to bring down Sadat in blood since 1974. In 1977 they had kidnapped Sadat's former Religious Affairs minister, Hussein el Dhahaby, to exchange him for *Takfir* men imprisoned, but Sadat would not deal. So *Takfir* strangled the ex-minister ritually, then shot him through the left eye. This man too had been shot through the left eye. It was a signal. There were all kinds of languages.

'Where are you, Raafat?'

'Downstairs, the 'Asr el Nil side. I've been phoning you for the last five minutes, but I couldn't get you. I have the car here ready, mounted on the pavement.'

'The traffic police will shoot you through the left eye for that. I was with the Film Star. I'll be there at once.'

Running on the way to the lift, he checked in his waistband for his Browning. It was there, nestling between his underpants and his belted light-grey cotton slacks. Daniel Gad wore a lightweight pale-grey bush-shirt over that, comfortably masking his automatic. That was the best place to carry a handgun for a quick draw, much better than in a shoulder-holster (which tended anyway to stimulate sweat in a hot climate) or in a pocket; this way you just flipped the bush-shirt away with your left hand and the Browning practically leapt into your eager right palm all on its own. Gad was happy with his Browning. He carried it with its magazine loaded with thirteen 9 mm shells, but none in the chamber. This meant that to load he had to pull back the charger and release it as he drew the pistol, but through years of practice he could do this very rapidly in one fluid movement. A Browning was not a Walther, and he did not like to carry his with a round in the breech. A Browning just might go off like that, and Gad had no desire to lose valuable parts of his anatomy. He checked too in his slacks pockets; the two spare loaded magazines were there. All this was no more than a mere instinctive reaction, he knew, like looking to see if his hair was properly combed. He was probably not going to need all this effective armament. From the sound of it, all the shooting had already been done.

He closed the hall door behind him, with the improbable title neatly lettered on its frosted glass: THE GREATER EGYPT EXPORT CORPORATION. All we ever export is Egyptians, thought Daniel Gad unkindly; there was never enough work to go round at home.

He leapt for a lift, magically appeared. It was full with perhaps sixteen Egyptians in it, well over the safety limit marked on the panel. The sixteen men and women chatted animatedly, wasting no time at all, as though this were indeed their last ride on earth. There was a heavy aroma of humanity and cheap perfume. A small man in a uniform worked the panel of the lift; fairly unnecessarily, since the controls were clearly automatic. It was the policy of full employment wherever humanly possible. With nearly one and a half million new Egyptians appearing every year, there was no choice.

Most of several years' crop seemed to be clustered now round Raafat Khalil's car, whose nearside two wheels were mounted squarely on the pavement, causing some compression. Two traffic police figured prominently, in their smart white summer uniforms and black berets. Gad flashed his secret police colonel's card at them and they backed off, suitably impressed.

'Quick, away. Before they change their minds.'

He sat in the front with Raafat.

Sergeant Raafat Khalil drove precisely and decisively, like someone writing a very clear letter in singularly neat handwriting. He did not fling his car about all over the road in a display of machismo like most Egyptians, hooting his head off. It was too nice a car to do that to, still very new and shiny black, a Fiat two-litre saloon, manual, locally assembled, and very highly tuned. It did not even look like a police car. Raafat loved it passionately. He practically slept with it. The car would have been lucky if he had, for Raafat Khalil was an extraordinarily dignified, decent and gentle man. Daniel Gad glanced at his profile now. It was pure Arab. He had nicely chiselled features, a straight nose, dark-brown eyes, a clear brown skin, and a full moustache. A fez would have sat well on this beautifully sculpted head.

Raafat Khalil was as Arab as he looked. His family had lived in Haifa for more generations than they could trace. His father had been a sergeant in the Palestine Police under the British mandate. When the British left, and Ben Gurion broke the five Arab armies to create the State of Israel, the Khalil family left. They had nothing against the Jews as such. They had lived and worked cheek by jowl with them in Haifa, and there were Jews too in the Palestine Police. But the Arab defeat had humiliated them. Moreover there were uglier sides to the thing than straight military defeat. There were also the actions by Jewish extremist groups, like the massacre by Begin's *Irgun Zvai Leumi*, the Army of the People, of some hundreds of men, women, and children in the tiny and non-strategic Arab village of Deir Yassin. That sickened them. So they moved to their sister Islamic country of Egypt. Raafat's father served in the Egyptian Police, and grew old and died. Raafat, becoming naturalized as an Egyptian, followed in his footsteps. He had married another Palestinian refugee, but that was the only link he had left with his former land. God only knew who occupied their house near Haifa Port now. Gad had seen photos of it when he had been asked for dinner to Raafat Khalil's flat in Shubra, one of the poorer parts of Cairo.

The two men were of the same age, thirty-nine. They had met first in the army. Raafat had been Daniel Gad's tank driver in those first four glorious days from 6 October 1973 when the Egyptian commandos and armour had broken clean through Israel's Bar Lev Line, and indeed almost right through Israel. For all his gentleness, Raafat Khalil had other qualities. He was a brave man, and his personal loyalties were absolute. His build was deceptive too. He was of middle height, and quite slight, but Daniel Gad knew that he had muscles like whipcord, and quite extraordinary powers of endurance, those of a Bedu in a desert. As a good Muslim, Raafat Khalil was quietly religious, and Gad had never seen him touch a drop of alcohol. They differed on both these points.

'They're keeping him there?'

'Yes,' said Raafat, not taking his eyes from the road. 'They said they haven't moved him.'

By now Raafat had driven them east through Mustafa Kamel Square and was coming up into the Opera. He turned left into Sharia Gumhuria, past the Opera Cinema, then right at Opera Square and past the Post Office to Midan Ataba, then half right into Sharia el Azhar. Cairo's millions thrummed about them. At the start of El Azhar a donkey cart blocked their path, its skull-capped driver impervious to them, his broad robed back square on to them as a wall above his load of vegetables and overripe tomatoes; he sat on his rights. Daniel Gad rolled down his window and stuck his head out. The heat, after the car's air-conditioning, hit him like a fist, and he swore richly and loudly. The squat shoulders lifted upwards fractionally, the cart moved a little to the right and they were past. Ahead of them was the light-blue metal pedestrian bridge over the road with its white-painted legend in Arabic:

MINISTRY OF DEFENCE
ENGINEERS' ADMINISTRATION.

And now to the right was the small square before El Azhar, and there was the splendid building itself, the Gate of the Barbers, and above the crenellated horizontal line of the wall the twin soaring pencils of minarets and the twin warm breasts of domes, all four thoughtfully tipped against Shaitaan with the steel crescent of Islam. The thin street up to the right past El Azhar led round to Suleiman Talkhan's lodging, but Gad's men had found no one there that morning.

Across left, across the high steel fence that divided the two lanes of this heavily transited street, were the Scent, the Spices, the Goldsmiths' and the General Bazaars of Khan el Khalili, for Gad the greatest rip-off centre in the city. Two hundred metres ahead they came to a main crossroads with Sharia el Mansuriya running at right-angles across them. A policeman stood there directing the traffic. Raafat drove straight on, then dipped down under the wide Salah Salem Avenue which ran north to Nasr City and the airport, south to the Citadel. Now, east of that Avenue, they were already in the Northern Cemetery. They left the domed tomb of the Tartar Princess Tolbay on their right, the ribbed tomb of a second fourteenth-century Princess, Umm Anuk, on their left. The desolate yellow Hills of Muqattam rose ahead of them like a wall, the rim of this great arid dust bowl. Raafat drove on towards them for two hundred metres, then turned left for another two hundred, to the fifteenth-century complex of the Qaitbai Mausoleum and Mosque and Oratory and Gate. This was the magic grave Islamic silhouette of soaring slim jets of minarets, rich domes and crenellated walls that probably bound Daniel Gad most profoundly to Egypt, Copt or not.

The group of people were this side of the horizontal grey and white stripes of the Mausoleum. Raafat stopped the car and the two men got out. The group opened to them, like a ballet. All were male, down to youths and one or two small boys. There were two armed civilian police, one a corporal. Except for these, probably all the rest were squatters, living decorously side by side with the dead, in the cemetery's tangle of tiny houses and myriad small domes. Even here the dominant masculinity of the society had imposed itself. Violent death was men's business. Women would kindly stay at home. Clearly, the community had also determined that not too many men should attend. There were proper proportions to all things in the Islamic universe.

Daniel Gad showed his card to the corporal, and the corporal straightened up and saluted. Gad bent over the body.

It was Suleiman Talkhan all right. There was no doubt about it. And considerably the worse for wear. The body lay on its back. Talkhan's right eye was open, and bulging slightly. The corner of the left was badly puffed, almost certainly from burning. The eye itself was not there. Gad went down on one knee and saw the sticking-plaster at the back of the head, and the seepage of blood. So he had been shot from exactly in front, and probably from some metres off; those did not look like powder burns on his skin. That was unpleasantly good shooting.

Daniel Gad looked at Talkhan's chest, and saw the eruptions in the skin round his nipples and across them, on his throat, and down on his stomach. He lifted the body's left arm carefully, and the shirt fell away. Yes, they had worked on the armpits too, they had known where to go. There would be another place –

He pulled the zip down carefully. There was an immediate subdued muttering, almost a roar, from the ring of men about him; a man's genitals were his final pride, deserving some respect even when he was dead. Talkhan's final pride was looking pretty grim. The entire head of the penis, the underneath, and the scrotum had all been badly burned. Gad could feel the audience pressing in on him in horrified fascination. He looked up at the sea of faces.

'You see the manner of people who are concerned? Can you tell me anything which could help me trace them?'

The faces hung above his as if on strings. None of them said anything.

The police corporal pressed between them.

'*Yafendim*, the people here say they saw nothing, and know nothing. Men going to work this morning found him here, is all.'

'At what time? We know who found him?'

'At six; they go to work early from here. They called us at once, four men together. So we know them, we took their statements. But they gave us nothing.'

Daniel Gad got up, dusting off his knee, and glancing round the faces again. A conspiracy of silence? It could be. The men would know that this had the marks of a political execution, the work of revolutionaries, perhaps Islamic Fundamentalists. They would not want to mix in that.

He thought that the smaller of the two boys looked particularly noncommittal. With his small white skull cap on the back of his head, and in his grey *gandoura*, or miniature galabiah, he was observing the Muqattam Hills, his lips rounded in a soundless whistle. As Gad watched, he disengaged himself from the group, and walked off nonchalantly past the car, disappearing then from sight.

'All the same, I'd better just glance through those statements,' said Gad.

'*Effendim*. They're in the big Khan el Khalili station. I took them. My name is Corporal Ali Fathi.'

The two men climbed into the car and Khalil drove it back two hundred metres over the dirt road, then turned ninety degrees to the right and went another three hundred dusty metres until they were passing again between the tombs of Umm Anuk and of the Tartar Princess Tolbay.

'Somebody's not telling all he saw,' said Sergeant Raafat

Khalil gloomily, from above his steering wheel.

'What makes you think that?'

Khalil glanced to the right at him soberly.

'The smell of fear, *Yafendim*. Somebody there saw them dump him.'

'So they didn't kill him there?'

Khalil glanced at him again, and with the index finger of his left hand drew the skin under his left eye down slightly; Arab for who are you trying to fool?

'With so little blood there? And no signs of a struggle? They tortured him there? Stuck the patch on his head there, in the dark?'

Daniel Gad smiled.

'You'll make lieutenant yet, Raafat.'

So he would, if Daniel Gad had anything to do with it.

The small boy with the white skull cap on the back of his head and the miniature galabiah of light-grey cotton was standing on the right-hand side of the road just after the tombs of the two fourteenth-century princesses, before the great Salah Salem Avenue, observing the massive traffic thundering along it in both directions with detached interest.

'Draw up by him, please.'

Daniel Gad twisted round to open the rear right door and the small boy got in swiftly, practically without taking his eyes off the murderous traffic.

'*Zayak, ya walad!*' said Daniel Gad. 'Better you sit down on the floor, if you don't want them to see you.'

'*Taayib, Yafendim,*' said the small boy, and got down onto the car floor. Even there, he gave away no dignity at all.

'*Ismak eeh?*'

'Said Farag,' said the small boy. 'I live by the Mausoleum of Barquq with my family. We are near the Camel Police Outpost. They know me thereabouts.'

Having decided to turn King's Evidence, as it were, thought Daniel Gad, the lad was going for broke, holding back nothing at all. If a man committed himself, he went all the way. It was a point of honour. He must have been all of eight years old.

'So you saw them drop him off?'

Sergeant Raafat Khalil was driving the Fiat 2000 steadily along Salah Salem Avenue now, towards Heliopolis. There was a slab of the Old Wall of Cairo to their left.

'I saw them,' said Said Farag. 'It wasn't late. Not more than eight-fifteen. Though people go to bed early in the cemetery.'

'No one else saw this?'

'Others saw this. Not many, two or three.'

'And who were they?'

'I'm not at liberty to say, *Yafendim*.'

Daniel Gad, his neck twisted uncomfortably left and downwards, stared down at the small boy. Said Farag met his eyes levelly. Ten to one he wouldn't talk even if you beat him, thought Gad. Maybe there was hope for Egypt yet.

'So what did you see?'

'Not too much of the two who dropped him, *Yafendim*. They had covered their faces. But I can tell you what they were like. One was short and thick, a strong man, with big shoulders. He was dark. The other was tall, with fair hair like the *khawwaghat* and very light eyes, perhaps even blue; I couldn't be sure in the dark –'

'What sort of age? How were they dressed?'

Said Farag observed him diplomatically.

'Not so old as you, *Yafendim*.' He used the Arabic *kabir*, which meant old, but also powerful, eminent. 'Their dress? Shirts and slacks. And they had wound *kefiyyaat* round their heads and faces.'

'They saw you?'

'No, *Yafendim*, they saw nothing of me. I didn't like the way the car was coming, so I hid behind a wall.'

'There was a car, of course. Did you see the number plates? You can read?'

The boy stiffened.

'I can read, *Yafendim*. I go to school. Only not today, because of this. But the car was without lights, though it came quite quickly. It was a taxi. It stopped with the driver's side nearest to me.'

'And?'

'The two men got out on the other side. They pulled the dead

33

man from the car and threw him onto the ground, as though he was *zibaala*, garbage. They got back at once into the car. They said no word all the time. The car went away fast, and again it showed no lights. The driver had never once moved from his seat.'

There was a silence. Said Farag communed politely with the car's roof. He might be only eight years old, but he already showed all an Arab's innate genius for story-telling. Nobody had to teach him how to build his suspense.

'And? There's something else important, isn't there?'

Said Farag relaxed slightly. He made his point.

'The driver hadn't covered his face with a *kefiyya*,' he said. 'I could see the driver's face all right.'

'And?'

The boy looked straight at Daniel Gad.

'I know the driver.'

'*What?*'

'I know him. He's a bad man.'

'My God, where do you know him from? Who *is* he?'

'A *saydaliyya* near Bab el Louk. He works there.'

'You can take us there?'

'Of course.'

Khalil had not needed to be told. At the first opportunity he had taken the Fiat left at a roundabout and round back on their tracks, then to the right and back into the Sharia el Azhar, the university and twin minarets and domes on their left, Khan el Khalili on their right, through Opera Square, down Sharia Adly to Sherif then hard left there.

'So why do you tell us this, Said?'

The boy locked eyes with Gad again. Then suddenly he twisted his body on the car's floor to the left, and with his right hand pulled up his grey galabiah sharply. Across his right thigh above the knee was a heavy straight scar.

'He did that?'

'He did that, because I entered his chemist's shop. He screamed that I had gone in there to steal. I had not. I was to buy aspirins for my father.'

'A bicycle chain?'

34

'A bicycle chain, and he gave me no chance to explain myself.'

'Then it's right that you tell us of him.'

'Also he called me a little black nigger from '*Issi'iid*.'

'You're in fact from Upper Egypt?'

'Yes.'

Indeed, he had the dark skin from there, where Egypt starts to shade into Black Africa. But he still had the fine features of the Nile.

'Aswan?'

'Aswan.'

'I know Aswan, and the High Dam, and Lake Nasser. It's a fine place.'

The boy beamed.

'What's he look like, this chemist?' said Daniel Gad.

'A small, thin man with black hair and a short black beard. He's never quiet. He's always moving something, looking about.'

Sharia Sherif had blended now into Nubar Pasha.

'The next one ahead is Muhammed Mahmoud,' said Sergeant Raafat Khalil. 'Running across the entrance to Bab el Louk Station.'

Said Farag glanced out of the window.

'We should stop here. It's just round the corner.'

'You heard what the man said,' said Daniel Gad, and Khalil glanced round and smiled slightly.

'We'll have to double-park, then,' he said. The traffic was horrible. 'The traffic police will hate that.'

'So they send us a ticket, and we give it to the Film Star to pay.' Police General Naguib Abd el Nour would just love that too.

Said Farag led them down a lane, round a corner.

'There.'

The chemist's shop faced onto the road; two doors, windows packed with the world's drugs and cunning imitations of them. The Egyptian consumption of drugs was hugely higher than most nations', and Egyptian chemists dispensed them much more lavishly, easily outprescribing their own doctors. There was movement in the shop.

'You're coming in too?'

'I should point him out to you, for it to be certain.'

To be certain also, thought Daniel Gad, that the bearded killer would know who had put the finger on him, just as the police took him. Arabs had a developed sense of vengeance.

'One at each door,' said Daniel Gad. 'We try to take him alive.'

'Of course.'

Daniel Gad and the boy went in through the left-hand door. After the summer blast of the sun outside it seemed shadowed and submarine inside the shop. Gad made out the three women buying at the long counter; two men behind it. Both wore white cotton smocks. The man further away was big and gross and clean-shaven.

The nearer man was rocking on his feet, concentrating on the woman counting her change in front of him. He was communicating his sardonic sense of mild contempt to her quite successfully, for she dropped two ten-piastre pieces and picked them up hurriedly. The man was slight and dark and vibrant. He had a short black beard.

'This is the man. This was the driver.'

The slight man's face was onto them like the flash of a silver fish jumping at dusk, and his vault over the counter seemed simply part of that swift fluid movement. As he straightened on the floor from that spring, facing Daniel Gad, his left leg shot out like a snake's tongue in a karate kick at the groin. Gad twisted to the right, but the blow still caught him high on the inside right thigh and flung him against the wall behind him. The slight man was out of the door like a bullet, the opened back of his white smock flying. Gad ran to the right out of the door after him, his right thigh screaming.

The white-sheathed figure raced ahead of him, a white blur of a black-framed face tossed rapidly round checking on him and Khalil pounding along behind him and the small boy behind that. So the quartet streaked and twisted through side alleys, skirting the packed Bab el Louk market and into and across Midan el Falaki, Falaki Square. Pedestrians spun from

36

their path, some falling, and cars braked in shrill cacophony to miss them, horns braying and drivers leaning out to curse at them. Gad was still amazed that the man had taken off so fast, the moment he had seen the boy. Said Farag could have been wrong; the killers might after all have seen him the night before when they dumped the dead Talkhan. It would not have worried them provided he had not identified them; they had evidently wanted that mutilated body to be found. Or else this secret organization, whoever they were, already knew who he, Daniel Gad, was, from photos and descriptions; a chilling thought. Or both those suppositions were true –

Their quarry was still running very strongly, now into Sharia Tahrir, Liberation Street, some eight metres ahead of Gad. They were hammering along the street itself; the pavements were thronged. This was a one-way street, the traffic against them, the blaring Cairo cars. And the trams, for there were still trams here, on the left side of the road, what the Cairenes called the *turumwaay*. This was where their quarry now ran mightily, along between the steel rails. Daniel Gad, still just holding the distance, was beginning to feel his sides bursting with pain.

They broke suddenly into Midan el Tahrir, Liberation Square. Once the British Kasr el Nil Barracks stood here, torn down when they left. Now it was the real hub of the city. From this wide circle Cairo's great arterial streets spun off, Kasr el Eini, Muhammed Mahmoud running into it past the American University, Tahrir into and across it then between the Egyptian Ministry of Foreign Affairs on the left and the imposing and now unoccupied buildings of the Arab League on the right, and so onto Tahrir Bridge across the Nile to Gezira; and Sharia Talaat Harb, and finally Ramses, leading north past the Nile Hilton and the Egyptian Museum. In Liberation Square broad phalanxes of cars, taxis, lorries and buses hurled themselves round and round a Wall of Death with ear-shattering intensity, slowed only perfunctorily by donkey carts, the long lethal steel columns of trams, and armed policemen with whistles.

As some faint last gesture of mercy to Cairo's massed

humanity, most of which seemed to congregate here at any hour of the day and half of the night, the authorities had built a steel pedestrian bridge right round this huge traffic circle. Raised some five or six metres above the murderous level of the street, this walkway was some three and a half metres broad, a raised and reasonably safe ring 150 metres in diameter. Stairways led up to it at strategic intervals, so that you could drop down as you wished to the fine shops along Talaat Harb, the airline offices along Ramses, the concave high Mugamma Police Buildings to the south, or the great bus terminus to the west. This benign elevated ring probably carried a million pedestrians a day.

They were all up there as the black-bearded chemist, his white smock tails fluttering behind him like wings, swung to the right into Talaat Harb, scrambled over the steel wire fence between it and the pavement, and reverse-raced past the pursuing Gad, and up the stairway to the raised walkway. Daniel Gad was over the steel fence swiftly too, his 9 mm Browning automatic digging him in the stomach. He looked back quickly; Khalil was just behind him, still on the other side of the fence.

'See which way he takes. Then go up the next stairway.'

'*Hader.*'

Daniel Gad raced on up the stairway, the sweat now pouring from him, drenching his chest and shirt under the arms. At the top of the stairway his heart plummeted. This walkway was solid with people, men and boys and women, mainly men, rushing in either direction, without pattern; no one here by training kept to the left or the right. This was Egypt. But he could not see the black-bearded chemist. He had lost him. He would never be able to look Khalil in the eyes again. Or Abd el Nour. He had failed dismally. Daniel Gad sweated.

Then he saw him. He had been looking left, towards the Mugamma building, assuming automatically that his quarry would go on in the same line, projected unstoppably forward at the top of the stairs. But the man had doubled back, cunning as a fox. Gad found him to his right, forging towards Ramses, shoving his way through the blunt mass in savage desperation.

Khalil had seen him too, at the right of the bridge, for when Daniel Gad looked down he saw Khalil racing across Talaat Harb, fending off the irate cars with his hands and feet; a true Egyptian crossing. He would be aiming at the next stairway up in Ramses, forty or fifty metres ahead. Gad saw the boy Said Farag, racing Khalil sturdily as his shadow. He saw Khalil reach the Ramses pavement and draw his handgun by the foot of the stairway. Khalil was a Colt .45 man.

Gad thrust himself forward again. It was heavy work, like shoving in a scrum. Egyptian men cursed him. One Egyptian woman in a black abaya, whom he had spilled to the ground, got up with alacrity and thrashed at him with her hands, screaming. But he was getting no nearer to the white-winged chemist, whatever he did. It was a pursuit in a nightmare.

Then quite suddenly he saw their quarry slow, perplexed, frozen there abruptly outside time, a black pinnacle of rock totally static while the wild seas of people swirled all about him. His face, looking to Daniel Gad's left, showed utter fear and helplessness, total indecision. His hands were still in front of him; Gad saw them slim, long-fingered, nervous, quick. At once the face resolved, like the image in a camera viewfinder. The man now knew his course. Startled, Gad saw this pinnacle of rock forge back suddenly towards him. At the same time, a kind of huge sigh of awe went up behind the black-bearded chemist. Looking there, Daniel Gad saw Khalil. His Colt had had a magic effect on the populace. They had opened up respectfully in front of him, like grass beneath the scythe. It's an idea, thought Gad, and drew his own Browning. Indeed the mass fell back now obediently before him, muttering.

But the chemist came on at him steadily, nothing in his hands. In his eyes either, for this lean black-bordered face was again curiously vacant. It did not seem to notice Gad. The man could have been sleepwalking, or hypnotized, or in a trance.

'Stop!' shouted Gad.

The man came on blithely. Maybe nothing could stop him.

In odd fear, Daniel Gad slashed at this face suddenly with his pistol. He saw the nose explode outwards in red. The chemist reeled to his left and brought up against the thigh-high side wall of the bridge. From there, his left hand over his shattered face, he looked swiftly round and up at Gad. The effect was extraordinarily crafty and evil. The eyes were very sharply back in focus again, in total intelligence. The left foot snaked out again at Gad, incredibly fast, but Gad jumped back. As he recovered, the man was over the side. He was always vaulting something. Daniel Gad ran to the side wall. He sensed Khalil to his left. The man would kill himself, thought Gad. He looked down.

But the chemist had landed like a cat. As they watched, he was up from all fours and sprinting forward. Ahead of him in Ramses was the long steel cylinder of a tram, the torsos of its sitting passengers painted tritely on its many windows. As usual, it bulged with standing passengers too, some even hanging on at the doors. It was grinding towards the Sharia Tahrir, and all other traffic gave its iron power precedence, halting before it.

But not the white-winged chemist. Gad's gorge constricted. He knew where the man was going. As Gad raced from the Ramses stairway, Khalil and the small boy somewhere behind him, he saw the chemist below him dive literally at the tram, about two-thirds of the way along it, where there was an opening just in front of its rear wheels. The tram went on serenely, the driver having seen nothing. Probably the passengers within it had not even felt the bump.

When Gad and his companions reached the tramlines the body of the black-bearded chemist lay before them like a lesson in anatomy. The two legs had been sliced off precisely just below the knees and were ranged neatly parallel. The headless torso, still pumping out blood mildly from either end, lay in the same exact line. Only the head had moved. It had rolled away a metre or so, and fetched up on its side facing its body, as though modestly admiring its own expert handiwork. The eyes were open and bulging a little above the broken nose, and the lips were set in a rictus. You might even, Daniel Gad supposed, have called it a smile.

# 3
# The Waterwheels of the House of Gabriel

'He died as a martyr,' said Fuad Wahbah, the boxer. 'He put Islam first.'

'Not like Talkhan,' said Omar el Masri, Omar the Egyptian.

'You should not mention the two men in the same breath,' said Abbas Sidki gravely.

The three sat in his room in Bab el Louk, on the second floor, its one window looking out on a tangled side-alley. Its front steps led out to Bab el Louk market, full of filth and life. The room itself looked as austere as its tenant. It had an iron bedstead, a mattress and sheets, a jar and wash-basin in a corner, a square table and several straight-backed wooden chairs. No pictures or plants softened the room's straight lines and flat surfaces. A single light hung from the dead centre of the ceiling, a shallow white porcelain cone shouldering a bright naked bulb. It hung from a vertical black flex. A telephone and a transistor radio stood on a small table in a second corner. In this taut room that radio could only be for news bulletins, that phone only for duty calls.

'Abdallah Hassan knew that he couldn't escape,' said Fuad, 'so he killed himself, rather than risk talking when they tortured him. He died for Islam.'

'Though he couldn't have revealed much,' said Omar. 'He knew only us in the Angels.'

'But us he certainly knew,' said Fuad, 'so he gave his life for us.'

'There's no doubt it *was* he who killed himself this morning?' Abbas Sidki asked.

'None,' said Fuad. 'I tried to talk to people who saw it. But they were frightened, they feared the police. I found only one. He described Abdallah accurately, talked of his white chemist's coat. I also got a friend to go into the chemist's shop and ask carefully what happened. They wouldn't talk much either but they confirmed it was indeed he who died, chased by two men in civilian clothes and a boy who had come into the shop evidently searching for him.'

'Then at least his place in paradise is assured,' said Omar, 'so we should not be sad for him, even though for us it's a bitter blow.'

'Remember Hassan el Banna's words,' said Abbas. 'That Allah granted the noble life only to those who knew how to die a noble death.'

'Abdallah did that,' said Fuad. 'He was a good man. But we are now two men short.'

'I've told the Upper Council that,' Abbas replied. 'We'll get two replacements at once. There's no lack of volunteers.'

'You acted fast,' said Fuad.

Abbas looked at him.

'We need that speed. We want no police follow-up on Abdallah. We must clear his lodgings of all his things. By first thing tomorrow morning.'

'I'll see to that,' said Fuad.

'There are other things we must do fast,' said Abbas. 'We can allow no one to harm an Angel and escape any less harmed.'

'We know the two men who chased Abdallah,' said Fuad, 'the two with pistols who caused his death.'

'Yes,' said Abbas. 'Colonel Tarek Daniel Gad and Sergeant Raafat Khalil.'

'You want them both?' said Omar.

'Let's take the bigger fish first. You two have a look at the Colonel's flat. You know the address. How easy would it be to

42

enter it, say, with him in there late at night?'

'We'll look carefully tomorrow,' said Fuad, 'when he's away at work.'

'Good,' said Abbas. 'Please let me know the possibilities. Say at eight tomorrow night. I'll be here.'

The two men got up to go.

'Oh,' said Abbas, 'I forgot to tell you. One of the two replacements will be a girl.'

'A *girl*?' said Fuad.

'Well, a young woman. You don't like the idea?'

Fuad eyed him cautiously. 'Not much,' he said. 'Would she be any good in this?'

'A girl could be good,' said Abbas. 'Think about it a bit. Think of any of the attacks we may have to make. A bank. Police station. Shop. If we put a girl in first, a sub-machinegun or pistol in her bag, the guards pay her only half the attention they would pay to any of us. That edge could make all the difference for us between success and failure.'

'If she can use that gun,' said Fuad.

'This one's been trained to use a gun all right,' said Abbas. 'Have no doubt of that.'

'If you say so,' said Fuad.

'I say so. This one you're going to have to hold back. A great sense of mission. I've read her file.'

'How's the other replacement?' said Omar the Egyptian.

Abbas glanced at him.

'Good too. He's been with the Angels awhile, in another cell. You'll see them both soon.'

'Good,' said Fuad.

'Talking of missions,' said Abbas, 'you've got a couple on your hands now, haven't you?'

'Missions?' said Fuad. 'Yes, so we have.'

'Fine,' said Abbas Sidki. 'Let me know how they go.'

Muhammed Abbas Sidki had known about senses of mission from as far back as he could remember. He had a high threshold for suffering and pain. He was born in 1955 in the Delta village of Beit Gibriel, the House of Gabriel, two-thirds of the way from Cairo to Port Said, but well off the main roads. The House of Gabriel was a fine resounding name; Gabriel was a senior executive in the Islamic celestial hierarchy too. That was the nearest that the village ever got to excellence. Abbas Sidki had learned poverty and the bitter struggle for survival in it from his earliest days. His father was a second-class clerk in the post office at the nearest town, eight kilometres away, to and from which he walked every day, except Fridays. The family was Egypt in microcosm: there were too many in it, with too few resources. Muhammed's father exhausted himself to keep his wife and nine children alive, always marginally undernourished, never quite satisfied. Among Muhammed Abbas Sidki's most compelling memories of his boyhood were those rare occasions when the family really ate well. This was forced on them four or five times a year by their own iron Islamic laws of hospitality, because they were receiving some important visitor, possible the Imam for that group of villages. (For Beit Gibriel, of some five hundred souls, was too small to carry an Imam of its own.)

Muhammed Abbas Sidki, though the eldest of the nine children, had always stood in great awe of this holy man, who, on such official visits, wore a fine gold or silver-brocaded galabiah, with a gold sash and a red turban. He invariably carried a beautiful set of worry-beads with him too. They were of cedarwood, finely carved in whorls and arabesques, and they had a clean sharp scent, that of woodsmoke on a hill. The Imam could click them through his fingers to mark his prayers at astonishing speed. Otherwise the holy man maintained an impressive impassivity.

The boy's awe was contagious, or his mother was naturally terrified of the Imam too. Herself illiterate, like eighty per cent of Egypt's rural population then, she treated the holy man with extraordinary deference. She always wore her cleanest clothes for his visits and her best *hegáb*. This was a finely engraved amulet of gilt, cylindrical, ten centimetres long. It hung at her right side on a silk string over her left shoulder, and contained a tiny scroll on which were written the ninety-nine names of the Prophet. She even served the Imam the delicious roasted chicken or stuffed pigeon in plates which she held by the rim from inside her abaya, so that her hand's naked flesh might not contaminate him. The Imam took all this in his stride; he had no doubt at all of his own value in himself, or as the official representative of Islam in that village.

Nasser's agrarian reforms had not yet really reached this village. Here the fellahin, the peasants, were riddled with bilharzia, and prone to cholera and any other major disease that came along. There was no effective sewage system, just as there was no electricity. What sewage there was was shallow, and seeped easily into the village's shallow wells. The fellahin drank from them, or from the Nile's waters.

Still, there was one huge security to the place, as warming as the light of the kerosene lamps with which the villagers lit themselves by night, as warming as the *furn* – oven, breast-high and bench-like and taking up the whole width of the far wall facing the entrance – in which the fellahin lit an evening fire and on which they slept. That security was Islam, the one great certainty and reassurance, the one source of fortitude and inner dignity in an otherwise totally humiliating and bone-crushing world. For you learned death early in the House of Gabriel. People and animals died quickly, from overwork or sickness. Besides, you were always at the edge of the desert here, you could never really forget it, and the desert itself was a form of death. Where the life-giving waters of the Nile reached, the land showed a vivid green, crops of cotton, wheat, rice, lucerne or market gardens or fruits. Where the waters ended, the green stopped short, in a cruelly exact line. It could have been slashed there with a steel ruler, the passionate green on one side, on the other sharp yellow, a colour of death.

Years later Muhammed Abbas Sidki, after he had seen men die in battle and formed his own knowledge of fate, used to think back quite often on that incisive colour change. Here was the reason, he thought, why the typical Egyptian was so endlessly patient, long-suffering, law-abiding, submissive. It was not that he was a coward. On the contrary, he could be an extremely good soldier. He was a very good gunner, particularly anti-tank gunner. He was great at dying at his post obliterated by overwhelming forces. The point was that he was a naturally *defensive* soldier. It was really quite hard to teach him to attack. (Which was why Abbas, who needed to reform things, had become a commando.) To understand that, you just had to look at where the yellow started. In its seven thousand years, this civilization had always had to live concentrated in these tiny ribbons of rich green alongside the Nile, hemmed in ineluctably by the eternal burning sand; for only four per cent of all Egypt's huge surface was arable land. If you had to live that tightly that long with your fellow men, you learned to watch how you moved your elbows. You learned to be orderly. You could not afford the luxury of tempestuous outbreaks. There was not the space for them. It was hard to be violent. If you killed a man, where did you go? If you ran into the desert, you died, painfully.

The fields of the House of Gabriel rambled across absolutely flat land, patterned with irrigation canals like a framework of veins, on one side of this confluent of the Nile Delta. In the old days the Nile had risen every year to flood these fields and irrigate them. Once those floods dominated, that water still had to be raised if men here were still to live. First, machines called *noria* or *sa'iya* were used, fashioned entirely of wood, great wooden waterwheels, with wooden buckets. An ox, harnessed to a long sweep, would circle round and round at its outer edge, the inner hub turning the waterwheel. For these batteries, for this unending task of Sisyphus, cool and shaded places were needed along the bank. When they, older than the Bible, were superseded, they left behind them along the edge clusters of *sant* or mulberry trees reflecting themselves in the waters. Men began to replace animals in this work, and about the end of the first quarter of the twentieth century more efficient leather buckets began to replace the wooden buckets on the rim of the wheel, in a system called *'ilbi*. Finally waterwheels made completely of metal, like children's watermills, were introduced.

The type of water-lift which Abbas Sidki knew best at the House of Gabriel was that with leather buckets, worked with a long counterweighted sweep, a shadoof. In all, there were nine *shawadif*, in three divisions of three each. In each division there was a shadoof and a man to operate it at each of three steps going down to the water. Working a shadoof wrung the sweat from you like a tight mangle. Inevitably the greatest need for irrigation seemed always to fall precisely on all the hottest days of the year, when the temperatures were 40°C or more. Then under the murderous full sun from noon till three in the afternoon the fields seemed like strips of living skin, flayed and blackened in agony. You could almost hear the earth pant like a beaten dog. The small round stones in it were boiling. If you trod on one it would burst the tough skin of your sole.

Abbas Sidki had worked in these *shawadif* in the House of Gabriel with men from the time that he, a lad big for his age, was eleven years old, and he was still working with them when he was eighteen, before he left for his military service. He knew the merciless iron hand of that heat, and the stupefying depression of utter fatigue, but he also knew the marvellous exhilaration of working in absolute physical harmony with other men, in a team unity of eye and skill and sinew. Sometimes the men, at the peak of their young strength, raced one another with their *shawadif*, scorning to husband their reserves of energy, throwing them away royally, with gusts of laughter, in companionship. Sometimes the sheer rhythm of that work was a joy, the pure mastery of it, and sometimes the sweet mesmeric small crescendoes of the *shawadif* as they lifted could lull you in poetry past all sense of tiredness.

He remembered the feluccas too, the fine ageless wooden hulls with their tall single sails, high and white like a sharp curved spearhead. The single mast bent back under bridges. The crews were so practised that seen from the side they brought their mast and sail down flush with the deck so near to the bridge and put them back up so close to it that they gave the impression of sailing clean through it, like a knife through butter. A felucca needed no more than one sail. It had no great need to tack. Egypt's prevailing winds blew south, upriver. The feluccas only needed their sails going that way. The current brought them back downstream, from south to north.

It was one of those happy small geographical accidents that may launch a civilization.

He had watched the feluccas from his post at the shadoof. Other parts of the world of the House of Gabriel unfolded about him here. After dawn every day, and in the evenings after dusk, the women of the village came to the Nile, to draw their needs of water. The men at the *shawadif* worked almost naked, their muscles knotted and twisting. The young women of the village would let down their *khumour*, their long veils, over their faces, between them and the men. They would go down the bank to the water, and before they entered it they would roll up the sleeves of their *thawbs*, and as they went in, little by little and with great care, each would lift and roll her *thawb* up over her thighs, so gradually that only a minimum of white flesh would be bared at any one time between the dark dress and the dark water. Then they would bend fluently and fill their tall jars. When they came back to the bank, and let their *thawbs* fall free again, it was as if they had been renewed, as if that touch of water had washed all parts of them. Their faces glowed with life, their strong black hair flowed in great silken waves down their backs, and their eyes were bright. They lifted the filled tall jars onto their heads with the casual grace of dancers, and walked off in their own good time, their necks regal, their backs straight, and, seen from behind, their hips swaying effortlessly and beautifully from side to side. Abbas Sidki always felt that this ageless female ballet, older than Abu Simbel and Luxor, was somehow a fraction more unabashed, more wanton, even, when the great red disc of the sun hung at the sharp yellow line of the horizon, a few tiny black silhouettes of palm-trees cut out from it, at dusk.

He had other images of the House of Gabriel, as human, as true, and more cruel. One was of the village men, and some women because men were short, working in the fields. It was midday and the sun filled the sky. There was no slightest breath of breeze. In their work, hands and feet put up dust. It hung in the air like a stain. The world baked. The ground itself seemed on fire. The fellahin worked with Egyptian hoes and scythes. In use, they curved the body. They and the murderous brass blast of that sun bent the bodies to the ground, nailed the bodies to the ground, draining them even of sweat. That was the image, that curve of prostration. Their future held only that.

The House of Gabriel was also its evenings. It was the fellahin coming back at dusk from the fields, the youths from the *shawadif*. The beasts of burden seemed easy then, the oxen walked relaxed. The fellahin seemed to be pulling their bodies by sheer will-power, or through fatalism. They walked on a dusty and crooked road. The village showed no neater geometry. They came to huts of reed and clay, houses made of mud bricks, built from the silt of the Nile – another reason why Egypt, always needing *more* arable land for its fatal population explosion, was always having to make do with less – and they entered the House of Gabriel. Now the village streets, no more than mean alleys, twisted in on themselves like entrails. They were charged with filth, packed down in diligent layers, old papers, dried bone, rotted vegetables. Sometimes the feet sank into doughy patches. There were pools of stagnant water, clouds of gnats and mosquitoes shifting above them like gauze curtains. In these narrow, crooked lanes, filth was a kind of comfort. The smell of stale urine and faeces hung in them like decayed incense. Eyes watched all the time from dark doorways.

The village had its fecklessness too. Goats roved freely among these curved fermenting passages, and chickens pecked gaily between their feet. The children ran as untrammelled among them, as naked as their fathers had been, and no less filthy. They would bathe naturally no more often than wolves or foxes. Flies festooned their eyes, causing them no evident concern. Mangy dogs scavenged, their backs slouched in guilt. Old men sat in chairs against walls, most smoking narghiles, tangible proofs of the sheer survivability of Egyptians, against all the odds. At this hour the silver of the evening sky could tighten the heart, giving it a brief sense of contentment. It was a social hour of the day, that of the evening meal. There were still few women about; Islam had made their first duty to their husbands and children in their homes, permitting them only that subterranean existence.

An alley led to the small prayer-house. It should have been a mosque. The village had begun to build it many generations before, but resources and energy had run out. The prayer-house stopped just below waist height. Habit and time lent it veneration. To the villagers it *was* their mosque. They sat and prayed in it on Fridays, facing the *Ka'ba* at Mecca and the speaker, who would address them from his slight elevation on a mud brick platform at the southeastern wall, where the orthodox *mimbar* or pulpit would have been. He reminded them vigorously of the major duties required by the ritual and moral laws – prayer, almsgiving, fasting, and the Haj pilgrimage, none of which they were likely to forget. Muhammed Abbas Sidki often went to the prayer-house on Fridays. If there was space the men, exceptionally, would let him in, wearing his very clean *gandoura* and his skull-cap, very awed and contained. Most often he would stand quietly outside and watch. Seen thus, the packed prayer-house would look then like a single many-headed wall, the turbans of its worshippers projecting just above it, static in piety.

Quite often the speaker from the substitute *mimbar* would be Abbas Sidki's father himself, for he was a deeply religious man, and therefore held in high esteem in the village, as he was for his rare literacy, which made him an honoured employee of the *miri*, the government. The villagers also respected him profoundly because they knew him to be a member of the *Ikhwan el Muslimin*, the Muslim Brotherhood, beloved of the people, founded by the saintly Hassan el Banna in 1928, whose *jawallah*, rovers, dedicated young men, had done so much for the fellahin during the terrible cholera epidemic, and which had brought schools and clinics to all the poor parts of a land which had never seen them before. Yet as far back as Abbas could remember, the Brotherhood was mentioned only in hushed tones. It had been outlawed by the government after one of its members had tried and failed to assassinate Nasser in Alexandria in 1954.

The subsequent witch-hunt of the members of the Muslim Brotherhood had coloured the boy's childhood, finally traumatically. In 1966, in that huge upsurge in Nasser's persecution of them, someone gave false information against Abbas's father. As was their custom, Nasser's secret police, part of that vast and efficient repressive machine built by the paranoiac side of this great and messianic Arab leader, came for their quarry during those sad early hours of the morning when all men's spirits are at their lowest. Abbas Sidki was not to see him again for five years. When he did, it was after Nasser had fallen dead of his heart attack in 1970, and Sadat had taken power and released many of Nasser's political prisoners. But this grace came too late for Abbas's father. Nasser's infamous desert detention camps had marked him too deeply. The lashes from those camps had scarred his back indelibly, as their studied and unremitting cruelty had broken his spirit. Now he no longer wished to fight anyone, for any cause. He wanted only to be left alone, to die gently.

So Abbas Sidki had learned a sense of responsibility young. At the age of eleven he was effectively head of the family. He worked in the fields and on the *shawadif* when he could, and his mother earned food and a pittance by working as a domestic servant in the town. The boy's education did not suffer much. Before his arrest, as if he foresaw it, his father had made Abbas promise that he would at all costs go on with his schooling, even if thereby his mother and younger brothers and sisters must suffer to some extent. Only by education, he said, did the child have any chance at all of fighting his way out of that will-sapping and humiliating poverty which was all that his father, with his elementary primary schooling, had ever known, and all that the vast majority of the other village children would ever know. So the boy, whose *kuttab* religious education, that first step when he was six to ten years old, had already been very intense, grounding him so solidly in the Koran and Sunna and Hadith that he would never forget them, that they would always be the core of his life and its lodestone, went most diligently through his primary schooling in the town where his father had worked, then through his *thanawiyya* or secondary school in a bigger town near to that, emerging from his leaving examination with the outstanding mark of ninety-five per cent, enough to get him into virtually any faculty he chose at university. But before he could think seriously of that, military service caught him.

He made no attempt to avoid or postpone it. After his intensive studying to get that high leaving mark, though he had kept working manually in the village when he could, he welcomed a change to hard military discipline. Also, like many young Egyptians and Arabs, he felt Israel's blitzkrieg and total defeat of the Egyptians, Syrians and Jordanians in the 1967 Six Days War as a deep personal affront. In that war, Egyptian and Arab officers and men had been forced to lie face-down in the desert sands as prisoners to be guarded by female Israeli soldiers. The infidel Jews had dragged Arab pride in the dirt and they had stolen and held on to Arab lands in the Sinai, Gaza, and the West Bank. The Arabs had to win those lands back; the Koran was categoric. So Abbas Sidki volunteered for the commandos. He was big and muscular and fit, and he had that excellent school record. The commandos were glad to have him and they trained him very thoroughly. Abbas's sense of history was good, for he started his military service in 1973, and that was the year of Sadat's surprise war of 6 October when he got his armies massively across the Suez Canal and broke the Bar Lev Line and, almost, Israel.

Abbas Sidki had got right into the act. He was in one of the Egyptian commando groups dropped behind the Israeli lines. In an early action, when the Israelis were still hurling their armour pell-mell into the battle in a desperate attempt to stop the Egyptian advance, Abbas knocked out three Israeli Centurion tanks one after another with Sagger wire-guided anti-tank missiles. It was a feat, or great good luck, or both, for a Sagger firer had to expose most of himself to enemy fire while he wire-guided his missile on its flight. Fortunately for Abbas, his commanding officer had seen his performance and reported on it. As a result Sadat, then on the look-out for national heroes to boost his fighting men's morale, promptly commissioned Abbas Sidki in the field, acclaiming him loudly in all the Egyptian media of communication. He also later awarded him a Star of the Sinai, which became Egypt's highest military decoration, a handsome silver-edged eight-pointed black star, with only the words 'Sinai, 1973' in silver on it in Arabic. Ironically, Sadat was wearing one at his throat himself, over his resplendent blue field-marshal's uniform, when Khalid el Islambouli and his three fellow-assassins from the *Jihad el Jedid* had shot him to death in the reviewing stand.

Abbas Sidki saw no more action in the 1973 war, for Sadat took him out of the line at once and showed him off round the country, to keep the home front's spirits up too. Abbas had become quite a valuable property. Here, as Sadat displayed him, was the new model of the Islamic warrior. Little did Sadat know how right he was. For Abbas's head was not turned by this quick fame. If you looked closely at any of the many photographs of him taken at that time, you could find an edge of mistrust in those very compelling eyes, a rejection, almost a contempt. Certainly, he had sold out nothing in exchange for Sadat's honours. He was still his own man. And that man did not look much as if he liked what he saw.

Indeed, the big cities to which his sudden stardom had brought him, like Cairo and Alexandria, had shocked Abbas beyond words. He had just distinguished himself in a war whose importance and repercussions were international, but he himself in worldly experience was still a country boy fresh from the sticks. The huge garish posters in the streets advertising films, actually showing the naked flesh of women's arms and legs and sometimes something of their throats, even some hints of cleavage, in alluring and provocative poses, seemed to him a blasphemy, and so did the way some young women, many clearly Egyptian, dressed for the streets. He was dismayed to find that, while Muhammed had categorically forbidden alcohol to his followers, some of the Egyptian officer and civilian celebrities with whom he was now supposed to fraternize in his new heroic role at governmental or army receptions could be seen imbibing with gusto and without visible compunction. Moreover, he instinctively felt such social circles alien. The physical mixing of the sexes was far too close, the atmosphere seemed to him illicitly charged, too veined with slick sexual innuendoes, too busy with the brushing of hands, eyes, shoulders. The whole style was wrong. No more did he like what these people talked of, which was power, riches, rewards. He heard too many comments about corruption, these quite explicit, sometimes apparently well documented, and usually admiring, about men in high places.

Abbas Sidki found great metropolises like Cairo no more lovable even outside such gatherings. Cairo's massed tinsel materialism jarred on him. It was a monstrous rats' nest of concrete and mud brick and packed tombs. There were corners here for quick evil and robbery and murder. It was brash and snide. Characteristically, it boasted the world's cleverest pickpockets. Yet for him the place had no identity. You were hard taxed to put a shape to it, lost in its seething mass. It was anonymous and impersonal and malign. It did not know you from Adam. It crushed you without comment. It fell on you like a rock face, choosing just that moment and not budging a millimetre afterwards. It was hell, in a neutral way. It was annihilation, the ultimate void. It was the new *jahaliyya*, the world before Muhammed, the world without God. It obliterated you, but it had not deigned to notice you.

He hated this society at once. He knew that truly it was this society as a whole, not just that of that one man Nasser, which had taken and tortured and broken his father — in fact that gentle man was to die six months later, for once quietly being just what his heart desired: an old man who died in a chair in the sun, at one moment just ceasing to breathe. It had broken him for no other crime than that of being a profoundly humanistic Muslim. Abbas Sidki was not going to forget that. He had a tenacious memory. For him there was something deeply wrong with a world that could do that, while exhibiting those Western vices of limitless material ambition, sexual indecency, corruption and general godlessness that he had seen or heard of in Cairo. This was true even though that world now cosseted him, offering him all its honours and charms, including those of sex, should he now want them.

There were reasons for the world's marked generosity to him at this time. First, it was always heartening to have national heroes around. Second, there was that impact he had upon people. He was a big man and he had a trick of immobility. He did not go away discreetly if you averted your gaze scrupulously from him for long enough. His black and brilliant eye compelled your attention. It tended to accuse you anyway, whether you were guilty or not. Your instinctive reaction was to offer him something. If he would not join you, maybe you could join him.

Abbas Sidki listened to all these offers politely, accepting none. He did not want to be beholden to this society. His mission would be totally to change it. So the photographs of him at this time, while they clearly paint the striking and dark and determined face, hesitate at the eyes. They still show these penetrating, but also, and above all, watchful. It is as if there were a cold film over them. It was not that Abbas was reserving his judgement. He had already made that, irrevocably. Rather, he was waiting until he could carry it out most lethally. Like a good soldier, he was holding his fire.

When Sadat's October war was over, Abbas Sidki asked one favour of the commandos, that they second him to Cairo University, to take its degree in Technical Military Science. He would engage to remain in the army and return to the commandos when he had graduated. His battalion accepted at once, keeping him on his full officer's pay and allowances, and he found a small room in Bab el Louk, the Gate of Louk, quite near to Midan el Tahrir, Liberation Square, the true hub of Cairo.

From Bab el Louk station stubby metro trains left constantly and cheaply, going south to Maadi and Helwan. Across the road from the station, a broad and badly paved street led seventy or eighty metres to the Midan Falaki. By day the pocked street was one of Cairo's busiest open-air markets. The sun beat down on stalls on either side, of watermelons and sweet melons, marrows, aubergines, tomatoes, potatoes, peaches, oranges, bananas, eggs and round flat loaves of *baladi* bread of ruddy cherubic complexion which the government subsidized heavily and which sold per unit for one piastre, say one US cent or one British penny. There were glass-counter restaurants where the customers stood, and naked chickens revolved on spits under the glass, turning brown over red-glowing charcoal fires. Here too huge quantities were sold and eaten of baked Egyptian *fuul* beans and fried *taamiya* cakes, and of pressed orange and melon juices. Raw meat hung, and the black moving pencil-points of flies fretted it, and the eyes of small children. Men crowded the restaurants and cafés, mostly Egyptians in shirts and slacks or galabiahs, a few Saudis and Kuwaitis on the loose. Men, and women in black abayas, shopped at the stalls. This marketplace never lacked its compressed layers of old newspapers, cigarette packs, fruit rinds, bones, condoms and other nameless filth, made respectable by the weight of time.

Despite his critical faculties, Abbas Sidki felt almost at home immediately; this was the comfortably ingrained ageless dirt of the House of Gabriel. His room was just off the broad and leprous street of the souk, up two narrow flights of stairs, above the workshop of a man, diligent and dedicated, who spent his entire life repairing typewriters, living in harmonies of keys and spools and bright wires. Abbas shared the second floor with this artist and his family. A toilet and small kitchen were shared with the two tenants on the floor above. At least Abbas's room, its window looking out on roofs and a choked side lane, was his own. For Cairo, that was a luxury.

Now began a year when Abbas Sidki ate alone. He brought his cooked food down from the kitchen to eat it in his room, or he went on his own to one of the restaurants in the Bab el Louk souk, or to one of the marginally grander ones in the Midan Falaki where you actually sat down at a table and ordered from a young Egyptian waiter, and where a meal of *adas* or lentil soop, *taamiya* fried cakes, salad and *baladi* would not cost you more than thirty piastres or US cents. That was in the evenings. At midday he would get lunch at a students' canteen. There too he generally ate alone; he was too mature, a little too forbidding, to make friends easily. He studied hard and brilliantly. His private life, though, was anything but brilliant. Abbas was bitterly lonely for the first time in his life. He had never used, nor ever even thought to use, those splendid social contacts with Egypt's élite which his wartime fame and Star of the Sinai had so easily made for him, and who would have been delighted to accept him back permanently into their circles. He would have seen such social climbing as a betrayal. They were not his universe. He found them alien, the enemy. They were gracious and graceful and corrupt, Shaitaan's tempters and temptresses.

Abbas Sidki kept his sanity that first year by going back twice to the House of Gabriel, where he saw his mother and his younger brothers and sister and left them money, and rediscovered his identity. The only pain to these small rebirths in his village came from the thought of going back to Cairo. There his consolation became more and more that most integral part of his village life, his basic training in his *kuttab* religious instruction. Islam was the one abiding certainty. He fell back on it more and more. In Cairo, he had always gone regularly to his Friday prayers, often to a mosque much frequented by university men. Now others began to notice his piety.

At the start of his second year of studies a tall young man left the mosque with him one Friday after prayers. Abbas had noticed him standing near the previous Friday. The second Friday, the tall young man, respectful and friendly, invited him to a coffee. Over it, he sounded Abbas out on his political views. It was skilfully done. It was apparent that he already knew virtually everything that there was to know about his guest. Had the latter proved hostile, the young man could still have withdrawn, intact. Instead Abbas Sidki, impressed, replied fairly frankly, though with equal care – the tall young man could always have been a police spy.

Within two weeks the Angels of the Sword had recruited Abbas Sidki. He sat at a table in a darkened room and swore on a Koran and the naked blade of a dagger that he would serve the Angels faithfully until his death. He had not needed much converting. He was already profoundly convinced of the Angels' main doctrine: that the only answer for Egypt, indeed for any Muslim country, was to turn it urgently, and at literally any cost, into a fully Islamic state, like el Khoumeni's Iran.

And he had no reservations about committing his soul and his sinews totally. The Angels, like every other militant Islamic group in Egypt, saw themselves proudly as direct spiritual descendants of Hassan el Banna's Muslim Brotherhood. By joining them, Abbas could pay tribute finely to his father, that gentle Muslim Brother, by carrying on his same work, if almost certainly more bloodily. So he discovered a deep identity. He swore his dread oath to the Angels almost gaily, with a sense of boundless relief. He had found himself, even in the hideous massy brick and concrete labyrinth of Cairo. His identity was that of the Angels of the Sword. They were young Egyptian men and women like himself, with strong beliefs in Islam and the good of their country. They were a brave and goodly company.

In turn, the Angels found him a good troop. Absolutely secure now in his path in life, he redoubled his studies in Technical Military Science at the university, and excelled in every trial mission that the Angels gave him. They saw the natural leader in him quickly. There was in him that chill innate need to exercise power, that imperious ambition, not necessarily egotistical, to use high talents – as if, if the talents were there, they had objectively to be used, by some irrevocable external law. The man was single-minded, not to be deflected. He might have been designed to perform only one great act in his life, and afterwards be discarded, as he would strictly discard everything leading up to that act that was not absolutely essential to it. The tasks which the Angels gave him in the first year or two were not great, mainly espionage, to find out army strengths, orders, dispositions, strategies, political sympathies. The Angels were still quite a small organization then, but from the start they had looked on penetration of the armed forces as important, and particularly of the army High Command. Thus Abbas Sidki, as a rising young army star, had great value for them.

During his second long Cairo University vacation, from mid-August to end September, the Angels' Upper Council flew him to Beirut, where a Palestine Liberation Organization official met him, and drove him to one of the PLO training camps north of the Litani River. The camp taught sabotage by explosives, and Abbas's specialization, sniping; he was a fine shot. They could not teach him much in this skill, but he did learn a fair amount about the PLO's strategy, organization and operational methods, and a deep sympathy for their cause. He demonstrated this by volunteering for two *fedayeen* raids on Israeli settlements in High Galilee, where he was credited with three kibbutznik kills, all shot neatly through the head. He did not go again. Abbas Sidki liked to test out what he could do, he liked to know his powers. But he was a classicist; he did not exaggerate.

The Angels made Abbas Sidki a cell leader after only three years. A year after that he graduated as top student from Cairo's faculty of Technical Military Science, returning then as a captain to his commando battalion's camp on the city outskirts. The Angels kept his room in Bab el Louk for him. It made a convenient base. He had lived austerely as a student, saving most of his salary. In his first year back with his battalion, 1979, he bought a Fiat 127, 1975 model. Its coachwork was beaten up, which was almost inevitable in Cairo's anarchic traffic, but it was mechanically in very good shape. He generally found it easy to get his battalion's permission to come into the city in the evenings. That, with his Fiat, gave him flexibility. It was needed; the Angels were growing. They were still too young to strike, however, when the New Holy War killed Sadat, provoking the fierce repression that had driven them underground.

But that was not an end; Abbas Sidki knew that the hour of the Angels could be at hand. Militant Islamic violence had burst out three times now, every three or four years. Last time *Jihad el Jedid*, the new Holy War, had killed Sadat in October 1981. It was now 1985. True, Mubarak was not Sadat. He was still the absolute ruler, but less blatantly. Mid-1984, Mubarak had even enlarged the Egyptian National Assembly from 392 to 448 seats and allowed some parliamentary opposition to appear, including the old Wafd Party. But the move was mainly cosmetic; there was never any real chance that he would allow the National Democratic Party to be seriously challenged in its totally dominating role. Again, Mubarak was not so histrionic and he had not sold himself to the West as far as Sadat seemed to have done. But there was still too much Western influence, atheistic consumerism and sexual permissiveness seducing Egypt away from her true Islamic identity. Mubarak had not *made* the peace treaty with Israel, but simply inherited it. But he had not broken it. He had just pulled his ambassador out of Tel Aviv. To an Islamic Fundamentalist, that was far from enough. The Israelis still held the Arab lands of the West Bank and Gaza Strip, didn't they? Far from giving them back, they were going on settling them intensively. And what about Jerusalem? The Golan Heights? Lebanon?

Nor were Egypt's structural faults really any better now than they were under Sadat. The economy remained a disaster, with its massive food and fuel subsidies, crippling bureaucracy and hideously inefficient public sector. The population explosion was still fatal and unstopped. The universities still produced tens of thousands of graduates annually, more than the country could place. Against that certain prospect of permanent frustration, impotence and uselessness, reversion to the only other certainty of Islamic Fundamentalism was irresistible, and the living example of Iran proved it dazzlingly practicable. Abbas Sidki was sure that the Angels of the Sword would take Egypt to that change, ideally turning this society into a purely Islamic state. At the least, they would execute some great Establishment leader in a *ghadhbah lil-Allah*, an Outrage for God, which would be great propaganda for Islam by deed. For Egypt, the beloved land. For that beloved land, Abbas Sidki was ready to pay any price, run any risk, murder any mere policeman.

# 4
# A Dive into the Void

What kind of organization was he facing? He didn't even
know its name.

Tarek Daniel Gad stood at the outer rim of his balcony at
1121 Bis Corniche el Nil. It was like standing braced outwards
on a ledge in a sheer rock face. Nine stories vertically below
him the cars, the black-and-white-painted Cairo taxis and
bulging buses and lorries pulsed blaring along the Corniche in
both directions. The fact that it was already ten-thirty at night
had hardly lowered their intensity a jot. Fifty metres out from
the foot of this cliff-like building, across the Corniche, was the
Nile. Moored directly in front at floating quays were four long
slim launches, metal-roofed and glass-windowed, river buses
which transported tens of thousands of workers for a subsidized tiny fee by day. Daniel Gad looked out ahead, across
the shimmering black ribbon of the Nile. He saw a felucca on
its central stream. It was under lights but bare of sail, moving
steadily from left to right, making sound economic use of the
current.

But perhaps it was the island which made the greatest
impact. It was two hundred metres across the dark river and it
blazed with light. Gezira was a long island. He could see the
Gezira Sporting Club straight across from him. Down to the
left of Gad's building, from the other side of the Corniche, a
new bridge lanced across to the island. It was the 6th of
October Bridge, named after Sadat's much publicized war and

supposed victory. To the left of where it reached the island was a tall circular tower. That was the Cairo Tower, boasting a revolving restaurant which sometimes revolved, and a view of Cairo which was invariably epic. A burst of illumination shone now from its top twin rings of observation windows. There was illumination too from the Anglo-American Hospital just west of it. To the left again came a spray of light from the Borg Hotel, the Tower Hotel, which was just to the right of the next bridge as it reached the island. This was Tahrir Bridge, leading straight west from Tahrir or Liberation Square. Presidents Carter and Sadat, standing up in their open car, drove exactly that route over Tahrir Bridge and past the Borg Hotel in 1979. Gad had seen it.

I wonder if we'll ever see that again, he thought.

He leaned forward deliberately from the waist, and looked straight down at the pavement rock-hard nine stories directly below him. Its mesmeric grip held him, mounting inexorably. The top of the balcony's brick outer wall caught him just above his knees. He leaned forward against it. A fraction more, and the surface tension of his soles on the balcony floor would no longer hold him. The balcony wall would serve as a fulcrum. He would topple beautifully forward, and drop like a bird, his arms outstretched, his head proudly back, his clothes fluttering. Suddenly he saw the pavement immediately below him most intimately. He penetrated it like a laser beam. He knew its inner being instantly. Its structure showed a minute and extraordinary beauty, that of a mathematician's perfect equation. It sang silently. It called to him most powerfully. It was an ultimate reality. Why not go down to it?

Why not?

The brash huge roar of the traffic smote his ear suddenly, as if abruptly plugged in from dead silence. It stunned him and impelled him. The cut of the wall top against the front of his legs was now a sharp pain –

To hell with *that* for a game, said Daniel Gad to himself, hoiking himself back a centimetre or two into relative safety, and taking some of the pressure off his bullied legs. Daniel Gad liked to force himself to dice with death like this from time to time. He had the theory that it hardened his nerve. He was, however, remarkably accurate in his assessment of the true risks. He never pushed his luck too far. This habit of Gad's could nonetheless be unnerving. Another manifestation of it was his lust for overtaking in Cairo traffic against all the odds. He only exhibited this mania once a month or so, but what it lacked in frequency he made up for in high drama. He would tuck the shiny new black Fiat 2000 in ahead of the vehicle in front of him just in time, a matter of whiskers separating him from the oncoming monster, which would invariably be a massive lorry or oil bowser, or one of the Cairene buses which were driven by men of steel who deviated for nothing, not even Leopard tanks. This particular dance with destiny could reduce Gad's colleague Sergeant Raafat Khalil, himself normally a man of iron equanimity, almost to tears.

As one last muscle-tone heightener, apt to concentrate the mental vision, Gad now commanded himself to look down, not just vertically, but slightly backwards into the balcony of the flat below. This time, however, he allowed himself actually to grasp his own balcony with his hands, and moreover to bend his knees somewhat to keep his centre of gravity comfortably in his own domain, so that he looked rather like a man getting on his marks at the start of a race. Comic though Gad's posture might have seemed, it did however permit him to confirm what he already knew, which was that the balcony below was identical to his. It was vast, some eight metres broad and four deep in the centre, where glass doors led back to a sitting and dining room. It narrowed to the right, where another windowed room abutted on it; a bedroom, probably the main one. Cane armchairs lolled about this balcony, as on Gad's, like benighted sunbathers. The flat below's only apparent difference from his, indeed, lay in its occupant.

She was not like Gad. Life had passed her by, or she had passed life by. She must then have been in her early forties, though the point might seem irrelevant; she had already assumed the parched agelessness of papyrus, which indeed her skin, or what little of it could be seen, closely resembled. She was an Arab lady of the Egyptian lower middle class, who had achieved to perfection that high ideal of total female self-effacement decreed by the most puritanical and exigent of that cultural level. As Gad knew, some ninety per cent of all Egyptian Muslim women were still circumcised. This Arab lady could have been the high priestess of that cult of fervently willed and dedicated sexual insipidity. Her clothes seemed as deliberately colourless as her sexuality. She always wore pastels, very light greys or browns or almost imperceptible pinks. She covered her broad body completely, from high-collared neckline to the floor. Her slippered feet peeped out demurely; her sleeves were long; you saw no flesh. She gave the effect of a slightly elongated oildrum on small feet. A wimple-like head-dress covered her hair scrupulously, and her forehead. Black Arab eyes, an aquiline nose, quite generous lips, gazed out at you as through a visor. That was as far as she went. Married at sixteen to an enterprising Egyptian entrepreneur three times her age, she had popped babies out for him for four years with machinegun regularity. He had then fallen dead and left them the flat and his reasonable fortune. Resoundingly celibate, she had devoted herself to her four sons, the last of whom had left Egypt two years before to help the Kuwaitis to run their oil ministry. She had stopped there, modestly striking her colours, frozen in time like a gnat in honey. Gad had never since then seen her afford herself any sensual satisfaction, save for the huge one that she visibly gained from eating *baklawa* and similar sticky sweets, which she did monotonously at all hours. For all he knew she was doing that in bed now, for he could see that the light of that room under him to his right was on.

Gad drew himself up and back from his racing crouch, massaging his aching calves, then sat down carefully on one of his own cane armchairs. He put his hand down to his glass, which he had set on the balcony tiles next to the bottle of Russian-formula vodka, can of orange juice, and ice-bucket. His glass was still half full. Back late from the office, he had been enjoying his first drink of the evening with well-earned gusto, minding his own business, when that familiar appeal to fence with fate, this time by balancing at the edge of his balcony, had smitten him. Now nothing could keep him from that drink. He savoured it richly, in no hurry. It was mellow, and very satisfying. There was the smooth silky caress of the orange, with somewhere in it the only just perceptible bite of the vodka, thin and clean, like a slim rapier of reality at the heart of things.

He bent to replenish it, and hesitated. He got up then and went back through his opened glass doors and through his sitting and dining rooms, then ninety degrees left into his hall, then to the right off it into the kitchen and to its refrigerator. He took out a chilled bottle of Giannaclis Villages and uncorked it. For Gad's money it was the only good dry white wine that Egypt made, from the Giannaclis vineyards near Alexandria. He took it and one of his tulip-shaped Orofors crystal wineglasses from Stockholm back to the balcony and put them down on the tiled floor before lowering himself back slowly into his long cane chair. Maddening connoisseurs, Daniel Gad was not averse to a little ice in his dry white wine, especially on a warm night like this. He leaned over and served himself liberally. Less lethal, the Giannaclis would also be crisper to the palate than vodka and orange.

Gad took another sip. The wine, that view, were both superb. It was a great life.

He sighed. But, brutally, life was not just a matter of Giannaclis and skittles. It was just three days since the bearded chemist had neatly severed his head and lower legs from his torso, ending up very much with the laugh on the authorities. Police General Abd el Nour, General Servant of Light, had not been at all amused by the death of the black-bearded and white-winged chemist, following so hard on Talkhan's. He was fast concretizing his hypothesis that Gad, aided and abetted by his fanatical and unhealthily loyal ex-tank-corps mate and driver Raafat Khalil, had set out to deprive his commanding officer of merited honours before Mubarak. Cunningly, and with incredible speed and efficiency, Gad was wiping out every member of this sinister new Militant Islamic cult, one by one, the very moment that each first raised his head, and before he had a chance to speak a single word out of it. Indeed, despite and in fact during the ferocious rockets that Police General Abd el Nour had delivered him in his sumptuous tenth-floor office in the Sharia Kasr el Nil, Daniel Gad was sure that he had several times discerned in the Servant of Light usually metallic eyes a look of distinct awe, not to say alarm. Gad had done what he could to re-establish his and Khalil's professional credibility. They had most thoroughly interrogated the owner of the chemist's shop – the gross man who had also been behind the counter when the black-bearded chemist sprang over it in his lightning reaction and sped off to his smiling double-guillotine act. They had done the same to the gross man's other assistant. These two had however not seemed to know much about the black-bearded man, except his name, Abdallah Hassan, and the fact that he had come to the shop the year before looking for work, with such excellent qualifications from Cairo University that the gross man took him on at once, at a salary of £E60 a month, say $US60.

It was extraordinary what a sparse picture they painted of Abdallah Hassan. Clearly he had kept his inner self virtually entirely from them. For them, he might have been the original Invisible Man; an outline, then, shockingly discovered, nothing within. It seemed that they were making that haunting discovery only now, as they talked of him. They looked concerned and somewhat guilty. No, they had never had any cause to complain of him as an employee. He was always very punctual and punctilious in his work. He smoked quite heavily, but they never saw him touch a drop of alcohol, even beer. He was clearly a religious man. Two of a Muslim's five sets of *salah*, daily prayers, fell within his normal working hours. These were those of just after *dhohr*, noon, and *'asr*, mid-afternoon. He always performed them most scrupulously in the shop, whether there was a crush of customers clamouring for service or not, and he kept his small prayer-carpet behind the counter for this purpose; nor did anyone ever gainsay him in this his strict observance. Abdallah Hassan cut no corners. Whenever he could he also did the Muslim *wudow* ritual prior to praying, in the kitchen or toilet, washing his hands from a copper basin, then his mouth, nostrils, face and forearms, then drawing the fingers of his wetted right hand over his bared head and from underneath forward through his beard, twisting his forefingers in his ears, drawing his fingers over his neck from the back, and washing his feet up to the ankles; all this in two minutes, demonstrating the skills of long piety.

No, they never saw him with a woman. Nor, now that they came to think about it with *anyone*. Though he was always polite, he wasn't really sociable. They did not recall his ever really talking about himself. He often seemed restless. He was obsessional about order. For a religious man, he showed no instinctive sympathy for the weak. He was hard on beggars and little boys. The salary wasn't much, though he could have been making a little on the side short-changing the customers – particularly the *khawwaghat*, the foreigners, who never knew any better and could afford to lose a bit anyway. But he had never asked for a rise. It was as if he didn't really *care* about the money; an extraordinary attitude. And, though he was always very knowledgeable and conscientious in his work, he some-times gave the impression of not really being *there*. It was as if all the time he really had his mind on something quite different.

Gad sighed. He recognized the signs.

Yes, the gross man did happen to know Abdallah Hassan's address; he had had to take him back there by taxi one afternoon when Hassan had had a very bad flu. It was in the Sharia el Maqsi in Rod el Farag on the other side of Shubra, near the Faculty of Art of the Ain Shams University. The gross man gave Gad the street number.

Gad had driven there with Khalil that same afternoon, which was the day after Abdallah Hassan's suicide – Hassan, Daniel Gad felt sure, would have called it his martyrdom, a straight jump to God. They arrived half a day too late. That morning a friend of Hassan had called and taken all his things. There hadn't been much, mainly books, and it had all gone into Hassan's one small suitcase. The friend said that Hassan was moving in with him. Didn't the landlord think that a bit odd? Not at all, said the landlord. It all seemed perfectly regular. Hassan had paid his rent up to the end of the month anyway. Besides, the friend had a note from Hassan. No, he hadn't kept it; why should he have? The friend had taken it away with him. No, it hadn't been handwritten, but typed in Arabic, and it had a scrawled signature which looked like Hassan's. Why shouldn't it have been?

The landlord had also known the friend perfectly well by sight. He had visited Hassan in his room several times, always at very respectable hours. The landlord knew the friend's name then? Well, no. Wait a minute; he thought he remembered Hassan once calling him Fuad. And what was his surname? No, the landlord couldn't help there. What did Fuad look like? Well, he was quite a short man, but he looked very strong. In what way? He had big shoulders and a big chest, like a wrestler or a weight-lifter. He was a dark man, no beard or moustache, perhaps twenty-four. He talked like an educated man. Maybe he was a doctor from the University. No, he didn't know the Doctor's address. Did he know anyone else who might? Like, had he ever seen the strong man, the Doctor, with anyone other than Hassan? Well, as for that, the landlord couldn't be sure. He would have to think about that one a bit.

That was about as far as Daniel Gad could decently go on that tack for the moment. You couldn't get blood out of stones, only out of decapitated and amputated Islamic Fundamentalists, which he already felt certain that Abdallah Hassan had been. Gad put plainclothes tails on Hassan's landlord and the two chemists, just in case, for the sake of good order, though he doubted that they would lead to anything very productive. He had the same sentiment about the corpses. He had had the mutilated body of Suleiman Talkhan and the four bits of Abdallah Hassan sent along to the civil police's forensic specialists, who were really quite hot at their jobs. Here too he doubted, however, that these gentlemen would be able, by some brilliant matching of hairs, threads, cigarette ashes or tramwheel tracks, to point infallibly to the monstrous leaders of this murderous lot. Life was not like that. He was up against a highly dedicated and intelligent group, ruthless in using torture and killing, including self-killing, when it deemed that expedient, and adept and extremely rapid in covering its tracks.

On a hunch, Daniel Gad had gone back the next day with an Identikit, and coaxed Abdallah Hassan's landlord for two hours until he had a visual picture of the heavy-shouldered Fuad, if Fuad it was, front and profile, that the landlord swore was the spitting image of him. This Daniel Gad then copied and got out very promptly to his agents and, more confidentially, to all police stations in the country – which is to say that he asked all civil police station commanders in his accompanying memo to ensure that all their men saw the pictures and knew that they must most urgently advise Gad through their commanders if they came across the supposed Fuad, but *without* hanging these portraits up in the usual Station Rogues Galleries where non-police passers-by might see them and bring Fuad the exciting news that he was famous. Gad wanted to keep that as his own surprise.

Daniel Gad gazed across the unseen thundering metal herd below him and the shimmering black water of the Nile to the rich scattered lights of Zamalek, sparkling like sequins. He bent and filled his glass, then leaned back and took a long pull of the chilled and chaste Giannaclis Villages.

It would be great thus to take an unsuspecting Fuad, unravel that torturing and murder and that suicide, discover the secret grave form that united them all. It would be satisfying as a work of art. But they were going to have to battle for it.

This was what police work really was in the end, thought Daniel Gad; not at all glamorous, simply a discipline of meticulously checking every detail and painstakingly following up every possible clue, even when the boredom of it maddened you. In life, even in what at first sight looked most inchoate, shapeless, merely accidental, there was almost always a form somewhere, at some level; a causal pattern, if you could only find it. Sometimes that could take you years. Sometimes, twenty years after some cataclysmic but apparently motiveless and meaningless event, one tiny fact would turn up and jerk all that long massy seeming chaos suddenly and uncannily into icy ringing focus, so that you said to yourself: No. Indeed. It could not have been otherwise. It was like, in infinitely slow motion, juggling a negative in a developing tank, and abruptly seeing the clear image swim up to your sight in that one magic instant, fixed then for all time. Gad could think of no other experience quite so richly rewarding. An orgasm, though exquisite, did pass kind of quickly. He could understand what Beethoven meant when he said he saw a symphony in a second.

Me and Beethoven, thought Gad, gazing at the glitter of Zamalek, which he knew had no less than fifty-five embassies and ambassadorial residences. That delight in form was what police work, well done, could sometimes bring you, provided you scrupulously applied all the disciplines. The rest was intuition and luck, but these you could not depend on. You had consistently to use each single strength and skill and technique of your organization. For your adversaries, the men in the black hats, had huge advantages. Among these were the great powers they gained from working in the shadows. Your enemies were faceless, you could not see them. They operated by a different moral law. And in this case, feared Gad, which had started in two days with the torture and murder of Talkhan and the sacrificial self-murder of Abdallah Hassan, they worked with a deep sense of purpose, an evident dedication, intelligence and efficiency that made them professionally admirable. Also possibly lethal for his country, and even outside it. They knew what they wanted. They had conviction and brains and power. They walked and they worked sure as cats in the dark. Knowing who you were, they could hit you at any time. They had the supreme advantage of dealing. They named the game and called the wild cards. One of which could be a Jack with a knife.

At any time, they could hit you –

What the hell, thought Daniel Gad resolutely, this was mere morbidity. And he had after all just won a self-test trial. He finished his glass of Giannaclis Villages – the third – and swung manfully to his feet. He kissed goodnight to the sequin-lights of Zamalek and went back into his sitting room through the glass doors, which he locked behind him thoughtfully. Umm Samir, his daily, could remove the bottles, ice-bucket and glass in the morning. Gad turned smartly left at the end of his sitting room. On the right was the loo and a monumental bath, served by a shower and a liquid gas geyser that protested with moans and a fan of blue flames if pressed too hard for hot water. He brushed his teeth. An early night was no bad thing these telling days.

Across from the bathroom, parallel to the sitting room, was his bedroom. As wall decoration it carried a Gauguin print of naked Tahitians and a long horizontal Modigliani nude with a knowing look, superb breasts, and a triangle of pubic hair intriguingly off centre. The classical simplicity of Gad's taste in paintings set the tone of his bedroom, most of it taken up by a double bed of heroic proportions. He took off his dark-grey bush-jacket with its two breast-pockets and two hip-pockets, and his neat light-grey trousers – Simpson's, from London – taking everything from the flank pockets, including his handkerchief, keys, and the two charged spare magazines for his Browning 9 mm automatic pistol. He slipped the bush-jacket and trousers onto separate hangers and put these back in the far corner cupboard, taking particular pains to leave the trousers hanging exactly on their knife-edge creases; Gad hated blurred lines. He went back to the bed and took the Browning from it and put it under the pillow on the right-hand side nearest to the door and windows onto the balcony, then he put the other contents of his pockets on the small table beside the bed.

He took off his singlet and underpants, since he always slept naked, and got into the right-hand side of the bed, under the single sheet which was all he could bear in this heat. On his right side, he slipped his left hand under the pillow, and felt the hard butt of the Browning.

Good, he thought, and switched off the bedside light. He fell promptly into a deep sleep.

It was an odd dream. Three men half-circled him. They were dressed like Tuaregs: flowing robes, the lower parts of the face masked by the ends of the head-dresses pulled across. One was squat, with a knife; one a big man. All he could see of the faces were the eyes. The three Tuaregs had some hypnotic power over him. He seemed paralysed before them, on a lower level, subordinate to them. They were bearing down on him from some height. The big man said, very softly, in Egyptian Arabic: 'Get his gun first. Probably under the pillow.' Powerless, Gad watched the third Tuareg, slim and quite tall, advance upon him and put a hand down under his, Gad's head, then go away silently with Gad's Browning automatic in it. 'Now the knife,' said the big one, still in Egyptian Arabic. The squat Tuareg advanced.

In Egyptian Arabic –

*This was no dream! These were no Tuaregs! And that was his, Gad's, pet Browning being carted off there!*

As the squat man with the knife bent over him, Gad drew both his legs up like lightning to his chin under the loose sheet, then lunged them straight with a mighty effort, projecting the squat knifeman like a shell rolled up in a sheet at the big leader. The two cannoned into the small dressing-table at the far wall, and Gad heard the big mirror snap in two. But this he registered in mid-air, for he had carried that lunge through into a fluid movement off his bed, stark naked. As his feet hit the floor he saw the third man come at him raising the Browning, and Gad managed to sink one fair left hook into his general torso, wilting him. Gad could spare no more, for he was on his urgent way; this was no place to be with that loaded Browning around and once those two torpedoed men got back on their feet. So Gad leapt for his bedroom door and got it open, slamming it shut behind him as he sprinted the four metres to the centre of the balcony where he had stood that evening. He heard his bedroom door crash open behind him. He had almost no time left.

Gad mounted his balcony wall like a cat. He caught one hideous view below of the murderous black street nine stories down. A shot whistled past his ear – from his own gun, the ultimate insult. Gad was over the wall and hanging from its top in a flash. Now he did not dare look down, or the vertigo would snatch him off. He swung his legs inwards experimentally. He had got it about right, but only just; the ceiling line of the balcony below cut just across the middle of his stomach; any lower, and he would never be able to swing in, but must fall straight and break his back forty metres below. Even now, the margin was terrifyingly slim –

He swung and let go, hearing an enraged shout straight above him. *Remember to half-twist in the air*, he told himself. For a moment he seemed to hang unsuspended but motionless. He had got it wrong. It was impossible to get enough foward movement from such a swing to take him in. Twisting in the air, he knew that at best he would fall across the balcony wall below. He could as well break his back there as nine stories down, and they could still shoot up what was left of him there from above –

In fact his confused twist, which he would certainly never have been able to repeat, took him in right side up just inside the balcony wall below and parallel to it. On his hands and knees, he scampered swiftly inwards like a joyful infant; he was taking no chances lounging about by the balcony wall where they might still get at him from above.

Daniel Gad stood up by the glass doors leading in to the Arab lady's sitting room. They were locked. Her flat was completely dark and silent. There was no light or sound from his flat above either. People were reconsidering plans. He had better keep moving. One of their plans might be to come down and get him in here – if not by his route, then by the stairs and front door.

Gad looked hurriedly about the balcony for some sort of cloth or towel. This had to be the barest balcony in Cairo. He saw nothing. Gad shrugged mentally; he had work to do. He sidled along to the right to what he guessed was the Arab lady's bedroom, and tried the door. Happily, like his own above, it was unlocked; after all, one hardly expected night visitors from that direction, except on flying carpets. Gad opened the door very quietly; with luck, he could find something modest to put around him before he came back onto the balcony and knocked on her door decently. But as, very slowly, he eased the door open, and stepped cautiously in, a huge clatter arose at his feet, of upset and no doubt shattered crockery and glassware; undoubtedly the remnants of the lady's supper which she had treated herself to in bed; he could feel the queasy clutch of a sticky pastry under his left sole. The bedside light went on at once, trapping him in its full glare. And the Muslim lady. She evidently slept half sitting up, for she had two huge bolsters behind her, as if trying at all times to maintain her daytime decorum. Gad noticed too that she appeared to be wearing exactly the same clothes as she did by day, perhaps for the same reason. Her hair was still fully covered, and her forehead, and all of her body that he could see, save for her hands, now drawn up protectively before her breast, and her black-Arab-eyed face, now transfixed by an expression of utter horror, her mouth locked open so tight that she evidently could not even scream through it.

'Pardon me, Madam,' said Daniel Gad, his left hand spread out prudishly over his genitals, 'but are you sure that your front door is soundly locked?'

Only later did Gad realize that he had sounded like some eager lock salesman, demonstrating to the public by live example how much it needed him. The Arab lady if anything looked even more horrified.

'It's really quite all right, Madam, I'm a police officer,' Gad went on in a conciliatory tone, adding superfluously: 'Though I don't happen to have my card on me at the moment.'

But this reassurance was lost on his hostess, who had now fainted, defensively and clearly, and with a nice economy of movement. Her head was in exactly the same place on her top bolster, her eyes shut, and her mouth still locked open. Gad eyed her swiftly. There was at least one virtue to her state. He did not have to do anything about her. He could instead jump for the bathroom, in the same geographical position as his, and get a towel and wrap it round him, then to the phone:

'Police Emergency? Police Colonel Tarek Daniel Gad, Special Section T, Terrorists. You want my police number. It's 843753. You can check that. And my flat is No. 40, ninth floor, 1121 Bis Corniche el Nil, between the Ramses Hilton and the Television Building. Get a patrol car to it absolutely at once. Maybe two or three. There are three terrorists inside, armed and dangerous. Oh, ah, and could you get a couple of men to the flat just underneath it too? With a spare Browning 9 mm pistol and a shirt and a pair of trousers. What's that? The *number* of the flat under mine? How should I know? What *size* of trousers? Hell, I don't know the number, but I'm a metre 83 tall and I weigh 78 kilos. What *kind*? Hell, *any* kind; just trousers. *Why* do I need trousers, a shirt, and a pistol, you ask? Sergeant, is it? Lieutenant. Lieutenant Tonsi, just do as I say! *Act*, and now! Or I'll have your head!'

In my position, I could hardly have said Balls, thought Gad reasonably, putting down the phone.

By the time the reinforcements arrived, the Muslim lady had recovered her consciousness and got her voice operating. She wailed loudly until the towelled Gad calmed her with repetitive teas and *baklawa*. But she needed to have no fear of high-pressure lock salesmen. After the phone, Gad had immediately checked her front door lock. It was indeed very sound. Far sounder, evidently, than his had been. When the reinforcements came, and Gad was again decently trousered, he and three armed police went up the main stairs to his flat. The door was still open, as if left so in deliberate contempt by the terrorists; they didn't mind your seeing how they got in, how efficient they were. The interior of Gad's flat confirmed that; the fingerprint experts came in in droves, and found nothing. The only thing that Gad had actually seen them touch was his beloved Browning 9 mm automatic pistol, but that, as he knew painfully, they had of course taken away with them. Their drugging of the building's *bawwab* had been as neat; no one knew how they had administered it to his midnight cup of tea. So they left no trace, except for Gad's broken mirror; nothing disturbed. It was almost polite, certainly very confident. It was as if they said gently, Well, never mind. Anyone can fail once. Another time, We'll be back. See you around . . .

The next day was no picnic for Daniel Gad. Despite his fraught night he got to his office immaculately on time. He had managed to get some sleep from 3 am when the fingerprint experts had finally left. One of the armed police had stayed till the morning on guard at Gad's lock-picked door. Police General Abd el Nour, groomed as a bank manager, received him quite promptly in his ample office. It seemed to Gad that his boss fixed a fairly jaundiced eye on him. He quickly learned, indeed, that the Servant of Light had received a very full and mocking report on the incident earlier that morning at his opulent house in Maadi, from the general in charge of the regular civil police in whose jurisdiction Gad's flat and the emergency police service fell. This general was at exactly the same level as the Servant of Light in the police hierarchy, and every bit as competitive for advancement and presidential or ministerial favours. He was clearly one-up in this case. The report was already going the rounds to a restricted but very select audience. It bore the title of Naked Courage, Abd el Nour told Gad grimly, and it suggested that several useful maxims might be extracted, such as, When fighting terrorists, never scorn to reconnoitre under ladies' beds.

Gad had been about to give a slightly different picture of his own attempted murder, in which he might just have mentioned in passing the initiative he had displayed in conserving this valuable government property by diving over the balcony, but after the Servant of Light's tirade he limited himself to answering his questions; it seemed evident that Abd el Nour could have borne that loss to the State, and might have preferred to see Gad end his dive nine stories further down.

'No,' he said, 'I got no clear perception of them. It was dark, remember, and their faces were masked.'

'Nothing at all?'

'Well, of course it's logical to infer that the squat man with the knife is Fuad. That's how Abdallah Hassan's landlord described the "Doctor", short but heavy-shouldered and heavy-chested, who collected Abdallah's things – and so took him right out of history, leaving no trace – just the morning after Abdallah decapitated himself. Which he did to stop himself being forced to tell us who were in his cell and why they tortured and murdered Suleiman Talkhan. It's clear now that they must have found out that he was contacting me. Talkhan would have been a cell member too.'

'Cell?'

'Cell. Of five members. Talkhan, Abdallah, Fuad, and the other two mystery men last night. A five-man cell. Pretty standard, wouldn't you say?'

'Standard for what?' said the Servant of Light foxily.

As if you didn't know, thought Gad.

'For Islamic Militants,' he said.

'You're sure that that's what they are?'

'That's how it looks. Top marks for dedication. Very strict standards, for friends or enemies. High intellectual levels – Abdallah had excellent qualifications at Cairo University in pharmacy, one of the four most exigent faculties. Abdallah's landlord talked of Fuad as a doctor, a very educated man. And they shot Talkhan through the left eye; almost a ritual murder. That's what *Takfir wal Hijra* did to that Wakf minister, remember?'

'Yes,' said the Servant of Light, 'I remember.'

'After they'd strangled him,' said Gad. 'That was a signal. Someone meant us to read it.'

'Which you didn't,' said the Servant of Light, automatically making that sound like an accusation.

'No,' said Gad, 'because instead of letting things lie Khalil and I found out about Abdallah and chased him until he killed himself. Then we went and dug up his landlord and started asking him awkward questions. Somehow that leaked back to our friends, either through that rooming-house or the chemist's. Or they had men watching either or both. So they saw we might get on their tracks. So, very swiftly and efficiently, they tried to eliminate us.'

It was really hard to read from the Servant of Light's expression if he was glad that they had failed.

'Fundamentalists again,' he said. 'Mubarak won't like that.'

'That's too bad,' said Daniel Gad. 'That's what it seems.'

'There aren't supposed to be any Islamic Fundamentalists worth mentioning left in Mubarak's world,' said Abd el Nour. 'Not any more. There's no reason for them. After all, Egypt's a fairly happy country overall these days, wouldn't you say? A fair amount of brotherly love about. Prosperity –'

Prosperity, my foot, thought Gad, too tactful to say it aloud. Abd el Nour was really working on his special pleading. It was the official line. In fact, as Gad knew, there was still a frightening amount of poverty and suffering about, and it could never be markedly reduced while some 1½ million new Egyptian mouths came on stream each year to be fed in the population explosion. And, shambling as it was, the Egyptian economy would collapse utterly and probably irremediably if the US ever stopped injecting its $2.4 billion of economic aid a year.

'It's even a democracy now,' said the Servant of Light tenaciously. 'Since Mubarak's constitutional reform and expansion of the National Assembly seats – even allowing the old Wafd Party to reappear in opposition.'

This time Gad could not forbear to comment. 'Not very far,' he said. Mubarak's National Democratic Party still reigned absolute in anything that really mattered. It just looked good to have a mildly lively opposition. For the gallery. To please the Americans.

The Servant of Light came back to the attack. 'Well, then, Colonel, where are they? This is your job, isn't it? What you're supposed to be employed for, right?'

'Who?'

'Your Fundamentalist friends. I expect some *action*! You should go out there and *get* them. As it is, I'll have to give Mubarak some sort of preliminary report on this, my God.'

'Well, you already have two heads out of five. I don't think that's too bad.'

'Yes, but neither of them was exactly a *talking* head when we got it, was it? I mean, you haven't really got *on* to them out there, have you? Got a *grasp* of them.'

'No, not yet.'

'But,' riposted Abd el Nour nastily, 'they've got onto *you*, all right, haven't they? I mean, we can't deny that. Got onto your flat all right, didn't they?'

'Yes. No, we can't deny it.'

'Apart from double-securing that front door, we'd better have a hard look at the flats above you. We don't want any rope-tricks from there, do we, emulating your example? And we'd better have an armed policeman in your flat all day, three shifts of eight hours each, until further notice –'

'Yes. Thank you.'

His girlfriend Bridget would just love that. Still, Gad could park the policeman in the kitchen at the back. He could do a superb job from there guarding the front door. And, no doubt of it, having an armed guard posted round the clock would be a reassurance. Though Gad doubted that his enemies would strike again there like that. From the feel of them they were professionals, artistic in their work. If they tried for him again, it would probably be something quite new.

'And your pistol?' said Abd el Nour, with his genius for putting his finger on open wounds.

'Yes, General. They took it.'

'My God, a police colonel who loses his pistol to his enemy! Doesn't that rate a court-martial in the army? Well, write me a report on it. Short. And a requisition form for a replacement. I'll sign them, this one time.'

'Sir. Then, if I may, I'll get the replacement this afternoon. I feel –' he hesitated a moment at the word '– naked without a pistol.'

'You're obviously critically less effective without one. All right.'

Gad leapt at the opportunity.

'Then perhaps I might be excused the reception this evening, General? I may be late back from the armoury and range.'

The reception was in honour of an arriving US expert in training security corps. His rank was equivalent to general, so a good part of Egypt's top police and army brass would be there, and some of their managerial talent in the form of rising stars. It was at 7 pm at the El Salam, the grandiose new hotel in Heliopolis. Daniel Gad loathed such all-male festivities, which he found excruciatingly boring.

'Certainly not, Colonel!' said the Servant of Light, the steel back in his voice. 'I shall expect *all* my officers to be present at that ceremony! *Abd* on time!'

Well, thought Gad in resignation, it was natural. Abd el Nour would see his status as partly judged by that.

Gad had quite a good afternoon. He had drawn his new Browning 9 mm with its two spare magazines and 100 rounds of ammunition from the central police stores, and driven to a police training school barracks at the edge of the city. The barracks had a 25-metre underground firing-range. Daniel Gad knew it well. He came here at least twice and preferably three times a week in the late afternoons or evenings whenever he could, and fired three magazines or thirty-nine shots at the black-painted standing metal man at the far end of the range. Pistol shooting was like any other skill – it paid to keep in practice. Gad counted the time spent a very good investment. His Browning had saved his life before. If you ever had to use a pistol, that need tended to be urgent. It helped to be prompt and accurate. So Gad took his pistol training seriously, as he did his thrice-weekly sessions in the police gymnasium.

The man who had taught Gad most about using pistols was the barracks' sergeant-armourer, who was also its shooting instructor, and had been the Police's champion pistol shot for years. He was a big and gentle man called Ismail, from the Delta, with a huge moustache like a Pasha from the Ottoman Empire, and broad hands. He had disabused Gad from the start from standing side-on to his target – we're not *fencing*, he would say – and taught him instead to stand square-on to it, his feet planted solidly apart, his body laterally rock-steady. He had Gad extend his master right arm straight ahead, his right hand gripping the Browning most firmly with the index and lower fingers, the forefinger and thumb riding fairly free, so that the pistol sat back precisely into the hinge tendon between them, and straight in line with the extended arm. Now came the secret: Gad learnt that even pistol champions never had absolutely still arms. Even theirs moved in from the left or right in tiny jumps onto the target. To shoot well, you tightened the pad of your forefinger very gradually on the trigger as your foresight moved in from one side onto your target, and you simply maintained the pressure as you went past. As you came back on, you tightened the pressure again, and so forth, until the pistol just about shot itself, usually with remarkable accuracy. After three years at about a hundred shots a week, Gad could do all that in about half a second, almost intuitively.

The gentle Ismail also trotted Gad once a week or so round the barracks' semi-commando surprise range, which was filled with dummy trees and bushes and thin and twisting alleys of mock plywood houses. A fairly high surrounding stone wall saved innocent bypassers in the world outside from being shot by mistake. As you moved in war-like crouch through this bogus universe, your loaded Browning at the ready, amazing targets jumped unpredictably up at you on springs. All, sadly, whether crouched, standing or charging, bore the form of that most murderous and deadly of enemies, man. Here the drill was to lunge straight back at your assailant, the body thrust forward on one foot directly at it, the right arm rammed out as in the standard firing-range, the extended left arm out supporting it; like an arrowhead. You always shot twice, the first and a cover; once you got the hang of it, one of the two almost always hit. The trick was to point with your whole body, instinctively; as even a poor shot, if he points instinctively at a flying bird, will generally do so with astonishing accuracy.

'You're pulling them all a little left, Colonel Tarek,' said Ismail.

'Hell,' said Daniel Gad. 'This trigger is as stiff as a young girl! A real virgin!'

He had just fired a first complete magazine of thirteen. He had felt that he was pulling his shots. Now, by peering, he could see where he had hit, on the white-painted stone wall to the left of the black silhouette, chest-high. The eagle-eyed Ismail had seen them seconds before him.

'Still, you've got a nice grouping,' said Ismail. 'All in a circle of ten to fifteen centimetres, Colonel Tarek. That's not bad. It shows you're pretty consistent.'

Though he had known him twelve years, this was the

nearest that Gad could get to having Ismail call him by his first name: Colonel Tarek. It was a nice Arab blend between the strictly formal and the friendly, while as a good Muslim Ismail had chosen the Tarek from Gad's first names, not the *khawwagha* and Christian Daniel. But Ismail would no more drop Gad's title when he talked to him than he would shave off his own resplendent Turkish moustache.

'That would just make me a pretty consistent misser in a fire-fight,' said Gad, 'so a dead duck. It's nothing like as sensitive as my last pistol. By God, I wish I could get that back! *Yareet!*'

'A pistol becomes part of one's body, one's life,' said Ismail. 'One grows into it as one grows into a wife.' He eyed Gad briefly. 'Or, say, into a close lady-friend, Colonel Tarek.'

These cunning bastards certainly keep up with the news, thought Gad. Aloud he said: 'So how do we get it right, Ismail?'

'Look, you've said it already, she's too stiff for you. You know, these Brownings come out of the factory with the triggers set like the brakes on cranes. The manufacturers don't want you to make any mistakes about pulling them free. So they make it hard. So even a good shot like you, you keep squeezing like the textbook says, and nothing happens. In the end you get a kind of agony, and you give a sudden little pull, and off she goes. It almost always throws them left. We can fix that, Colonel Tarek. We just file the trigger mechanism down a bit, like we did with the last one. Give me ten minutes. After all, you're not driving a crane, are you?'

He was back from his armoury in less time than that. While he was away, Gad had walked up to the black metal man at the end of the range. There was a little pot of black paint and one of white in a niche in the left side wall. Gad took the white and painted out the thirteen black holes to the left of the target's chest. At least they made a nice grouping, as Ismail had said; the widest two were some twelve centimetres apart. But that was hardly good enough in the cold world of reality. In a live fight, you did not disable your enemy by near misses. Gad walked back up the range with the target area behind him recomposed into clear black and white, so there would be no doubt where his shots landed the next time.

This brought him more joy. Ismail had judged the new pistol and Gad, and matched them uncannily. For Daniel Gad the hair trigger was now set so right that he felt himself shoot exactly as his eyes looked. He was aware of no effort linking brain and muscles. It was as if the Browning was simply an extension of his hand or his eyes, an intuitive part of him. Using it now brought a marvellous exhilaration, that of an athlete very highly trained and performing well, in absolute and precise control of his body. The feeling was so acute and intense that Gad wanted to laugh with it. He took the first five shots steadily, nicely balanced, with the single-handed grip. Ismail said:

'Colonel Tarek, this is very pretty. You've made a fine rose, all on the heart. You have it now. Why not try it rapid?'

So Gad took the double-grip, left hand straight out and under the right, supporting it, and fired the next eight shots about as fast as he could. The silence fell.

'Six of the rapid on, all chest-high. No, seven; one's just on the edge at the right. So seven out of eight. Not bad; you were really shooting fast.'

'It's thanks to you,' said Daniel Gad. 'You got that trigger-pressure dead right. Just like that! You're a bloody genius, Ismail!'

Ismail beamed behind the huge black fan of his moustache, and pushed both palms out at Gad in a self-deprecatory manner.

'It was nothing; you did the shooting. Always *taht amrak*, Colonel Tarek. At your service.'

And thank God for that, thought Daniel Gad, for Ismail had really turned the new pistol into a jewel for him, even more lovable than the one he had had before. I must lose my pistol more often, thought Gad, reloading his two magazines and pushing one back up the Browning's butt. Then he walked back to the end of the range. A black-paint man now, he thought happily, and took that can first and pointed out the twelve silver impacts on the black metal silhouette. He went

83

back for the white paint and erased his single miss; it had been about thirty centimetres left, a little wild. Now the target and target area were ready and waiting for the next customer. As he walked away, Gad was thinking that he was going to have to leave cleaning his nice new Browning until he got back to his flat that night after the reception. It was a service that he always liked to carry out himself, just as he preferred always to paint out his shot marks at the range himself, whether on the target or off, instead of having Ismail do it. Both taught him things about his pistol, and that was a vital preserve. It was better to do some important things in life personally. After all, you didn't delegate the act of making love, did you? But this key rite with his pistol took boiling water and ten to fifteen minutes, and Gad was already cutting it fine if he was to get to the reception on time. So he looked in at Ismail's small armoury beside the range and borrowed a rag to wipe down his Browning, which he then parked as usual in his waistband just under his bush-shirt. The creases in the trousers, now thankfully his own, had emerged impeccably from his prior night's ordeal, and his bush-shirt was fresh. So he could skip going back to his flat to change. That evening uniform was optional, which suited Gad; his personality did not depend centrally on one. But the Servant of Light, he guessed, would certainly wear his, with all his medals. Abd el Nour just loved his general's uniform.

Gad slapped the seated Sergeant-Armourer Ismail heartily round the shoulders and thanked him again warmly, dropped into the barracks toilets to pee and wash his hands and comb his hair, and jumped cheerfully into his Fiat 2000.

He was of course quite right about Abd el Nour. Still, Gad had beaten him to the punch by arriving at the El Salam Hotel in Heliopolis at three minutes to seven, so actually being within the reception salon on the first floor when the gong officially went. This gave Gad a fine moral edge. He nonetheless found it hard to maintain against the sheer exuberance of the Servant of Light's uniform. It fitted exquisitely, like a glove, not a wrinkle showing. Clearly, he had had it individually tailored.

He wore his gold general's epaulette with its Egyptian eagle and crossed muskets, and the downwards gold piping at the top of his lapels. On his left breast he displayed three full rows of medal ribbons. They were dazzling; conceivably he had had them hand-painted. He had a wide selection; from Nasser, from Sadat, from Mubarak. Abd el Nour was a man for all seasons; he knew how to sow his seed efficiently in all. Mere changes in command did not deter him. He had the self-sufficiency and indestructibility of a bulldozer. Also there were few there to compete with him visually. With his cinematic silver hair and multicoloured splash of gold insignia and medal ribbons, he looked like an extremely elegant, ludicrously expensive and brilliantly packaged bottle of French perfume, topped by a platinum stopper.

For the rest, Gad found this resolutely all-male gathering quite as boring as he had feared, anyway to start with. There were generals and admirals all over the place, and three or four ambassadors. The spooks were also well represented, as usual cunningly disguised as first or second embassy secretaries. Among others, he noticed the MI6-SIS man from the British Embassy, the KGB's Head of Mission, and a pack of CIA operatives. The spooks were a fervent little community, generally not doing much real harm. Few spoke or read more than a bare smattering of Arabic, which helped cushion them comfortably against local realities, making them even more dependent than in most other countries upon the private mythologies of the profession. They were thus something of a mutually self-sustaining élite, often even frequenting the same bars, and notably the excellent and expensive French-cuisine Arabesque Restaurant in Kasr el Nil, where a skilled eye could discern them entertaining actual or potential agents and, tangentially, one another; Gad had once seen men from three separate intelligence services lunching clients there at one and the same time. This could keep them very busy. It was too much to expect them always to be right too. Gad did not know of any Caucasian intelligence service that had predicted Sadat's assassination. Still, they were in good company. It had surprised the Egyptian security services too. Only Israel's

Mossad had seen it, and warned Sadat of an Egyptian plot on his life two months before the event. But Mossad, thought Daniel Gad, was another kettle of fish. They were tuned scrupulously in to this whole region. They had to be.

One advantage to having so many Caucasians at the party was that hard liquor was abundant, and Gad solaced himself with four straight whiskies. Thus mellowed, he met the guest of honour, the American general who was going to teach a trick or two to Mubarak's security guard. He was a tall man with a suntan and a sharp blue eye. Gad talked to him affably, instead of doing what he wanted, which was to wish him better luck with his results than the Americans who had just spent some hundreds of thousands of dollars training Sadat's security staff when he was shot. A little blurred, Gad then drifted up against the last person that he would ever have sought out in his right mind, Abd el Nour. The Servant of Light was talking vigorously to a man whom he appeared to be monopolizing. Gad did not need to ask himself what Abd el Nour was selling. That was obvious: Abd el Nour. But he wondered who the man with him was. Abd el Nour must have been convinced that he was very important indeed.

Then he saw why. The man was wearing the Star of the Sinai at his throat, the eight-pointed silver-edged medal some five centimetres across from point to point, the centre jet-black with just the Arabic words in silver: Sinai, 1973. Anyone who wore that medal was very important.

But this man was impressive in his own right too. He was big, taller than Daniel Gad by a few millimetres, and broad. He had a short black beard, a full moustache, and very penetrating and compelling black eyes. He wore a commando's camouflaged smock and pants, pressed and neat, and paratrooper boots. His contrast with the gaudy Servant of Light was acute. Whereas Abd el Nour had crammed on to his chest every medal to which he was possibly entitled, and probably a few more, the man beside him wore only that Star of the Sinai at his throat, and his paratrooper's wings on his left breast. Gad knew that he could have put more medals there if he had wanted, those of the 1973 campaign at least. But this man went only for the top. Of course Gad knew him. He had read and heard about him and seen his photographs. But he had never met him.

So he stayed solidly planted there on his two feet until even Abd el Nour had to admit him. Abd el Nour said ungraciously: 'Colonel Gad, one of my staff. Major Muhammed Abbas Sidki.'

The big man turned square on to him. The shining black eyes were very level and steady. This man made an impact that you felt almost physically. He smiled, very slightly, and put out his right hand. Gad shook it. Abbas Sidki had a strong grip, a dry hand.

'The general here's been telling me something of your work, Colonel. It sounds fascinating. And highly dangerous. I don't think I'd have the stomach for it.'

Well, if the Film Star can talk about it, thought Gad, I suppose so can I. He gestured towards Abbas Sidki's throat.

'They don't give those away with the rations, Major. You did something to earn that.'

Abbas Sidki screwed his eyes down towards his medal, then raised them again. He looked faintly surprised.

'I sometimes feel a fraud,' he said. 'You know, we did a tremendous amount of training with those wire-guided missiles. Most of us were qualified engineers. We worked until we could use them against tanks almost instinctively, without thinking. It was automatic. My action was like that. It was all over in sixty seconds. I happened to be seen. I wonder if one can really call that bravery?'

'I would,' said Gad. 'What would *you* call bravery, Major?'

Abbas Sidki's eyes locked on to Gad's.

'Not just a matter of having good reflexes,' he said, 'as it was with me in that case. No, something much longer-term. Fighting on your own for a cause, say. Over years, against very great odds. Terrible doubts. But still going right through with it, at any personal cost. I'd say that's nearer to it, Colonel.'

'Any cause?' said Gad.

The other's piercing eyes continued to measure him. Abbas Sidki gave the impression of weighing everything that Gad and he said very carefully, but also of not avoiding or holding back any worthwhile truth himself. He looked a very honest man. Gad noticed that all this seriousness had proved too much for the Film Star. Abd el Nour had wandered away in a sulk.

'Any good and genuine cause,' said Abbas Sidki. 'Not something purely egotistical, for one's own advancement, say; I don't mean that. For something other than oneself, and *great*. Say for a community. Say for *the* community, the Islamic *Umma*. But I see, with respect, that you've a small cross at your throat, Colonel –'

'Purely decorative. But yes, I'm a Copt.'

'Then for a nation, let's say. For Egypt. For all of humanity.'

'Unfortunately, people tend to be on different sides.'

'Yes,' said Abbas Sidki, 'I think that that can sometimes be a truly sad business. I don't know the answer to that. All you can do is your best, as you most honestly see things. But it can be sad.'

'*Kisma.*'

'Yes.' Abbas Sidki was watching him very steadily, very seriously. 'You could call it a kind of fate.'

Then, as if out of instinctive politeness wanting to give Gad his turn at glory, he switched sharply:

'But you would have been there too, Colonel, in the October War?'

'Yes, though not with the commandos. With the tanks.'

'Ah, you Tank Corps boys did a magnificent job those first days.'

'Well, it was training again, what you said. But once we'd bust through the Bar Lev Line we didn't know what on earth to do next. We'd never trained for a second stage. So we sat on our bottoms for four days and allowed the Israelis to take the initiative. We never got it back. A pity.'

'A grave pity,' said Abbas Sidki, 'for ours was a just cause. To win back Arab lands taken by an enemy.'

Gad glanced at him.

'Yes. Of course.'

'Well, there'll be another time.'

'I hope not,' said Daniel Gad. But the other made no

comment. Well, he's a soldier, thought Gad. Soldiers like wars. They're part of their job. Then Abbas Sidki switched again.

'What's your ideal in your anti-terrorist job, Colonel? Your cause?'

'Oh. Law and order, I suppose. It's not very inspiring, or dramatic, I'm afraid.'

'I think it can be inspiring. A fair and just order?'

'Yes.'

'I can believe that,' said Abbas Sidki.

'A drink of some kind?' said Gad, needing one himself.

'Thank you, no, Colonel.' Abbas Sidki looked around him. 'I don't much like these things,' he said.

'Join the club,' said Gad.

'I had to attend any number of them,' said Abbas Sidki, 'when Sadat pulled me out of the line. He paraded me around. I loathed it.'

'I can bet.'

'He should have sent me back to the line. There were a lot of good people there.'

'Yes,' Gad agreed. 'There were fine men there. It was a great time.'

'I'm leaving, Colonel,' said Abbas Sidki, off on one of his tacks again. 'I've done my duty for the day. It was good to talk to you.'

'Yes,' said Daniel Gad, 'it was very good to meet you. Let's keep in touch.'

'Yes, we'll do that all right.'

'I'll ring the commandos. Then let's meet.'

'That would be good,' said Abbas Sidki. 'In peace.'

'Yes,' said Gad. 'In peace.'

They shook hands.

Driving back afterwards to the Corniche in his shiny black new Fiat 2000, Daniel Gad said to himself: That is really quite one hell of a man. He looked forward to seeing him again.

The eyes bothered him slightly, though. He had the feeling that he had seen them before somewhere.

Maybe the photos, thought Gad.

# 5

# *A Meeting for Murder*

'I accept that there is a risk.'

Mainstree was still in control. But there was not much in it. The tension between the other two men was electric. They could be at each other's throats in a second, blowing the meeting up in his face. Mainstree had chaired many gatherings, but few so lethally charged. He looked from one man to the other, then rested his gaze on his hands on the table. They were slim and strong, an ally; a musician's or a surgeon's hands. He leaned back then slightly in his chair, affecting ease. Now he seemed fully in command; the secret of transmitting confidence was to look as if you had it yourself. Such postures of power suited Mainstree. He had the experience, and he had the build for them. Mainstree was lean, long and elegant, like his hands. He had a managing director's eyebrows, silver-grey, like his thick and rather long hair. He wore a pearl-grey summer suit and a darker grey tie with light-blue polka-dots on it. Mainstree looked sixty and physically very hard.

'Good of you, Sir John.'

That was the Israeli, Avram Ben Yehuda, who had injected just enough contempt into that title to make it unmistakably an insult. Ben Yehuda was as tall and slim as Mainstree, and probably ten years younger. He was bald, except for a narrow horseshoe of iron-grey curls carried low, and very brown. That dark complexion and quick face suggested Sephardic origins. The man was in fact Ashkenazi, from Poland. He was dressed with the arrogant informality of the Israeli rich: faultless gabardine slacks, polished Egyptian sandals with interlacing straps, a dark beige Dior shirt with sleeves. He wore a gold chain bracelet on his right wrist and a tiny silver Star of David on a thin gold chain round his throat. Hair showed on his barrel chest at the open Vee, like massed rolls of barbed-wire on a battlefield.

'My point is that the objective, I think, justifies that risk.'

Mainstree made this reply with a deliberate lack of aggression, diplomatically, gently, even soothingly. He knew that that thrust of pure hatred from Ben Yehuda was not really against him at all. At the moment, Ben Yehuda was hardly even aware that he existed. His naked hostility was directed exclusively at the third man in the room.

'A high one, I should have thought,' observed that third man. 'You are after all talking of murder, are you not?'

Again, that criticism, opposition, taunt, while ostensibly replying to Mainstree, was really aimed point-blank back at Ben Yehuda, at whom the third man stared without deflection. He too was using Mainstree simply as a lightning-conductor. For the moment.

'I can easily think of cases where murder would be fully justified,' said Ben Yehuda as provocatively. 'Even quite close to hand.'

'Any time you like,' said the third man, interpreting him accurately. 'Really, any time at all.'

His tone was silky and his English, which was the language in which all three spoke, fluent and almost accentless; certainly remarkable in a Libyan. Wahid Hakki was as Arab as his name. He was strikingly good-looking. Perhaps forty-five, he had a high brow and abundant black curled hair, and a fine nose and mouth. Again, the tall trim body added an impression of class. He was dressed as smartly as the other two, but less soberly. There was no wrinkle in his white linen suit. He wore slim brown hand-made shoes, a pale blue sea-cotton shirt with a brilliant multicoloured silk tie, like a splash of many paints at his throat. He had a gold Patek watch on his left wrist, and a heavy black sapphire set in a gold ring on the third finger of his right hand.

'I suggest we think about that somewhere outside,' said Ben Yehuda.

'Agreed.'

The two of them had been sniffing round each other like that from the moment they had come through the flat's door five minutes before and discovered that one was Israeli, the other Libyan. They were like two highly bred dogs, circling, feinting, testing each other out, the challenge accepted, one or the other bound fatally sooner or later to spring for the jugular, trapped by this absolute imperative of the tribe or the skin. Mainstree watched them in some disgust. At least he suffered from no self-recrimination. Mainstree was of the kind who would always forgive himself more easily for a sin of commission than for a sin of omission. He had tried out his bravest formula here. It could have led to a fantastic and resounding triumph. Now it looked like leading to a fantastic and resounding defeat. And promptly.

'Can you two prancing gladiators not have the nous to see,' he asked, more brutally frank in his disillusionment than was his custom, 'that, however mortal enemies you may mutually be, it is at least logically possible that there is a third and far more mortal enemy of you both whom it is in your best interests jointly to annihilate *now*, *however* you may massacre each other afterwards?'

The two heads swung round to him, registering him fully for perhaps the first time.

'Almost anything is logically possible,' said Avram Ben Yehuda. 'But, tell us, who is this third enemy so mortal that he is greater than each of us, Libyan and Israeli, Arab and Jew, is or could be to the other? *Is* so much more mortal an enmity in fact possible?' He glanced reflectively across at Wahid Hakki, and added: 'Frankly, I doubt it. A greater enmity than between Israeli and Libyan? I don't see it. I seem to remember that you mentioned Mubarak. I don't see the relevance. How?'

Clearly, he was still antagonistic. But no longer totally. He had said 'Tell *us*' and not 'Tell *me*' and 'each of *us*, Libyan and Israeli', thereby actually accepting Wahid Hakki's existence as a human being. It was a small step forward.

'I second that,' said Wahid Hakki. 'What's the purpose of this meeting? Why have you brought *us* together like this? Why *us*?'

Mainstree glanced down at his hands in front of him, sinewed and still. He looked up again.

'I hope I can answer both questions to your satisfaction,' he said. 'Let me lead off by repeating my first statement to you after you came through that door, just after I had introduced you, and before you had had the time to work up your fury at your discovery of your colleague's nationality –'

The moment trembled, fragile as an eggshell. Then, faintly, each of the two men addressed smiled. It was another small progress. The two were laying down their arms, however temporarily. They were listening now.

'I said something like: "Gentlemen, I felt it useful that we should meet, briefly to consider whether President Hosni Mubarak of Egypt has not perhaps outlived his usefulness –" '

'You plan to assassinate Mubarak,' said Wahid Hakki. 'It's as I thought.'

'Mubarak?' said Ben Yehuda. 'Why should Mubarak be the greatest enemy?'

Mainstree looked at him. It was a moment to challenge. Mainstree could feel the current suddenly in his favour.

'You ask that?' he said. '*You?* A Tehiya man? Really someone fairly far to the right of that party? Tehiya, Renaissance, which was Prime Minister Begin's fiercely nationalistic ally in his governing Likud coalition from 1982? Let's remember Tehiya's ideals and passions, its deep Biblical feel for Israel, for "Greater Israel", as a dedicated and ever-expanding power-bloc that should immediately annex the West Bank and Gaza Strip outright, then take back the Sinai as part of Biblical Israel, and finally Lebanon, the land of Ashur and Naphtali. *Your views on Israeli foreign policy, Mr Avram Ben Yehuda, are as aggressive as these, or more so!*'

Ben Yehuda looked back at him levelly. *It's the only way,* Ben Yehuda thought to himself with cruel incisiveness and no doubt at all. *War and the threat of war, fear always. For the*

*Arabs will never truly accept us in this area of the world,
however long we stay. So Sadat cheated, consciously or not,
when he addressed the Knesset in November 1977, offering to
let Israel live in peace among the Arabs, even welcoming it, so
that some Israelis there wept. For that peace is not for us. We
must walk always with our weapons in our hands, sleep
always with our weapons by our sides –*

It was a rocky, narrow path across the sheer face of a
precipice, its jagged depths sheathed in cloud when you looked
down. Ben Yehuda knew that if you fell, no miracle saved you.
You got no second chance. The path was as exigent as tragedy.
But at least it had the clean hard edges of tragedy, its stature
and its dignity. You did not relax. The Jews had relaxed too
often in their history, most recently between the two world
wars. Then those in Germany had reclined into the fond
illusion that the Iron Crosses they had won in the First World
War would preserve them for ever in peace and honour. That
path had led the Jews in Europe to the long peace of the
Holocaust. You won, you survived, only by unremitting
vigilance, poised always to attack, to move forward, your loins
girded.

Today too, peace was a luxury Israel could not afford. As
Ben Yehuda saw it, after bitter years of experience and
thought, the moment the pressure lifted from Israel's borders,
she was undone; Israel the Brave Nation would seep out
centrifugally and dissipate, like the spume of the sea upon
sand. A Saladinic tranquillity would annihilate her, just as
Saladin had finally killed the Crusades with peace, at no cost,
when, having thrashed the Crusaders at Tiberias and retaken
Jerusalem, rather than knock them all off messily, he instead
left them quite free and unmolested on an unused strip of the
Palestine coast. After a hundred years or so it struck them that
they had no purpose there, so they got up then sheepishly of
their own volition and went home. Ben Yehuda did not want
that kind of peace for Israel.

He looked suddenly at Wahid Hakki opposite him, and read
in that sculptured shut face what he saw as full confirmation of
his thoughts. Neither Ben Yehuda, nor any Israeli, or any Jew,

would ever really belong to the very Arab world of this man. He glanced back at Mainstree.

'Yes, perhaps those are my views. But, again, why should Mubarak be my first enemy? We're after all at peace with Mubarak, with Egypt. At least technically.'

'For precisely that reason. Because Mubarak, though he will keep picking away in criticism of your West Bank settlement policies, and chatting ostentatiously to Yasser Arafat in public from time to time, and doing his best generally to sidle back into the bosom of the Arab family of nations, will most certainly *not* go so far as to break the Camp David peace accords with Israel; Mubarak does *not* want another military defeat. So he is the major obstacle to your achieving that cornerstone of Tehiya's and your expansionist policies – the recovery of the Sinai. With his dogged insistence on peace, Mubarak has you checkmated; it takes two to make a fight. Without genuine provocation and open hostility from him, it's politically virtually impossible for you to take back the Sinai by · force – even your great lovers and protectors, the Americans, wouldn't stand for it. Just to get your Greater Israel policies off the ground, you've got to get rid of Mubarak first. To achieve your expansionist aims, you need a thoroughly bloody-minded Egypt, spoiling for war, and you need the world to see that.'

'You have a point there,' said Ben Yehuda, 'but how does that explain the kind of thieves' alliance which you appear to be promoting between Libya and Israel?'

At the word 'thieves' he had glanced across at Wahid Hakki. The man's dark Arab eyes had stared back at him stonily, not a muscle in that finely etched face moving. He would probably be quite good with a knife, thought Ben Yehuda.

'I can think of two reasons,' said Mainstree smoothly. 'Immediately, because Ghaddafi and Libya have every cause to dislike Mubarak as much as you do. Ghaddafi's basically a puritanical Islamic Fundamentalist, pan-Arabist and anti-Western. Mubarak's a moderate, pro-Western, with an English wife, and the heir to a peace treaty with Israel – anathema to Ghaddafi – which Mubarak will not break.

Mubarak vigorously opposes Ghaddafi's – shall we say? – somewhat strong-arm methods, and has been particularly rough on any of Ghaddafi's hit-men that he has picked up inside Egypt; and Ghaddafi knows this. He also knows that Mubarak has always leapt promptly and volubly to Numeiri's side at every real or imagined Libyan attack on the Sudan or threat of invasion of it. And that Mubarak rigidly opposes his designs on Chad.

'The second reason is linked with the first, and is absolutely basic, geopolitical, and long-term. It is that Libya and Israel – the Tehiya thinkers in Israel particularly – are natural allies to destroy Mubarak *because their logical and desired areas of expansion are complementary, not antagonistic*! Mr Ben Yehuda has already agreed that for him Greater Israel is today's Israel, plus of course the West Bank, Gaza Strip and Golan Heights, and the Sinai and Southern Lebanon. What about Libya? Surely the striking thing about Muhammar Ghaddafi's territorial ambitions *are that he wants an African empire* as well as North African Arab unity. He wants Chad, and some or all of the Sudan, and, ideally, a vassalized Egypt. Would that be about right, Mr Wahid Hakki?'

The Arab smiled slightly.

'Yes, that would be about right, Sir John,' he said. 'That would do fine.'

'You see the geopolitical beauty of it?' said Mainstree. 'It has something of the same sweet inevitablility about it as the swings in Egypt's alliances. Egypt has always tended recently to swing one of two ways in her alliances – northeast to the Fertile Crescent, or south and southeast through the Sudan and, ideally, Saudi Arabia – the most recent example of the northeastern swing of course being her integration with Syria in the United Arab Republic from 1958 to 1961, and of the southeastern swing precisely what Mubarak is trying for now. If you will do what I shall dare to suggest, your countries will, I believe, be able in harmony to achieve these your great ambitions, and emerge more powerful than ever before.'

'In harmony?' said Wahid Hakki. He looked across at Ben Yehuda and went on mockingly: 'Even though Israel here doubts that she could possibly have any more mortal enemy than Libya?'

Mainstree came in quickly.

'Would you *really* say, Mr Ben Yehuda, that Libya is and will remain for the foreseeable future Israel's most dangerous enemy, in the sense of an actual armed threat on the ground, in the air, on the sea?'

Ben Yehuda frowned at Mainstree, then looked for long moments at Wahid Hakki, and back at Mainstree.

'Certainly not. We don't like Libya's fanatical pan-Islamic fundamentalism and we thoroughly dislike Libya's export of terrorism and backing of Palestinian Arab terrorist organizations with money, arms, explosives and training. And we'll go on shooting down without mercy any Libyan we find involved in such activities. Let there be no mistake about that –'

'It's thoughtful of you to be so explicit,' said Wahid Hakki.

'– But,' Ben Yehuda went on, ignoring him royally, 'clearly Libya's not our most dangerous enemy among the Arabs, as an immediate armed threat against us. Our most deadly enemy in that sense is of course Syria. And will be for the next twenty or thirty years.'

'You see?' said Mainstree. 'There again is my point. Once Mr Ben Yehuda and his colleagues have achieved their Greater Israel, their fighting stance must remain oriented predominantly towards Syria, northeast. While Libya's whole thrust must be and remain south into Chad and Africa, southeast into the Sudan. The two postures are compatible. Your two nations can coexist. You can afford an armed truce.'

The representatives of these two proposed bedfellow-nations continued to stare balefully across the table at each other.

'It's true that Mubarak's maintenance of the Camp David peace accords is a serious obstacle to our taking back the Sinai,' said Ben Yehuda, glancing at Mainstree as he did so, 'but who or what do you see in his place?'

'Let's ask Libya that question,' said Mainstree. 'Mr Wahid Hakki, what would you think that Colonel Ghaddafi would like to see instead of Mubarak? Whom or what would *you* like to see?'

The Arab turned fully to him.

'Clearly, we'd not weep to see Mubarak go. Not that the man's brought in any really new policies of his own. He's probably not capable of it. And he *did* say on the night of Sadat's execution that he proposed to go on carrying out Sadat's policies unchanged. Including the Camp David accords and peace treaty. And selling out Egypt to America. That's about what he's done. Mubarak is Sadat's bagman, the poor man's Sadat. For that alone he deserves to be shot. I've no doubt at all that that's what Muhammar Ghaddafi thinks. He has only loved one Egyptian President, and that was Nasser – you'll know of course that as a very young and fervent leader, Ghaddafi offered Libya to Nasser on a plate, to make, with Egypt, a great new Islamic Republic. That pan-Islamic ideal still stands. In the Greater Libya concept that you mentioned, Sir John, we'd like to fuse Egypt too, but *provided* their leadership was right. We could never have achieved that with Sadat, nor could we achieve it with Mubarak –

'So, what would we like instead of Mubarak's Egypt? A full-blooded Islamic Fundamentalist leadership. A full-blooded Islamic Republic, like Khoumeni's in Iran.'

Wahid Hakki studied the Israeli opposite him.

*Doesn't he realize what could happen then?* he thought. *That could trigger off a sweeping bushfire of Islamic Fundamentalist takeovers right through the Arabian Peninsula and Fertile Crescent, even into Saudi and the Emirates and Kuwait and North Yemen and Syria and Jordan and Iraq. That would give us finally that one absolute Arab unity which we have always tragically lacked, and which we must have ultimately to wipe Israel off the face of the earth forever –*

But if Ben Yehuda did not see that, so much the better. It would then be well worth working with him in the most loyal cooperation to destroy Mubarak's Egypt until he *did* see it, when it would be too late. Indeed, there would be an irony to that alliance really worthy of the best traditions of Arab vengeance –

'Then we probably could work together,' said Ben Yehuda.

'Good,' said Hakki, and Ben Yehuda looked at him and smiled slightly in friendship.

*Fool!* thought Ben Yehuda. *Don't you see it? We'll work with you while it suits us, then annihilate you.* Aloud, he said: 'If your aim is to get rid of Mubarak.' For an Islamic Fundamentalist government in Cairo would petrify the Americans. It should then prove easy to find a moral pretext for Israel to attack it, and retake the Sinai. That should create a big enough diversion and tie up enough Egyptian troops for Libya to move against Chad and Sudan – and Egypt's western border if necessary – with relative impunity.'

Ben Yehuda was beginning to bite.

Wahid Hakki glanced at the flat's opened windows deliberately, careful as a good Arab souk trader not to show his quickening interest in the business at hand. Instead he looked back at Mainstree and said:

'Why us, Sir John? What made you bring the two of us here?'

Here was this large and comfortably furnished penthouse flat on the corner of Patriarco Ioakim and Marasli at the edge of Kolonaki, that fashionable and glittering quarter of central Athens. It looked down on the sun-drenched green square of Maraslio, bounded by Souidias and Genadiou, and it was only eight minutes by foot west-southwest down Ioakim to Kolonaki Square with its groomed shops and restaurants, and its very Athenian habit of watching the beautiful people, particularly the beautiful Greek women, saunter past in the deliberately opened reviewing passage in front of the restaurants in the evening and right through the night into the early morning. It was about another eight minutes to Syntagma, Constitution Square; down Koubari, then to the right into the superb wide avenue of Vasilissis Sofias, some of the world's great embassies along on your right hand, the National Garden across the avenue on your left, with its manicured tree-lined walks this park a tryst for all three sexes. On your left, before you crossed Leoforos Amalias to reach

99

Syntagma, was the Prime Minister's office, Parliament, and the Tomb of the Unknown Soldier; an august heartland of the establishment in which to plot the overthrow of an establishment.

'Because of your affinities,' said Mainstree.

'Affinities?' said Ben Yehuda, looking hard at the Libyan across the table from him.

'Let me tell you a little about your companion,' said Mainstree. 'Then judge for yourself.'

Ben Yehuda glanced back at him and shrugged.

'And with your companion's permission,' said Mainstree, and, when the Libyan opened his hands outwards towards him in a gesture of assent, went on: 'Wahid Hakki Pasha here, then, comes from a good Tripoli family. His father's in big business – a major motor agency, shipping, construction. He was also one of Libya's first ambassadors, to Paris, for six years. In education, Wahid was internationalized, I think we might say. He was at school in French lycées in Paris, then he went to Jesus College, Cambridge, for four years. Where he read law, I think it was?'

'Yes, it was law.'

'He nonetheless stayed a strong nationalist throughout, and after Cambridge came back very willingly to Libya, and entered his father's businesses in Tripoli, most successfully. In Sadat's October 1973 war with Israel, Wahid Hakki volunteered for the 100-tank Libyan Armoured Brigade which fought on the Egyptian front. He had two tanks shot from under him, and was wounded. It was his exploits as a tank commander that brought him to Ghaddafi's attention. I believe we can say that this was where Wahid Hakki really found himself – in politics. Quite a strong personal identification with Ghaddafi, I think? Yes. And with his pan-Islamic line, of course. Wahid had a hand in the attempted Libyan coups in neighbouring Niger, Tunisia and the Sudan. He was one of Ghaddafi's closest political advisers on the Chad enterprise. And we may not yet have seen the end of that; Ghaddafi's a remarkably tenacious man. As is Wahid, who is also particularly well versed in the intricacies of Sudanese politics, and has the aim of one day at last breaking the Sudan away from Egypt. How should I put it? In summary, a strong Libyan patriot, internationally educated, very close to Ghaddafi, with deep-rooted pan-Arabic ambitions? Would that be fair?'

'Pan-Islamic might be better,' said Wahid Hakki.

'Pan-Islamic, indeed,' said Mainstree.

'And your affinities?' said Ben Yehuda.

Mainstree glanced back at him.

'You haven't seen them? Take your own history. If I may turn to you now. You were born in Warsaw in 1934, of very orthodox Jewish parents. They saw the Holocaust coming. They had also been profoundly moved by Theodor Herzl's vision of Palestine as The Jewish Homeland, and even more by their compatriot Zvi Jabotinsky's passionate right-wing clarion-call to all Jews to go for a 'Greater Israel'. It was thus logical for them to get out of Warsaw early in 1939 and to get into Palestine, via an illegal immigrants runner.

'But a British patrol-boat stopped you three hours out from Tel Aviv, so that you and your parents spent your first month in your supposed homeland behind barbed wire. Then, in one of those inscrutable switches of British policy in those days, they suddenly let the three of you in. You as a child of five were still somewhat under age for it, but your father was an immediate recruit for the Revisionist terrorists. He grew with them. He became one of Menachem Begin's lieutenants when Begin came to lead them and to forge them into the Irgun Zvai Leumi, the IZL, Etzel, the Army of the People. Your father was personally credited with killing thirteen British, between Army and Palestine Police – not counting his share of the casualties caused when he helped organize Etzel's blowing up of the King David Hotel in Jerusalem and their hanging of the two British sergeants in Naharia. He died fighting with the Etzel forces against the Arabs in Sheikh Jarrah in Jerusalem in 1948, after Ben Gurion had declared the State of Israel. At least he saw that State created.

'That left you at fourteen with a mother and quite a lot of money – for, unusually, he had got out of Europe far enough ahead of the SS to carry his wealth with him in precious stones and gold – and, above all, an inspiring heritage of revolt against seemingly impossible odds. You built up his jeweller's and diamond-cutter's business in Tel Aviv shrewdly in your teens, with your mother's help, but all the main thrust of your ambition went into Herut, Freedom, Begin's political party, consistently impotent in the political desert until 1977, when its hour at last struck. You rose with it, then outstripped it. You've always been a spearhead man – with Dayan's paratroopers in the pivotal and bitterly costly taking of the Mitla and Geddi Passes against the entrenched Egyptians in 1956, opening the whole northern Sinai up to the east bank of the Suez Canal to the Israelis in a mere couple of days. In the Six Days War in 1967 you were with the assault group that took Sharm el Sheikh at the southernmost point of the Sinai Peninsula, securing the whole of the Gulf of Akaba for Israel. In 1973 you were an Armoured Brigade Commander with Sharon's full tank division which by 18 October he had got back across the canal through the Deversoir-Abu Sultan gap to destroy several SAM missile sites. By 22 October he had completely encircled the Egyptian 3rd Army round Suez, so that Sadat had no option but to sign an immediate ceasefire at Kilometre 101 on the Suez-Cairo Road, there being virtually no Egyptian forces left then between you and the capital –'

'So you were with Sharon's tanks,' said Wahid Hakki, an edge in his voice. 'I lost several friends to those tanks, killed or maimed for life.'

Ben Yehuda kept his eyes levelly on him, not looking away. He shrugged very slightly. Ben Yehuda was not offering any apologies.

'You've shown the same approach to your politics,' said Mainstree quickly. 'You bypassed Begin's and Shamir's Likud coalitions. And, of course, the Peres-Shamir deal. An individualist, you didn't mind the free-competition Liberals. What you couldn't stand was the National Religious Party and ultra-orthodox Aguda Israel. The fact that Aguda could have forced Begin to stop El Al flying on the Sabbath struck you as ludicrous old-world sorcery which was ruinously costly in lost efficiency. You're hardly religious, Mr Ben Yehuda. Your very real biblical feel for Israel relates exclusively to Greater Israel as a dedicated and expanding power bloc. As I've said, Tehiya's the political party nearest to you, and you're already pretty far to the right of that –'

There was a silence. The flat's windows were opened onto its balconies, but at this penthouse level little sound reached it of the traffic down in Ioakim and Marasli. The three men sat rather formally on straight-backed chairs at the mahogany table by the sitting room's windows. Wahid Hakki pulled out a gold cigarette-case from his inner right breast pocket and offered it to the other two. They shook their heads.

'Do you mind?'

'Of course not,' said Mainstree. 'Please do.'

Ben Yehuda had noticed the brand: Benson and Hedges. He saw Hakki light his cigarette with a gold Dunhill lighter. Hakki's English university education had evidently left its traces. Ben Yehuda looked back at Mainstree.

'Well, you've done your homework.'

'Most of it is right, is it?'

'All of it that matters.'

'It wasn't so hard. You've reached a level. You're something of a known figure now.'

'Indeed? Well.' He glanced at the Libyan and back at Mainstree. 'With respect it still looks to me a very odd alliance. The two of us are supposed to have sufficient affinities to serve for your plans. How far is that really true? All right, we're both patriots, ambitious for our countries, expansionist. That's enough?'

'You're both also, by your records, men of action of considerable stature. You have to translate your convictions into hard facts in the world. You don't just dream. You've both often made strongly personal decisions against the prevailing expert advice, which is never easy, and come out much more often right than wrong. And you're both profoundly committed to this region of the world –'

Wahid Hakki was stubbing his cigarette out very carefully in the heavy Swedish glass ashtray in front of him. Ben Yehuda noticed that he had smoked it down to exactly half its length. Hakki, he thought, would never smoke too much. He would discipline his body scrupulously, professionally, using his mental and physical assets to the maximum, but carefully.

'You're both then obviously extremely strong-willed individualists,' Mainstree continued, 'and you both have power and money in your own right. I understand, Mr Ben Yehuda, that your jeweller's shop in Dizengoff, plus your diamond-cutting atelier, grossed $US50 million last year, and gave you a net post-tax profit of twelve per cent. That's good money. And, Mr Hakki, I believe that the annual gross of your and your father's businesses in Tripoli is in the hundreds of millions of dollars.'

'That's correct,' said Wahid Hakki.

'I didn't think that even the Israeli tax authorities knew those figures,' said Ben Yehuda. 'I shall have to sack my Chief Accountant.'

'You're both also very strong,' said Mainstree, 'in your friends and contacts. Through them you can quickly multiply your own already remarkable power and riches. I've no doubt of my choice. You're both very valuable men, highly original. You were by far the best two prospects I could find in the entire area.'

'Why two, Sir John?' said Wahid Hakki. 'Why not three?'

'Because I think you two, with me, will form the perfect group, powerful enough on our own to bring off this magnificent coup, this splendid change to the face of the world and its history. Three's a lucky number. Four's already a crowd. For the same reason I've avoided any thought of bringing in Russia. Like Mr Wahid Hakki, I see the ideal replacement to Mubarak as an Islamic Fundamentalist government in Egypt. The Russians might not like to promote Islamic Fundamentalism too much here, for fear of the fall-out effect on the huge Muslim minorities in their own vast territories. And if they *did* want to take an active hand, and we succeeded, we'd be beholden to them and, believe me, we'd have to pay a heavy price for that. No; we don't really need them. Three's the right number. The three of us.'

'You called us originals,' said Ben Yehuda. 'You have some claim to originality yourself. Yours was a novel approach: a letter in your name saying that you would greatly value the opportunity of a talk with me on a matter of great moment to my country and the region. You included a first-class air return ticket to Athens, and a booking at the Grande Bretagne in Constitution Square. And the name of one person to refer to about you.'

'The letter I got was identical,' said Wahid Hakki, 'and the reference impressive.'

'So was mine,' said Ben Yehuda. 'Professor Yuval Neeman, ex-President of Tel Aviv University and an eminent physicist, and sufficiently able to have been Minister for Science and Development and a Tehiya member of the Knesset.'

'I hope he gave me a good report,' said Mainstree.

'Yes, by implication,' said Ben Yehuda. 'Whatever you had to say, he said, you certainly wouldn't bore me. And he sent his regards.'

'I hope you give me as good a write-up in return.'

'I doubt that I'll go back to him on this,' said Ben Yehuda. 'His having been a Likud Cabinet member could make it delicate. No, but I have other good friends.'

He glanced at the Libyan, addressing him as a near-equal for the first time.

'And your reference, Mr Hakki?'

'Oh. Well, it was Ghaddafi himself. He knew Sir John at once, from his oil deals. Yes, he thought I should certainly come.'

'I see,' said Ben Yehuda. 'Sir John, you have set out to show that the two of us here have certain basic affinities, and that our two countries have a deep identity of interest under your plan. But three of us are sitting here. What do we know about you? Save the bald facts in Who's Who – good county family, good public school, excellent war record, chairman and majority shareholder of quarter-of-a-million-barrels-a-day Mainstree Oil, UK-based and selling about a hundred thousand barrels a day there, the rest in Europe, 1984 turnover some £2.8 billion and post-tax profit £25 million. That makes you a very rich man. But what else? What moves you, Sir John. What caused you to call this, well, *uncommon* meeting? What's there in it for you?'

The Englishman boxed his fingers, making a church steeple of them, the points of his elbows resting on the mahogany table. He looked back from them to Ben Yehuda.

'Quite a lot of money,' he said. 'I would make many millions of pounds a year more if we successfully went the route which has been mentioned – replacing Mubarak and all his system by a full-blooded orthodox Islamic Republic like Khoumeni's Iran. So huge a new advance of militant Islamic Fundamentalism, after the living proof of its victory in Iran, would carry the threat at once to the whole soft underbelly of the Arabian peninsula – Oman, the United Arab Emirates, Qatar, Bahrain, Kuwait, Saudi Arabia itself. We all know how near to taking power Islamic Fundamentalism has been in various countries in the Middle East over the last few years – we've seen the occupation of the mosque at Mecca and the consequent savage fighting and killing; we here in this room will have known that to be a determined and very nearly successful attempt to unseat and destroy the ruling feudal Saudi hierarchy and replace it by a Khoumeni-style Islamic republic.

'My many new millions of pounds of profits? Because the Arabian peninsula, the Middle East, is one of the world's greatest oil-producing regions. Certainly the most economic; compared to the North Sea, say, your crude oil production costs are almost nothing – you push your finger into the sand in Saudi Arabia, just about, and the crude comes squirting out. All the major Middle East producers are of the Organization of Petroleum Exporting Countries. OPEC's not a very happy family today. She has cut herself to a production quota of 17.5 million barrels a day – even down to 16 million latterly – as against the 30 to 32 million barrels a day OPEC was producing before the recession. It's poetic justice; OPEC *caused* that world recession by their goddamned greed for higher prices. Consider that in the three months from the October 1973 war *they quintupled the price of crude*, from around $2 to $10 plus per barrel. By 1979–80 they had tripled it again to about $30 per barrel. In some agony, the world learned to do without oil partly, and to replace it by cheaper sources of energy.'

'I think I can guess your point,' said Ben Yehuda. 'You must benefit from a major Middle Eastern conflagration, because Mainstree Oil gets its crude from some *non*-OPEC source.'

Mainstree looked at him and nodded.

'You're just about there. Of its modest need of a quarter of a million barrels a day of crude oil, Mainstree gets two hundred thousand barrels *from its own non-OPEC British North Sea concession*. We get the remaining fifty thousand that we need generally from non-OPEC sources, sometimes through joint ventures, say in Norway or Mexico. But we've also been good customers of Libya's 40 API Brega crude, which is how I got to known Ghaddafi.

'So what happens if we nudge world history a little along the path it was going to take anyway, just a little later, by unleasing Islamic Fundamentalism in Egypt, then in the rest of the Arab Middle East? We cause some confusion, until after a few years the place settles down to being a nice new and secure Fundamentalist world. But during that confusion the region's oil production drops vertically, just as in Iran and Iraq at first in their war. Who makes up the shortfall? No one, because the world's *non*-OPEC production is already fairly fully stretched at 23 million barrels a day. What happens if an essential commodity is suddenly scarce, with no short-run alternatives? For those that still *have* that essential commodity, as Mainstree Oil would, its value and market price would go through the roof. There, gentlemen, are my many new millions.'

Ben Yehuda looked at Hakki, then back at the Englishman.

'It's an extremely interesting exposition. I'd guess it's very probable that your economic prediction's right. You'd get your new millions. But is that really all you want?'

As Mainstree turned to answer him, Wahid Hakki came in quickly: 'I'm not so certain that Sir John *would* get his many new millions. Suppose we *did* liquidate Mubarak and put in Islamic Fundamentalists, then carry the Islamic Revolution into the hearths of all the major oil producers in the Arabian

Peninsula, cutting off their oil production, anyway in the short term, mainly in Saudi, Kuwait, and the Emirates – even then we'd only be knocking out some 7 to 8 million barrels a day at the present production rates. But surely the rest of OPEC – major producers like Nigeria and Indonesia – would be only too glad to make up that shortfall. As Sir John has said, OPEC has been holding its total production back to 16 or 17 million bd by a strict quota system to keep its price levels from eroding. But it *could* produce around 30 million bd at very short notice. So the rest of OPEC ought to be able to replace the lost Saudi, Kuwaiti, and Emirates production promptly. Why then should the price levels of Mainstree's oil suddenly go up? I don't see it.'

'Your point is perfectly valid,' said Mainstree easily. 'The rest of OPEC would be delighted to try to make up that 7 to 8 million bd shortfall, and they could go some way to doing so fairly fast, *but probably only at a significantly higher cost.* Because Saudi and Kuwait are by far the world's lowest-cost producers. And the rest of OPEC would want to pass these higher production costs on to crude oil buyers and the public, and this pressure would draw Mainstree's crude oil and refined product price levels up in its wake. The public, unnerved by the sudden disappearance of traditional and hitherto secure suppliers, would probably readily pay these higher prices. Now Mainstree's own production costs shouldn't have gone up by one red cent, so that this increase in general market price levels would go straight into our pockets as extra profit. No, if we could help history along a bit, by replacing the feudal and semi-feudal governments in the Arabian Peninsula with full-blooded Islamic Republics, that upset would quite certainly increase the world price of oil, and thus Mainstree's profits, have no doubt.'

'Yes, I suppose that's logical enough,' said Hakki, 'by say twenty, thirty per cent.'

'Though the last two major price rises, in 1973 and 1979, caused in whole or part by similarly cataclysmic political events, were of four hundred and two hundred per cent? But let that go. Even an increase of only twenty per cent on today's price of almost $30 per barrel is some $6 per barrel. My small company produces 250 thousand barrels a day. With no rise in my own production costs, I suddenly have an additional income of $1½ million a day. An additional gross income of some $550 million a year, at no cost, just for my small group. I'd say that gave me good and sufficient grounds to get rid of Mubarak if I could, wouldn't you?'

Hakki smiled slightly. 'It's a powerful argument.'

'More than half a billion dollars a year,' said Ben Yehuda, 'is a powerful argument for practically anything.'

'But would the Americans let us do it?' said Hakki. 'Put Islamic Fundamentalism into power in Egypt? Help put it into power in Saudi Arabia?'

'Could they stop it taking power in Iran?' said Mainstree. 'We'd not be injecting something alien from outside, would we, but simply unshackling a huge power already innate in these countries. The Americans will lose in both countries, in the entire area, because they're constitutionally incapable of recognizing genuine grass-roots revolutions that grow inside countries whose ruling establishments the US supports. Instead they insist against all the evidence that such revolutions have been packaged, sent in, and backed virtually completely by some other international or local power, like Russia, China, or Cuba. We round this table probably understand the colossal latent power of Islamic Fundamentalism in a country such as Egypt because the great bulk of her citizens, however talented they may be, know that they are completely excluded from any real exercise of political or economic power under their existing establishments, which are increasingly identified with the US – rigid, autocratic, and not always innocent of corruption. These citizens believe that their only possible route away from this total frustration, and towards any sort of self-expression, identity and human dignity would be by breaking and completely restructuring their present societies, preferably to create purely Islamic states like Iran. *And they are almost certainly right!*'

'Yes,' said Hakki, 'many Arab peoples in the Middle East want political and economic power in their *own* hands now, not their rulers'. I travel a lot amongst them. I've seen the strength of the desire for change.'

'There's no doubt of that power indeed,' said Mainstree. 'It nearly shattered the Saudi Establishment by its bloody occupation of the Mecca Mosque. It came close to destroying Sadat's on October 6 and 8 1981 by its *Jihad el Jedid* assaults in Cairo and Asyut that killed some 70 and wounded more than 200. You'll probably also know that the New Holy War in fact had *ten* attack squads ready in Cairo on October 6, not only to execute Sadat but also to take by storm the TV and radio stations, key police stations and headquarters, the main central security military camp at Shubra, and the main mosques. They had their TV and radio broadcasts already recorded. By these, and from the mosques, they would announce the Islamic Revolution and push the crowds out into the streets to attack and tie down the rest of the security forces. After Sadat's death the arrests came too thick and fast, the plan collapsed. But it nearly succeeded; the Asyut fighting showed that, and the mass police raids turned up 19 caches of *Jihad* arms, ammunition and explosives in Cairo. It was a close call four years ago. Next time, *this* time, it *must* succeed –'

His words hung in the air. Hakki said: 'I'd like to repeat a question already asked. Money, the many new millions, is that really all you want out of this? What for? Don't you already have all you can want?'

'Oh, surely one always wants more, doesn't one? Can one *ever* really have enough? It's all a game of numbers in the end, isn't it? Fascinating, like poker. One always wants more money, influence, power. What else is there?'

'You're not in this only for the money,' said Ben Yehuda deliberately. 'There's something else, isn't there? There was too much passion in your voice.'

Mainstree looked at the other two for some while, then he shrugged and smiled very slightly.

'All right. Yes. But the money side is important. At least for me. That probability of huge neat financial gain gives the whole project a good solid formal structure, makes it a kind of classic. It aches to be done. It's almost respectable. Were the probability financial *loss*, then I'd think twice before going ahead. What else draws me, then?'

He looked carefully at the other two, from one to the other.

'Put it this way. I feel as fully committed to this region as do you.'

'Yes, one can feel that,' said Ben Yehuda. 'But why is that?'

'A detail you may have missed from *Who's Who*,' said Mainstree, 'is that I was born in Palestine, in 1923, in Jerusalem. My father was an officer in the British Palestine Police. He had his baronetcy; he didn't have to work. But he had long been a friend, I suppose you could say disciple, of T. E. Lawrence. My father had been an Arabist at Cambridge. He was with Sir Ronald Storrs in Egypt in the First World War, and I imagine that his Arabic and his sympathy with all things Arab made him a logical choice as a Storrs contact officer with Lawrence. Those years would have been where he formed his mystique about Lawrence, which I suppose I inherited from him as a mystique about the whole of the Middle East. At the war's end my father transferred to the Palestine Police when that corps was created; by then he couldn't stand the idea of living in England, if the alternative was an Arab land.'

'You suffer from that too?' said Ben Yehuda. 'You're a professional exile too?'

Mainstree looked back at him quite seriously.

'Yes, it's a feeling I share in part. My first view of the world was pretty Arab. I lived in Palestine until I was ten, you see. My brother and I were probably unusually close to my father, because my mother died when I was two. So our house in Katamon, that hilly and very Arab part of Jerusalem, was my first home – I even used to talk some pretty basic Arabic to Jamil, the son of my father's Arab orderly, and my great friend –'

'*Ya salaam!*' said Hakki. '*Ehlan wa sehlan!* Welcome back!'

'*Khetar Kherak, ya Sayed,*' said Mainstree. 'Well. At ten I went back to England to boarding school, and I matriculated just after the Second World War broke out. My brother, who was four years my senior, and I got back once on holiday to Jerusalem in those six years; the Colonial Office wasn't all that generous with family passages in those days. Still, that one time was a coming home. It confirmed everything I felt at school in England: Palestine, the Middle East, was my world, where I belonged. No hard feelings to Britain, but the Middle East was home.'

'So you would have found your way back here in the war,' said Hakki.

'Yes, in the army I wanted something with a Middle East, an Arab touch to it. I found it in the LRDG. Do you know of it? The Long Range Desert Group. Our job was almost entirely to operate behind enemy lines in North Africa. There was quite a strong Rhodesian contingent with us. It was dangerous, and a magnificent and unforgettable experience. A handful of us would often be out for months at a stretch in a jeep, seeing nothing but the deserts and their Bedouin; we were after intelligence about the Germans and Italians. I think we did a fair job. We certainly learnt a great deal about the deserts, often painfully. But they're very honest places, you know; a kind of ultimate honesty. They've a harsh purity; a chastity, even, clean as sudden death. And of course the nights, particularly in the Western Desert. The air had that charged luminosity, vibrant. It was an uncanny, unearthly beauty, out of a fable. You always remembered it.

'So it must have been a war quite like Lawrence's, I suppose; long periods of movement and hardship, very solitary, then short bursts of action, generally very bloody. But there was a sweep, an austerity, a grandeur to it that I'll never forget.'

Also an MM and an MC which I'll spare them details of, he thought to himself.

'But you went back to Britain after it?' asked Hakki.

'Not in the first years,' said Mainstree. 'No, I stayed on in the army, and in the Middle East. I got myself seconded to the Sixth British Airborne in Palestine. Till 1948 I saw from first hand, and generally violently, the bloody drawing of battle lines for the classic war between the Jews and the Arabs in the Middle East that we've been watching now for the last thirty-seven years. But in the two years that I was there the main thrust of the battle was between Begin's Etzel and the even more extremist Lechi, the Stern Gang, on the one hand, and the British Mandatory Power on the other. Ben Gurion's Haganah moderates at times came into the fight on *our* side against Etzel and Lechi.'

'Where did you find that your sympathies lay?' said Ben Yehuda quietly.

Mainstree looked at him, then at Hakki, and back at him.

'In the Arab-Israeli war of 1948? With the Arabs. They had totally underestimated their enemy. They were badly organized, and the liaison between the five invading Arab armies was lamentable. They got it all wrong. So they were the underdogs. My sympathies were with them.

'But, perhaps to compensate for that, Mr Ben Yehuda,' Mainstree went on, 'had I been Jewish, I would have backed the most extremist, Lechi. Not even Etzel. And certainly not Haganah.'

'Ah. Why?'

'Because I personally have little time for moderates. They never really change the face of the world. They only seem to, for a short while. I can't think of any really great man who was moderate, ever, at any time in history –'

There was at least that, thought Ben Yehuda suddenly. They had at least that affinity. None was a moderate. Each, however sophisticated, was a natural extremist. Each was tall, seemed physically fit and trim, and evidently used power effectively in his field. All three might belong to one of the oldest universal guilds. All moved and thought instinctively like predators.

'What happened after 1948?' he asked.

'In my life?' said Mainstree. 'Oh, I stayed in the army. I was in the disastrous 1956 British-French attack on Suez. That was my final disillusionment with British foreign policy. With postwar Britain, say. I resigned from the army in 1958. Then for a year I was, in Mr Ben Yehuda's words, a professional exile – always in Middle Eastern countries, Jordan, Syria, Iraq, the Lebanon, the Gulf. By then my brother had proved himself a natural tycoon. He had created Mainstree Oil and was its majority shareholder. He had never married – he never had the time – and in 1959 at the age of forty he had his first and final heart attack. That left me sole heir. I've been trying to look like an oil company chairman ever since.'

'And you've not forgotten your first love, the Middle East?' said Hakki.

'No.'

'And precisely what is the charm for you,' said Ben Yehuda, 'in moving the levers that kill Mubarak?'

Mainstree looked at his chapel of fingers on the table in front of him.

'Look, it puts you back in the game. In the Big League. You're back in the swim, the world stream of events. Doing something that really matters. You can not only help history along. You can *be* part of history.'

'Like Malraux,' said Ben Yehuda, 'who said of Lawrence that at least he left his name on the map.'

Mainstree stared at him, looking a little surprised.

'Something like that,' he said.

'All right,' said Ben Yehuda. 'Well, we can probably work with you, then.'

He glanced at Wahid Hakki, his eyebrows raised.

Hakki gazed back at him, with no expression at all. Yes, my friend, thought Hakki to himself, we can work with you, *Kafer*, ungodly one. Until we have Islamic Fundamentalism throughout the region, a multitude of Islamic Republics united splendidly to destroy you, to avenge the many humiliations of our defeats, to avenge your taking of good Arab lands, your Deir Yassin massacre of our wives and our children and our old men – to wipe the abomination of Israel finally and forever from the face of the earth. Don't you see it, fool? We'll work most gladly with you till then –

Aloud he said, turning from Ben Yehuda to Mainstree:

'Yes, we can work with you. With you both.'

Mainstree was silent for some moments, contemplating the chapel of his hands, then he smiled brilliantly.

'Good!' he said. 'And where do we go from here? We start recruiting?'

'We shouldn't need to,' said Hakki. 'We cover what's happening in Egypt pretty closely from Libya, you know. And

I can see no need to put in men from outside.'

'No?' said Mainstree.

'No,' said Hakki. 'Though we'll need some money.'

'What's your plan?' said Ben Yehuda.

Wahid Hakki glanced at him in veiled dislike.

'Not to make the mistake Sir John attributes to the Americans – failing to recognize genuine grass-roots revolutions that spring up within countries. There already *is* one in Egypt. And a militant Fundamentalist organization to carry it out, already powerful, well trained, and well armed. Our intelligence is probably the one group outside it to know anything about it. I don't think that even Egypt's special security men have tumbled to it yet. That will make the impact of its execution of Mubarak and general uprising all the more devastating.'

'How much money will we need?' said Mainstree.

'Three million US dollars each should be ample to get things moving. We'll need more later. A militant organization carrying out a coup will need big money to buy information, connivance from key men in the police and armed forces, all sorts of unforeseeable items.'

'On the backs of these visiting cards,' said Mainstree, 'you'll find the number of our account at the Banque Indosuez, 4 Avenue de la Gare, CH-1002 Lausanne.'

'How could I draw money from it?' asked Hakki.

'Any of the three of us already has the right to draw from it. If you gentlemen could just give me your specimen signatures, I'll send them on.'

Ben Yehuda laughed. 'You've judged our reactions well, Sir John. I'll send my three million by telegraphic transfer tomorrow.'

'I'll do the same,' said Hakki.

'Mine are already deposited,' said Mainstree.

'What is this organization?' said Ben Yehuda.

Hakki shrugged.

'The title's melodramatic, I'm afraid. But they're very serious people indeed, the Angels of the Sword.'

'It goes with a swing,' said Mainstree. 'Where's it from?'

'It's something Hassan el Banna, founder of Egypt's Muslim Brotherhood, once said. He was rebutting the theory that Islam was a religion concerned only with the spiritual and ritualistic side of things. Not so, he said, it was all-embracing, covering every aspect of a man's life. "For Islam", he said, "is a faith and a ritual, a nation and a nationality, a religion and a state, spirit and deed, holy text and a sword." That's as I remember the text.'

'Tell us about it,' said Ben Yehuda. 'Tell us what we're buying.'

Hakki looked at him icily. 'I'll tell you what we'll *not* be buying,' he said, 'because it's not for sale. That is their faith, their dedication. These men, once committed, will not permit themselves to fail. But if you want to know how their structure operates, it's built on five-men cells of activists. Organizationally, the Angels of the Sword is –'

# 6

## *Fund Raising for a Better World*

'It's time,' said the girl. 'I'll go in now.'

The three assailants were from Abbas's cell. It was five to eight in the evening.

'You've got your gun?' said the heavy-shouldered man, Fuad.

'Yes. In my handbag.'

The gun was a 7.65 mm Italian Beretta automatic, black and beautifully made.

'We stop ten metres before the shop, as planned,' said the driver of the taxi, Omar the Egyptian, 'and we wait there till you signal.'

'By putting my head out of the door, which will have been shut till then, to keep out all others.'

Ironically, the jeweller's shop was in the same street as Abdallah's chemist's, off Muhammed Hahmoud, not far from Falaki Square.

The girl got out and walked to the shop. They had assured themselves that there were no clients in it. The jeweller always shut at eight. They knew all his habits. They had watched him for weeks past from a room hired opposite.

By the door the girl's nerves tautened. She would underscore this date deeply: her first mission. By its violence she would mark and remember it. She glimpsed her reflection in the shop window. The window was quite small, three metres wide, two and a half high, one deep. It held necklaces, rings, bracelets, a few expensive watches, mounted on royal blue. The stones were all good. This jeweller was renowned; many *khaw-waghat* bought from him. A steel shutter came down over the window at eight, though this was not where the best goods lay. Like the one- and two-carat diamonds and the gold bullion and the krugerrands. They were inside. The cell knew that. She saw herself superimposed over the jewellery display. Her image was like the falling shadow of some bird of prey, light and silent and swift and lethal. She reached the door, beyond the window, pushed it, and went in. A bell tinkled above her.

'Just closing,' said the jeweller, in Arabic, then stopped, looking at her. That was what they had planned. She was superbly dressed. That richly flared flower-pattern skirt was Dior. He could not place the sheer white blouse with its bouffant sleeves and the neat black bow at her throat and the intricate classic lace across the bosom, but he knew that that meant money too. The sheer black high-heeled shoes with their broad gold buckles were certainly hand-made. The rather large and very supple black leather handbag hanging from her left shoulder was Spanish or Italian. She wore no jewellery. She had no need to.

'I'm sorry,' she said in English, her American accent marked.

'It's nothing,' he said, his own English good from practice. 'I was in fact just closing. But of course for you –'

'Why don't you do that?' she said. 'Close, I mean. For the rest of the world. I don't like competition when I'm buying. And it'll probably be worth your while.'

'Of course,' he said. 'What might you be wanting?'

'A one- to two-carat diamond, mounted on white gold or platinum. If you have such.'

'Certainly,' he said, and went promptly to the window. He turned on a light. She watched him let down the steel shutter, then close the shop door and shut one of its three locks. He left the bundle of keys hanging from it. Good, she thought.

He came back behind his counter. He was a short man, pot-bellied and bald, aged fifty or more. His two bands of remaining hair, very black, perhaps dyed, crept over his skull from back to front, close to it as paint. He had quick black eyes and small white teeth. You could smell his love for money. She would find it no pain to kill him.

'A moment. Here are the one- and two-carat stones, and sizes between. And here's the tray of my best two-carat stones. Not many but as I think you'll agree, impressive. All these are exceptional white plus, certificated finest quality round, and internally flawless.'

He was letting her into the secrets of the trade, a sure-fire way of influencing her to buy. Well, she had achieved her aim —to get the trays of his best diamonds out there in front in the open. She took his jeweller's loupe from his hand and examined the diamonds methodically. It magnified to the power of ten. She saw that his diamonds were brilliant cuts, their surfaces trimmed to a perfection of fifty-eight facets which brought out the best in them. She judged carefully, by the four C's – cut, colour, clarity and carat weight. She looked *through* each stone towards what remained of the daylight visible through the wire-meshed door, keeping a wary eye open for any yellowish-tinted stones, or any carbon spots, inner flaws, or surface blemishes. She ended with five exceptional stones. The jeweller observed her selection with some awe.

'You know your stones. You like the best.'

'One always searches for the ideal.'

'Indeed. This one might interest you. Practically flawless. And 1.65 carats.'

'Ah. And at what price? $US13,000 per carat?'

'*Madam! These* days, with the Gulf War and inflation? I would ask more than that!'

'Well, we can talk. And what about these five that I've put aside? I'd like you to make a special price for them, not more than $US25,000 a carat.'

'Well, I must think about that. Meanwhile, should I put all the other stones away?'

'No, no, let's leave them all out for the moment. Meanwhile I'm sure you must have some gold bullion? Krugerrands?'

It was pushing her luck. He froze at that, curved over the counter across from her. She saw the small gold cross on the pendant round his neck flicker and be still. He was a Copt. That made it easier. He was famed for selling to the richest *khawwaghat* too, the foreign guests from the Meridien and Hilton and Sheraton and Mena House and Salam and Shepheard hotels. That helped. She knew where the gold was. The cell knew most things about this man. In the safe behind the counter there was one gold bar of 12.5 kilos or 400 troy ounces worth some $US130,000 and about fifty krugerrands at say $US400 each. She had to talk that safe door open. The cell could have tried explosives, but blowing a safe open in situ was not easy – or criminals would have done so successfully more often. And explosives made a mess and a noise, and the Angels were fastidious and disliked both. She looked back at the little Copt with his pot belly and his two painted black strips of hair.

'What's the matter? You don't trust me? You think I'm going to try to rob you or something?'

How could he not accept her? With that perfect American accent? Those splendid clothes? That virtual acceptance that she would have to pay up to $US25,000 a carat for those five exceptional stones? His quick black eyes relaxed. His small white teeth smiled. They were like the tabs of a cash register flashing on a sale.

'Of course not. Of course it's all right. A moment, please.'

He turned his back to her and she heard him spin the combination wheels. The door clicked open. She saw him burrow into the safe. He came out with the 12.5 kilo gold bar and set it on the counter in front of her. He had left the safe door open; he would want to get the gold bar back in there promptly, in company with the krugerrands. That miserliness would cost him dearly. She gazed down at the gold bar, the serial number stamped on it, the Springbok head, the words Rand Refinery Ltd. Black and white men had blasted and dug and lifted and refined more than 1,500 tons of ore from down to 10,000 feet to produce that.

'And your price for this?'

'A moment while I check today's quotations. Of the order of $US150,000, I should say. A moment, please –'

'No, stay still, please. Your hands on the counter in front of you. And stand *absolutely* still –'

The jeweller's small white face froze on her in horror, the thin black eyebrows ludicrously high, almost meeting their twin black painted brothers above. His mouth was open, his sharp black eyes clamped on the Beretta in her right hand, the 30 cm silencer on it.

'But –'

'Shut up. I don't mind killing you. I know you have an alarm bell behind you under the counter, to your right. Don't be so stupid as to try to make for it. I repeat, stay quite still. I'm now going to take a few steps backwards to your front door, which I shall open. I shall be covering you with this pistol all the time. I'm a very good shot, and, remember, no one outside would even hear it –'

She backed away slowly over the tiled floor. It was clear of obstacles; she had made sure of that. She kept the Beretta dead steady on the jeweller. But he clearly loved his life. He was not moving.

The pistol in her left hand, she turned the key with her right, and opened the door very slightly. Her heart plunged in shock. The head was at the crack of the opening at once; a young Egyptian, well dressed.

'*Elhamdullilah!* Praise be to God! I must buy a present! For my wife, you understand! Her birthday!'

She kept her grip ramrod stiff on the door handle. That way he could not see into the shop, or the pistol.

'I'm sorry. We're shut. Definitely shut!'

'But look, this is one key day in the year! I must insist!'

'So must I. We're shut. Get the hell out!'

He stared at her face, rigid against him, then he swore and turned away. She switched back swiftly to the jeweller, her heart still thudding. He had not moved, like a rabbit before a snake. His quick rodent's eyes observed her with respect. Before, her perfect American rich girl's accent had impressed and persuaded him. Now he had just heard her use completely colloquial Egyptian – indeed, almost gutter Egyptian. She was clearly a girl of many parts.

121

He knows that now, she thought. Already he knows too much about me.

'Not the slightest movement, remember –'

This time when she opened the door there was no one at it outside. She showed her head, lifted her free hand. She heard the car door open. She came back a little into the shop, her Beretta still pointing. Fuad Wahbah and Omar the Egyptian were beside her in half a minute. She talked to them swiftly in Egyptian Arabic; *that* disguise was already blown –

'The two trays of his best one- and two-carat diamonds are on the counter there. And the gold bar. The krugerrands will be in the safe –'

'Open?' said Fuad.

'Open.'

Fuad went fast round the counter. He had a leather attaché-case. He bent to the safe.

'Fifty-two krugerrands,' he said, and she heard him spill them into the case and the gold bar and the two trays of diamonds with them. He snapped the case's combination locks shut and left the case on the counter.

'Now?' said Omar.

'As planned,' said Fuad. 'We take him to the back and tie and gag him.' He turned to the girl. 'You heard anyone there?'

'Not a soul,' she said.

'His *khadama*, his cleaner, comes at seven tomorrow. She'll free him.'

'You don't have to tie me up!' said the jeweller. 'I'll call no one!'

'You have to, for the insurance,' said Fuad. 'Fine, but tomorrow.'

The small man swallowed. She saw that he was shaking.

'All right,' he said.

'And you're to give no accurate description of us,' said Fuad. 'Tell them we were masked. Or we'll come back and kill you, slowly. We'll know if you've talked. We have our friends in the police.'

The jeweller pressed his pot belly against the counter. Sweat showed now on the bald curve between the two black bands on his skull.

'I know what you can do,' he said.

'All right, round the back,' said Fuad. He turned to the girl. 'You'll watch things here? And the case?'

'Yes,' she said.

Alone, she checked that the front door was locked, then sat in a chair by the counter, within reach of the suitcase. She had put out the shop's main light, leaving only the side light on the counter. She could relax a little now. The first part of the job was done. She would have to manoeuvre to do the second. But it was vital for her. The other two need not even know about it. But this was her first mission. She had to mark it irreversibly, for herself.

Zeinab Marzuk could only act totally and incisively, for she had little power for compromise or nuance. She usually wore, not these chic Western millionaire's garments, which she termed contemptuously her working clothes, but her *ziyy el Islami*, her sexually neutralizing Islamic robes. She was striking even in these. Zeinab was tall for an Egyptian woman, about 5 foot 8, or 1 metre 73, and even that full-length body veil could not totally stifle the full curve of her breasts and swell of her hips. From the stamp of her expression, she took no trace of coquettish pride in these female attributes; rather, she bore them without comment as axiomatic, perhaps with slight contempt. It was a good, rather regal face, beautifully structured, with a high and wide brow and salient cheekbones, the eyes placed wide in it, the nose straight and thin-bridged, and the lips clearly cut, a little thin. She had a fine olive complexion. There was a glow to it, and to her dark-brown eyes. It was as if by it she sought in some small measure to emulate the glitter in Abbas Sidki's.

Zeinab was thirty years old. Daughter of an eminent physician from Heliopolis, she had read a brilliant degree in sociology at Cairo University, then gone on for a year to the city's stylish American University. Here she had won a scholarship to Harvard, where she had graduated as brilliantly in anthropology. There too she met her husband. Already violently pro-American, she found him the epitome of all things excellent. Indeed, two years her senior, he was already renowned in the university's law and debating societies, and qualified *summa cum laude*. From a centuries-old, and acutely right-wing Massachusetts family, he slid effortlessly into the family's law firm in Boston. Their lives seemed fixed smoothly and for all time on an ideal of patrician American life, exhibiting its oldest and most solid values and traditions. She was ecstatically happy with him. He was a big fair man with honest blue eyes.

The discovery that these could lie outrageously without the slightest change in expression – had indeed been doing so for a full year – broke her and caused a sixth-month miscarriage that nearly killed her. But the mental shock was worse. She had simply not been equipped by her upbringing for the West's double standards in such matters. She listened incredulously in silence as her husband advised her, in really quite a friendly way, that for a man in his position to have a mistress or two was in a sense just part of the life style, and not to be taken too seriously. Zeinab took it seriously. She left him. He did not contest the divorce. Back in Egypt she gravitated naturally to the Angels. Her passion for America and all Western values had switched completely to hatred. If this was arguing politics from the vagina, it was none the less fervent for that. Abbas Sidki, after examining her file, accepted her for his cell in place of Suleiman Talkhan without demur. She had the fire he liked. Moreover, his Islamic Fundamentalists on principle did not discriminate against the use of women as terrorists. For equality of opportunity, any Women's Liberation movement would have been proud of them.

So Zeinab sat calmly in her chair by the jeweller's counter, the locked case of treasure safely on it. She gazed down comfortably at her blue-black 7.65 mm Beretta automatic with its 30 cm silencer. She found it a slick and seductive messenger of death. Killing, effective violence, could be a route worth travelling. It was an exigent but privileged universe, filled with its own cold meaning. It had the charm, perfection, and inevitability of pure mathematics. Its devotees reached it through life's cruelties, betrayals, humiliations, and deceptions. It was the one grave certainty. If you could never be sure in life, you could always be sure of death. These then were a select small company, an ultimate élite. Zeinab, recently converted to it, glanced from the locked and loaded case to her pistol, that miniature precise engine of destruction, and felt the warm glow of one performing her duties completely.

Well, almost completely. She still had that one key thing to do privately.

It amused her that the thought of carrying out this violent act caused her no compunction at all, though she had come back to the most orthodox practice of Islam. But if skilled violence was now clearly her only trade, Islam even supported her in it. She knew that the Angels of the Sword had in fact, somewhat ponderously, checked with their Imam in Minya, halfway to Asyut, for his Islamic approval of their robbing banks and jewellery and similar shops to get the funds needed for their operations, even should this provoke bloodshed and death. The Imam, a gentle elderly man, whose left thigh had been permanently maimed in a riot in his youth against the British-backed Egyptian police, had come back from his consultation of the Koran and Sunna and Hadith to tell the Angels to go ahead; the cause was after all unobjectionable. Naturally, it would be better if any people damaged were non-Muslims, but Muslim casualites were also acceptable in a pinch.

This one was a Copt. And one who simperingly sold his jewels and himself to the *khawwaghat*. In a way she would be doing it for Abbas. A sacrifice for Abbas. No one could deny that it would make things safer for all. But above all for Abbas, the cell leader. For him she would do anything.

She looked up at the slight sound.

'It's done,' said Fuad Wahbah, the heavy-shouldered boxer.

'He's tied securely and gagged?' she asked.

'Like a fowl,' said Omar the Egyptian. 'On his bed, and a broad strip of sticking plaster over his mouth. He'll not be doing a thing until his *khadama* finds him in the morning.'

'Let's go,' said Fuad, and picked up the case. Omar watched

him. He said: 'That's a great haul. Two hundred and fifty to three hundred thousand dollars. Even after our fences take their very fat rake-off. And all done in ten minutes. We'll not make more than two raids this good in a year.'

'He won't talk later?' she asked.

'No,' said Omar. 'He's terrified.'

'Let's go, *now*!' said Fuad, opening the front door's lock.

'I'm staying,' she said, 'just a minute. You go on. I just want to see how he looks.'

'What the hell?' said Fuad, half-turning back. 'You're checking on us? You're not in charge here!'

'No, no,' she said, 'I just want to see. We're all in this together. I did my part at the start all right, didn't I? I just want to have taken part in everything.'

'Please yourself,' said Fuad. 'We're not waiting. The vital thing is in this case. I'm getting it away *now*!'

'I'll walk,' she said. 'I'll come right after you, to Abbas's room.'

They were gone. She shut the door and turned one lock. She went then to the back. The jeweller was in the first room behind the shop. They had left the light on for him. He was flat on his back in the bed. There were about fifteen metres of light rope round him, round his wrists and elbows and knees and ankles. The flat pink plaster cut off his mouth. His colour was high. Well, it wouldn't be for long –

His head and mobile eyes had swivelled to her. He was beaten. Even his twin black strips of dyed hair were awry. She put her pistol down on the side table and came close to him, her loins by his head.

'Listen. Pray to your God if you have one. I'm going to kill you. You see, I think it's right that you die.'

The small man writhed in his bonds. He reminded her of a netted fish. He would die soon. He could not get off his back. His eyes were horrible in their intensity. A whinnying sound came from his nose.

'No, no, you have to die. Be reasonable. You've sinned too far against Islam, sold too much to the *khawwaghat*. And you're a danger to us. Who's to guarantee you'll not talk when the police really get to you? No, I assure you this is the best way.'

He screamed through his nose; she had not thought that possible. She took the heavy pillow and got atop of him. She rammed the pillow down over his face. She clamped her body down closely over his, her crutch tight down over his, snug below the pot belly, like a wrestler in a hold. It was an ironic reversal to the usual sexual posture. His body curved and bucked beneath her. She echoed him perfectly. For a small man he showed great vitality. She thrust powerfully down onto him, her pillow inflexible, riding him mercilessly. Afterwards she would untie and ungag him, leaving him dead with no mark of violence upon him. For his *khadama* and the world he could have died of a heart attack. Even Abbas and the Angels would never really know what had happened. His death was her own private monument. And by it she would have made them all safe.

A sudden final climax galvanized him. She straddled him close, bouncing identically with him. Now the great ecstatic warmth flowed beautifully about her arched loins. Abbas! She shouted silently, I do it all for *Abbas*!

# 7

# *A Man for the Bath*

'So I told him to take his hand away at once,' said Bridget O'Shaunessy. 'At a Faculty dinner too! Can you imagine it?'

Daniel Gad could. He knew his fellow countrymen.

'Or?'

'Or,' said Bridget, 'I'd go on saying that again and again, louder and louder. I said.'

'I'll bet that shook him.'

Bridget cocked her head slightly and looked back at Gad, possibly discerning the thinnest vein of mockery.

'Well, the President of the University was there with his wife. I mean, it couldn't have made him look too good, could it?'

'No.'

'Also, I picked up my fork.'

'That was when he got the message,' said Gad.

'Well, he did kind of loosen his grip then.'

'At least it speaks highly for Colloquial Egyptian.'

'How's that?'

'He's your *Fus'ha* teacher, isn't he? You can never tell with these Classical Arabists.'

'Is that so?' said Bridget.

'It's their formal structure,' said Gad. 'It binds them rigid. They're always trying to rebel against it.'

There was nothing wrong with hers. Gad could understand the academic who had made his pass at her thigh. Egyptians,

Arabs, were generally brought up so strictly veiled and purdahed off from their females that when they did finally come across American girls, like this one, or Europeans, who flung fair expanses of their naked flesh around in the open air and appeared to think nothing of it, they tended to go berserk. It was like putting a large juicy steak in front of a starving man.

The two sat companionably in the bath, facing each other, in Daniel Gad's flat on the ninth floor of 1121 Bis Corniche el Nil. The warmish water, a defiant challenge to the summer heat outside, reached to comfortably above their waists. The first time they had made love, they had thought as one to bathe together afterwards. It was a way of prolonging communion, of not breaking contact. Then by inspiration they had decided jointly to reverse the order, and it became established as part of their ritual. They sat at each end of the bath, facing inwards on each other, embalmed in warm water, their bare toes touching. They were like two curiously carved chess pieces locked in amiable confrontation. It was a cheerful and easy intimacy, apparently without limits. In the bath they talked to each other about anything at all, she about her studies and friends and teachers at the American University and the trips about the city and Egypt which it arranged, and, with disarming frankness, about her past and her love life in the States. Gad had given her to understand that he worked in the government, fairly high up, something in the Ministry of the Interior, to do with law and order. It was one way of putting it. This was the first time that she had come to the flat since Gad had got his police guard. She accepted the one on shift in the kitchen, a chubby sergeant, without demur, even looking impressed. Clearly, Gad must be high up indeed. Bridget was a slight girl, with long dark-brown hair, deep brown eyes, and a very pretty small face, with small and very regular features. Her complexion was milky white; her skin did not take the sun well. There was a little saddle of freckles across her nose about which she was inordinately self-conscious, and an almost exact replica of it on a larger scale across her full and beautifully shaped breasts. She had receptive nipples with quite broad red-brown circles round them. Her waist was small, and after it her hips flared out handsomely. Slight she might be, but she was all female, with all systems set to go. Her legs were nicely modelled. The hair over her mound of Venus was a rich luxuriant black, a startlingly accurate jet-black isosceles triangle, the difference with the shade of the hair on her head so acute as to make one or the other inevitably appear fraudulent – though Gad knew that they were not.

Bridget O'Shaunessy was as Irish as her name and complexion. She was passionate and diffident, carnal and innocent, Catholic and pagan. More and more he had found her an affectionate and attentive companion, outgoing and fascinated by the Egypt she saw about her, and particularly by the medieval Cairo that he, himself a great lover of it, could show her; for if a European city might boast ten buildings from the Middle Ages, Cairo had them by the hundred. Medieval Cairo was a city of the *Elf leila wa leila*, the Thousand and One Nights, its medieval monuments not torn down like Baghdad's or Damascus's by Mongol invasions. Bridget visited them with him and had the good taste to love them.

Bridget was twenty-eight. She was Boston Irish, though not exactly of the Kennedy set. Her father was a travelling salesman, retired. Bridget herself was a bright girl, and she had done well in high school, gaining a scholarship to Berkeley, always with a secret ambition to write creatively. After taking a good degree in English, she had come back to take a job on a small paper just outside Boston. She worked on hard news, which she liked. The job gave her independence, her own small flat in Boston, and a car. She kept on good terms with her family, visiting them diplomatically two or three times a month.

Only her love life seemed a little lacking. She had been going with her current boyfriend, so she told Daniel Gad, for four years. He was a Kennedy Democrat, a youngish politician at City Hall, seven years older than she. He came from a poorer family than hers, was extremely ambitious, and worked fanatically hard. He saw his social contacts as essential stepping-stones in his political career, so his social life was vigorous, and his friends many, and politically significant. He took her often with him to these gatherings, though her role was subsidiary.

He had one other salient characteristic. He was pure Boston Irish and Catholic like herself. Her parents were heavily in favour of him as a suitor, impressed by his position, his ambition, and his Irish Catholicism. They had a great sense of clan. Bridget's great-grandparents had been the first of the family to emigrate. Their descendants had married pure descendants of Irish Catholic immigrants like themselves. So her boyfriend qualified in all respects.

Except one. So exclusively projected was this powerhouse on his future prominence that he seemed to have no time or energy left for sex. He made love to her about once a month, in her flat, never in his. It was crisp. He was not a man to believe in foreplay or in expressing tenderness afterwards. He was emotionally too muscular for that. It was done too much on the wing, in passing, between bed and dressing-table, as it were. It was a convention, just something you did now and then, rather like paying the electricity bill.

As for herself, Bridget was miserably dissatisfied. There ought to be more to the performance. When she had graduated from home and orthodox Catholicism, she had gone on to lose her virginity quite pleasantly at Berkeley. Even her few amateur and fumbling experiences there had proved a good deal more rewarding than this. Yet she did not quite know how to get out of it. Her relationship with the young politician had surreptitiously become one of the most difficult things of all to break – a pattern, entrenched by approval. His friends generally approved of her for him. Her parents approved of him for her. He had, after all, some excellent qualities. And he never actually beat her. She was sunk. Recently, too, he had muttered about marriage once or twice. That would be the ultimate disaster. It would simply put a permanent legal seal on her state of unhappiness.

The Daughters of the American Revolution rescued Bridget O'Shaunessy, to her amazement. She had just published in her paper a telling exposé of the secret love life of another City Hall politician, rather senior to but happily quite unconnected with her boyfriend. This gentleman, the respectably married father of two teenage daughters, had had a relationship with his mistress which, ironically, was the exact opposite to Bridget's. From the evidence, it was clearly fully, even rambunctiously, satisfying to both sides. Wondering how far she was driven by sheer envy, Bridget felt some pangs of conscience in writing this piece. Still, it won her salvation, anyway temporarily. The Daughters of the American Revolution were delighted with it, and at once generously offered her a scholarship in recognition. Inscrutably, it was for a year's full-time study of Arabic at the American University in Cairo. It covered all tuition, travel, and reasonable living expenses. Never mind that it was the only scholarship the Daughters had to hand at the moment, and that they had had some difficulty in finding a recipient. Bridget leapt at it. She was glad to distance herself from her current situation and reflect on it. She had never been outside the States in her life. Here was an entirely new culture. Maybe she would even convert to it.

Daniel Gad stopped her from going that far. He was himself an odd blend of East and West, but he did not believe in easy conversions. You were generally what your culture had made you. There were no short cuts.

Gad, who knew a fair number of the teaching staff at the American University, both American and Egyptian, sometimes went to their and the students' parties. There was good sound sense to that. Although Gad liked women, he was far too wily a Copt to take on the Islamic Establishment head-on by making passes at their women, married or not, rich or poor, educated or simple. The constraint was absolute. It was not much better with the Copts, whose community in Egypt numbered some five million or seven million souls (depending on which Copt you spoke to) of Egypt's total population of 48 million. The Copts might be Christian, but they often seemed very nearly as hard on unauthorized sex as were the Muslims. The taboo seemed to have drifted across and stuck firmly on them by osmosis. This tended to be hard on a man like Gad, who was not naturally monogamous. Thus he wisely restricted his hunting to Western circles.

Bridget met him at her first party in her first week in Egypt. It was in the rather elegant furnished flat of one of the richer American students she had met in the Arabic Language Unit, located on the fourth floor in Saad Zaghlul in Garden City, facing south. She saw a tallish man on the balcony, and went out to have a look at him. He had snake hips and good shoulders and he was quite elegantly dressed, in knife-creased light cream slacks with a thin dark-brown leather belt, slim brown shoes and a light-blue short-sleeved cotton shirt which showed a brown throat and some muscular brown arms. He wore a thin gold chain round his neck with a small Greek cross at the end of it, and a gold watch on his left wrist, she thought Rolex. He had the face of a slightly worn Red Indian: very high cheekbones, very olive skin, a buccaneering broken nose. After that his eyes startled. In that context they should have been black or dark-brown. They were instead bright blue, ultra-marine. They had been observing her too. She could not recall her politician's eyes lighting up like that.

'New?'

'Yes, four days ago. So it's still hard for me to find my way about. Though I had a map tonight.'

'It's wise. Cairo's a tricky city. No tall mountains as landmarks, for one thing.'

'No. You know it well?'

'Fairly well, I suppose. Let me get you a drink.'

'What's that you're having?'

'Egyptian vodka, genuine Russian formula. It's really great stuff. And only six or seven dollars the bottle. Black market rate for the dollar, of course.'

He smiled. He had a good smile. He meant it.

'Of course.'

'Best thing the Russians left us, before Sadat flung them out. Of course, they're back now.'

'Yes. That's with orange, is it?'

'Yes. That the way you like it?'

'That would be fine.'

He went into the flat, leaving his glass in her hands. It was a pleasant way to stake a claim. She took a sip. The Russians had really done a great job there.

People eddied out onto the balcony. The party was warming up. Most of the students were Americans. Easily next in numbers came the Japanese, from their diplomatic corps and major financial institutions like the Bank of Tokyo, and big trading companies like Sumitomo; after the two oil price explosions the Arabs were going to go on being very powerful people for a very long time, and the Japanese were far too shrewd to miss any opportunities with them through not knowing how to read, speak and write their language fluently. The Europeans came a long way behind, a few English, French, Germans, and Belgians. In the large sitting room that led out to the balcony two of the younger American students, dressed in galabiahs, were executing their version of Arab dancing. Some, she had heard, took their passage to Egypt very literally, searching for their souls. Some, men and girls, converted to Islam. It could seem an attractive abdication.

The party host, a tall young man from Yale who had told her he was on the American University's CASA programme of advanced Arabic studies, drifted out onto the balcony, checking to see if she was happy. She thanked him prettily, but not too prettily. Seizing her meaning accurately, he smiled and drifted off again. The Red Indian was enough for her evening. She had come to the party modestly covered, in dark-blue linen slacks and a long-sleeved and fairly high-necked white blouse. She had been warned to avoid eye contact with Egyptians in the street and not to dress provocatively because, being literal-minded, they were provoked, and lunged their eager paws at any proffered half-bare breast or bounding buttock. The Red Indian had nonetheless undressed her politely, with aplomb and speed. He would know the colour of her panties and her weight to the nearest pound.

'Your drink.'

'Oh, the Russian vodka. And here's yours.'

He made no comment on its perceptibly lower level.

'Us,' she said. 'It's just struck me.'

'Pardon?'

'Knowing how to make it was the best thing the Russians left *us*, you said.'

'Oh, the vodka. Yes, so I did. Ah, you don't agree?'

'No, it's not that. But you said "Us". You mean you, the Egyptians?'

'Yes, that's right.'

'But you're English! You're a lecturer, aren't you? I mean, you have that Oxford accent and all –'

He laughed.

'No, I'm Egyptian. I carry an Egyptian passport.' He glanced at her. 'But you're about half right. My mother's English. And I did in fact go to that place.'

'Place?'

'Oxford. Though I wasn't at one of the glamorous colleges. A modest one, called St Edmund Hall.'

'Oh. And you studied Arabic there? A doctorate?'

'That would have been coals to Newcastle. No, lady, I'm no lecturer. I read a thing called PPE. That's Politics, Philosophy, and Economics. I concentrated on the Politics.'

'That's your interest?'

'Round here,' said the Red Indian, 'politics tends to be everybody's interest. Sometimes, too often, a question of life or death.'

'So what brings you here?' said Bridget. 'Nobody's running any elections here tonight.'

He smiled.

'John,' he said, gesturing towards a willowy and nice-looking man with brown hair and glasses who was standing in the sitting room drinking Coca-Cola. 'The director of your studies and fate at the university. I'm a friend of his.'

'You're an active politician?' she asked, wondering if she was ever going to break out of this bracket. 'I didn't think you had so many around here.'

'We don't. They're still quite a rare animal. This is still basically a police state. Oh, we have our *Maglis esh-Shaab*, our People's Assembly, and so on, but mainly they just do what they're told. If Mubarak, like Sadat before him, really wants to push some measure through, the voting in favour tends to be pretty decisive.'

'Yet you still work for it, rigged votes and police state and all?'

He looked at her very seriously.

'Oh, yes,' he said. 'I think it's probably the best we can do at the moment. You can't really run a full-blown democracy when two-thirds of your population are still illiterate.'

'And what do you do for it?'

'For my police state? Oh, I work in a government department. On the side of law and order, you know.'

'Wasn't there more of that in England? Weren't you tempted to stay there?'

'After Oxford, you mean. No, not really. England's a very civilized country, but —'

'But?'

'But it's not my country. *This* is my country.'

'Because your father's from here? What does he do? Is he in the government too?'

'Because I'm from here too. I was born here in Cairo. We've been here quite a long time, you know. You can call Egyptian civilization 7,000 years old, if you go back to the Pre-Dynastic prelude to the Pharaohs. Relatively, the Muslim Arabs were latecomers. They only got here in the seventh century AD with the armies which spread out in waves from the Arabian Peninsula after Muhammed's death. We were here long before that. We, the Copts, I mean. You know what a Copt is?'

'Well, to be honest —'

'We're Christian Egyptians. Like the Greek Orthodox, only different. For one thing, we have our own Pope. When we can find him, that is. When he isn't being banished to desert monasteries at Wadi Natrun. We have our little run-ins with the Islamic Establishment from time to time.'

'Ah.'

'Was my father in the government, you asked? That's a laugh. Father's anti-government on principle. No, he's a neuro-surgeon, very independent-minded. Also a bigwig on the Council of the Anglo-American Hospital in Gezira. You've heard of it? If you have to fall ill in Egypt, which God forbid, either go there or get out. My family's full of medicine. Two of my brothers are doctors and even my mother was a defenceless nurse when my father met her. He always says that it was wooing her in London that made him need two shots to get his FRCS. Father sees me as a disappointment. He wanted me to take medicine too. He thinks I'm wasting my modest talents.'

'Are you?'

He looked at her again. He had that trick of suddenly turning very concentrated. After the light chat and flippancies, it was somewhat forbidding.

'No. I don't think so. For what worth they may have. I said I was on the side of law and order, just now. That is true. I hope a fair law, a fair order. I think it vital that we have moderate men at the springs of power here today. Without that we're lost.'

'And you're a moderate man?'

He looked at her steadily.

'Fanatically moderate, you could even say.'

'And who are the enemies? Israel?'

He shook his head.

'No, and I say that after fighting in two wars against her. Not Israel. Not the *concept*. Israel is most basically organization and order. Orderliness. She's Western Europe, development, democracy. Of course she has her Greater Israel side, which is abrasive and deadly dangerous. But she has her moderate men too, to control that. They exist. We can talk to them. We can make a deal with men like that. With them in power, we can live with Israel. It was because he saw that that Sadat made his incredible flight in an unarmed aircraft to Israel in 1977 and addressed the Knesset, offering peace. Sadat may have been a charlatan and a fraud in some of the other things he did, but in that one political move he was a genius. It was *the* key move, changing everything. No one else saw that, and acted; only Sadat. For that he deserves his Nobel Prize and his eternal fame.

'No, our true enemies are nearer home. Much nearer home. Among the Arabs. Among the Egyptians themselves. Ironically, in Islam. In one lethal extreme of Islam. How much do you know about the *Ikhwan*?'

'Sorry, I'm new around here, remember? I don't even know

what it means.'

'Of course,' he said. 'I'm sorry. Brotherhood. It means the Muslim Brotherhood.'

'That, yes. Our hackles are trained to raise at that. Blood and terror, not so?'

'In Egypt it was in fact founded in 1928 by rather a saintly man, Hassan el Banna.'

'Oh. Not a born killer?'

'Hardly. He was always a deeply religious man.'

She realized from the emotion in his voice that she was talking to a very serious man. And, she found, an attractive one. Here was someone through whom she might really come closer to Egypt.

'You mean he was rather like our Martin Luther King?' she said. 'A man of peace, but prepared to fight for it?'

'Yes,' he nodded. 'Banna wasn't ever violent just for the sake of it. Rather he was always a puritanical reformer. He came from his village as a very young man to a great religious school here in Cairo in the Twenties. That moulded him, not Cairo itself, which shocked him badly. He saw the city with the eyes of a pious villager. Banna wanted social justice. He was always in favour of the poor and underprivileged everywhere, and particularly in the *rif*, the countryside. He astounded the fellahin. No one had ever done a goddam thing for them before. You said that the words Muslim Brotherhood made you think of blood and terror. Yes, Banna's organization had a capacity for violence; his times were violent. But at the human level he knew all about humiliation and suffering, and he did all he could to eradicate them. Banna was a good Muslim. You know that all Arabic words stem from an *asl*, a root, of three key consonants? The *asl* for Muslim – or Islam for that matter – is s, l, and m. Remind you of anything? *Salaam*, peace. The connotation is peace. Banna was a good man of peace.'

'You know,' she said, 'you sound as if you were in love with this man.'

That brought him up with a jolt. He gave her another of his jet-like penetrating looks. Then he laughed suddenly.

'You're probably right,' he said. 'Love and hate. You know,

I've read every single thing he wrote that I could get my hands on. And everything that's been written about him. He's a fascinating man. Basically one of us.'

'One of us?'

'A moderate.' He smiled. 'All right. Maybe sometimes fanatically a moderate. That makes him a good guy in my book.'

'Oh? Being moderate is so difficult? So worthwhile?'

He turned his searchlight look on her again. He literally almost lit up with it.

'It's probably the most difficult thing in the world,' he said soberly. 'Certainly the most worthwhile thing. Even if you fail trying.'

'So Banna's not your villain? Not your true enemy?'

'Banna? This great man who gave the poor here an identity, a purpose? A kind of pride? No, Banna was never my villain, my true enemy. The murderousness grew up inevitably alongside him, like a weed, so close and naturally that I don't think he really noticed it.'

'How's that? How do you mean?'

She saw him look down at his almost empty glass. The sounds of the party beat out at them now, in top gear, a very high hum. She felt in its pressure a curious intensive impulse to frankness, honesty. She had to keep talking to this odd man, and to keep him talking. For he seemed to be trying to tell her deep truths as he saw them. She could only respect that. Indeed she felt called upon to reciprocate in kind. She could match his uninhibited intimacy courteously by bursting into tears or telling him her own life story. She was certainly moved, yet also comforted; as one who, in some burning desert, stumbles round the next sand-dune to find an old and warmly trusted friend, in fine physical nick and of smiling countenance, and moreover amply equipped with camels, water and tents. Only two other couples remained out on the party's balcony now, possibly similarly locked in impromptu communions.

'Late 1942 Banna sensed danger,' said the Red Indian. 'Earlier that year Sadat, with whom Banna was closely linked, was jailed for his connection with two farcical German spies

139

who lived on a Nile houseboat hired from a belly-dancer and frequented a nightclub called the Kit Kat, flinging sterling banknotes printed in Greece about generously. The British trapped them. Banna feared the British, and their puppet Egyptian wartime governments and police. So in defence he built his terrorist group, his Secret Apparatus.'

'It stayed under his direct command?'

The Red Indian looked at her sharply. 'There lay the trouble. By its very nature the Secret Apparatus tended to slip out of Banna's control.'

'Like the FBI under Hoover?' she said. 'Or the CIA in the 1960s?'

'Yes,' he said. 'The Secret Apparatus also tended to cultivate paranoia, keeping the hands of their creators clean by monopolizing the dirt themselves. An élite trained in espionage, the use of arms, the techniques of terror. They took an oath of obedience and silence before a Koran and a pistol. They developed their own mystique. Their leadership, by murdering a prime minister, provoked Banna's own death. It was a most bitter loss to Egypt.'

'This now is your true enemy?'

'That's near it; the Secret Apparatus side, not Banna's marvellous and humane social pioneering. Today, the enemy is Islamic Fundamentalism, and it's all the more deadly because it's so easy to sympathize with some of its aims. For me, at least. It's élitist, with some of our best young talent. Dedicated, ready literally to die for their cause –'

'Wait a minute. You've made quite a jump there. You say that Islamic Fundamentalism is the true enemy, and deadly. Yet just *why* shouldn't they govern that way if they want to? It's their country, isn't it? And you've made it sound a philosophy of great austere beauty, a selfless puritanical return to first principles, a purposeful drive for social justice. What's wrong with that?'

'Yes, that's how it looks to its followers. What's wrong with it? Well, I'll buy you a drink on that. I'll go in and get some refills.'

'I'll come with you.'

'You haven't had enough?'

'Vodka?'

'Talk.'

'No.'

'Fine. Then into battle.'

They went in, weaving through the milling students to the bar in the kitchen. The tall Yale graduate replenished their vodkas, showing no ill will. On the way back they passed near the Red Indian's friend John, who raised his eyebrows above his Coca-Cola.

'Miss O'Shaunessy, I should have warned you.'

'Doctor?'

'As your spiritual guide. Daniel Gad is a kind of natural hazard to young lady visitors to Cairo. Be on your guard.'

'Oh.'

'I take no responsibility for him, mind.'

'No. Thank you.'

'My children.'

'Daniel Gad, is it?' she said, back on the balcony.

'Yes. My father's very anglophile in his medicine, but totally francophile culturally. Hence the Daniel, and the fact that I was schooled at *lycées français* by strapping great Christian Brothers, a permanently unsettling experience. The Gad's Coptic. Then they stuck Tarek on as a front-end loading, I suppose to make me look a bit more Egyptian if they could. And your first name, Miss O'Shaunessy?'

'Bridget.'

'Ah. Bridget. And where are you from?'

'Boston.'

'Boston, that's fine. I've heard it's a majestic city. Bridget, you asked what was wrong with Islamic Fundamentalism? I don't believe that you can go back in history. Not healthily, I mean. Look, I have infinite sympathy with the Fundamentalists' integrity, their drive against corruption, their dedication to a just society. But can we honestly go *back*? To cutting off the hands of recidivist thieves, and stoning adulterous women to death, with golden swords for princesses? I can't believe it. It's my French schooling, you see. It's made me Cartesian. I'm suspicious of myths, particularly beautiful ones. I just don't think you can deliberately go back in politics. Maybe not in human relationships either.'

'How powerful are your enemies?'

He looked down at her.

'Inside Egypt? Well, we've had three pretty bloody upsurges of it since 1974. Say 100 killed in them, 300 to 400 wounded. Of that order. Then around 15 executed, and hundreds imprisoned. But much more violent each time. And all this interacts with what must be easily the most disastrous economy in the world, and an exploding population.'

'I'd no idea the situation was that grim, or the Fundamentalists that dangerous.'

'Well,' said the Red Indian, 'neither Mubarak nor the Americans are going to tell you about it too loudly, are they? The name of the game for them is to get the world's fullest confidence back in the place. But of course the Fundamentalists are still dangerous. If only because they have that trick of attracting such damned good young people, serious, highly intelligent, of deep social purpose. One other thing –'

'What's that?'

'They're also wrong. Their route takes us straight back to institutionalized barbarism. And/or to World War Three. In this region, they could set off World War Three at almost any time.'

'Have another drink.'

He looked at her and laughed.

'You think I'm exaggerating?'

'No, no,' she said, 'but I've made you talk so much.'

'I did, didn't I? You were too good as company. I must be boring you silly.'

'Quite the reverse. Look, I was very moved, above all by what you said about Hassan el Banna. And the heritage he left to the Islamic Fundamentalists. It's a great story. People just don't know about such things in the States. I'd like to write about it –'

'Write?'

'I'm a journalist, you see. A small paper outside Boston.'

She told him its name. He had never heard of it, which did

not surprise her.

'You wouldn't mind?'

It did not seem so. He looked rather pleased.

'Not at all. You'd not quote me?'

'Not if you didn't want me to. And I'd check the copy with you.'

'Fine,' he said. 'Well, yes, I've personally always found it a fascinating subject. It's very much of my country, you see. Of my times.'

'Yes.'

'You'd need to read up some background. I'll give you some names.'

'What a very serious man you really are,' she said.

He laughed again.

'Perhaps in this. But a gay, light-hearted dog in everything else. As your spiritual mentor John implies.'

'Your flat's here in Cairo?'

'Yes. Come, I'll show you if you like. It has a fine view over the Nile. And you could pick up a couple of books on Banna. We can have that third drink there.'

'Why not? I'd like that.'

They said goodbye to the man from Yale. Spiritual mentor John had already left.

# 8

# A View from the Top

Down in Saad Zaghlul, Daniel Gad opened the front right-hand door of the car for her. He had brought the Fiat 2000. He drove down west, and turned to the right into Kasr el Eini. It was ten o'clock; it had been a post-dinner party. Kasr el Eini was still charged with cars and taxis and buses and bright lights and pedestrians and noise and colour. The cafés and restaurants were open and busy. It was like a scene from the Arabian Nights. When they reached the People's Assembly building on their right, Gad turned left through the break in the central traffic island and went past the reconstructed Barclays Bank into Kamel el Din Salah. They dipped down under the Tahrir Bridge and Sharia and lifted up into the Corniche, the Nile immediately on their left. Then on their right the Nile Hilton, then the building of the Arab Socialist Union with the Egyptian Museum behind it, and the 6th of October Bridge over their heads, then the massive new Ramses Hilton. A hundred metres along Gad said: 'That's my building to the right. You see? That small Porsche showroom on the ground floor. And a rather classy curtains shop.'

'Ah. But we don't stop here? I'm for white slavery instead?'

'No. We're cunning. We park round the back.'

A hundred metres on they came to a tall circular building with sandbagged gun positions on the pavement outside it, sober-faced and steel-helmeted troops manning them, armed with Kalashnikov Ak-47 automatic rifles and sub-machine guns. There was even a heavy-calibre machinegun manned on the first-floor balcony.

'You know the place?'

'No,' she said.'

'The *Bineyat el Television*. Television building. It's a useful landmark.'

'Why all the muscle?'

'Oh. Well, terrorists have an obsession about it. Whoever's trying for a coup d'état feels he must have this, so he can tell everyone why he's liberating them. Quite a democratic impulse, really.'

'The group that killed Sadat didn't try to take it?'

'*Jihad el Jedid?* The New Holy War? Yes, they did. They had several other hit-teams ready to go that 6 October in Cairo, to take the TV and radio stations, key arsenals and police stations and military camps, to incite the crowds to rebellion, and to wipe out most of Egypt's top leadership. They'd thought it all out.'

'But? A little bird sang to you?'

'No. As soon as we got Sadat's killers, things cracked, and we kind of got to the others first.'

He turned the car hard right just before the Television Building.

'Brace yourself now to see something of the true face of Cairo,' he said. 'Of Egypt, for that matter.'

'Meaning?'

'Well, we've just seen a fairly presentable Corniche, wouldn't you say? With a fairly good restaurant on the last corner and my Porsche agency and Arab Socialist Union Building and all. Quite a fancy façade. Now you'll get an idea of what lies just behind it.'

Indeed, she could already observe a sharp difference between the reasonably elegant Corniche, asphalted and miraculously free of potholes, and the thin lane in which they now rolled. The moment they were past the Paprika Restaurant on the corner they were on packed earth. It was as if Cairo, immediately it had come off the Corniche, and thus off duty, had whipped off its tie and shirt, loosened its belt several notches, and mounted a chair back to front to sprawl at ease over a narghile. For this lane was certainly at ease, particularly when Gad turned his car to the right again, so that it was running, or better crawling, back behind the line of tall buildings and parallel to the Corniche. Here the thin road was undisguisedly of naked earth, and deeply rutted at that. It was decorated at intervals by small ponds.

'I thought you had so little rain here?'

'We do. That isn't rain.'

'Oh, shit.'

'Yes, but processed. The fact is that our sewers leak. Sometimes we have major outbursts in main streets. That can hold traffic up for hours. Talking of Sadat –'

'That association's intentional?'

'No, natural. But it's ironic; Sadat literally created the Frankenstein that slew him. When Nasser fell dead of his heart attack in 1970 to everyone's surprise, no one felt more lost than Sadat when he succeeded him. Sadat had no followers. The great political powers against him were the Nasserists and the Marxists. He chose his troops: the Islamic Fundamentalists. He gave them money and backed them heavily, especially in the universities. There the Fundamentalists assumed Banna's mantle and developed their own Secret Apparatus. Then they turned against Sadat and killed him. Going their own goddam way.'

'Raising their own Banna, as you might say.'

'*Merde.* You know, Bridget, I think that I'd have probably guessed that you were a journalist. You have that bitchy curve to your questions and comments now and then. Oh, one thing I forgot to tell you about the building we passed, the Television Building. The government's Press Centre's on the first floor. They'll get you Press cards, invitations to Press conferences, authorization to buy hard liquor duty-free, that sort of thing.'

Daniel Gad stopped his car. He was not alone; the whole large rectangle behind the tall buildings was a mass of tightly packed cars, with slim manoeuvring lanes between the blocks. Gad threaded his way, to the right again, into the last of these. Now he killed the motor, took out the keys, came round and opened the door for her, then gave the keys to the skull-capped and barefooted man dressed in a dark galabiah who came to him from the half-lit back of the building. He was a slight man, dark-skinned, his face cavernous and deeply lined. 'Friend Abdou here,' said Gad, 'looks about sixty-five, wouldn't you say? The life expectancy for this class of my countrymen is now probably about forty. Which is what he says he is. Then just a year older then me. It makes you think, doesn't it?'

It did. She glanced again at Abdou, and saw a tired old man.

'Next bit of true Cairo tour,' said Daniel Gad, and led her left across the dirt road. There was still a lot of action. She could see that the dirt alley ran on parallel to the Corniche for perhaps another three hundred metres, then hit a busy main road. Just past the car parks, the alley was charged either side with ramshackle shops, with the accent on food and drink. Every third or fourth unit was a coffee house or very simple eating house. There were only men in them, in galabiahs and slacks. The few women she saw were walking or shopping. They and the men examined her.

'Up here,' said Gad, and they went now up another dirt alley at right-angles to the first, directly away from the Nile. Here there was filth packed in layers under the foot, newspapers, bones, rinds of fruit and vegetables, part of the alley. Again small fragile shops abounded; she could make out engineering and motor workshops, tailors and grocers and lodging houses and always coffee-houses and simple restaurants. The many men watched her curiously without hostility. The alley twisted to the left, to the right, blended into others, curled back in on itself. Lights and Arab words and music beat at her. Within minutes she was lost. Men, small boys, a few women in black, pulsated past her, from behind, from in front. Here they could jump and rape and kill her and who on earth outside would ever know? This was a pullulating world all on its own, impervious to strangers.

'Okay,' she said, 'I think I have your point. Can we please go back now?'

'We are,' said Daniel Gad nauseatingly, walking tall beside her. 'We're already going back.'

'You often wander round in this jungle all on your own?'

'Now and then,' said Gad. 'It's a good antidote against bureaucratic piety.'

'And students' parties,' said Bridget. 'It surely has cleared my head.'

Gad was looking apologetic, a trifle hangdog. 'Jungle's a little rough, though,' he said tentatively. 'I have to admit that. But they're a pretty amiable lot, really.'

She could see that he thought that. Quite a few of them had greeted him.

'All things considered,' said Gad.

'Certainly quite a community,' she said, relenting. 'There must be a hell of a lot of people in here.'

'It's an equilateral triangle,' he said, 'with no paved roads in it. Each side's about a kilometre. There must be tens of thousands inside. Maybe hundreds of thousands. You have seven or eight sleeping to a room, you know, and say three or four families to a toilet. They don't have it easy. You just don't know, from the outside. They're like an island, and there are many of them in Cairo. They're often just next to you. You remember when you looked up at the first alley to that main road two or three hundred metres off? Well, on the right just before that main road is the back of the Ramses Hilton. Just next door. But in there they won't know about this, of course.'

She glanced at him. But he wasn't making any accusations. He was just stating facts.

Bridget's shoes were pinching and her feet beginning to hurt. She was tired. She wished to God that Gad would get them out of this place. She glanced at him appealingly.

As if by pure witchcraft, by a magician's swift twist of the wrist, he met her wish in that instant. By a devious side route she had not even noticed, he had brought her out to the very mouth of the second alley. There to her left was the main road again, and, she now knew, the back of the Ramses Hilton with its politically ignorant inmates. She could have jumped straight into Daniel Gad's arms.

But Gad had moved on, so she followed him instead. At the back of the building they entered the garage. There was no sign of Abdou, but the black Fiat 2000 had incredibly been inserted under cover between two other cars with no trace of a scratch upon it. At the back of the garage Gad had mounted some steps and dissolved into the wall. His voice floated out to her:

'You have to take this part on faith.'

Mounting the steps, she pressed herself into the narrow and lightless crack in the wall. Sightlessly she followed it round to the right, then round to the left. She burst out into a foyer. On her left was a cubicle containing a chair and table and glassed in from the height of the waist of a man sitting up. Evidently from this redoubt had emerged the huge man who was now talking to Daniel Gad by the nearer of the two lifts. Presumably he was the *bawwab* of the building. He was seven foot tall and broad in proportion. He wore a dark-grey galabiah and a round white turban. His skin was black and his features fine and rather Pharaonic. She had no doubt that he was a good guardian. To subdue you all he would have to do would be to lean or sit on you. He looked down from miles away and nodded courteously to her when Gad motioned to her. He would know her next time.

The lift was less monumental. It was an ornate nineteenth-century cigar box full of gilt and panels. These were lavishly inscribed with Arabic graffiti, both written and drawn, only the first of which did she fail to understand. Clearly the male and female organs were seen much the same way the world over.

'Sorry about that,' said Gad. 'And these are even advertised as luxury flats!'

'Who lives in them?'

'Mostly respectable middle-class Egyptian families. A few foreigners. Oh, and a block of them are leased highly profitably short term to young Saudi and Kuwaiti bucks sampling the fruit forbidden at home.'

They reached the ninth floor. There was a landing with four numbered doors. A broad flight of stairs led up through it. She saw little concentrations of dirt at the corners of the stairs, like silt deposited when a flooded river ebbed, and scraps of paper here and there. She heard a series of clatters and grunts and looked back. It was the lift clearing its throat before descending. As it moved down she could see its top through the glass panel in the landing door. It carried a curious load. Fascinated, she watched the decoration of used tissues, empty cigarette packs, orange and banana peels, and what appeared to be condoms thoughtfully knotted after use, sink gracefully out of sight.

'People *will* throw rubbish down the lift shafts,' said Daniel Gad, not visibly dismayed. 'Come and have that third drink.'

She was going to need it.

Still, a colleague at the American University had warned her on her second day that Egyptians often did seem to have a definite need for dirt. It was as if they were never completely happy if it was totally absent. They had to have just a little about to be able to move their elbows around and feel at ease. For the Cairenes, that colleague had added, you could see this as straight realism. For Cairo, locked in its huge dustbowl, received contributions from the desert winds night and day. However scrupulously you cleaned and polished a table top in your Cairo home, kept all your doors and windows securely shut, it would still within hours be filmed with dust when you came back to it.

Gad's flat was clean and trim.

'How do you do it?'

'Keep it tidy? I have an old duck from Shubra, Umm Samir, who comes in early every morning, gives me breakfast, cleans the place, and sometimes gives me lunch. She's a great character.'

'Umm – ?'

'Umm Samir. The Mother of Samir.'

Through the entrance hall, the flat developed to the right, towards the Nile. To her left, a window looked back to the convulsive maze in which they had wandered, and down on a dirt side road which ran alongside Gad's building to the start of that labyrinth from the Corniche in front. The first room to her right, about five metres deep by four wide, was a dining room. Indentations from the walls marked it off from the next identically shaped room, with sofas against the long walls, and armchairs in the free spaces. The last wall was glass.

'Come out and have a look while I get the drinks.'

He had opened the glass doors, and she went out with him onto the broad balcony. It thinned to the right. She saw windows and a door; another room. They stood at the balcony's edge. The view was breath-taking. The traffic roared in twin steel streams nine stories below her. Ahead, beyond the cluster of long moored launches, was the broad glinting black band of the Nile.

'That's Gezira, straight across,' he said, and she looked at the four-kilometre-long island, glittering like a fairground.

'Gezira Island?'

'Gezira's enough, really. That's how Island's pronounced in Egyptian Arabic. From here we're looking across immediately at the Gezira Sporting Club, rallying-point of Cairo's social climbers and a few athletes. See over to the right of it, on the river front? *There.* That tall line of buildings rather like ours here. That's Sharia Sarai el Gezira. Halfway along that block, the penthouse, that's my parents' flat.'

'My God, they could see everything you do here!'

'My God, so they could. Still, they must be hardened by now. Down there left's the start of the 6th of October Bridge, that we passed under. And, left of it on Gezira, that tall lit tower. See it? Very famous; the Cairo Tower. You go up in a lift and get a fabulous view. You should do that. The Anglo-American Hospital's next to it. Then next left's Tahrir Bridge, halfway along it the Borg Hotel, Tower Hotel. Carter and Sadat drove over Tahrir Bridge past it six years ago, taking bows.'

'What's the blaze of light down there hard left?'

'That's about due south, on our own bank again. That'll be the Meridien Hotel. And Shepheard's just before it. You know, from here you can see about ten kilometres south and north along the Nile. But you haven't asked about the pyramids.'

'All right, I'm asking.'

'Almost due west, almost straight out from here. Sometimes I can see them on a very clear day. Now you get your drink.'

He went back through the sitting and dining rooms; perhaps to his kitchen and bar there. Bridget relaxed. She bathed her mind in the huge and sparkling view, thinking of nothing at all.

'Here's your vodka and orange,' he said. 'Your good health.'

'Thank you. It's beautiful here. Tell me, what did you do when you got back here from Oxford? You went straight into the Government?'

He looked at her over his glass. Vertically below him forty metres down the streams of traffic rushed at each other, like two great metal chains ceaselessly turning.

'No. It was 1967. There was a war brewing. It was the Six Days war. So I joined the Army.'

'And?'

He shrugged.

'I got a hell of a lot of military experience in a very short time. Nasser had bitten off much more than he could chew. The Israelis beat us very soundly. And the Syrians, the Jordanians, the Iraqis. In only six days.'

'Was it very bitter fighting?'

'More, it was very bitter walking. In the Infantry, where I was, it was mostly slogging back across the desert, under shelling and air strikes. The way back was marked for you by army boots. It was a sad sight. Most of the Infantry had thrown away their boots because they felt freer to escape in their bare feet. None of us was very highly trained, you see.'

'You talked of being in two wars against them.'

'Oh, yes. Well, the other one was a bit different. It was Sadat's 6th of October War, in 1973, the Yom Kippur War. That's their holiest feast day. We attacked them when they weren't really looking, as you might say. This time *we* hammered *them*, anyway at first. At two in the afternoon when the sun was right in the Israelis' eyes – we didn't miss a trick – Mubarak, then commanding the Egyptian Air Force, sent over about 220 jet aircraft to blitz the Israelis' Bar Lev fixed defence line, then we packed our shock troops across the Canal in their little rubber boats – they'd been jumping in and out of them and paddling them for two years on the Great

Bitter Lakes where the Israelis couldn't see them. Some 8,000 of them went across the Canal under a barrage which started at five past two from 4,000 guns, mortars, and rocket launchers – the heaviest since Alamein. It and the prior air strike bust up the Bar Lev Line enough to let our shock troops through. They had to run four kilometres inland and take up position for the Israeli armoured counter-attack. It came soon, and our shock troops murdered the Israeli tanks with their Sagger anti-tank missiles – you know, it's wire-guided, the infantryman fires it from his shoulder.

'Meanwhile we got assault bridges and our tanks and heavy equipment across the Canal – finally five army divisions and well over 1,000 tanks. We had all trained very intensively for this, and it worked. We were winning, and against the Israelis. It made a nice change. We'd even shown a little genius; to cut our way through the seventeen-metre sand ramp on the east bank of the Suez Canal to let our tanks and heavy equipment through, we used high-pressure hoses powered by West German water pumps we'd been buying quietly for years. For four days we slaughtered the Israelis, with their exclusive faith in the aircraft and the tank. Our Russian SAM batteries on the west bank of the Canal cut swathes in the attacking Israeli aircraft, protecting us. Meanwhile their tanks charged gallantly at us, contemptuous of any infantry or artillery support, to blot out our infantry armed with their Saggers, and our infantry and tanks annihilated them. Then we suddenly went to sleep for four days. The official phrase for it was re-grouping.'

'You sound bitter about it.'

He looked at her, and wondered why he was talking so frankly. This was not his usual line of conversation with Western girls.

'It was a grave mistake,' he said. 'You see, we had only really trained for the first bit. And in those four days the Israelis could re-equip and rethink. They were no longer reacting by piecemeal and suicidal counter-attacks. They had become an organic force again. Now they waited for us twenty kilometres inland, by the Mitla and Geddi Passes. When we finally lumbered forward to them – and moved out from under the protection of our marvellous SAM missile umbrella – the Israelis were ready for us, with their tanks and aircraft and helicopter- and ground-launched missiles which created havoc among our tanks. Then began one of the biggest and deadliest tank battles of all time. After it the Israelis set the pace. By then they had already also thrown back the Syrian and Iraqi and Jordanian and other Arab forces on the Syrian front, after savage fighting. By the 15th of October Sharon had counter-attacked across the Suez Canal and by the 18th he had a full armoured division across. Four days later Sharon could have walked into Cairo and taken it had he wanted. For us, the party was over.'

She was quiet for a while, looking out over the spangled city. Then she said: 'You were still an infantryman?'

'No,' he said, 'I'd gone armoured. I had a tank. Well, a squadron of tanks. We had some fantastic experiences in those first four days. We were among the forces that took Assaf Yagouri prisoner, commander of the crack Israeli 190th Armoured Brigade. He looked round once in anguish at his 115 tanks, all knocked out, some burning. We'd done that in twenty minutes; Sadat claimed it a world record. There must have been some of those. Do you know how many tanks were knocked out in all in these huge tank battles on the Egyptian and Syrian fronts, on both sides? More than 3,000. That's in a sixteen-day war. It took six months of fighting between Montgomery and Rommel in North Africa in World War Two to knock out 650 tanks on both sides.'

The brilliant city sang and sparkled below her. She listened to it. Directly out from the balcony, in the black water, where the light from the Corniche and landing stages still reached, a man rowed in a small boat, in a valiant line straight across the river. He wore a dark galabiah and a dark skull cap rakishly to one side, and his legs were parted and barefooted. The ripples stemmed out very regularly from his oar tips. He looked like a zealous waterbug on a still pond. Bridget finished her drink.

'Look,' she said.

'Yes?'

'It's really splendid up here. I was wondering what you would like from me?'

He considered her. The question did not seem to surprise him.

'Oh. Well, not necessarily anything at all, really. No cover charge.'

'No?'

'No. Well, it did strike me that it would be very nice to make love to you.'

Her heart leapt like a young lamb.

'Again, repeated, no hint of obligation, of course. I could drop you back at your flat whenever you wished, quick as a flash.'

She examined him in turn. If you ignored that shockingly broken nose, he was not really so bad looking. He was tallish. He seemed bright, chatty, and outgoing. He could show her Egypt. There was that car, and it was a nice flat, even including the lift shafts. All in all, he was certainly more attractive than her politician.

'All right,' she said.

'Oh,' said Daniel Gad. 'Well, splendid.'

'On one condition, though.'

'Oh. Yes?'

'That I can get into bed first.'

He looked mystified.

'After all,' she said, 'I hardly know you.'

'That's true,' he said. 'Well, it's just along the balcony here. The door's not locked, and the switch is just inside to the left.'

Clearly eager to please, he demonstrated this by opening the door and switching on the light. She went in past him.

'There's a side light just by the bed,' he said. 'You may find it a little less glaring.'

She did, switching it on as he switched off the main light. It was an improvement. The room could stand subtle treatment, for the double bed in it seemed huge, exactly square, like a boxing ring.

'The loo's straight through there,' said Gad helpfully, 'and the bath.'

He disappeared tactfully onto the balcony, to where she could not see him through the room's glass windows. Still, he seemed already intimately linked to her, by some skilled personal radar or sixth sense, for it was within a minute of her coming back from the bathroom and slipping into the double bed on the side of the small lamp that he reappeared through the balcony door. He smiled at her affably and took off his clothes without undue haste, folding his pants neatly and carefully observing their orthodox creases. Such was his aplomb that she had not even thought to offer to switch off the bedside lamp. At least he was lean and hard; he was not going to die on her from a heart attack. Her Boston politician, for all his relative youth, already had an incipient pot belly, which leapt into prominence if he leant forward in one of his rare naked appearances. She noticed that Gad had a burst of scars in the small of his back, across his spinal column. She also saw that he was circumcised; presumably that was another old Coptic custom. He advanced upon the huge square bed, smiling cheerfully. She was terrified.

It was he who now, lying beside her on the other side, leaned gently across her and put out the bedside lamp. He then held her for some while, his right arm under her body, his left over it, but so quietly and for so long that she was sure that he had gone suddenly and soundly to sleep. He had that trick of inscrutability. Her politician was not like this. Once into the act he tended to romp through it at speed and without pirouettes, like a man performing a necessary but somewhat disreputable digestive function. Perhaps it was all her fault. She should have stimulated Gad. She began therefore to move her right hand slowly over his left shoulder and arm, then down to his waist, and over his left flank, near his genitals. The effect was magic. His own left hand moved down companionably to her loins, and he began to massage her. His aim was unerring. Moreover, his patience seemed inexhaustible. He went on and on. It was as if he had simply misplaced his script for the moment, and now, reminded, was diligently carrying it out to the absolute utmost. She was in raptures.

He sprang about, following his own logic and sense of

timing, his head down, and, squealing faintly with delight, she felt his tongue. She blew up. This seemed to please him. She could see him above her, arched back, his head slightly to one side, commending her. Then, giving her little quarter, he was upon her, rampant. Yet he was still reasonably considerate, he still had her on his side. The evidence for that was that she exploded again, this time exactly in harmony with him. He stayed with her for a while, courteously. In due course he rolled over to his side of the bed and lay on his back.

'I think the sheet's enough, don't you?' he said. 'It's still quite a warmish night.'

He lay with his head propped up on one elbow, looking at her. He seemed clearly interested in what she thought about it.

'Yes, indeed,' she said.

It had all been quite a matey affair.

Afterwards they went by common consent and had their first joint bath, establishing that happy custom. Subsequently she saw him quite often, two or three times a week, sometimes coming to his flat by day. Then she got to know Umm Samir. Umm Samir looked very old, if agile. She was slight and wiry, and very dark. Her face was hollow-cheeked and wrinkled as a prune. She had two visible teeth, which did not meet. Barefooted and totally illiterate, she had the cunning of all the fellahin from all time. She was a great sitter and thinker. This was her favourite pursuit when alone in the flat. Work did not count for her unless somebody saw her doing it. When Bridget or Daniel Gad was there, Umm Samir was a blur of movement, sweeping the balcony or on her hands and knees polishing the linoleum inside. If someone watched she could make even cooking look athletic. Umm Samir had two speeds only: full ahead and full stop. Bridget had tumbled on her dread secret often, for Bridget had her own key. She would generally find Umm Samir in a cane armchair on the balcony, facing out upon the epic view, sound asleep under a beatific smile, or in the same state of suspended animation on a chair with her feet up on the kitchen table. To the old lady (and Gad said that though she looked all of seventy she would hardly in fact be half that; that was what excessive childbearing, malnutrition, and lack of hygiene did to the human frame) this place must have been pure bliss after her home in Shubra.

Umm Samir also had a true Egyptian's deep sense of fellowship with dirt. Dirt, in reasonable proportions, was nice to spread around, like love and friendship. In the kitchen on the side of the building was a rubbish chute, in the wall by the sink. You pulled a lever and a metal recipient swung out. You put in your garbage and pushed the lever back, and the garbage fell obediently, presumably to some communal nether room from which little men in caps and carts collected it efficiently. Anyway, it passed totally from your ken. But Umm Samir scorned this prosaic route. There was a window in the kitchen's side wall, above the dirt road nine stories below. This window was formidable, of steel. You needed real muscular effort to operate it. Yet Umm Samir always went this way. She would beat her way through all the steel catches, and the flat's contribution of torn paper and bones and vegetable and fruit rinds would flutter or plunge down to join their mates in the mounting piles in the side lane below. If Bridget was in the kitchen when Umm Samir had just completed this exercise, Umm Samir would invariably shoot at her the proud glance of one who had discharged a useful duty well. Bridget never had the heart to suggest that she used the chute instead.

'Could I have the soap, please, Daniel?' she said now, in what must have been about their fifteenth connubial bath.

'Oh, sure,' said Daniel Gad, parking his vodka and orange – another vital element in this pre-love ritual – and twisting heroically for the fanged metal soap holder behind him by the taps; this, the spiky end of the bath, was traditionally his. 'Though why don't I soap you? How about that?'

'Oh, thanks.'

The two stood up, and he began to soap her slim shoulders and under her arms and across her full breasts, watching her nipples perk up promptly. Their broad circular bases, he noticed, shaded from the centre in almost perceptibly separate rings of colour, like archers' targets. She looked steadily up at him above her, with her deep brown eyes and her long brown hair and her pretty small face, backed up by her twin saddles of freckles, the first over the bridge of her nose, the second inverted, climbing up the inner curves of her breasts, in that fine milky white skin that the Egyptian sun murdered. He turned her gently and soaped her back. From there too he put his hand down and soaped her trim black bush. Then he slipped his hand with the soap between her legs. She was like warm silk, silk at blood heat.

'Fancy his putting his hand on my thigh at a Faculty dinner!' said Bridget.

'Fancy.'

He had got down to her knees.

'Now legs and feet and toes.'

'No, that's easier when we're sitting down again.'

'Oh. OK.'

'So now it's your turn.'

Gad submitted without a struggle. As a valuable civil servant he reflected that, should she indeed scrub him too violently, he could always scream for help now from his freshly installed police protection.

# 9
## Saints and Sinners

'We're not equipped to handle saints,' wrote Bridget O'Shaunessy. 'Our Western Democracy is built about averages. But Hassan el Banna, who founded the Muslim Brotherhood in Egypt in 1928, was in no way average. Nor was he any abstract ideologue, but a very practical saint, with high aims. He strove for strict personal morality, ascetic public service, the spiritual values of Islam, and against corruption, secularism, and foreign influences. He was a fervent Arab nationalist, strongly backing the Arab revolt in Palestine against the British Mandate in 1936.

'Egypt's recent history was bitter. By 1875 Britain and France dominated her economically. She owed them £100 million and was in effect bankrupt. They imposed controllers on her, who ran the country and cut money to the army and public works. When Egypt rejected them, British-French gunboats shelled Alexandria on 11 July 1882, and Britain began a seventy-two-year armed occupation, sometimes harsh. In June 1906 British officers were hunting pigeons in the Delta. They wounded a woman from Dinshaway, whose villagers then attacked them. An officer opened fire. They hit him in the head with a rock. He later died. The British tried fifty-two villagers, hanged four and flogged many publicly and imprisoned them. Dinshaway became a symbol of revolt. And World War One simply replaced autocratic Ottoman rule by British-French. In 1919 all Egypt under Saa'd Zaghlul and his

Wafd party rose against the British. The British crushed them. The 1922 Anglo-Egyptian Treaty left Britain controlling communications, defence, interests of foreigners, and Sudanese affairs. The 1936 update just exacerbated nationalist sensitivities; Britain still kept her heavy troop concentrations in the Canal Zone and jurisdiction over Sudan. Humiliated, lacking a national identity or purpose, the Egyptians fell back on their first certainty – Islam. The Muslim Brotherhood met a deeply felt need.

'Banna had begun it modestly. He was born in 1906 in a Delta village, where his father was Imam, an El Azhar graduate who mended watches to swell his slim pay. At eight Banna went to the *kuttab* Koranic school, and at twelve to primary school, where he led a religious society. He saw *dhikr*, where the worshipper concentrates on God to reach ecstasy. This Sufi mysticism linked people directly with God. It was key to Banna and his Brotherhood. Mysticism can imply withdrawal, the hermit in the desert, but Sufism was centripetal. It drew people together by a powerful sense of fraternity. The Sufis recited their liturgy *in groups*, often backed by rhythmic deep breathing, dancing, or whirling – hence the Whirling Dervishes. In 1923 Banna came to Cairo for deeper religious studies. Cairo dismayed him: the savage fighting between the Egyptian political parties in their anarchic struggle against the British, what he saw as the lewd immorality of the Cairenes in their books, papers, salons, and behaviour. He preached the vital need to purify Islam by worship, love, and selfless service, through his fellow-students in the streets. Graduating in 1927, he taught at a school in Ismailia, again preaching widely through mosques, schools, coffee-houses. Next year he took on the first recruits for his Muslim Brotherhood, Egyptian labourers from the British Army camps in Ismailia and the Canal Zone.

'In Cairo from 1932, Banna built up his Brotherhood. Refined, it was a cell system, each cell of five to ten, collectively responsible with an elected head. Cells fitted upwards through clans and groups into 1,000-member battalions. It was a tightly knit structure, its chain of command crystal-clear, its members physically highly trained. With it, and his fit and zealous 40,000 young rovers, Banna ran the Brotherhood's 2,000 branches, each with one school at least, 500 welfare centres dispensing food and clothing to the poor, and its clinics in every province, so realizing his deep passion for social justice. By World War Two the Brotherhood was a major political force with members everywhere – students, civil servants, fellahin, urban workers, young professionals, even armed forces. It had arrived on the main street, owning office buildings, with full-time paid staff. It had two vigorous publications. It held conferences – one in 1935 on stopping Christian missionaries – lectured in mosques, sent arms and volunteers to Arab Palestine, harassed the British, and wrote bulletins of advice to the heads of Arab governments. Banna meant it when he said that Islam should cover every aspect of a man's life. By 1948 the Brotherhood claimed a million active supporters.

'What went wrong? Tragically, Banna's fine movement carried the seeds of its own destruction. Banna himself created his terrorist wing in 1943 as a shield against the British and Egyptian rulers. The world knew it as *El Jihaz es-Sirri*, the Secret Apparatus. It became a very secret élite, its greatest loyalties to its own leadership. This lethal élite was probably 1,000-strong by 1948, totally committed frontline shock-troops, highly intelligent, excellently trained and equipped, almost indestructible in their five-men-cell system, each a time-bomb on his own. Behind each could be tens of thousands in support. Just four such activists of the New Holy War led by Khalid el Islambouli shot down Sadat and 35 others in 1981 right in front of virtually the entire Eygptian Armed Forces, knowing they would die themselves. The numbers are not decisive. That dedication is.

'Banna died suddenly. In December 1948, a youth in officer's uniform – certainly from the Secret Apparatus – shot Prime Minister Nokrashi Pasha dead. He had just banned the Brotherhood, as grown too strong. Almost certainly Banna knew nothing of this murder before it. He was shot fatally six weeks later, undoubtedly by the Political Police. The terrorist wing he had created had caused his own death. The Brotherhood lived on under a successor, but its power declined. Bitter persecutions split it, particularly under Nasser.

'But its heritage survives, passionate and powerful. Militant Islamic Fundamentalist groups have picked it up three times in the last decade. A future article will deal with these. Let me now just set that scene.

'The Islamic Fundamentalists first rebelled bloodily against Sadat in April 1974, only six months after his fairly successful war against Israel. The *Faniyya el Askariyya*, the Technical Military Academy group, stormed the military academy in northeast Cairo in broad daylight. But they delayed then and lost, with over 40 killed, wounded and executed. *Takfir wal Hijra*, Atonement and Holy Flight, erupted in July 1977. They set out to destroy an entire evil society, not just one corrupt political regime. Their band of believers living the True Islam at the desert's edge would surge out to annihilate the whole external rotting world. They kidnapped a former cabinet minister to trade for imprisoned *Takfir* men. Sadat refused. They murdered the minister. Sadat killed and wounded 63 and executed five in reprisal. Four years later *Jihad el Jedid* made their lethal forty-second assault on Sadat's reviewing stand in Cairo. Two days later they killed more than 60 police and army in Asyut, 370 kilometres south, losing seven killed themselves. The Establishment first tried 24 and executed five. It held 3,000 suspects. It then tried 302 more over three years, asking the death penalty for 299, finally in September 1984 sentencing 16 to life imprisonment and 91 to terms up to 15 years.

'The rocketing rise in ferocity in these recurrent bloody assaults and reprisals argues a growing intensity to Islamic Fundamentalism in Egypt today. And Sadat's peace with Israel aggravated the Fundamentalists' hatred of him. The Brotherhood's journal *Dawa*, Religious Call, condemned him curtly:

"... What is the *Shari'a* here, the Islamic Law? 'If land is stolen from Muslims, and they cannot get it back for any reason, they are not to blame if they get back what they can, with the firm resolution to recover all their rights, and take all the necessary steps to demand and get the rest of their rights . . . (But) if land is stolen from Muslims and they could get it back but do not, then all are evil . . .' "

'The West Bank and Gaza Strip, *at least*, are enemy-occupied Arab lands. Sadat, to get back the Sinai, implicitly accepted by the Camp David accords that Israel would not return these lands fully and at once. The *Shari'a* was clear. The sentence was death.

'Finally, three sociological factors keep Islamic Fundamentalism dangerously volatile in Egypt. First is the huge influx from the countryside. The culture shock can be traumatic. The fellah coming to the metropolis finds a concrete jungle, murderously competitive and impersonal – unless he can live with a group already established from his village, rare today. No one knows him. He doesn't exist. So he falls back on his *kuttab* childhood faith. His renewed Islamic passion tells him to destroy this cruel and evil society that rejects him. Big cities are clearly corrupt; wanton women display and sell themselves shamelessly. Godless Western consumerism saps the true Islamic character. The leadership has even made a shady deal with Israel. Our fellah is ready to revolt.

'Secondly, the young intelligentsia is driven back to Islam too. Nasser made all higher education free – which puts 100,000 new university graduates on the labour market every year. The competition for entry is brutal. Even if a country student gets into a top faculty he may end bitterly frustrated as well as alienated. On qualifying brilliantly as a doctor after eight years, say, he may find no job, or one for $US60 a month as a kind of government clerk. His total disillusion can easily turn him into a violent Islamic Militant too. Just what an intellectual élite these Militants are in Egypt is shown by groups put on trial. The 15 Muslim Brothers tried for the Nokrashi killing in 1948 comprised six university students, five civil servants, one engineer, and three small businessmen. The 24 first tried for Sadat's killing included three from the army – two officers – two university professors, one doctor, one engineer, one pharmacist, nine students, and seven artisans; hardly throwaway lots.

'Thirdly, this iron-grim framework cannot improve radically or soon. Mubarak created more Assembly seats and *some* opposition in mid-1984. This was mainly cosmetic; the average Egyptian still has no real political power. The economy stays bleak. Nasser made the monstrous bureaucracy, now 3 million, and nationalized everything in sight and reduced it to utter inefficiency by price subsidies and controls, now basic structural faults. The infrastructure – roads, telephones, sewers, unmaintained in the 30 years war with Israel – stays fragile. Some 48 million Egyptians overload it, multiplying at a net 1.4 million annually. So Egypt has to run desperately to – at best – stay on the same economic spot. So stop overbreeding? But by Arab *machismo,* the more man you are, the more children you have. And the fellahin still see them as good life insurance against old age. But what do you feed to these new 4,000 Egyptian bellies daily? Egypt already imports some 75% by value of her food. Less than 4% of her land area is arable and that drops yearly; the fellahin still build their mud-brick huts from Nile silt. From exports? But Egypt's traditional exports – cotton – have not risen in 27 years. Her four main hard-currency earners – remittances from 3 million Egyptians working in the Arabian Gulf; oil exports; the Suez Canal; tourism – have probably already peaked. Even with them, Egypt's current account deficit is $US2 million. What keeps her afloat? We do. We, the US taxpayer, with $US2 to 3 billion of economic aid a year. For how much longer?

'So the prospects look gloomy. How then dare we deny the Islamic Fundamentalist who says: Give us our chance. We can hardly do worse than you. Can we ignore their right to wield the sword of reform, to prove that they too may be saints, not sinners?'

Bridget sat back from her typewriter. It was six weeks since she had met Daniel Gad and absorbed from him her abiding fascination with Hassan el Banna. She had needed that period for research; her Arabic studies took up most of her time. But her article gained most from Gad. His patience amazed her, and the depth of his knowledge.

'Have a vodka,' said Deborah, sounding sophisticated.

'Yes. Thank God. That's the first article, anyway.'

Deborah got up and went out to the kitchen. She was slim, blonde, quite tall, nice-looking, Scots, and twenty-one. The two had met when the term started and, liking each other on sight, found a flat together. It was halfway along Sharia Hassan Hagazi, five minutes' walk south of the American University. Though convenient, the flat was scruffy. Also, like Umm Samir, the Egyptians above discarded their garbage through their windows. The municipal minion due to remove it had an irregular schedule. As the girls' flat was on the first floor the smells could smite.

'With orange, as you like it,' said Deborah, holding two glasses.

'Great,' said Bridget. 'Though Daniel's still got to check it.'

'Ah, the article?' said Deborah, sitting on the moulting sofa, 'Yes, of course.'

She sounded impressed. She was still somewhat in awe of Gad, who was due to collect Bridget that evening in fifteen minutes, and of Bridget for having a full-blooded affair with him.

'After that I'll send it to my editor express,' said Bridget. 'Now that I'm out here, he keeps pressuring me for material on Egypt.'

# 10

# *A Trick of Focus*

'Fantastic!' said Bridget O'Shaunessy, superbly naked on Daniel Gad's vast square bed. 'It was only three nights ago that you checked my article, and you know I got it off to my editor the next morning, by a student who was flying back to New York that day because his father was sick. So this morning already I get this telex from Boston through the American University –'

'This morning? That's brisk!' said Gad.

'Yes. So this telex says,' said Bridget, undeflected, ' "Your article outstanding stop. Printing uncut in Political Section next week-end magazine stop. Eagerly awaiting next instalment stop. Then suggest something about Egyptian Armed Forces stop. Say human interest story on war hero or heroes. Congratulations, very pleased your work." Isn't that *something*? I've never had an editor telex me congratulations before!'

'It was an excellent article and you deserve it,' said Gad. 'And the next one on the militant Islamic Fundamentalist groups will be just as good.'

'It's because you've helped me so much,' said Bridget. 'I would never have managed it otherwise. I was very lucky to meet you.'

Daniel Gad writhed mildly in embarrassment.

'Look, Bridget, I get a lot out of this, you know. You give me a great deal.'

'Nothing,' said Bridget stoutly.

'Ah, and the third article,' said Gad. 'Maybe I could help you there.'

'Oh? Marvellous!'

'The man I have in mind is a certified wartime hero all right,' said Gad. 'From 1973. He knocked out three Israeli tanks in a row with Sagger missiles. And he's a pretty striking character too. A big, trim man, with a short black beard and powerful eyes. He won the Star of the Sinai. That's the highest Egyptian medal for bravery. Your paper ought to love an article about him.'

'What's his name?' said Bridget. 'Daniel, you could really fix it for me to interview him?'

'I'm sure I could,' said Gad. 'His name? Muhammed Abbas Sidki. He's a commando major. I'd read about him, but I didn't meet him till a week ago. He seemed very friendly. He –'

But then he saw that Bridget had fallen beautifully asleep, deeply content. When Gad was sure that she was soundly away, he got up very quietly, put on the Chinese silk dressing-gown that his father had given him inscrutably on his last birthday, and went out onto the balcony, taking his empty glass with him. From there he could go safely without waking her through the French doors into the sitting and dining rooms and thence to the fridge in the kitchen where, resplendent in his shining white Chinese silk, he greeted armed Police Corporal Ali and emerged with dignity and a full chilled bottle of Giannaclis Villages. Back on his balcony, it struck him how nonchalantly he – and indeed Bridget – had taken this armed police incursion into his domestic life, twenty-four hours out of twenty-four. He was also much more devious now about his daily programme, going to work never by exactly the same route any two mornings running, or at quite the same hour. He was already quite attuned to it, without drama. You became used to living under the constant threat of death like this remarkably quickly, less out of gallantry than out of boredom; the danger had simply become another standing condition of your life. Nonetheless Gad had his new Browning 9 mm automatic fully charged in the right pocket of his Pekin gown, just in case a terrorist might try diving in on him from the balcony above.

Seated on a long cane chair in the centre of his balcony, he let his eyes stray across to the Cairo Tower ahead and slightly to the left. The guide books put its height at 187 metres, say 610 feet. The rotating restaurant was on the 14th floor, the bar on the 15th, and the fabulous view, aided or not by the telescope, from the 16th. He really owed it to Bridget to take her there one of these days, or nights.

Gad took a delicious long cold pull of the Giannaclis and thought about Bridget. He knew that he was getting very fond of the girl. Her dazzling bath techniques, and the bliss in bed thereafter – well, that was part of it, even a good part. But there was also Bridget as Bridget. She had a kind of very fresh and pleasant mental temperature, a warm way of looking at life, a new dimension to his.

East and West had something to do with it, and so did virginity. Bridget was no virgin, no doubt about that. Virginity was by definition a restriction. Once she liked you, Bridget was very generous with herself, as much out of bed as in it. She didn't mark out frontiers with little flags.

The only girl that Daniel Gad had ever loved (*other* girl?) had been a virgin. Resoundingly a virgin. She had also been Arab, and Muslim, of a good, rich and powerful Cairene family. Her name was Magda. Gad had met her at the American University in Cairo when he was back on vacation from Oxford. Both were eighteen. Magda was vivacious. She was also extraordinarily beautiful physically. She was of medium height, slim, and opulently curved. She had long rich black hair and, by contrast, a startlingly fair complexion. Her very black and sparkling eyes were set wide, against that sheer white skin, her nose was aquiline, and her lips full and red. She was like some ripe exotic fruit.

But with fierce thorns about it. Daniel Gad discovered slowly and painfully that Magda had chosen to study psychology at the American University in Cairo, and her indulgent parents had approved that, mainly because it was socially smart, like choosing the right Dior dress for a reception, and not at all because she had any profound interest in humanity, or sense of mission to help it. She was indeed the last person in the world to have deep insights into or intuitions about others. No more were her high-pitched giggling sessions with clutches of other young Egyptian ladies of her ilk in the tree-shaded courtyard by the cafeteria on the Sheikh Rihan side of the American University, nor their expressive, elegant and enticing jouncing of breast and buttock as conversational aids as they strolled or stood and chatted, to be taken at anything like their face value. These were simply the iridescent and mesmeric flourishings of the peacock's tail. Under them Gad gradually discerned in Magda the contours of the most lacquered character that he had ever met, already set iron-hard for life. It was like a little mobile computer, designed for only one language. Its one command to her was to marry a rich and powerful man, or one who with mathematical certainty would become rich and powerful, of her own or a higher social standing. So seen, Magda was a superlative construct, totally efficient, not carrying an excess gram of mental fat.

The proposition was categoric, as discreetly relayed to Gad by Magda and her parents. There was no souk bargaining here; a few points about dowries. The central deal was straight. In return for marrying her, Gad would get Magda's virginity, her full-time care of their children, and her occasional use as a social decoration. Magda's father – a man simultaneously powerful in banks, cotton and a major motor agency – had no need to stress to Gad that Magda's virginity was authentic, though in Cairo doubts on this score might sometimes be pardoned: some doctors there made quite a speciality of sewing back hymens ruptured by chance or by design; the standard fee was £E40, say $US40. But Magda's parents would have engineered her too perfectly for her not to be genuine. As Gad knew to his chagrin, Magda was never allowed out with men unless most scrupulously chaperoned.

There was one other small point, Magda's father had remarked one day, which Gad of course already knew about. He would have to convert to Islam. For, while Islam had no real objection to its young men remaining Muslims but still marrying non-Muslims – say other Peoples of the Book like Christians or Jews – it did not permit the reverse. If a non-Muslim man wanted to marry into the tribe, he got himself converted to being an orthodox Muslim first.

The basic inequity of this point teased Gad's sense of tidiness. He went away and thought about it.

It was not, however, until the whole thing was over that it struck him one day that one question that neither side had ever even raised was whether Magda and he suited each other physically and psychologically. The point simply was not pertinent; it was as if women had never really been designed to be full companions to men, but rather their sexual vessels and their children's mothers; many Muslim women themselves seemed to subscribe to this thesis.

Magda still represented for Gad agony and platonic ecstasy over fifteen months between two Oxford summer vacations. It was a saga of visits, phone calls, letters and telegrams. There was a certain pleasantly heady note of doom to it from the start. Gad certainly loved the girl most passionately, but, secretly, also hopelessly. His stance was indeed far more a comment on himself than on Magda. He was at that teething stage in life when he had for a while to seek the impossible, as if privately needing to test or to punish himself. He could as easily have been trying to scale an unconquerable rock face or to win some tragically lost political cause. After those fifteen months Magda, her inner computer still fixed unerringly upon her single aim, her mental antennae quivering, saw what was happening, and promptly married one of the richest chemists in Cairo, to whom she presented a squadron of children. She appeared perfectly happy at her glittering receptions. Gad's parents, who had been most diligently noncommittal throughout the affair, now gently released a deep sigh of relief, while Gad came down from Oxford and went off to war. Gad still thought nostalgically of his love for Magda from time to time. He was used to the exercise, which afforded him a mild blend of pleasure and sadness; perhaps one always loved one's lost ideals, however impossible they might have been. And

Gad was under no illusions; his marriage with Magda would have been impossible, a total disaster. They saw that from the start, he thought, looking now slightly right to his parents' penthouse flat in Zamalek; the wise old medical owls.

Bridget O'Shaunessy would be a full companion, though. *Was* already a full and equal companion. Maybe that was a key difference between East and West; some Western women really could be cheerfully equal with you, losing no femininity. Maybe laying no claims on you was part of it. Certainly Bridget had laid no claims on him that he could feel. The idea did not seem to have crossed her mind. While Magda – Magda had been *all* claim.

Daniel Gad bent and filled himself another glass of clean ice-cold Giannaclis. Sparkling Zamalek, to which his eyes now went back, contained interesting people beyond his parents. Gad had got a message that day about one. This man had an elegant flat in Zamalek's Sharia Saleh Ayoub. The message had been by telex, coded, and it had come from Jerusalem. It had said:

'For Salah ed-Din: Believe Abdel Aziz Fawzi may be preparing to fly. Regards, Absalom.'

It was enigmatic and, to Gad, electrifying. It was indeed a double code in the sense that, even when the original scrambled Latin letters in which it had been sent internationally had been clarified into standard English by the key to the agreed code, the resultant information was not breathtaking, save to the initiate. In this second and subtler code, Gad himself was Salah ed-Din, Righteousness of the Faith, which the West had corrupted to Saladin, that great Kurdish general who won Jerusalem back for Islam from the Crusaders in 1187, and by his Ayubid Empire centred in Cairo brought Islam to its medieval heights of cultural glory, and who had left his name in Cairo in a square just outside the Citadel and a well inside it, and in a stretch of the city walls to the south. Coptic or not, Gad had no objection at all to that code name.

The signature was no less intriguing. Absalom was a major in a counter-terrorist unit in the Mossad, the Israeli secret service. His name was Uri Allon, he was a Sabra, Israeli-born, and Gad knew him only by his reputation, which was very good. It was perhaps not altogether surprising that the counter-terrorist organizations of these two countries which, whatever their treaty relations, were not at the official governmental level exactly the most ecstatic of bedfellows, should nonetheless be so close and cordial. A strong sense of profession could sometimes cut right across national boundaries. And Israel had as much trouble with its extremist fanatics as did Egypt. Further, this close professional relationship was not new. As far back as August 1981, two months before Sadat was shot, when Begin met Sadat in Alexandria, he had given him warning of the assassination plot which Mossad agents had learned about in Egypt. For of course Mossad operated in Egypt, and sometimes discovered secrets even Egyptian Intelligence itself did not know, just as Egyptian agents operated in Israel, often as effectively.

The third and clinchingly dramatic double meaning in this superficially trite message lay in the phrase 'preparing to fly'. In the inner code that signified 'preparing a coup d'état'. Now that, if it was accurate, and the subject was indeed Abdel Aziz Fawzi, was hot news without any shadow of doubt.

Daniel Gad had a thick file, deservedly thick, on Abdel Aziz Fawzi. He was a highly impressive and possibly very dangerous figure. Abdel Aziz Fawzi was a man of deeply puritanical cast of mind, of considerable professional and political stature. Born in Alexandria in 1922, he was a strong nationalist, and profoundly religious. These characteristics had come to him from his father. The family was rich in cotton, but his father had felt called upon to become one of the *'Ulama*, the Religious Learned, and thus had trained in El Azhar as a Doctor in Theology, and later taught there. Abdel Aziz had first trained as an engineer in the Egyptian army, and there he had become one of the first Free Officers, with Sadat, Nasser and Khalid Mohieddin, later to be known as the Red Colonel, founder of the left and centre-left political party called the National Progressive Union, whose members ranged from Nasserist to Marxist and religious progressive socialists, both Muslim and Coptic. Like Khalid Mohieddin, Abdel Aziz

Fawzi joined the Muslim Brotherhood as a young officer, and always stayed loyal to its ideals of social justice and an independent and purified Islamic State. He was given leave of absence by the army to specialize in metallurgical engineering at Cairo University; later he was to achieve professional renown by being among the leaders of the team that put the steel mill at Helwan successfully into operation. At the height of his career, after he had finally left the army except as a reserve officer, he became a consultant in metallurgical and mechanical engineering, self-employed, well off, and always busy. He had gone back into the army before Sadat's October War in 1973 to help intensively to train the Egyptian shock troops in using the Sagger anti-tank missile.

Politically, Abdel Aziz jumped about, but never very far; he always stayed between the broad frontiers of Egyptian nationalism and militant Islam. Nasser impressed him greatly by his handling of the British-French-Israeli attack on the Suez Canal in 1956, turning what could have been a military disaster for Egypt into a crushing political victory, hastening Egypt's total independence and rocketing her international prestige to the skies. Consequently Abdel Aziz became a passionate disciple of Nasser, transferring to him some part of his fierce loyalties to the Muslim Brotherhood. He became one of the three or four most powerful men in Nasser's all-embracing political party, the Arab Socialist Union. Abdel Aziz went along with, though he never liked, and did everything within his power to soften, Nasser's ruthless persecution of the Muslim Brothers, and the harsher cruelties of his secret-police state.

Abdel Aziz stayed with Sadat at first when he succeeded Nasser, particularly attracted by Sadat's partial dismantling of Nasser's police state, his release of many of the Muslim Brothers whom Nasser had imprisoned, and his heavy and sustained support of the Islamic Fundamentalists in the universities, even at the expense of the Nasserist and Marxist organizations there, which Sadat now banned. But by 1974 he had begun to have his doubts about Sadat. He did not like his Open Door economic policy, so he could sympathize with the militant Fundamentalist group called the Islamic Liberation Organization when in April 1974 it marched on and took the Technical Military Academy in Abassia in northeast Cairo after a fairly bloody fight, then rested too long and fatally on its laurels at the Academy, failing in its plan then to wipe out or imprison Sadat and the ruling élite, and to declare a pure and full-blooded Islamic Republic. Abdel Aziz expressed the same sympathy (so police informers recorded) when *Takfir wal Hijra*, Atonement and Holy Flight, kidnapped and killed their former cabinet minister for Religious Endowments in 1977.

By the end of 1977 Abdel Aziz Fawzi was totally disenchanted with Sadat, whose traitorous flight (so he saw it) that November to Jerusalem to make a deal with the Israeli enemy was the last straw. So he turned hard to his old Free Officers and Muslim Brotherhood colleague, Khalid Mohieddin, the Red Colonel, and rose swiftly to the top layer of command of that gentleman's National Progressive Unionist party. There Sadat's paranoiac raid of 5 September 1981 – a month and a day before Sadat's killing – caught him, with 22 others of the NPU's leadership, as part of the 1,536 figures whom Sadat, finally panicked, arrested that day from every single shade of his political opposition, thus guaranteeing his own execution. Abdel Aziz suffered what he felt were deep indignities in Sadat's prisons, and it was not until February 1982 that Mubarak released him. The delay was in part because the police, including Gad's specialized unit, were busy investigating any links which Abdel Aziz, among many others, might have had with the militant Islamic Fundamentalist group that shot Sadat, the *Jihad el Jedid*, the New Holy War. As Gad knew, there was no doubt at all that Abdel Aziz sympathized fully with this murderous group. It was very nearly as certain that he had been personally in contact with their leaders. It was only fractionally less probable that he had given them material aid, including money. But there was no cast-iron proof.

Almost the first thing that Abdel Aziz had done on his release from prison was to quarrel fundamentally and break decisively with Khalid Mohieddin. This was because

Mohieddin, impressed by Mubarak's modest bearing, deliberately low profile, and evident sincerity, had accepted the appeal Mubarak had made to almost all the sectors of Egypt's political spectrum to enter into a dialogue with the new government. Khalid el Mohieddin and senior men from his National Progressive Unionist party had even accepted Mubarak's invitation to attend the intensive government study group which met in February 1982 constructively to consider Egypt's economic problems, which were as cataclysmic as ever and which, short of shooting all the bureaucrats, wiping out the public sector and banning motherhood, were probably insoluble. Entering into the spirit of the thing, Mohieddin and his NPU had even thoughtfully presented Mubarak and the meeting with a fat blue-covered book of 118 pages originally entitled 'Egypt's Present Economic Crisis and the Road Out of It'. This was too much for Abdel Aziz. For him Mubarak, whom Sadat had first selected when a mere obscure bomber pilot, and slowly groomed until he had finally made him his vice-president, was just that: no better than a total political creation of Sadat's.

Since March 1982 Abdel Aziz Fawzi had stayed very busy with his engineering consultancy, politically inert, but not dead. He was like a big gun, fully primed, held in reserve, ready and waiting.

Physically, Abdel Aziz gave an impression of extraordinary solidity, as if he were made of some almost impenetrable wood, like teak or mahogany. Not tall, he was thickly built. He was a very still man. Abdel Aziz watched and listened, a little monumentally, then spoke deliberately. He was olive-skinned. His face seemed nearly rectangular, as if echoing his short strong body. He wore no moustache, and his cheeks were very smooth – again that impassive sheen of very hard wood. His nose and lips were rather thick, boldly marked, and the eyes a clear light-grey. His hair was black and lank and close to his skull, brushed forward, without a parting. If he sat and talked to you, his hands would rest on his lap, or more often, quite motionless, on his knees, with the broad backs and stubby fingers of a forceful and practical man. If he was seeing you in his elegant flat in Zamalek's Saleh Ayoub – there were even green trees about in these wide and quiet streets – his wife would not be in evidence. Abdel Aziz Fawzi was still traditionally Arab, very Islamic in this. He would have shown you his two sons with pride, had they not already long since grown up and become professional men and left home, but you would never meet his wife. Her job was to look after the children when they were young, and her home and her husband always; but off scene. She was not for the light, or heavy entertainment of guests. At that level she did not exist. Under his lofty ceilings, set among his dark and sober furniture, Abdel Aziz had some deep need of such inexorable formalities, of a purity, an austerity. He was a formidable man. There could never be any doubt of his stature, or his strength.

Daniel Gad had had one other piece of news that day, just before he had left his office. At his request, Egyptian Immigration had accepted from him a short list of key political figures in Egypt and in the other main countries of the region. Immigration's job for Gad was to let him know anything they could about these key people's movements. Their report this day was that a certain Wahid Hakki, Libyan nationality, had flown in first class on the Jordanian Alia airline from Amman. Egypt's diplomatic relations with Libya were still interrupted, as they were with all the other so-called hard-line Arab states, but Egypt was still fairly liberal about letting the nationals of such states into the country – just as she still let in young men from Saudi, Kuwait, and the Emirates to study for years at her universities. Wahid Hakki had asked for and got a tourist visa at the international airport, then gone on by Misr Limousine taxi to stay at the Mena House Oberoi Hotel in Giza, within a stone's throw of the Pyramids. Gad knew Wahid Hakki's reputation as a ruthless and imaginative business tycoon, as a good and highly decorated tank commander in the Libyan Armoured Brigade with the Egyptians on the Suez Canal front in Sadat's October 1973 war, and subsequently as one of Ghaddafi's closest political counsellors, and strongest supporters of his militant Islamic line.

Now what precisely would so high-powered a gentleman as

this be wanting in Cairo right now? Some new and huge inter-Arab business deal that would make the financial world gasp? He couldn't really have come just for the tourism – that would hardly be Wahid Hakki's style. If he had chosen to stay within spitting distance of the Pyramids that more probably meant simply that when the Egyptians woke up the next morning they would find that Cheops, the bulkiest, was gone, transferred lock, stock and barrel to Libya overnight.

Or was it politics?

Gad's mind ranged back lazily to the other powerful political figure he had been thinking about that evening, Abdel Aziz Fawzi. Then he sat bolt upright so suddenly that he nearly broke his glass.

Christ Almighty.

Any connection?

And with the headless chemist and eyeless and cigarette-blistered Talkhan?

It was probably nothing. Just a wild hunch. Still, there did seem to be some kind of magnetic pull between these three events, or clusters of events, only ten days apart in time.

Gad was anyway profoundly glad that his instinctive reaction that day when he had heard about both Abdel Aziz and Hakki was to bang a plainclothes tail on each. You never knew. Sometimes routine procedures actually paid off.

# I I

# *For the Good of the Country*

'To my mind, there's no doubt that Sadat deserved to be killed,' said Abdel Aziz Fawzi, in his flat in Sharia Saleh Ayoub, Zamalek.

'Then we two will see eye to eye,' replied Wahid Hakki, alone with him.

'From the first time I knew him,' Abdel Aziz went on, 'he was always a charlatan at some level. Flamboyant, personally profoundly ambitious, not too scrupulous. He was always something of an actor, with an actor's multiple identities. In the end he had sold all of them, to the Americans. What was more grave was that he had sold them Egypt's identity too.'

The phrases were measured, the passion in them ruthlessly disciplined. Abdel Aziz Fawzi, dressed very formally in a dark-blue suit and a conservative dark tie, delivered them sitting in his big deep brown leather armchair in his vaulted big-windowed sitting room, with his squat powerful hands planted solidly on his knees like a Pharaoh in judgement. Abdel Aziz would always be the man in the dark-blue suit, thought Wahid Hakki, himself distinctly more racily attired, in a light-grey cotton suit, a pure red silk tie at his throat, elegant narrow brown shoes, his gold Patek on his left wrist and his black sapphire ring on the third finger of his right hand. He had not met Abdel Aziz Fawzi before, though he knew a great deal about him. He found him of even more stature than he had expected. He would make a great leader. He had an implacable honesty that attracted and convinced. It went beyond mere courage or daring. It was the core of his being. He looked exactly what he was, and meant exactly what he said.

'Yes,' said Wahid Hakki. 'And perhaps his flight to Jerusalem was the worst betrayal of all.'

Abdel Aziz looked at him steadily, then shrugged his strong shoulders. His hands did not move.

'Particularly since the Egyptian people didn't even really get their promised payoff. If you sell your soul to Shaitaan, you should at least ensure that Shaitaan pays the price. You'll recall Sadat's constant song to the people to justify his peace process with Israel? This was that *Abnaa es-Shaab,* the Sons of the People, wouldn't have to die again in war, and instead all the war money would come to them for peaceful development. So 1980 would be the year of prosperity, abundance for all. It wasn't. In 1980 bread prices doubled and meat was short. There was inflation. Wages didn't keep up with prices. Professionals and skilled labour emigrated. Why? Because Sadat was still in fact spending 15 per cent of the GNP on the army. He saw a new road to fame now – to champion Africa against Russia, to offer an army of a million men to the US to fight Russia. As you know, we very nearly went to war with your country, Libya; maybe the Sons of the People were going to have to die in war again after all.'

'Yes,' said Wahid Hakki, 'Sadat had taken you right out of the Arab family of nations by then.'

Abdel Aziz's heavy face observed him.

'They were right to reject us. Israel humiliated us, and thus all Arabs, time and again. When she bombed the nuclear reactor in Iraq, and the PLO and Lebanese in Lebanon. When it became obvious that she would *never* give real self-rule to the Palestinian Arabs in the West Bank and Gaza Strip. Meanwhile Sadat let the US grow dominant in Egypt. You want our million men to fight the Russians? he said. Go ahead. You want to store your arms here? Go ahead. Our strategy is yours. You want to send me thousands of highly paid US advisers to run my country? Go ahead. You want Egypt as a staging-post for your helicopter attempt to rescue the

American hostages in Iran? Go ahead. That last was the most unclean; Iran is a sister Islamic country. That really soiled our national honour. Also there was suddenly too much corruption. Not just baksheesh. Corruption on a big scale, at high levels.'

'And all for the cause of Western democracy,' said Wahid Hakki.

'That may have been the story Sadat was selling to the American Embassy,' said Abdel Aziz, 'but in fact, as I'm sure you know, Sadat was always autocratic, and in his last years in power he became really dictatorial, intolerable. You'll know of his Law of Shame, by which the public prosecutor could on his own pull in suspects for real or imagined offences and decide their punishment, and to hell with any formal and fair court procedure? And his Law 2 of February 1977 by which anyone initiating or taking part in a strike could get up to 25 years' hard labour? And Sadat's so-called People's Referendums were always a farce. I know of a recent one in Khalid Mohieddin's native town, which gave the usual something like 99.7% in favour of Sadat's measure. Why? Because in fact almost no one deigned to vote. Of the 6,000 registered to vote only 20 did – or 0.3%. Democracy under Sadat! If one were looking for justice, one would do much better under Islamic Law.'

There was a silence. Abdel Aziz Fawzi sat rock-like.

' "Unclean", I remember you said,' said Wahid Hakki.

Abdel Aziz examined him.

'Yes.'

'Concerning Sadat's letting the Americans use Egypt as a springboard for their – happily failed – attack on our sister Islamic Republic, Iran.'

'Exactly.'

'I am reminded of the Prophet's saying, to all Muslims.'

'Ah?'

' "Whosoever amongst you sees an abomination, he must correct it with his hands; if he is unable, then with his tongue; if he is unable, then with his heart." '

Abdel Aziz shrugged again, his eyes and manner steady as

his own hands. He was not a man who feared to carry his thoughts through to their logical conclusion.

'The man was an abomination. Sadat was that abomination.'

'Then *Jihad el Jedid* were correct to execute him?'

Abdel Aziz weighed him up with his light-grey eyes. Wahid Hakki felt his own tall lean body light in the balance. The impact of this man's personality was immense. If they could get him for this task, he would achieve it. Only a thick brick wall, or very bad luck, would stop him –

'*Said* Wahid Hakki, if you are a true believer in the Koran and the Sunna, as I think you are – and as, indeed, you mentioned to me earlier this morning that you were – then that conclusion is really inescapable, isn't it?'

Wahid Hakki smiled, but the other did not respond to that. The heavy, smooth face simply looked back at him impassively. It did not even look irritated at what it could have read as an impertinently direct question. It was just experienced and certain.

'We heard in Libya, indeed, that you were supporting them.'

'Supporting *Jihad el Jedid*? Presumably you don't mean in the sense of being one of their execution or other activist squads? Wouldn't my age – though I'm grateful for the implied compliment – count a little against me? And you'll not be forgetting, will you, that I was in one of Sadat's more unpleasant prisons uninterruptedly from the 5th of September till the 15th of February, so that I could hardly have been on stage for the execution on the 6th of October? Or do you mean did I support them with sympathy? But I think I have already answered you that.'

'You have, *Yafendim*, very clearly. Our information was that you had, as well, contributed money to their worthy cause. Possibly also arms.'

Abdel Aziz observed him for some while, then he said: '*Said* Wahid Hakki, don't you think I've already declared myself far enough?'

'Indeed, *Yafendim*, just as you think best. Then if I might perhaps be permitted to ask you a slightly different question?'

'*Etfaddal.*'

'You have, I think, been very explicit in your condemnation of Sadat. Would you consider that Mubarak was significantly better?'

So immobile had Abdel Aziz Fawzi now become that Wahid Hakki thought at first that he had just not heard him. Then Abdel Aziz gave a great sigh.

'Better, certainly,' he said, meticulously. 'Mubarak is a much more modest man. Nothing like so passionately ambitious personally. Much more honest. More decent, even.

'But *significantly* better? Probably not. Consider that *he has not changed a single one of Sadat's main policies since he came to power*, nor will he. He has done exactly what he promised. Remember that he said on TV at eight on the night of Sadat's killing that *Egypt would go on following Sadat's course without deviation. This*, surely, is what we have got to watch. *This* is what matters. It means that Mubarak has not changed, *and will not change if he remains*, Egypt's orientation radically away from the US politically, militarily or economically. Politically, this means basically that we do what the US tells us in the Middle East. Militarily, they grant us huge sums, arm us, carry out giant joint exercises with us, use our country and stock arms in it, train our officers in their war colleges, and buy our loyalties; we end as their vassals. Economically, Mubarak's maintenance of Sadat's policies means that we remain crippled, only American handouts keeping us alive. Well, I suppose that's cheaper for them than another full-scale Middle East war. And the corruption is still there, even near the top.'

'And the Palestinian cause?' said Wahid Hakki.

'Ah, yes, the Palestinian cause,' said Abdel Aziz. 'That's another example, that sad story. Here too Mubarak never once really moved against Sadat's peace deal with Israel. Not even on Israel's criminal and murderous full-scale invasion and occupation of Lebanon. We withdrew our ambassador. That was enough? No, there is no way in which we can regain our dignity with Mubarak, and his years of leadership have proved it. With him, we are and shall remain critically dependent upon a totally alien materialistic culture which ceaselessly saps our own Islamic values. We trade our identity as the price of our survival. Meanwhile Arab lands remain occupied and violently settled by an enemy, and we, with by far the most powerful Arab army in the Middle East, and against the express dictates of the Koran, do nothing. What surprise is it that most of the Arab, the Islamic family of nations, still really rejects us? Nor will this improve significantly.'

'Unless Mubarak is stopped,' said Wahid Hakki.

Abdel Aziz sat like the statue of Abraham Lincoln and thought that over for fifteen seconds. Then he looked at Wahid Hakki.

'Another coffee?'

'With pleasure.'

The two tiny cups had sat empty now for the last half hour, on the small tables beside them. Abdel Aziz clapped his hands twice. The sounds were harsh and crisp, like pistol shots. Wahid Hakki jumped in his skin. It was the first time he had seen those two powerful squat instruments move in that same last half hour.

The *khadama*, the maid, came in at once. It was as if she had been waiting crouched on her marks behind the kitchen door. She wore a high-necked, long-sleeved and very faded dark-grey abaya, and a nondescript black headcloth knotted under her chin. Both of these could have been washed and bleached a thousand times. So could she. She could have been of any age between thirty and seventy. She was dark-skinned and very wrinkled, and her body looked as if it had lost any hint of feminine contours years before. They could no longer have been of any significance. She would have completed her required mass breeding many years since, she had satisfactorily discharged her natural function, so that there was now really no important social role left for her; she would be living on borrowed time until she died. This would be as good a way of passing that as any. She was cylindrical and resigned. Wahid Hakki knew that she could not be Abdel Aziz's wife because she was barefoot.

'*Masboot* again?' said Abdel Aziz.

'That would be fine,' said Wahid Hakki. *Masboot* was middle-sweet, what reasonable, moderate men took.

She brought the Arab coffee with a speed that argued a constantly boiling pot in the kitchen. Her broad flat feet sighed back there across open patches of tiled floor like a beggar's practised mutterings of humility.

The two men sipped their boiling hot coffee, staring courteously straight ahead, finishing about together. They put down their tiny cups, and looked at each other.

'Unless Mubarak is stopped,' said Abdel Aziz Fawzi.

Wahid Hakki felt a knot tighten in his stomach.

'*Yafendim,* how would you handle things if you were in his position?'

'Where Mubarak is? Well. After I had dominated my opposition – for there would be that, of course – I would without doubt go straight for an Islamic State.'

'Like Iran? Like Khoumeni's?'

'Look, that, perhaps inevitably – because it was the first – has been a bloody business. I have no love for spilling blood as such. But if it has to be done – yes. In the end. Like Khoumeni's: a pure Islamic State. There is such a need for that, you see. For honesty. You see,' he went on, painfully, as though he were apologizing for some grave personal weakness, 'I find that I have a kind of need for social justice. Which must be grounded in something – well, pure, unchanging. Like Islam. I know that practically it is impossible to achieve completely. But if at least everything is designed honestly for that, is pointed for that. I cannot truly feel comfortable in my skin without that. And, though I think Mubarak a good and sincere man, I do not believe that we yet have anything like enough social justice in Egypt. Mubarak's heritage from Sadat has simply been too heavy.'

'And Mubarak simply not Muslim enough,' said Hakki. Abdel Aziz looked at him and shrugged.

'So, first and last, I should insist categorically on Egypt becoming a full Islamic State, immediately, even if the way to it were bloody. The country's law, at once, would be Islamic

Law, with no exceptions. For us, there's no other way; we're Arabs, Muslims, not pseudo-Americans, poor men's Westerners. Only this way can we keep, and develop, our true Islamic identity. It follows inevitably from this that I should take Egypt out completely from her present total dependence on the US, politically, militarily and economically. Internationally we should be genuinely independent under all three of these headings. Politically we should be as Third World and Non-Aligned as we were in Nasser's great days of partnership with Tito and Nehru of the Bandung Conference. Militarily we should be allied with neither superpower, and *nobody* would stock arms or have the right to use bases in our country. Our most profound alliance would be that natural one of blood and culture – as fully returned members of the great Arab, the great Islamic family of nations. And in that role, in absolute consistence with the Koran, our attitude to the Palestinian question would of course be crystal-clear: Israel must at once give back *at least* the West Bank and the Gaza Strip to their rightful Arab owners, in *total* autonomy, and with *every* Jewish settlement evacuated, and must fairly compensate financially every Arab thrown out from his former property in other parts of Palestine. If Israel would not, then we and the rest of the Arab family of nations must force her to by all the means at our disposal, even war.'

'It would be a truly great endeavour,' said Wahid Hakki. 'And without doubt the way we should go. But the problems will be immense, and not just internationally. You would face huge opposition within Egypt herself, against your pushing through your Islamic State. And a sinking economy which, once the American and other Western aid had stopped, would sink ever faster.'

'Of course there would be strong opposition against our Islamic State within Egypt,' said Abdel Aziz. 'From the Establishment, from parts of big business and the armed forces. But there would also, I think, be huge support for us. Our governments have cheated the Egyptian people too long. They are still at base a religious people, profoundly Islamic. I think they are not happy in their blood at the way things go, at the bastardization of their Islamic principles, the whole grim Palestinian story. Once they knew that this was a sincere revolution for a pure Islamic State, for genuine social justice, I think most would support it. Else why was there such wide support for the New Holy War – which Mubarak at first called a mere mad tiny splinter-group of terrorists, and we then discover he's holding *three thousand* in jail for questioning – and why such wide support for the other militant Islamic Fundamentalist groups before them, Atonement and Holy Flight, and the Technical Military Academy Group? No, those groups, and their supporters, are not really dead. They're still very much alive and about, under cover. And,' said Abdel Aziz, turning his monolithic head directly onto Wahid Hakki for a moment, 'there may be others.'

'Ah, yes?' said Wahid Hakki.

'As for the economy,' said Abdel Aziz, 'in truth, yes. What a mess! But, if the economic problems are big, our Islamic government would also be very strong, with the full weight of the Koran and the Sunna behind it. We would take the draconian measures no other government dared consider. I think we would succeed because we would be totally convinced that we were doing something necessary and right. As certain as is Islam itself. It's hard to stop a really convinced man with strength and some experience behind him, you know.'

'Still, it would be bitterly hard when the US and West cut their aid to you.'

Abdel Aziz Fawzi shrugged. 'We can stand that,' he said, 'we'll just have to pull in our belts. We can do it, if we are convinced. And a little disciplined austerity would do no harm to the Egyptian people at the moment, provided it really applied equally to every social class. And we should see to that,' added Abdel Aziz, sounding rather pleased at the thought.

'It sounds exactly right to me,' said Wahid Hakki.

For the first and indeed only time that day, Abdel Aziz Fawzi turned his head and smiled marginally at Wahid Hakki. It was like seeing a dinosaur suddenly relax.

187

'But it doesn't look very likely that I shall ever in fact occupy Mr Mubarak's seat,' said Abdel Aziz.

'My friends and I could perhaps arrange it,' said Wahid Hakki.

'*Naam?*'

'I am one of a group who would back you as President of Egypt.'

'Oh,' said Abdel Aziz. 'Thank you, but it's not very practical, you know. Since I left the Red Colonel, I don't have any sort of party machinery. It would take years to build that up.'

'Indeed. And, even when you had so built it up. Egyptian democracy being what it is, there would be no guarantee whatsoever that you would then achieve power, however sincere and worthy your aims, and however wide your electoral support.'

Abdel Aziz sighed again.

'Yes, that's about the measure of it.'

'Moreover, we don't have years.'

'No, that's very true. The matter's urgent.'

'And there is only one route to an immediate satisfactory solution.'

'Which of course is?'

'Which of course is a coup d'état, *Effendim*. Just like the Technical Military Academy Group. Atonement and Holy Flight. The New Holy War. Only this one must succeed.'

'I see. Yes. But, tell me now, who *is* your group?'

'I am not at liberty to reveal their names and exact personalities. I can tell you that we are of three separate nationalities, and all intimately connected with Egypt. We are all convinced – you spoke of the value of conviction in such matters – that Egypt's survival as a healthy and dignified Islamic nation depends entirely upon your carrying out such a coup. There is no one else; you must know that yourself. No one else has the stature, the power, the known probity. I put it to you that it is a sacred duty, *your* duty. What guarantee do you have about us, if I cannot, and will not, tell you anything more about the rest of us? Well, you have me unreservedly as a hostage, you could betray me at any time to the Egyptian Political Police; they would be delighted to take me in, with a specific and provable charge against me – for, as you will see, I shall – I hope – be leaving you concrete evidence of my visit. I shall be your contact throughout, I shall always let you know where you can call me, and I shall come here at once whenever you want. So my life is your guarantee. And perhaps what little you may know of me may suggest that I am a truly devoted, if humble, servant of Islam. I would not cheat against Islam.'

'I know you fought the Israelis with us on the Canal front in 1973,' said Abdel Aziz, 'and I know of your services to Ghaddafi as a political counsellor since then. Yes, you have proved yourself a good Muslim. I believe I can trust you. Still, a coup d'état, a bloody matter –'

'Only you can lead it,' said Wahid Hakki. 'It's a very grave trust. Remember "Whosoever sees an abomination, must correct it with his hands . . ." And remember that it would, profoundly, be for the good of the country.'

'Yes,' said Abdel Aziz. 'Yes. But have we the weapon?'

Wahid Hakki, tall and elegant, slim and high-browed, fine-featured, looked back at him levelly.

'Yes,' he said, 'I think we have the weapon. It's a sword.'

Abdel Aziz's lack of motion had now become so total that it was deafening. After about a minute he looked at Wahid Hakki and said:

'Ah. A sword?'

'Yes. I believe the full title is the Angels of the Sword.'

The other looked at him again through his wall of silence, then said tartly:

'You are remarkably well informed in Libya.'

'Well, we try to keep up with local gossip columns, you know. How good are they?'

'It's impressive. Very few indeed have heard the slightest hint about them here, in government or out of it. How good are they? Very good. Carefully selected. Highly trained. Very intelligent. Above all, totally dedicated to Islam. Their objective too is the pure Islamic State.'

'As good as the New Holy War, say?'

'Probably better. You know that our Fundamentalist revolts have been recurring for the last decade or so? This would be the fourth. Well, each time the Establishment never quite annihilates them. Each time they go under cover, then spring back. And each time their newest representative has learnt just a little bit more. I'll need money for this, you know. Not only for arms, but for training, bribes, organization, information, propaganda, recruiting . . .'

'Of course,' said Wahid Hakki. 'These two Samsonite briefcases that I brought, on the table – each contains half a million dollars, in $US100 notes. They're not locked. My fingerprints must be all over those cases, and on some of the notes, so there's your evidence if you'd like to turn me in. That's just for a start, of course, you'll be needing more as things start moving. We'll back you all the way.'

'A million dollars is a lot of money,' said Abdel Aziz. 'Yes, we could start with that.'

'Will you?'

Abdel Aziz, his broad-backed and sinewed hands statuesque on his knees, stared straight ahead, deciding his life and his destiny, and perhaps that of his country.

'Yes. I think I have no option.'

Wahid Hakki's heart surged.

'Good. Then on the back of this card are two numbers, one in Tripoli, one in London. If I'm not there, they'll know where you can find me immediately.'

'Angels of the Sword, then,' said Abdel Aziz. 'For when?'

Wahid Hakki glanced at his beautifully manicured finger-nails.

'How about when the American President comes here in a couple of months?' he said. 'Still fairly fresh from the election results? Then you would get tremendous worldwide publicity. It could allow you to make the widest possible case for Islam.'

'There would also be tremendous security precautions here at that time.'

'The more reason for them least to suspect you then. Remember that Islambouli killed Sadat before virtually the entire Egyptian army and air force.'

'It's valid reasoning. Let me see what they think about it. But let's take that as the provisional date of – execution, shall we say?'

'They?'

'In the activist cells of the Angels of the Sword,' replied Abdel Aziz, then went on with a gift of irony which Wahid Hakki would never have suspected, without moving a muscle of his face: 'I regret that I cannot reveal to you details of their identities, but I can assure you that my communication with them will be total.'

'I've no doubt.'

'Oh, one other thing. You know these terrorists, particularly the assassins, tend to be extremely individualist – artistic, even – in their choice of their execution weapons. I have no particularly close contacts with international arms and explosive dealers. Do you think you could help provide whatever specialized weapon or explosive might be asked for in this respect?'

'Of course. We'll do everything we can to help.'

'I'll contact you by express letter posted from Athens. That will be safest.'

'I agree.'

'I'll let you know at the same time how things look generally, for the attack plan.'

'Excellent. Oh, perhaps after you've stored the money somewhere safe, you'd be kind enough to wipe off the briefcases. Just in case, you know.'

'Certainly,' said Abdel Aziz. 'In fact I had already thought to do that.'

'Thank you.'

'But in all conscience I should warn you,' said Abdel Aziz, 'that I had also considered, and rejected, the idea of wiping off the $100 bills too. There must after all logically be ten thousand of them. I mean, enough is enough.'

'Yes,' said Wahid Hakki, a trifle uncertainly, getting to his feet. 'Well, a most productive meeting.'

'Indeed,' said Abdel Aziz, rising too, and apparently enjoying his own private sense of irony. 'And all for the good of the country.'

Downstairs as Wahid Hakki got into his waiting taxi he noticed the man on the other side of the road in his dark-grey galabiah and black skull cap leaning against a spare treetrunk and diligently reading his *Akbar*. Now where have I seen *him* before? thought Wahid Hakki, his heart lurching suddenly.

# 12

# *The Road to Jerusalem*

'*Ehlan wa sehlan, ya Bey!* Welcome!'

The hearty Arabic greeting caught Daniel Gad mid-stride halfway down the disembarcation ladder of the Nefertiti flight just arrived at Lod, Tel Aviv's airport. Nefertiti was in fact straight EgyptAir, Egypt's national airline, in both aircraft and aircrew, coyly repainted and disguised in this manner under its new exotic title out of deference to the other Arab States' repugnance at Egypt's dogged maintenance of her non-war relations with Israel. By this polite fiction, EgyptAir could keep her landing rights in the other Arab States. Here was Arab realism.

The man at the bottom of the gangway seemed to have no need of such diplomatic posturing. He was beaming cheerfully up at Gad, evidently without a care in the world. Happiness, indeed, looked his salient characteristic. He was a chubby man, full-faced and balding, with no visible complexes about it. Though very brown-skinned, his cheeks were rubicund. His body was pear-shaped, but Gad guessed surprisingly tough, most of that apparent fat sheer muscle. He moved lightly on his feet. He looked like a rounded but bouncy Greek nun, commando-trained.

This was Absalom.

Otherwise Major Uri Allon, of Israel's Mossad.

'Daniel?'

'Yes. Uri?'

'Yes. *Mumtáz!* Excellent!'

Gad had at once followed Allon's convention with their names. Daniel and Uri were common enough names on their own, giving away nothing without the surnames. It seemed a nice balance of human warmth and security.

'It's great to meet you after all these years!' said Uri Allon, taking him by the left elbow and walking him towards the terminal building, then looking round and up frankly at him; he was eight to ten centimetres shorter than Gad. 'Yes, you're about as I thought!'

Gad looked back at him and laughed.

'You're about as I expected too,' he said, 'including your handshake.'

It had indeed been crisp and powerful.

'Ah, that's all my gardening,' said Uri Allon.

Gad would have betted that other forms of training had contributed.

'You've nothing else than that shoulderbag?' said Allon.

'No.'

'Good. Then if I might have your passport –'

'Sure. Here.'

'We won't stamp it, of course, so as not to embarrass you with your other Arab States. Just give it to you on a separate sheet of paper.'

'Fine.'

Allon took him through Immigration and Customs at double-VIP speed, but a regular Israeli policewoman, armed, searched his shoulderbag very thoroughly, and a male corporal searched him quickly and expertly in a curtained booth.

'Everyone gets the treatment,' said Uri Allon, 'my apologies. Even our film stars . . .'

Outside, Gad saw that he was keeping the visit low-keyed, as Gad had hoped. There was no official car and chauffeur, simply Allon's (presumably) own 1.8-litre metallic-blue Scirocco, in pretty new condition. Allon put the shoulderbag in the boot and opened the front right door for Gad from the inside. He saw Allon connect his safety-belt and did the same. Allon drove them out of the airport, in a measured way, respecting all the speed limits. Everything looked new, smart, clean and functional; these Europeans, thought Gad. At the main road, they turned southeast for Jerusalem. As soon as they were climbing steadily, Gad said:

'It was extremely good of you to accept my coming here to see you at such short notice.'

Allon glanced across at him very briefly from above the steering-wheel, then back at the road in front. He looked a very meticulous driver. He would probably drive a tank that way too, thought Gad.

'I've often had the impression, Colonel,' said Uri Allon, naming Gad's rank for the first time, 'that you and I are really on the same side.'

'Daniel would still do fine, Major,' said Gad, 'if it's OK with you. Yes, so have I.'

'Good,' said Allon. '*Beseder*. OK. So what brings you here, Daniel?'

'That telex you sent,' said Gad. 'Also the human curiosity to see what you looked like in the flesh.'

'Well, here I am,' said Allon. 'You buy what you see. That telex was some use to you?'

'Maybe a great deal,' said Gad. 'But could you tell us anything of the background to it? I mean, it was kind of sparse: "Abdel Aziz Fawzi may be trying a coup d'état." No more, no less. That's still a hell of a lot, of course, if it's right. But could you tell us how you got it, build it up a bit?'

Uri Allon thought about that one for a full thirty seconds. Then he said: 'He was having dinner with someone a few days ago in Cairo. He waxed very eloquent on the imperative need to do something drastic to change the Egyptian government's line. Egypt had sold herself out to the US. She had let in godless Western materialism to corrupt all true Islamic values. Free sex too. Corruption everywhere. And Egypt wasn't doing a thing really to stop Israel's creeping invasion of the Palestinian Arabs' West Bank. The only answer was a full-blooded Islamic state à la Khoumeni.'

'It's a song he sings,' said Gad.

'But this time so vehemently,' said Allon, 'that I thought I ought to drop you a line about it.'

'I'm damned glad you did,' said Gad. 'But might we know just a little more? Like, was the dinner in Abdel Aziz's flat?'

Uri Allon glanced at him again marginally from above the steering-wheel.

'Not in his flat.'

'Oh. In a friend's –'

'Or maybe a restaurant. As you know, Cairo has many good restaurants.'

'So it has. The kind of guy he would have been talking to like that could have been one of his old Free Officer pals from the 1940s.'

'Indeed, it might well have been a Free Officer from the good old days. Or not. Say a colleague from the Red Colonel's party.'

'And how would you have heard about it?' said Gad. 'A waiter? A third person at the table?'

'I'd back the waiter theory,' said Uri Allon. 'I mean, there are waiters everywhere, aren't there? Or maybe it was Abdel Aziz himself who told me.'

'You're a big help, Uri! Give us a break!'

'Not I!' said Uri Allon. 'Like a good journalist, I'm not revealing *my* sources! What, and have you, the moment you get back to Cairo, take out all that nice system of agents that I've installed there with so much trouble? No, sir, Colonel.'

'All right,' said Gad, after a few moments, 'Major.'

He had not really thought that Allon would concede, but it had been worth trying.

'It's not as though it were the really hard stuff,' said Uri Allon. 'Really *hard* information, I mean. A firm decision. A plan. An organization. A strategy. Arms. Target areas. Dates. Nothing of that. So much so that I was in two minds about contacting you. But I just had that feeling, you know, from something about that report, that this was, or could lead to, something really serious –'

'I'm still damned glad you did,' said Daniel Gad. He knew how valuable that kind of intuition was in his business, especially when the hard facts were slim. You developed it as a sixth sense over time, or you did not. It could lead you wrong too, of course. This time it looked accurate.

'Mind you,' said Uri Allon, now making a considerable concession after all, though ethical rather than professional, 'I think Abdel Aziz has a point there in his jab about Israel practically annexing the West Bank. I don't like that. We must be mad. We *really* want to take on feeding another 750,000 to a million Arab mouths? They're time-bombs. By 2015 the Arab population of the West Bank and Gaza Strip will equal Israel's entire Jewish population. Look, I can see the sense to Yigal Allon's plan of having a string of Israeli forts along the west bank of the Jordan River, then giving *all* of the rest of the West Bank to the Arabs. Because now the distance between Natanya on the Israeli coast and Tulkaram on the official Arab West Bank border is only 12 or 13 kilometres. An Arab armoured column could cover that in 10 or 15 minutes, cutting Israel in two. At least the Allon Plan would give us some 65 kilometres between our line of forts and the sea. It would give us *some* breathing space against an Arab armoured thrust from the east.'

'You may have a point there,' said Gad. 'Anyway geo-politically. Twelve kilometres *is* a kind of narrow waist to have to try to defend.'

'But this Likud policy of packing Jewish settlements into the West Bank as hard as we can go!' said Uri Allon. 'I don't like that either. Not a bit. Particularly when it's turned into a crusade by our Jewish religious extremists, like Gush Emmunim. Or the Nartorei Karta, so ultra-orthodox that they'll hardly let you breathe. These goddam Israeli Southern Baptists can be a real pain in the arse, believe me!'

'I believe you,' said Gad.

'In fact I sometimes think,' said Allon, 'that our worst enemies are our own goddam extremists. We ought to lock up the lot of them on sight!'

'I know the feeling.'

'The Arabs deserve a better fate than that,' said Allon. 'I rather like most of the Arabs.'

Gad said nothing, but his heart leapt out to Allon. Allon was a man after his own heart, a fanatical moderate like himself. And he probably really did like the Arabs, or some Arabs, if the way he used their tongue was any evidence. Gad had of course known from his records that Allon spoke Arabic fluently, but he had not expected him to be *this* fluent, and particularly not in the slushy and booby-trapped fields of colloquial Egyptian Arabic, which is what the two men had been speaking for the last fifteen minutes.

'How do you do it?' said Gad. 'We could pass you off as the genuine Egyptian article.'

Allon glanced at him and laughed.

'I deserve no great credit for it,' he said. 'My father was a merchant, and we moved about a bit. So as a boy I had four years in Arab schools in Iraq, and four at a school in Egypt, in Alexandria.'

Climbing now all the time, they had come to many curves. They were into the swelling green Judean Hills, veined with runs of wind-carved white boulders like bleached marble sheep. It was biblical country. Despite its great beauty, it was harsh land. Men would live hard in these bleak hills.

And die hard. Gad saw the occasional burnt-out carcass of a truck, mounted off the road at its side like a rusted monument. Allon must have seen or sensed the direction of his gaze, for he said:

'I think it's your first time up here?'

'Yes.'

'Ah. Then these are our relics of the 1948 war. You'll know that the Arab armies blockaded Jerusalem? It was touch and go if the Jews fighting there would survive, until we crash-built a secret new road from the coast through the hills. Till then, we pushed as much food, arms, ammunition up the blockaded route as we could. There were ambushes and blocks everywhere. We had heavy losses. These were some of them.'

'But some got through?'

Allon glanced at him again briefly.

'Yes, some got through. Enough.'

'You were in it, I believe?'

Allon smiled slightly.

'Yes, I was one of those up in Jerusalem. So I was damned glad enough trucks got through.'

'And you were with Palmach in Jerusalem?'

Allon smiled again.

'You've been reading up a lot, Colonel.'

'Daniel.'

'Daniel. Yes, I just made it on age, into Palmach.' Palmach were the Haganah's élite shock troops, who won a name for considerable bravery and tenacity. Allon went on: 'You'd have missed that, though?'

'The 1948 war? Yes, I was a wee toddler of three. Not much use with a gun.'

Though Uri Allon had hardly been middle-aged when he began his wars. Of Russian parents, he was himself a Sabra, born in Haifa in 1929. Despite his youth, he had had one invaluable strength for Palmach, beyond his courage and intelligence – his fluent Arabic. Because of it, Palmach had sent him in 1947 to buy arms for them for the imminent war from the Arabs in Benghazi, where the Allies, Germans and Italians had all bequeathed great quantities to the desert sands. With his £500 – a vast sum in those days – Uri bought vital quantities of Italian Breda ammunition and guns, since these were the most compatible with the arms which the secret army of the embryonic Jewish State already had. With his canny business sense and earthy wit, Uri did a superlative job for his country with the Arab arms dealers in Benghazi, one of whom had found Uri so sympathetic that at the last moment he refused any payment for his consignment of arms, telling Uri to take it instead as a contribution towards the formation of his new State, for use against the occupying British. Years later, Uri came across the same man as a penniless refugee in Israel, and secured him a good and stable job. Uri took the concept of loyalty seriously.

As he took the concept of confidentiality about his agents.

Gad said: 'Uri, you play a skilled game of poker. You deflected very smoothly there from the main subject. You wouldn't tell us just a little about how you got that news about Abdel Aziz?'

'Sorry,' said the Israeli. 'Anyway, isn't it about time you dealt me a good card in exchange?'

'All right,' he said. 'How's this for the Ace of Spades you need for your Royal Flush? Guess whom we tailed yesterday morning latish to Abdel Aziz Fawzi's flat in Zamalek?'

'Moses. The Archangel Gabriel.'

'Wahid Hakki.'

'Wahid *Hakki*?'

Uri Allon was so moved that he jammed his foot on the accelerator and the metallic-blue Scirocco leapt forward like an unleashed colt. Happily there was no car immediately ahead. Allon slowed the car again. It was some tribute to his control that he had kept going throughout in an absolutely straight line.

'My God!' he said. 'Now we really do have something! Wherever Hakki goes, like Ghaddafi, revolt and bloodshed follow not far behind. Did you get any line on what happened inside?'

'No,' said Daniel Gad. 'And it's not that I'm playing hard to get. But the meeting was too quickly set up. We had no prior warning of it. It couldn't have lasted more than an hour, then Hakki went straight back to his hotel, the Mena House at Giza, and left for the airport that afternoon. He'd flown in the day before from Amman. He flew *out* to London. Curious. And one other thing. He went into Abdel Aziz's building and flat with two pretty large Samsonite briefcases. He came out without them. Arms? Explosives? Key revolutionary documents? Money?'

'You'll know next time,' said Uri Allon. 'If it's anything, they're bound to meet again.'

'Oh, yes,' said Gad. 'We'll know every damned thing that goes on in Abdel Aziz's flat from now on. A little man with a telephone company cap will go in to check his phone, and bug it. Or we'll hire the flat next door and eavesdrop electronically. We'll know what goes on next time.'

'Those are two powerful people,' said Allon sombrely. 'If they're together, then something's up.'

'That's about as I saw it,' said Gad. 'That's why I wanted to come up.'

For he knew that Uri, with his excellent Arabic, was detailed in his Mossad counter-terrorist unit to keep a beady eye on developments among the Islamic Fundamentalists, whether in Syria, the Lebanon, Saudi, or – probably most explosively these days – in Egypt herself. There was good sense to that. Extremists, even of totally opposing nations, tended to reinforce one another. If Egypt's extremists suddenly went extra-violent, ten to one Israel's Nartorei Karta or Gush Emmunim would do so too, in some way or another, at some level or other, and sooner rather than later; in some sense they were all members of the same appalling club. So Allon was a good man to talk to, and keep in the picture. By his two-day-old telex he had just proved to Gad that his network of agents in Egypt, however small, was very alert.

'Thanks for being so open,' said Uri Allon.

'A pleasure,' said Gad politely. He noticed however that Allon was still not giving the slightest hint about his people in Cairo. Gad also knew that in telling Allon how he, Gad, would keep Abdel Aziz under surveillance from now, he too had really given away precisely nothing; it was standard procedure.

'It's good too that we met on this,' said Uri Allon, 'and it makes sense for us to work together. You know, I see two huge threats here in the Middle East, either easily able to trigger off a third world war. First, a sudden war of vengeance by Syria, fully armed and backed by Russia, starting with a massive surprise attack to retake the Golan Heights. Second, as sudden a coup d'état turning a key country like Egypt into the region's second major Islamic Republic, with Islamic Fundamentalism then sweeping into power in every other Arab state including Saudi and Kuwait, and the Emirates. Either threat's success would be very bloody, and I think a grave step backwards towards barbarism.'

'You don't have to convince me,' said Gad, 'I'll buy it. I'm not happy, but I'll buy it all.'

A last few twists, and Jerusalem lay before and below them, sloping down east and south, beautiful and tinged with pink from the faintly roseate Jerusalem stone. All this part immediately before them now was the Jewish New City. Allon drove them through and across streets whose Hebrew names sang – Sderot Weizmann, Jaffa, Sarei Israel, Ben Yehuda, Agron, King David. To Gad this New City hummed with efficiency. He was amazed to see no dirt. The streets were clean and smart. The traffic lights worked and the cars and buses and even the pedestrians actually obeyed them scrupulously. No wonder the Israelis had a habit of winning their wars.

'In which hotel have you put me for the night, Uri? The King David? or they tell me one called the Moriah is pretty good.'

Allon glanced at him.

'As a matter of fact, Dori and I thought you might prefer to stay with us. For one thing, we have an unparalleled view of the Old City Walls – and there they are now –'

Gad saw swiftly left the rough square of the Old City, the grave stone walls and spiked battlements, and far back the rich curves of the Dome of the Rock and near it El Aqsa Mosque, and the tall spires of minarets and churches. The Holy Sepulchre and the Wailing Wall were in there too; this small walled packed space held among the most revered shrines of the three great Religions of the Book. And enough seeds of conflict, thought Gad, to guarantee eternal war.

'It's very kind indeed of you,' he said.

Allon drove past the King David Hotel, then down.

'This is where we live,' he said. 'Yemin Moshe.'

It was a beautiful small quarter, purely residential. The houses had clearly all been rebuilt to maintain their original styles, in that fine pink-white Jerusalem stone. Its setting, thought Gad, was as dramatic as any in the world, and as significant. Yemin Moshe faced due east across the last wadi that had formerly separated the Jewish New City from the Arab Old, into Mount Zion and the southern and western walls of the Old City from Zion's Gate to David's Tower and Jaffa Gate.

'Yemin Moshe's the select suburb here these days, isn't it?' said Gad.

'Yes,' said Uri Allon, parking his Scirocco at the edge of a small square. 'Again it's no great credit to me that we're here. My father was very successful as a merchant, and he left my two brothers and me well off. I put most of my money into this – why not enjoy it in our lifetime? Also, you know, I fought quite hard under and across those walls in 1948 and 1967, so they give me memories. Besides, I just love that view.'

The setting of a rebuilt Yemin Moshe was significant, thought Gad, because no people in its right mind would have put that money into it if they thought it would ever be shot up again from those walls. The Israelis were not contemplating giving them back to Arab control, *ever*.

Allon rang the front door bell as he opened the door with his key, so that his wife Dori was in the hall to welcome them as they came in. She was in her early fifties, of medium height, still quite slim, with grey hair, and singularly regular and fine features. Her eyes were set quite wide, grey and gentle. That indeed seemed her predominant characteristic; a great calm gentleness. She was born Romanian, a child refugee to Palestine. They sat in the sitting room, whose large main windows looked straight across at the Old City walls.

'I'll leave you for an hour, if I may,' said Uri, 'just to call in at my office. If you'd like a shower or a rest –'

Dori had shown Gad his room.

'We don't need to talk any more?'

'I don't feel you and I *need* to talk much, you know. And you've given me the really vital bit, about that gentleman. I'll ask our people to watch out for him like hawks, everywhere, and report anything back urgently to me. Then I'll pass it at once to you.'

'Fine.'

'Perhaps the most useful thing we can do after that,' said Uri, 'is to show you the place a bit, so you get the feel of us. This afternoon I could take you to look at the Old City – on foot, of course – then by car round some of the new building in East Jerusalem.'

'Great.'

'Is there anything specific that you'd like to see?'

'One thing,' said Daniel Gad. 'Your Yad VaShem.'

This was Israel's monument to the six million Jews who had died in the Holocaust. It meant Hand and Name, perhaps because that in the end was all the concentration camp inmate had left of his identity, simply a number which a German tattooed on his wrist, for the short time before he was exterminated.

There was a short silence between the Allons.

'You don't have to do that,' said Uri Allon finally. 'It happened long ago, not in your time. A family thing.'

'It's as Uri says,' said Dori. 'It's an old wound. Leave it.'

'Yes,' said Gad. 'Nevertheless, I should like please to see it.'

'Of course,' said Uri Allon. 'Perhaps in the morning, before your aircraft.'

'Fine.'

'As for today,' said Uri, 'Dori has a lunch. So I suggest we go out. You like fish?'

'Sure.'

'Then we go to the Dolphin in East Jerusalem. It's the best Arab restaurant and the Arabs revere it. The Jews love it too, so much so that sometimes the front door opens and a grenade comes in. Still, the food's worth the risk.'

'Veterans like us should be able to take a chance like that,' said Daniel Gad.

So when Uri came back he and Gad drove together to the Dolphin and there they took their chances. They had an excellent fish lunch, laced with chilled Israeli white wine, which Gad found as good as, or better than, his beloved Giannaclis. He noticed that Uri, like many Israelis, drank sparingly. While they ate, no Arab grenades rolled in through the door.

Afterwards they went back and parked near Jaffa Gate, then walked through it and past David's Tower and into and down David Street and the Street of the Chain. There were Arab shops crowded on either side, restaurants, curio shops, traps for the tourist. It was another Khan el Khalili or Muski in miniature. They came to the Dome of the Rock and bought their tickets and took off their shoes at the door and went in. The mosque, with its octagonal base walls and voluptuous dome above, and its intricate mosaic patterns, was striking enough from the outside. Inside it blazed with beauty. The dome itself, seen from beneath, was an exquisitely illuminated complex in gold of interlinking circles and whorls and arabesques. In the eight walls themselves superb stained-glass windows were set, richly alive with reds and golds and blues and greens. An elderly Arab guide took them down curving stone stairs to Abraham's Rock, enchanted to talk to them in Arabic. Once outside again, Uri Allon took Gad out south then west through the Jewish Quarter past the Wailing Wall where the pious, divided into separate sections of the wall, by sexes, stuck their scrolled prayers reverently into it.

Uri Allon's next kindness, as Gad was quick to realize, was also politically shrewd. This was his display to Gad of the tremendous amount of new building that the Israelis had done on the eastern side of Jerusalem which they had captured in 1967 at a cost in blood. To the north, east and south of the Old City Gad saw a whole flood of pink-white new building. Uri told him that Jerusalem's mayor, Teddy Kollek, had strictly forbidden the use of anything but pure Jerusalem stone. Private enterprise had built thousands of blocks of flats of four to six stories, of clean and elegant design, and many government offices, including a new police headquarters, all on what had formerly been bare mountainside. There were, said Uri, some half a million Israelis living in this distillation of eighteen years' new building, beyond the half-million living in pre-1967 Jewish Jerusalem. Israel was never going to give this mass of superb new constructions, or the lands on which they stood, back to the Arabs or to anyone else, except over Israel's dead body. Their sheer visual impact convinced Gad of that. He noted that Israel was keeping a hard-nosed sense of realism here too. Every new building, Uri remarked, had to have its own atomic bomb shelter, with separate air supply and entrance. Israel, he said, had learned painfully and as recently as 1973, when Egypt had nearly beaten her, that it never paid to underestimate your opponent.

That night they dined at home, comfortably, at great ease with one another. Afterwards Uri took Gad to the sitting-room windows. Searchlights illuminated the Old City. The effect was ethereal. The crenellated battlements and famed gates and fine towers shone like the contours of a freshly minted coin. Israel was not going to give back this agate old citadel either.

Uri Allon drove Gad to Yad VaShem next morning. Gad had said goodbye first to Dori, for Uri would take him on later straight to the airport. The austere dark holocaust buildings stood on a green hilltop west of Jerusalem City, near Mount Herzl and Herzl's tomb. Uri walked through them with him. Gad saw the black-and-white photographic account of the Nazi German's meticulous massacre of six million Jews, by hangings, mass shootings, Zyklon B Gas, starvation and medical experiments. There was a huge photo of the swastika-bannered mass meeting in Berlin on 15 August 1935 shouting for a Germany cleansed of Jews. There was the Children's Choir at Warsaw Ghetto, the heads, through scientifically induced malnutrition, already appearing grotesquely too big for their bodies, some still smiling diligently at the camera. There were many other children's faces, this time non-Jewish, most transfixed with appalled fascination, one or two smiling even more horribly, at the public execution by hanging of three Jews in 1939. Gad saw the paintings and poems of the children of Theresienstadt Ghetto, to which 15,000 under the age of 15 went, and 100 returned.

A little garden,
Fragrant and full of roses.
The path is narrow.
And a little boy walks along it.

. . . When the blossom comes to bloom,
The little boy will be no more.

That butterfly was the last one.
Butterflies don't live here,
In the ghetto . . .

And there in sharply etched blacks and whites were the German Nazi *Einsatzgruppen* forcing their women and children victims to strip off their personal belongings and clothes, for loot, before machinegunning them into oblivion at the edge of mass graves, the victims staring into the lens of the camera, one still coquettish, one with utter hatred, the others in numb terror. Gad saw the platform at Auschwitz where the SS separated out the women and children and weak to die at once in the gas chambers, as unfit for work. There too was the still uncovered Nordhausen mass grave peopled by its thousands of naked bodies of men, women and children tumbled like the carcasses of chickens. The faces of this people, humiliated literally to death, emaciated, suffering, stoic, affected Daniel Gad the most. He could understand why men like Uri Allon were ready to fight to the death rather than let that kind of fanaticism win again.

At Lod Airport, through the emigration formalities, and sitting the last ten minutes with Uri Allon before he boarded his plane, Gad said:

'I cannot thank you enough, Uri. Not just for the news about Abdel Aziz, which may prove vital, but also for letting me see something of yourself, Dori, your country. It goes without saying that you and Dori must come down to see me in return.'

Allon brightened visibly.

'I'd really love to see Cairo again. After these many years. You mean it?'

'Of course.'

'You know, it could work then. I've a couple of weeks' leave in two months. Maybe a few days then?'

'Fantastic. The whole two weeks if you like. No trouble at all. Just let me know. You have my address.'

'*Mumtáz*. Excellent.'

'Ah, and I have a small thing for you here. Knowing your interest in Arabic –'

Gad pulled a stiff folder from his shoulderbag and opened it. There lay the first two pages of an exquisite illuminated manuscript in Arabic. Each page was about 40 centimetres deep and 30 wide. Allon scanned it and knew it. It was the start of the Koran's 15th *juz* or part, which included the *Sura Beni Israel*, the Chapter of the Sons of Israel, and the *Sura el Kahf*, that of the cave – the story of how Muhammed, pursued by his enemies, hid in a cave, and was there saved by a spider, who obligingly spun a web across the entrance, so that his enemies when they arrived took it as obvious that there could be no one inside. The chapter headings were illuminated in white and the pages in rich blue and gold. Blue and gold rosettes divided each verse line, and a gold oval circled by blue signalled each tenth verse. The text itself was tall, slim, and very elegant. It began with that mellifluous and benevolent phrase beloved of the Koran and Arab official document and letters:

*Bismillah er-Rahman er-Rahim* —
In the name of Allah the Compassionate and Merciful —
Glory be to Him who carried his Servant by Night
From the inviolable Place of Worship to the Far Distant
  Place of Worship . . .

'It's a gem!' said Uri Allon reverently.

'Late fourteenth-century Mameluke. It once lay in the mosque by Barquq's tomb in Cairo's Northern Cemetery.'

'A masterpiece!' said Allon. 'But how could I possibly accept it? You know that! How could I possibly accept it?'

'You'd honour me by accepting it. Besides, think how well it would go framed next to the Arabic books and scripts you have in your study.'

'Still —'

'Nothing official, you know,' said Daniel Gad. 'From me to you. You know Arab manners in these things. You'd dishonour me in not accepting it. Call it just a gift of friendship.'

'A gift of friendship, then,' said Uri Allon more happily, then walked out with Gad to the gangway of the aircraft, waved to him and watched him go.

# 13
# Pursuit and a Death in Berkeley Square

That afternoon Uri Allon sat in his small office in the cluster of new two-storied buildings off Ruppin on the western side of Jerusalem, a little past the turn-off to the Knesset and before the Ministry of Finance. There were only five Mossad men and two secretaries in this unit, whose main door bore the brave legend MAZEL TOV GEODETIC SURVEY. None of them had done a geodetic survey in the five years they had been there, and surprisingly few people had ever come or phoned or ask them to do one. They stayed busy nonetheless. Much of Mossad's work was counter-terrorist, counter-extremist; logically, since a main objective of surprisingly many people was still to annihilate Israel and any Jews in or out of it, if not by open war, then by any means they could think up, the bloodier the better.

Uri gazed out of his south-facing window towards the Shrine of the Book and thought about Wahid Hakki and his meeting with Abdel Aziz. Uri had urgently passed the news to his chief and colleagues the day before, but had had no playback yet. If Hakki was in the act too that made this the big time. Why had he gone on so swiftly to London instead of back to Libya? Who would he see there? If he went back to Abdel Aziz afterwards, Uri was sure that Gad would know about it, and Mossad through Gad. For the Egyptians had some very good modern electronic equipment for eavesdropping now. When Nasser called on Russia after the Arabs' shocking 1967 defeat, she not only rearmed Egypt completely and sent 15–20,000 advisers to retrain her forces, but also fully reorganized Egyptian Intelligence and supplied sophisticated electronic tools including radio interception and electronic surveillance and locating equipment. Those new skills cost Israel dearly, Allon knew. Egypt's whole attack in the 6 October 1973 war was based on Egyptian Intelligence's acquisition of the secret Israeli plan for Canal defence. Egyptian Intelligence even got hold of Israel's code map for all the Sinai with all the code names used in Israeli radio traffic, already translated into Arabic.

Uri was sure that his recent guest would know all about using such equipment. He had faith in Gad. Yet he wondered if Gad would get much higher than Colonel, for he was a Copt. The Egyptian Muslims were not diehard religious exclusivists, but they did tend to keep the top command posts for themselves; they were only human. So Boutros Boutros Ghali, Egypt's Minister of State for Foreign Affairs for many years, and an excellent one at that, would never make cabinet rank, because he was a Copt; the Foreign Minister, Abdel Meguid, was most doggedly and durably a Muslim. Uri did not think he minded if Gad never made General. He liked him as he was. He had been sure from what he knew of Daniel Gad's reputation before he met him that they would have things in common. They were professional policemen. Each had fought for his country. Neither was fanatical.

One of the unit's two secretaries came in with mail for Uri Allon's in-tray.

'Anything exciting there?' he asked her.

'Not really. Just your daily summary of travelling rogues.'

This was the airlines' playback to him from the shortlist he provided them, and constantly updated, of the twenty or so personalities which he looked on as most dangerous for Israel, and for that matter for regional stability as a whole. They included members of Nartorei Karta, Gush Emmunim, and Tehiya. Also included were some few fanatics so extreme that they fitted into no existing political party. There were some wild characters here.

'Anyone I know travelling?' he said to the girl, just at his door.

'Not really,' she said. 'There are only three of your list figuring anyway.'

'Oh?'

'Including that old friend of yours, Avram Ben Yehuda.'

'Oh, Avram. And where's he off to this time?'

'London, I think,' she said. 'The El Al flight tomorrow. But see for yourself, Major. It's all written down there in front of you.'

Uri Allon stared at his shut door. London, indeed. Why was Avram Ben Yehuda going there? He had no particular love for London, no very close friends there. If he was travelling on his diamonds business he most often went to Amsterdam. So why London, just now? Why would a really fanatic right-wing extremist, a Greater Israel hawk so far right that he had practically flown clean out of sight, want to go to London just tomorrow?

Who else of his rare stamp would be going there then, for example?

Major Uri Allon leapt to his feet, walked to his window, and stared out of it.

Wahid Hakki, for example.

Uri Allon felt himself sweating. It was only the vaguest possible supposition. Yet he knew he was right. That was the pattern. There was the form. He had to have the guts to see it.

He went back to his desk and the phone on it, and rang his boss.

'Dan? Can I come in and see you? I have something that I think is urgent . . .'

Uri Allon got his London taxi to drive on past and stop beyond Avram Ben Yehuda's to minimize the risks of Ben Yehuda seeing him. They were halfway down Hay Hill in Mayfair, having come to it from Claridge's Hotel in Brook Street via New Bond Street. At Claridge's seeing Ben Yehuda get his taxi,

Uri had asked the top-hatted doorman with the big silver buttons on his frock-coat to get him one too, then had given the driver the time-hallowed instruction: Follow that car. His whole day had been filled with this kind of vaudeville, ever since he had caught Ben Yehuda's El Al flight earlier, travelling tourist where Ben Yehuda travelled first class. They had met twice, and Uri did not know if Ben Yehuda would remember him. He of course knew a great deal about Ben Yehuda, since this was his business, and had several recent photographs of him in his well-documented file.

Uri's trip into London from Heathrow Airport had had the same touch of soap opera about it. He had again followed Ben Yehuda in a taxi, not knowing where he was going, then stood discreetly behind him in Claridge's foyer, but not so far that he could not hear the number of the room he was given, or his request to be called at nine-thirty that evening. Uri had himself then, with great luck, got the adjoining room. Then, fairly sure that his quarry was resting, he had gone out to the nearest public callbox and phoned his contact in the Israeli Embassy on a direct line with a request to get a coded message to his boss Dan Abromowitz in Jerusalem. By now, Abromowitz would know that Uri had followed his target to Claridge's, believed his target had a meeting at or after nine-thirty that night, would attempt to find out what it was about and who – which might include Wahid Hakki – was at it, and would then revert. He had also asked his boss to transmit the gist of this message to Salah el-Din.

After making that call, Uri had gone back to Claridge's, checked that Ben Yehuda's key was not in Reception, then quietly adopted a strategic position in the large lobby from which he could keep an eye on the lift, and settled down with that day's *Guardian*, *Telegraph* and *Times*, which he felt were still among the best newspapers in the world. At 9.45 Avram Ben Yehuda had appeared from the lift, in a nicely cut dark-blue suit, and a battleship-grey light camel-hair overcoat which hung faultlessly from his tall, lean frame; it was all he would need, for it was not a really chill night. Uri Allon sighed; he could not compete with Ben Yehuda. For one thing, there was the inescapable pear shape of Uri's body. For another, he did not like camel-hair, or camels. Instead he wore his trusted Burberry macintosh, and the grey trilby hat which he resuscitated only for his trips overseas. He looked, he knew, like a grocer on holiday.

Now in Hay Hill, out of his taxi, he watched Ben Yehuda's bald brown pate, rimmed by its narrow horseshoe of iron-grey curls, ride like a clipper's figurehead into the lobby of Berkeley House, his gold chain bracelet flickering round his right wrist. Once he was inside, before the door clicked shut behind him, Uri Allon bounded after him; Ben Yehuda could be going anywhere in this smooth tall building of many luxury flats. Holding the door, Uri watched the doorman show the visitor into the lift. What could Uri do now? He could hardly ask the doorman directly to which flat Ben Yehuda had gone. If Uri was due at the same meeting he was supposed to know that himself. He slipped outside again. He would simply have to wait and hope for a break.

It came soon. Within two minutes another taxi had drawn up at Berkeley House, from Dover Street. Standing a fraction further down Hay Hill, Uri Allon walked back up, at a pace calculated to get him to the heavy wooden Berkeley House door just as the new arrival got down at it. This figure, stooping slightly now to pay his taxi driver, was also tall and trim. A navy-blue overcoat clothed his athletic body closely, over a dark suit, the creases in his trousers knife-edged, the black shoes shining. He had a white silk scarf round his throat, no hat. It was a fine head, with a high brow and abundant black curled hair, aquiline nose and thin chiselled lips. As the man turned from the taxi-driver's window Uri saw the black sapphire ring on the third finger of his right hand. By his complexion the other could be Arab. And was; he would not know Uri, but Uri knew him, from photos and reports; he had a file on him too: Wahid Hakki, tank captain with the Libyan Armoured Brigade on the Canal front in 1973 and close political counsellor and friend to Ghaddafi ever since. Hakki's eyes had not even registered Uri, flicking over and dismissing him. Hakki went straight to the Berkeley House door. He had other things on his mind.

If Uri wanted to find out what they were, and where Hakki was going, he had only one course of action: to go in with him. This he did, just behind him, thus being nicely placed to hear him speak to the doorman who had left his glassed-in cubicle to the right.

'Flat 81?'

'Yes, sir. Eighth floor, to your right as you come out of the lift.'

The doorman took Hakki across to the lift, which was straight across from the entrance, and pressed buttons for him. Meanwhile Uri Allon examined the lobby. It had four pillars. Steps led down from the right of the lift, doubtless to a basement, perhaps toilets. Stairs went up at the left. There were mirrors against the left wall. Two chandeliers hung from the ceiling.

'Sir?'

The doorman did not sound as if he really meant it. It was a sharp drop down from Wahid Hakki's sartorial elegance to Uri Allon's Burberry and trilby. Uri watched Hakki disappear into the lift and the doors shut behind him.

'Oh. This is Berkeley House. I wonder if you can tell me how I can get to Berkeley Square?'

The faintest hint of a pitying smile played about the doorman's lips; these tourists.

'Just down at the bottom of Hay Hill, sir. Fifty yards. Turn right, and you're in it.'

'Many thanks.'

He went out, gave the doorman half a minute, then came back. He could not see the doorman through the side window. The heavy door was shut, but not locked. Uri opened it naturally. If the doorman reappeared Uri would be forced to some further gem like: 'Ah. And the Berkeley *Hotel*?' But no one came. Uri moved to the mailboxes. No. 81 said Sir John Mainstree. Mainstree Oil. Uri went left to the stairs and started climbing.

He reached the eighth floor panting slightly, and found 81 a little past the lift as the doorman had said. There seemed six or seven flats to every floor. This floor was very quiet. Uri took his three skeleton keys from his pocket and worked gently at 81's lock. For the flat of a big oilman, if that is what Mainstree was, it was a surprisingly easy lock to pick.

He opened the door with infinite precaution, stepped in, and closed the door behind him, so that it rested against the opened tongue of the lock; like that he could open it with a finger to get out. He was in a hall. Four doors led off from it. From one, slightly ajar, came voices:

'. . . So you feel that he definitely accepted the commission?'

That voice was very English indeed, very Oxbridge. Mainstree?

'That was my clear impression. I took along a million dollars in hundred-dollar bills, in two briefcases, just to get things started, and as some evidence of our seriousness. He would never have accepted them if he had not fully accepted our proposition.'

That English was only fractionally less perfect. It would be Wahid Hakki; his file said that he had been educated partly in England.

There was a laugh.

'Some men would. After all, if he just kept the money, and did nothing, what redress would you have?'

That was Ben Yehuda's voice; Uri recognized it. Then Wahid Hakki's tones came back, very gravely.

'Not this one. He is a man of stature. I tell you. A great austere Islamic idealist. Also, I think, a very practical man, who will be able to get things done for us, as we could never do them ourselves. With him representing us, with him as leader within Egypt, and with merely average luck, I think we must succeed.'

'It's a great relief, then,' said Sir John Mainstree's voice, 'that he has accepted our proposal. You did a good job, Wahid. Thank you.'

So far, thought Uri Allon, they could have been discussing any giant business deal.

Now things started to come a little nearer home.

'It's nothing,' said Wahid Hakki. 'I found it an honour. This is a man of destiny. He is a man called on powerfully to mould the destinies of his country, for Islam. Perhaps change the history of the world, anyway in the whole Middle East. This man has a prophet's utter need for purity in his people, for the sake of his and their God. And he has a great warrior's courage and cunning and tenacity to achieve it. When we last met, Sir John – indeed when we *first* met – you spoke of T. E. Lawrence, and of your father's and your admiration of him. Believe me, by this giant figure that we have chosen, by the movement that *you* have initiated, for a cleansed great world religion, a cleansed great way of life, you will have left your name on the map too, Sir John. You also will have turned the world a few degrees on its axis, perhaps for ever.'

There was a silence. From it it did not sound as if Sir John Mainstree were exactly displeased by this flattering interpretation. Then came the waspish comment from Avram Ben Yehuda, perhaps, thought Uri Allon, feeling left slightly out in the cold; the practical man of action, jerking them back to reality:

'And what about the tools for the job?'

For Avram Ben Yehuda would not have had much time for mystiques of austere Islamic purity, as a means to worship a singularly exigent God, and to scrupulously living out His iron will. Ben Yehuda's only mythology, Uri Allon knew, was that of Greater Israel. But that was a strictly political, not religious, philosophy. Ben Yehuda'a Bible had only three dimensions.

'He confirmed that the group I suggested was right, and would serve.'

'Ah. Just "would serve"?'

'No. As a matter of fact, he was rather more lyrical. He described them, if I remember right, as very carefully chosen, highly trained, intelligent, and totally dedicated, their objective being the re-creation of the pure Islamic State.'

'Ah. And as good as the group that had to do with Sadat?'

'He thinks probably better. He remarked that Egypt's militant Fundamentalist groups have exploded into action cyclically in the decade or so from 1974, every few years. This time would be the fourth. Each time the government thinks it has stamped them into extinction, they rise again, more powerful, more experienced, more able than before.'

'So, probably, do the government's anti-terrorist forces,' said Ben Yehuda.

'That's quite possible,' said Wahid Hakki easily. 'We shouldn't underrate our risks.'

'It still sounds fine to me,' said the voice of Sir John Mainstree diplomatically. 'And I think we've made remarkable progress. So, presumably, our friend will now arrange a talk with the Angels?'

'I'm quite sure he's in close contact with them already,' said Wahid Hakki. 'As he was in close contact with the New Holy War. Ah, and he asked one thing in regard to them –'

'Which was?'

'He stresses that the front-line activists selected may be mildly temperamental, and ask for special weapons or explosives for the, ah, execution of their mission. If they cannot get these locally themselves, they may ask us for help.'

'Of course we'll do what we can,' said Mainstree. 'And, between the three of us, I'm sure we're not entirely without resources. And a last question for the moment, Wahid –'

'Yes?'

'When's it for?'

'Oh. Well, you know that in this year after his elections the American President is due to make his Middle East tour? That puts him in Egypt in a month or two. At that time we should have the maximum possible publicity focused on Egypt. I suggest that is the moment. If Mubarak falls then, perhaps that in itself will ignite the whole of the rest of the non-Fundamentalist Middle East – Saudi, Kuwait, the Emirates – the possibilities are staggering . . .'

The meeting thought about that. Then Mainstree said:

'Well, if it's going to be that tight, we should meet more frequently. I suggest exactly two weeks today for our next meeting.'

'You would be very welcome in Libya,' said Wahid Hakki.

'With respect,' said Mainstree, 'too many people may be watching there. I suggest the same site as our first meeting, two weeks today, 10 am. I'll book you from the evening before in the same hotel.'

'Agreed.'

'Yes, agreed.'

'Then, if you gentlemen have finished your drinks, I suggest we disband. The less time we are together, the better our security rating –'

Uri Allon heard the chairs scrape back, and slipped out of the door, relocking it like an artist. He went along the corridor away from the lift to the first corner, turned it, and stood silent, listening, as the two men left the flat, rang for the lift, and entered it. Then he walked softly to the stairs and went down them. The doorman was not away for a pee again this time when he entered the lobby. He was intent behind the glass of his cubicle over a *Standard*. He raised his eyes vaguely and Uri Allon, in cavalier spirit, raised his trilby in return. The doorman's eyes did not unglaze; his mind seemed still on his paper. Uri stepped out into the night.

Immediately out of the heavy wooden door, just to his right, he saw the taxi. It had just dropped a fare at the restaurant there: Rififi's, Dinner & Dance, Cabaret. Uri's urgent aim now was to get his murderous and priceless information to his contact at the Israeli Embassy, for immediate transmission to Abromowitz in Jerusalem and through him to Daniel Gad in Cairo. It was well after the Embassy's closing hours, but Uri knew his contact's home number and the address of his flat in Hampstead. It would be most efficient to go straight to him. But Hampstead was miles away and Uri was tired. Moreover his contact was going to have to root out a secretary and come in to the Embassy to send the coded message anyway. If Uri went out to see him it would make his night's work that much longer. And he might not even be at home. Better to ring him; there was a public phone in the Washington Hotel in Curzon Street, just round the corner off Berkeley Square. So he let the taxi go.

It was not the best decision in his life.

As he turned left down Hay Hill towards Berkeley Square he saw Avram Ben Yehuda. At twenty yards, the tall hard body, the grey camel-hair coat, and the thrusting bold brown pate with the thin reverse horseshoe of iron-grey curls slung low round it were unmistakable. That was strange. Uri had given Ben Yehuda and Hakki all of a minute's lead; he would have thought that Ben Yehuda would be out of sight by now. And, while there were some smart car showrooms to look at in Berkeley Square, there wasn't much to loiter for where Ben Yehuda was: just Riché's Ladies hairdressers, and a window advertising Chanel. Still, Ben Yehuda was quickening his pace now.

Uri followed him automatically. It was slightly off the direction he wanted for the Washington, though it was the logical way for Ben Yehuda to go if he was walking back to Claridge's. Conscientiously, Uri's instinct was to make sure that the other was doing just that. Indeed, as he expected, Ben Yehuda crossed Hay Hill to the right at the bottom, and Bruton Lane just after it, then walked past the National Westminster and the Banque Indosuez and along the north-eastern leg of Berkeley Square. Uri himself, at the bottom of Hay Hill, would normally have cut half left through the Lansdowne pedestrian passage to Curzon Street for the Washington. Instead he turned right now with Ben Yehuda. It would only take him a few minutes more; that way he would simply continue on round the square and come back to his aim.

Just before the windows to the right opulently displaying their Rolls-Royces and Jaguars, Ben Yehuda crossed to the left over the road to the pavement next to the iron railings of the gardens. Uri did the same. Under the tall trees, this pavement was darker than the first. Uri saw no other pedestrians. The gardens were already shut, the gates locked. Cars tended to keep to the other side of the road, for traffic was one-way here, clockwise round the square. There were not many cars. At the end of this pavement, thought Uri, Ben Yehuda would curve round the railings to the left, then cross over to the right past Al Saudi Banque on the corner into Davies Street, and walk up it until he reached Brook Street and Claridge's.

But he did not. As Uri turned to the left round the railings, he found Ben Yehuda there, facing him and standing easily.

'*Tislachli*, pardon,' said Ben Yehuda courteously in Hebrew.

'*Bevakasha*, please,' said Uri Allon automatically.

'It's Uri Allon, isn't it?' said Ben Yehuda. 'I thought I'd seen you rather too many times today.'

And he nodded slightly past Allon.

Uri Allon swung his head back instinctively, to the left and up, but he never got it all the way round. He had simply a very swift image of a high and extraordinarily fine-looking Arab face, then he was hit with incredible force on his spine, in the small of his back. His body arched backwards in total agony. His eyes bulging, his breath sawing sadly as he sucked it in through his open mouth. At that moment Ben Yehuda stepped in close and hit him accurately in the solar plexus with the very slim-bladed dagger in his hand, pointed slightly upwards for the heart. The force of that blow, even without the stiletto, would have been enough to paralyse him. While Hakki held Allon from behind, Ben Yehuda withdrew the dagger easily. It had left almost no mark, the cut closing up immediately. Allon was unconscious within seconds, and dead very soon. He looked curiously bloodless, though almost no blood had come out of him; his stricken heart would have pumped it instead into the cavities within his body.

The whole murder had taken only twenty seconds. Most of that time the two men had been holding him closely. To any passing driver, they would have looked like friends fondly aiding a third who had drunk too much. They turned him and hitched the top of the railing spikes through the back of his beloved Burberry, straightening the trilby on his head. Then the two men walked away, each in his separate direction, quite gracefully, and without undue haste. No one stopped them. Uri Allon stayed on his railings, spiked on them like a frog. The two others had, however, done an artistic job. He looked very life-like. He could simply have been leaning there, thinking about life. So tranquil and contemplative did he look that it was some hours before anyone actually went up to him, touched him, and discovered that he was dead.

Daniel Gad did not learn of Uri Allon's death until late the next day, through Uri's chief, Dan Abromowitz. Ironically, at the same hour Gad received a small package by special delivery from Jerusalem. He opened it. It was an exquisite ring of filigreed silver and granulated gold, with a tiny model building in place of a stone. An explanatory note had thoughtfully been included: 'A Jewish marriage ring of the sixteenth century made in Venice, to be worn on the middle finger of the bride's right hand. Mounted on the wide band is a bezel, the model of a building with a cupola representing a synagogue or the marital home. Inscribed within the band is *Mazel Tov*, Good Luck. It can also be worn as a locket, the bezel being hinged to take a token.'

A separate note said: 'A Gift of Friendship, for your Lady – Uri Allon.'

# 14

# A Sword for the Angels

'You ask why I said nothing at the meeting?' said Avram Ben Yehuda, two weeks later, as he looked down from the large and luxurious penthouse flat in Patriarco Ioakim in Athens' Kolonaki, on to the sun-drenched green square bounded by Souidias and Elvetias. 'It was because I then had nothing to say, Sir John. It was only when I was going down in the lift afterwards with Wahid Hakki here that the thing struck me. In fact it was something that *you* said towards the end that triggered it. Do you remember that when Wahid suggested that we meet next in Libya you declined, saying that too many people might be watching there?'

'Of course,' said Mainstree. 'Yes, I remember.'

'Your word "watching" did it. The moment I got in the lift I knew suddenly that I was *already* being watched. By a stubby man in a macintosh and a grey trilby hat. He'd got out of his taxi just ahead of Berkeley House when I got there. He, or someone very like him, had been a little behind me when I registered at Claridge's. Again, he was somewhere in the lobby, hat in hand, when I left for Berkeley House. I couldn't recall him at Heathrow, but the huge crowds mask things there. However, I thought I *could* now half-remember him in the departure lounge at Lod. It was hard, because he was inconspicuous. So inconspicuous he was probably professional. Then I knew I knew him: Uri Allon, Mossad. I had even met him somewhere. Many Mossad people in Israel live under

222

the fond illusion that no one knows who they really are, but Israel is a small country, and *some* of us know who some of *them* are.

'So I told Wahid my fear. I couldn't be absolutely sure, but we could check. I asked Wahid to go up to the right when he left the building, and wait some twenty or thirty metres up Hay Hill. I'd be at the same distance the other way, looking ostentatious. We'd give it five minutes. If nothing happened, fine. If Allon picked up my trail again, that would be decisive, and we'd have to – deal with him. Within half a minute he came *out of Berkeley House itself* – where presumably he'd been trying to listen in to our meeting – and came straight after me. You know the rest. I phoned you an hour later from Claridge's, as a semi-warning, to say that we two had had a wild evening after we left you, but that you were not to worry, everything was fine, and the plans should stay just the same. So Wahid and I got off on our flights next morning as scheduled, no problems.'

'I took the meaning,' said Mainstree. 'Fortunately the papers didn't play it up much. He wasn't famous and apparently you didn't leave much blood around. The police have been making inquiries in the area, but not too hard. Maybe they see it as just another Israeli–PLO settlement of accounts. The Berkeley House doorman – so he tells me – identified him as a man who had come into the lobby at ten that night and asked the way to Berkeley Square. Presumably for the tryst with his killer. But that seems as far as it goes till now – no pointers towards us. Again fortunately; I'd hate to change my flat for jail. They're excellent flats.'

'They could of course track back to me, conceivably,' said Ben Yehuda, 'since Allon was staying in the room next to mine at Claridge's. I asked to see the register when I got back, on the pretext that I thought I'd written my home address wrong. If the police know that, they have only to ask if any other Israelis were staying at Claridge's that night, then to learn from the Berkeley House doorman that Allon came into the lobby within what must have been minutes of my going up to Flat 81. It could then get awkward for all of us. So I think I'll give the

UK a miss for a few years. It's no hardship. I don't go there much anyway – Amsterdam's my European city, for my diamonds business. But if the British police can't firmly establish the link with me, then I think that you are both fairly safe.'

'I have my diplomatic passport anyway,' said Wahid Hakki. 'That can cover a multitude of sins.'

'As a matter of interest,' said Sir John Mainstree, 'how did you do it?'

'Kill him? Well,' said Ben Yehuda, 'Wahid hit him hard in the back and held him, and I hit him in the front with this.'

Resting his left elbow on the beautifully polished dark mahogany table round which the three again sat rather formally, by the sitting room's wide windows, Ben Yehuda twisted his forearm upwards, slightly pulled back his jacket sleeve, and with his right hand pulled the dagger from its sheath. The dagger had a fine small guard of silver and a haft just thick and long enough to grip firmly, and covered with what looked like some non-slip material like shagreen, with a scrolled silver ball at the top. The blade was five inches long, two-edged, and extraordinarily slim, not more than a quarter of an inch across. Except for that noble handle, it looked like a flattened icepick. Both edges of this thin blade shone brightly, from evident loving care.

'God Almighty, man, you don't wander through Airport Security wearing that damned thing, do you? Don't their metal detectors pick it up?'

'No, no, be at ease. I always travel with it in my suitcase in the baggage compartment. I don't think they X-ray those so thoroughly, or perhaps I've just been lucky. But I haven't needed it yet during flights.'

'I hope that situation lasts,' said Mainstree. 'From the look of it, you could shave with it.'

'You could. It's very sharp. And quite effective.'

'Lethal. You've shown that. Fortunately for us.'

'Mossad must still be watching you,' said Wahid Hakki, 'and presumably with much more suspicion than before?'

'It's logical to suppose that, though I've seen no concrete

sign of them this time. They could have had someone on my flight here yesterday. I didn't try to cover my tracks at all to the Grande Bretagne. But this morning I went up to the Plaka and walked fast through its twisted streets and stairways and changed taxis three times before getting here. No one followed me here.'

'I've been keeping an eye down on Ioakim and the square,' said Hakki. 'I've not seen anyone steady down there.'

'They'll get tired of it,' said Ben Yehuda. 'Maybe they already have. They can suspect me all they like, so long as they have no hard proof. And they don't. Suspecting me won't break my bones. They'll drop it.'

'You don't think they'd ask Greek Intelligence to keep an eye on you if you come over here again?'

'Not a chance,' said Ben Yehuda. 'Greece has always hated Israel. They'd never cooperate.'

'Then if that's that,' said Hakki, 'I too have an item on lethal weapons.' Seeing that he had their full attention, he went on: 'Our friend from Cairo contacted me just as he said he would, by a letter which a friend of his posted to me in Tripoli from Athens. He says the method of execution and the executioner are already decided. It's sniping, and the sniper is one of the best cell leaders that the Angels of the Sword have. And, it goes without saying, probably the best shot. He would like a particular telescopic-sighted rifle which he says can be bought in London. Apparently he's used the type before, with positive results. Before I give you its details, let me stress one thing. The fact that Abdel Aziz has already gone this far this fast is the most conclusive proof we could ask for that he is now completely committed to our cause. And, incidentally, that the Angels of the Sword themselves are too. At this pace, I think that we cannot fail.'

'Excellent news,' said Mainstree. 'Things are moving indeed. Tell us now of this rifle.'

Wahid Hakki opened the left side of his very light-grey linen jacket. They saw the flash of darker grey silk lining. He brought out a folded sheet of paper.

'I typed it myself from the letter.'

Mainstree read it out aloud:

'Finland Sako Finnbear rifle, calibre .30–06, four-round magazine, overall length 1125 mm, barrel 610 mm, weight 3.7 kg, with German 'Original' (Japanese-made) telescopic sight with tube diameter 26 mm, and high ring mounts. Plus 50 Sako soft-nosed .30–06 cartridges. Available from Oy Sako Ab, SF 11100 RIIHIMAKI 10, Finland, Phone 914–37444, telex 15247, cables SAKO RIIHIMAKI. Also in London from Collins Bros (The Southern Armoury) Gun and Rifle Makers Ltd, 171 New Kent Road, SE1, Phone 407–2278, where approximate prices: rifle £350, telescopic sight £50, high mount rings £50.'

Mainstree looked up.

'The gentleman sounds as though he knows what he wants,' said Ben Yehuda.

'It's a very good sign,' said Sir John Mainstree. 'In shooting, it's really knowing your gun that matters.'

'That doesn't sound much for a specialist sniper's rifle.'

'It's not. A good London gunmaker's price for an equivalent of .30–06 calibre and telescopic sight would cost you up to £3,000, delivery six to twelve months. Say a John Rigby gun, from 13 Pall Mall. But I've heard that Sako make a good rifle. The price is lower because Sako's is more like mass production and anyway the Finns are keen on hard currency. John Rigby builds his guns by hand and he'll practically tailor your rifle to your individual needs. The important thing here is to give our Angel the kind of gun he knows and wants.'

'That calibre's big enough for what we need?'

'What d'you want, a .50 calibre heavy machinegun? A .30–06, particularly with a soft-nosed bullet, will bring down something much bigger than a President.'

'Like?'

Mainstree glanced at him.

'Like a very big buck, an eland, say. Or a lion, even.'

'It's that powerful?'

'Yes. Look, against lion I'd use a .470 double-barrelled rifle; like the one you may have noticed against the wall in my study. That's a Rigby, running at about £11,000 these days. But you know the most heartening thing about our Angel, the most professional? He's chosen a solidly mounted rifle which will be completely shot in when he goes into action with it. That is, it'll shoot exactly where he aims it. He's not gone for any of this crap of collapsible telescopic-sighted rifles which you just screw together the moment before you shoot your victim, as you see on the films. That's for the birds. You're almost *bound* to have sighting errors every time you stick one of those amateur toys together. And you've only got to have your sights a hair's breadth off line to miss a man by a full yard if you're shooting at a distance of two hundred.'

'How do we get the gun?' said Wahid Hakki.

'I can do that, or get it done,' said Mainstree, 'seeing that I'm the one of us who lives in London. And I know Collins of the Southern Armoury; I sometimes see him at Bisley Camp, in Surrey.'

'You don't have any licence problems with the police with a rifle like that?' asked Ben Yehuda.

'Not if you're a member of one of the National Rifle Association's rifle clubs, as I am. Then you simply register it with them.'

'What then?' said Ben Yehuda.

Mainstree shrugged.

'Then I just file off the serial numbers and report to the police that, most regrettably, someone has broken into the locked boot of my car and stolen the rifle and let's say some car tools while I was parked for a drink at a pub one evening on my way back from Bisley. I'll see that the story's credible too. I'll take the rifle down to Bisley with me in fact, and make sure some other members see me shooting it in – a job which I'd like to do for our friend the Angel anyway.'

'It's putting you to a lot of trouble personally,' said Hakki.

Sir John Mainstree smiled, turning his bushy silver-grey eyebrows at him.

'Not at all. I like rifles. It's a pity I didn't show you my gun room while we were in my flat. Also, the more we can keep this thing in our own hands in our own countries, the less chance there is of a leak.'

'True.'

'What concerns me,' said Mainstree, 'is how we get the rifle from me to the Angel.'

'I can do that,' said Wahid Hakki. 'I have to be in London again on Thursday next week for one of my father's companies. If you can have the rifle ready and shot in by then, I'll take it back with me by air.'

'If Colins has a .30–06 Finnbear with telescopic sight in stock, and I'll check that the moment I get back to London tomorrow morning, then I can certainly have it shot in and with the serial numbers filed off by next Saturday. You'll have no problems with Customs?'

'I think it's very unlikely. First, I'll be coming in my father's Lear Jet, because three of the other members of the company's board are needed in London too. And Customs are generally easy with private aircraft, certainly on those leaving, as regards security – with good reason, because if we *are* taking a bomb on board, the only people we'll be blowing up would be ourselves. And even if British Security *did* catch me with it, I'd just say I'd bought it from a man I met in the hotel bar, at a price I couldn't resist. I was taking it back to my own country to shoot desert foxes, meaning no harm, except to them. My story would be quite consistent with your report to the police, Sir John, because my unknown bar friend could perfectly well be the man who broke into your car, or his fence. No, I foresee no problem. Remember, I always have my diplomatic passport. And of course the Libyan authorities won't touch me.'

'Excellent. But then from Libya into Egypt?'

'Ah. Do you have a map of North Africa?'

'Of course. Just a minute.'

Mainstree got up and went to the bookcase at the far wall, and his tall body bent down to the lowest shelf, his silver-grey hair flopping forward over his forehead. He came back with a tall, broad hard-covered book.

'The New Oxford Atlas, Revised Edition, no less,' he said cheerfully, and turned to the country index on the back inner flap of the dust cover. 'Libya, North Africa, pages 78 and 79.' He opened the large volume at these pages and laid it before

Hakki. Mainstree stayed standing at Hakki's left elbow, and Ben Yehuda got up and stood at his right.

'We'll take off on Saturday about midday,' said Hakki, 'unless the weather's pretty dirty. The first Lear leg is six hundred miles London to Marseilles, where we'll land and refuel and probably have lunch, then fly on the eight-hundred-mile leg to Tripoli, getting in at say 3.30 pm. If you would be so kind, Sir John, as to have the rifle and telescopic sight and ammunition packed securely in a suitcase or bag, then as soon as we're clear after landing at Tripoli I can hand the bag on intact for its next leg on the relay to Cairo, that will be the six hundred miles or say nine fifty kilometres just about due east along the coast to Tobruk here; I'll use either a twin-engined Cessna for that, or the Lear Jet; I'll have to check to see if Tobruk can handle the Lear; probably yes. You could help with the suitcase, Sir John?'

'Of course,' said Mainstree. 'With pleasure. Now our Angel says that a Sako Finnbear .30–06 is 1125 millimetres in overall length. One metre 125 millimetres, which is – let me consult my pocket calculator – just over 44 inches. That, diagonally, still argues a fairly big suitcase; I'll check to see if the big Samsonite with the cypher spin-lock could take it. If not, some other rigid case that I could padlock and give you the key. No trouble.'

'*Taayib,* fine. From Tobruk the same agent that I've put in charge of the bag at Tripoli takes it in a four-wheel-drive jeep two hundred miles, let's say three hundred kilometres, just about due south into the Libyan Desert – there's a rough road, as you can see marked here – to Jarabub. Here my agent parks his jeep with a friend and changes into flowing desert robes with a headdress held down by black *ogals* and all until he looks just like a *Badawi.* Which is just as well, because that's effectively what he's going to be for the next twenty-four hours of his life or so.

'This is because two genuine members of the club, two full-time *Badu,* are going to trot him and his bag across the border into Egypt on their camels, somewhere south of Jarabub. The Egyptians won't stop them? You're right; they won't. Libya has eleven hundred kilometres of frontier in common with Egypt, all of it desert. You can't patrol all that desert efficiently all the time, particularly not against *Badu*. The Bedouins don't recognize frontiers. They define themselves by their tribes and blood loyalties, which can overlap many boundaries. The Egyptians tend to leave them alone, particularly in the deep desert. They find them alien. The Egyptians have never really understood the Bedouins, or wanted to. At worst, they develop a self-protective contempt for them. Having spent all their seven thousand years of civilization clinging desperately to the ribbon of arable land on either side of the Nile, the blister of El Fayyoum to the west of it, and to the green fan of the Delta to the north, they are probably the Arab or Islamic nation which has the least natural affinity with the desert or its nomadic Bedouins. They fear them both. The *Badu* know that. They know too that, on their own terrain, they can always outwit the Egyptians. So these two *Badu* will get my agent and his precious suitcase through all right. Where to? Waahit Síiwa, Siwa Oasis, you see it here? About a hundred kilometres from Jarabub as the crow flies.'

'I see there's a road marked from Jarabub to Siwa Oasis,' said Ben Yehuda. 'They couldn't take that?'

Hakki looked up round to the right at him.

'They could,' he said, 'but the Egyptian Frontier Police aren't entirely cretinous. They put on a good show on things like roads, at frontiers. They would certainly be inquisitive about what was in my agent's bag.'

'I retract,' said Ben Yehuda.

'Siwa's a great place,' said Hakki informatively, perhaps to make up for the slight acerbity of his previous words. 'It goes back a long way in history. Did you know that Alexander the Great went there in 331 BC, after he had defeated Darius at Issus, probably to ask the Oracle of Ammon to confirm that he was the son of Zeus? Alexander and his party took eight days to cover the 300 kilometres southwest from Mersa Matruh on the coast. They got lost in a desert sandstorm. In a few days their water was gone, and they faced a terrible death by thirst. It clouded over, and a storm broke "not without the help of the gods". They refilled their leather waterbottles and pressed on through hills and down a ravine to sandy plains covered with shells which at night reflected the moonbeams so that all the plains glittered and shimmered. They passed through a gorge black as Erebus. They were lost again. A pair of talking snakes put them back on the track. Alexander never told what the Oracle revealed to him in the innermost shrine of the Temple of Ammon, but from Siwa he went on to conquer the whole known world, and die –'

'May our secret Finnbear rifle, passing through Siwa too, cause as epic a change in the world's history,' said Mainstree.

'My second agent will wait there,' said Hakki. 'He's based in Mersa Matruh and he's worked for me for years. He'll take the rifle by taxi back from Siwa to Mersa Matruh – still a rough eight-hour trip – then along the coast road through Sidi Abd er-Rahman and El Alamein. Egypt has police and army roadblocks along all that coast out of fear of a Libyan putsch, but my man's well known, and for any dangerous trip I always fit him out with lots of *Playboys* and *Penthouses* –'

'What on earth's the sense of that?' said Ben Yehuda.

'Most Egyptian troops will do almost anything for a couple of cigarettes and a good girlie magazine,' said Hakki. 'The language doesn't matter – they probably can't read anyway; it's the pictures they like. My man'll be OK. Before Alexandria he'll turn off southeast at El Amariya into the Desert Road to Cairo. Mersa Matruh–Cairo's some 500 kilometres, say another seven hours. I don't want to *fly* the rifle-suitcase that stretch; too conspicuous. Anyway, the whole trip from my landing at say 3.30 pm at Tripoli on Saturday next week to delivering the goods in Zamalek shouldn't take much more than two days. So I'll reply today from here to Abdel Aziz's letter telling him to expect a package on the Monday afternoon or evening following my Saturday arrival in Tripoli. He'll be a happy man.'

'So will our Angel,' said Mainstree. 'So should we all be. It's working out.'

'It's as well that we're moving fast,' said Ben Yehuda. 'You've seen the latest dates for the American President's visit to Cairo? October 6 to 8. That's only a month away. It's another thing too. Have you noticed?'

A few seconds later Wahid Hakki said:

'My God! Of course, October 6, the anniversary of Sadat's launching of his nearly victorious war against Israel in 1973. *And* the anniversary of Sadat's own execution. What an irony if we could kill Mubarak on that same date!'

'Why don't we make that our aim?' said Avram Ben Yehuda.

'Indeed,' said Mainstree. 'It's totally logical. A little uncanny, even. It's as though this thing is now generating its own fatality.'

'All the more reason that we should keep meeting regularly, then,' said Ben Yehuda. 'When and where do we meet next?'

'Perhaps here's safest,' said Mainstree. 'Again at 10 am in two weeks? Then say weekly?'

The other two nodded.

'Good,' said Mainstree. 'By the time we next meet we'll have delivered our Angel the sword he wanted. From then on it will be up to him, Abdel Aziz, and the gods.'

# 15

# *A Walk in the Hills*

Muhammed Abbas Sidki, major in the Egyptian Commandos, holder of the Star of the Sinai, had seen the flicker of movement a hundred metres away, just as he rounded the rocky outcrop. He froze at once himself, and sat down very quietly indeed, three-quarters behind the outcrop, the large hard-composition suitcase which he had been carrying completely behind it. He spun the six-digit code to open it. The Angels' sponsor in London, whoever he was, had set the number at 061085, clearly for 6 October 1985, the target date. No doubt, to be practical, he had chosen these figures as ones they would be unlikely to forget. Perhaps he had also wanted to show his solidarity with them in this date which could change the face of the world.

The Sako Finnbear .30–06 rifle, the telescopic sight fixed on its high ring mounts, was packed in two towels so that it sat diagonally very snugly in the case. The fifty rounds of soft-nosed ammunition, the screw-in sections of the cleaning rod, the detachable wire brushes, pull-through cord and packets of four-by-two cleaning felts, and the bottles of rifle oil, were also packed in a towel and set firmly in the case in the triangle under the rifle. His body half twisted round, Abbas Sidki unsheathed the rifle and put three rounds in the magazine, then closed the bolt on the first to set it securely in the firing chamber. He put on the thumb safety catch. Abbas could shoot from either shoulder, though he preferred the right, but here he was at the left of the outcrop, so he peered round it very gently with the Sako to his left shoulder.

The desert fox, a respectable hundred metres away, was brought sharply forward by the telescope; he could have been ten or fifteen metres off. He was sitting in the sun by another outcrop, which presumably contained his burrow, cheerfully minding his own business. Abbas knew that he was a *Fennecus zerda*, a small brand of fox about seventy centimetres or a little over two feet from the tip of his nose to the end of his tail, with huge rounded ears that carried a copious blood supply in their large surface area – a bright device for losing body heat fast. His fur was an elegant brownish-yellow, shading to black at the end of his bushy tail. *Fennecus* lived off jerboas, rodents, birds, lizards, locusts and fruits. He was normally a nocturnal character, but he was also acutely sensitive to cold. Perhaps his burrow had chilly drafts. Here anyway he was, basking unabashed in the sun, gazing to Abbas's left.

Abbas Sidki slipped off the safety catch and took up the pressure very gradually on the trigger with the ball of his left forefinger. The action was hair-fine. He had not altered the initial setting at all. The Sako Finnbear fired itself, practically all on its own. There was a sharp whipcrack. It echoed against the harsh light yellow hills.

The fox had disappeared. Disappointed, Abbas Sidki got to his feet. He had had the impression that he was dead on his aim when the Sako had fired itself. He had been told when the rifle filtered through to him two days before that it had been shot in by an expert in London. His miss now meant either that the sights had come off line in the voyage – though the rifle had been packed very firmly in the tough composition suitcase – or that he was shooting badly, or both. Either fault could be disastrous at this late stage; 6 October was in just on two weeks' time.

He walked forward to the other outcrop to see if he could trace where his shot had gone, still carrying the Sako Finnbear. It seemed a pity if it – or he – was shooting badly, for it looked a beautifully built rifle, with a pistol-grip chequered walnut stock and cheekpiece, a thoughtfully designed thick rubber pad at the butt to take up some of the recoil (which you noticed; there was a powerful charge in those cartridges), and that smooth glitter of high-precision engineering to its barrel, telescope, and bolt and trigger actions. He had been so impressed (now, it seemed prematurely) by his first look at it that he had at once ruled out any question of having a silencer fitted (which the Angels' Higher Council had offered; they had access to a reasonably good armoury). Abbas had reasoned that the Egyptian armourer, however good he was, was going to have to cut some sort of nicks or grooves in the Finnbear's barrel to take a silencer securely; if he did not, the damned thing would probably fall off each time he shot. But if the gunsmith started cutting into that barrel he would almost certainly thrown it or the telescope sight out of kilter to at least some degree, necessitating a complete re-shooting-in for the rifle. Abbas hated the idea of their doing all that, and still not getting the re-shoot completely right. His soul rebelled at the thought of spoiling, or of not handling completely pro-fessionally, what looked like a precision instrument.

If this was his conclusive argument against fitting a silencer, he had another, more private. If he did his sniper's work properly, he should need only one shot. That must attract attention, but not necessarily fatally, if the crowds were thick and the noise heavy anyway. As he was planning things, he would still have a fair chance to escape. Yet Khalid el Islambouli, when he ran over to the reviewing stand before virtually the entire Egyptian army to shoot Sadat to death, had no such chance and must have known he had none. How then could he, Muhammed Abbas Sidki, honourably add a silencer which could prejudice the success of this whole great act, simply to improve his chance of survival, already infinitely higher than El Isambouli's had been? Islam taught that there should be a just measure in all things.

Ten metres before the second outcrop he saw the small bundle of fur. It had fallen half behind a large stone. He walked to it and bent over it. He had aimed at the left side of the desert fox's chest. That was where he had hit. The right side was not there, nor was the rest of the right side of the body. Only the head was intact, neat and in repose. Poor small beast, thought Abbas Sidki, I should never have done it. He knew that *Fennecus* was a sociable sort of fellow, easily domesticated, then very affectionate. Yet the incident had seemed a token of some kind. It seemed no accident that the desert fox should have sat in the sun at his outcrop, and that Abbas should have rounded his, one hundred metres away, at just that moment. The small killing had been a test and a proof, a kind of dry run. It was symbolic of the eclipsing at another level of a life more resounding than the fox's. By it Abbas Sidki knew his rifle, and knew that it was absolutely true. It was a lightning discovery, a trust, an intuitive certainty. The rifle would work with him now, comfortably as part of him, like a hand or a leg. He knew now that he would not fail in his killing. He would hit where he aimed.

This sudden and, to Abbas Sidki, most encouraging knowledge made the rest of his planned trial of the rifle somewhat superfluous, but he determined to go ahead with it nonetheless. First, however, he disposed decently of the desert fox. He went to the nearest patch of soft sand and dug a hole in it with his hands, then came back and picked up the gutted fox carefully by its huge sound ears, parked it in the hole, and packed the sand back solidly over it. The small animal might well, after all, have its niche in Egypt's future history. Islam held that animals had souls too; a good Muslim, after cutting the throat of a sheep correctly for eating, would hold its body steady while it died, so that its spirit might escape from its body without let.

Abbas had set out that Friday after his noon prayers in the mosque. This was Allah's day but, as he saw it, what he was doing was very much Allah's work. He had come to a place of great beauty if, like Abbas, you liked the austere and majestic. At about Kilometre 80 on the 122-kilometre Desert Road from Cairo to Suez, there was a narrow asphalted road which led off at ninety degrees to the right. You could easily miss it if you were not looking out carefully for it. A small square blockhouse stood on one side at the entrance, and quite often this side road was shut by a wooden pole or by empty oildrums. Abbas Sidki had never seen more than one army private on duty here. This slim road ran for fifty kilometres across the Gebel Ataqa, Ataga Mountain, to a point forty kilometres south of Suez, on the Gulf of Suez and the Red Sea. Rather over two-thirds of the way along this side road, another asphalted road branched off, to the west, and to a fairly big cement works that could perhaps be seen as of some strategic importance. The troop at the blockhouse on the main Cairo–Suez road often, in any event, put on a creditable performance to any drivers trying to enter the slim road from there. The riposte, for any of the rare *khawwaghat* or foreigners who wanted to use this road, was the invariable two or three cigarettes and a girlie magazine.

Some of the more adventurous tourists or foreigners working in the country had discovered that this was a short cut through to the Red Sea, usefully avoiding the chaos of Suez. From where this side road reached the coast it was only some fifteen kilometres to 'Ein Sukhna, Hot Spring, just beyond which was a sea of so turquoise a clarity that the heart sang, and some superb white sand beaches. The huge popularity this area merited was denied because visitors still blew themselves up at times on the mines. From 1967 until the peace treaty of 1979 this was of course a front line with Israel. When it ceased to be the Egyptians found that they had misplaced the maps of their own minefields. From 'Ein Sukhna for sixty kilometres south the arid light-yellow mountains crowded down to the sea, whorled and eerie as landscapes of the moon, the wadis cut into them like deep dead tear ducts.

It was these mountains that fascinated Abbas Sidki; a forgotten stark face of his country. The hills of the Gebel Ataqa were like them, though not so high, 870 against 1260 metres, 2,900 against some 4,000 feet. But the magic was the same. From the blockhouse he had driven seven kilometres south across an arid plain flat as glass, then veered east into the first line of hills, sheer as the rim of the world. The thin road twisted and turned. It ran past beds of soda, floods of rock. The hills about him, above all to the east, carved and writhed in convulsions, were suddenly frozen terrifically for eternity, shrieked silently of some agony of the world an infinity ago. The light played tricks here. There was almost always a bloom to it, even to the stars at night. By day it made these grave and tortured lands a kind of silk carpet. Their aspect changed hourly with the fall of the light. At sunset they shaded from pink to purple. In the same spot you could be in two totally different worlds at dawn and at dusk. Probably the greatest error of people about deserts, thought Abbas Sidki, was to imagine them all of sand. This was not true, nor could you anywhere see that better than here. You could have whole runs of sheer hard rock, then whirls of cliffs, then great falls. You could find sudden sprays of great boulders. Indeed there was always sand somewhere, sometimes in patches, sometimes in great lakes, pure and white and soft, and fatal to vehicles.

Abbas did not take his Fiat 127 that far off any run of hard earth that Friday, though he did not stop till he was twenty kilometres from the main Cairo–Suez road, and two from the slim side road. This place's virtue was not just its harsh beauty, but also its solitude. Few would hear his spaced shots here, let alone challenge him. That last risk was anyway minimized by his commando major's uniform and Star of the Sinai. These had caused the soldier at the small blockhouse almost to break his back with the force of his salute before he wheeled an oildrum aside to let Abbas Sidki through; he had never before been so near to so much military rank and glory in his life. Few others who might meet Abbas Sidki so accoutred that Friday afternoon in the Gebel Ataqa would be likely to treat him with any less deference.

In fact he met no one. After the fox he shot only four times more; after that first shot, he did not really need even this small confirmation. He shot against nothing else living, but all four times against the metre-square canvas target he had taken from his camp; he had built a light collapsible wooden frame for it in his room in Bab el Louk. He set it up at the fox's rocky outcrop, then fired three times at it from his outcrop a hundred metres away, once standing, once lying prone, raised on his elbows, and once from a sitting position, which was his favourite, with his elbows resting on his knees. Then he shot once from two hundred metres, again from his favourite position.

He walked afterwards up to the target. All four shots were in the bull's-eye, no one impact more than ten centimetres from another. They made a pretty pattern. Abbas looked at the rifle in his hands, then round him at the rim of uncanny hills. He was supremely happy. He glanced then up at the sun, and down at his watch. It was already the hour of the 'asr, the mid-afternoon prayer, or a little after.

It seemed to him a very apt moment at which to pray to God. Since he had no water for his *wudow*, his preparation for prayer, he used sand instead, as was permitted. He went down on his knee at a patch of dry sand and struck his palms upon it, then wiped them over his face. He put his palms on the sand again, then with his left palm wiped his right hand and arm up to the elbow, and with his right his left hand and arm. His symbolic washing finished, he stood and turned to face south-southeast, which was where he judged Mecca to lie. He advised God how many inclinations of the head his prayers were going to represent, then, raising his open hands to each side of his head, said 'Allāhu Akbar!', 'God is great!' and, gazing steadily at the spot on the sand which he would later touch with his nose and his forehead in his prostrations, recited the Koran's opening and its 112th sura. He then said 'Allāhu Akbar!' again, and went into the standard series of inclinations of the head and body and other prayers, ending with the one hundred and two repetitions of the perfection and greatness of God which he patterned by clicking through his *sibhah* beads.

When Abbas had finished, he packed the Sako Finnbear back carefully in its suitcase. He would pour boiling water through the barrel and wire-brush it – very lightly indeed, for force here could spoil the rifling – then pull slightly oiled four-by-twos through it as soon as he got back to his room in Bab El Louk, and perhaps rub some wood oil into the stock to keep it at its optimum beauty. Abbas Sidki walked back the five hundred metres to his Fiat 127, a very contented man. He drove it back the two kilometres of hard earth and rock to the slim asphalted road, then the twenty kilometres north to the main road. The soldier at the blockhouse had evidently been waiting for him, for he had rolled the oildrum out of the way already. He performed more heroics in saluting Abbas. Abbas waited for a gap in the traffic, then crossed to the other side and turned left, to drive the eighty kilometres west to Cairo, into the eye of the sun. He pulled down the car's visor against that. Despite it he still felt that God was very good. It was as well, for he had more work to do for Him that night.

'The day is set as October 6,' said Abbas Sidki. 'And, as you know, our cell has been honoured with the noblest task.'

The three men and the girl, Zeinab Marzuk, gazed back at him. There was Fuad Wahbah, the civil engineer, dark, heavy-shouldered, the boxer. And Omar el Masri, Omar the Egyptian, the fourth-year medical student, taller, fair and blue-eyed, those features perhaps bequeathed him by some Napoleonic multi-great-grandfather or British equivalent. The third man, Ali Sarawi, replaced Abdallah Hassan the dead chemist. Sarawi was a modern-languages graduate, fluent in English and French. He was a small tight dark man, with very black hair and closely set features. He looked like a button. He was no new recruit, but had been with the Angels for two years, in another cell. After Hassan had killed himself to keep his Angels cell inviolate, and when the shape of the plan to assassinate Mubarak was already forming, the Upper Council transferred Sarawi to Abbas's cell. His huge worth there was that he was a department head in the Egyptian Ministry of Foreign Affairs, located on its triangular site in a gracious high-ceilinged building at the start of Tahrir Bridge and opposite the august and still sadly vacant headquarter offices of the Arab League. In his position Sarawi had access to the latest information about the American President's and Mubarak's route through Cairo on 6 October. The Upper Council had instructed Abbas Sidki to carry out his execution during this trajectory, when the eyes of the world would be most closely focused on Cairo and Egypt and the impact of a President's death at its most incendiary.

Wherever the eyes of the world might choose to focus, it was evident to anyone in this room that Zeinab had eyes for only Abbas Sidki in it.

The four men and the girl sat that day in the Angels' safe house in Sharia el Mansuriya. Abbas sat in the black wooden throne of a chair in which they had bound and killed Talkhan. The other four fanned round him.

'It's now certain, as from today,' said Ali Sarawi, the department head from Foreign Affairs, 'that they will take exactly the same route from the airport through Cairo as Sadat took with Carter in 1979.'

This news was invaluable. By getting it Sarawi had justified his whole existence.

'It seems incredible that they haven't changed,' said Fuad Wahbah, the boxer. 'Aren't they *asking* for someone to try to shoot or bomb him, if they stick to exactly the same route?'

'Maybe they see it simplistically,' said Omar el Masri, Omar the Egyptian. 'If nobody attacked on this route last time, then nobody attacks this time.'

'There's no change *at all*?' asked Abbas.

Ali Sarawi's small button face observed him alertly.

'One. From Ramses Square to the Ramses Hilton bleed-off they take the new flyover. It gives Mubarak a chance to show off how modern we are. Also, as you know, the Sharia el Gala'a alternative is bleak in the extreme. I don't think the new flyover was finished when Carter was here.'

'No. But the rest's the same?'

'Yes. The Americans confirmed it as suitable for them today. I dropped into the ministry on my way here and saw the telex. So they come off the flyover at the Ramses Hilton, then turn left and south past the Egyptian Museum – our visitor has to be made to feel he's seeing some of the right things, even if he never actually gets *inside* them – then up into Liberation Square, which all the guide books tell us is the heart of the city, then between the Arab League building and my ministry onto Tahrir Bridge. Splendid view of the Nile north and south. Past the Borg Hotel and the Cairo Tower and the Exhibition Grounds on Gezira, then across the bridge over the Nile tributary and left at the Sheraton Hotel into Sharia el Giza, and all the way out to Giza and the Pyramids and the Mena House Hotel where we lodge our distinguished friend.'

'This is music to me,' said Abbas Sidki. 'It's the centre that concerns me. And the centre seems sure.'

'Yes, the centre's sure.'

'And the times again?'

'Reconfirmed as: Arrival of Air Force One at Cairo Airport: 9.30 am. No customs or immigration formalities, of course. The cars pick up our visitors and their entourage at the plane. The leading car is of course open, and both Presidents will be standing, just like Sadat and Carter, in the centre of the city, from the bleed-off from the flyover up past the Egyptian Museum into Midan el Tahrir, then on to the bridge past the Borg Hotel and the tower, then off the other side into Dokki and past the Sheraton into Sharia el Giza. That's not so far to have to stand, when you consider that it's the only parade the public's going to get this October 6. For Mubarak's still opposed to any kind of military review or parade to mark that anniversary. I mean, Sadat was always insisting on those, and look where they got him! To complete the timetable, and it's only approximate, the leading car's due to reach Midan el Tahrir at 10 am and Mena House Hotel at 10.40.'

'*Mumtáz!*' said Abbas Sidki. 'Excellent!'

'Our cell's strike won't be the Angels' only action that day, will it?' said Fuad Wahbah, his body hunched, his powerful shoulders forward.

Abbas looked at him for a few seconds, then at the other two.

'What I tell you now I do not have officially,' he said. 'You know our cardinal operational principle: we in the activist cells never have a complete picture of the Upper Council's strategy and battle plans. It's our best self-protection, because if one cell is broken, and its members tortured – and, as you know, our enemies are certainly ruthless enough to do that – it *cannot* betray its fellow cells, and only the cell leader could betray his link upwards to the Upper Council, and that link is only one man.

'So I can tell you only what I think, and guess. You must take what I say as no more than that. Well then, I think that, the moment the execution of the Abomination is confirmed, at least twenty – and probably more – Angels activist cells or hit squads will attack and take the television and radio stations, then announce, by pre-recorded films and tapes, our objective of taking power and turning Egypt away from selling our soul to America, from corruption, and from betraying our Arab brothers in Palestine and the Lebanon, and towards and into a full Islamic Republic; and we shall exhort the people to rise with us, and overthrow their betrayers. The bulk of the hit teams will attack and take the key army camps, police stations and arsenals in and around Cairo, including those in Shubra and Giza. Some teams will take key mosques and spur our cheated population to take to the streets and to wreak vengeance on their traitorous masters. Other specialist hit teams will seek out the top three or four hundred leaders in the Establishment, men and women, politicians and senior officers and business directors and members of Mubarak's tame 'Ulama and journalists and academics, all who have been against us and whom we have watched for years, so that we know in all detail their daily – and nightly – timetables and patterns of behaviour. These we shall judge and execute summarily. We want none of them in our Islamic Republic; none can be saved. We have the organization, the knowledge and the weapons to do this in Cairo – we must have forty or fifty caches of arms, ammunition and explosive hidden throughout the city in safe Angels houses. And above all we have the will, our enemies can come nowhere near to us in that.

'Nor shall we strike them only in Cairo,' said Abbas Sidki, his black eyes glittering, his rich voice mesmeric, 'but simultaneously at every other major city and town in Egypt, including Alexandria, Port Said, Ismailia, Suez, El Mansura, El Mahalla el Kubra, Tanta, Fayyoum, Minya, Asyut and Aswan. It will be a total attack, and nothing will prevail against it. By and for God, we shall succeed. And our small cell is the cornerstone of this great mission.'

'Abbas,' said Omar el Masri gently, 'how shall we operate?

You must tell us how we must operate, what you require of us.'

'It is indeed a huge project,' said Fuad Wahbah, the boxer. 'We must not fail you in it.'

The girl Zeinab, diffident, said nothing, but her eyes were wholly on Abbas.

'Let me then say this also,' said Abbas Sidki. 'That as it is true that no Angels cell should know anything deep about the others, so it is true that there need be no secrets *within* an Angels cell. We are each brother to the others, in all things. Even life, even death. So let me tell you my plan. You know that I am to exterminate the Abomination by rifle, and that the day is October 6. You know too that I have received the rifle, which is telescopically sighted, from London. Well, early this afternoon I tested it out in the Gebel Ataqa, well off the desert road to Suez. This is a marvellous rifle. It will not fail in its aim. You know too, from the most valuable information that Ali Sarawi brought us today, that the two Presidents will be standing in their open car all the way from the bleed-off from the flyover by the Ramses Hilton to Midan el Tahrir, then over the Tahrir Bridge to the other side, and to the left past the Sheraton into Sharia el Giza, where they sit.

'It's simple, then. I just have to find an eyrie from which to hit the Abomination while the two of them stand.'

'Where?' said Fuad. 'Where, Abbas?'

'Ali Sarawi twice mentioned here tonight that in crossing the Tahrir Bridge the open car passes by the Borg Hotel. That is my eyrie, right on Sharia el Gezira, which runs at right-angles to Tahrir Bridge through to Zamalek. The hotel starts about seventy metres in from Tahrir Bridge. It's a broad narrow building facing onto the Nile. The first four floors or so are some kind of separate administrative building. To enter the hotel you actually walk *down* four flights of four stone steps each to a fairly ample lobby and reception. The top floor, the eleventh, is a twenty-four-hour coffee shop, and the tenth is the restaurant. I'd be interested in any room near the southern edge of the hotel – nearest the bridge – on the ninth, eighth, or seventh floors, facing the Nile, naturally. Each such room has a good balcony, quite private from all the others. Room 502 on the ninth floor, or near to it, would be ideal.'

'You seem to know the place already just about backwards,' said Fuad Wahbah.

'I had a look at it a week ago,' said Abbas. 'I got them to show me some of the rooms on the ninth floor.'

'Won't they know you if you go back?' asked Omar Masri.

Abbas glanced at him.

'No,' he said, 'because next time I won't have my beard. I'll be Abbas Yamasi, a first secretary in the Saudi Arabian Ministry of Foreign Affairs, just visiting to see what I think of Egypt. I'll have a diplomatic passport to that effect, too. The Upper Council is looking after that; you'll know that the Angels have some expert forgers of documents.'

'What's our job?' said Fuad, the boxer.

'I'd like you, Fuad, to go in as soon as you can, tomorrow even, and book me a room there for say ten days from October 5. Push your weight a bit about what a big shot I am in Saudi, with a lot to do about advising Saudis whether or not to come to Egypt on holiday. The Establishment here is still aching to be loved by Saudi, and the Borg loves to get Saudi visitors; they actually have lots of money and they really seem to like spending it. So push them into showing you their best rooms, and see if you can get 502 or near it. You're my great Egyptian friend, of course; I studied for a year with you at Cairo University. They'll want a deposit. I'd give them a hundred Egyptian pounds at once – here – they'll like that; they're about a forty-pounds-a-day hotel. *Tamaam?*'

'*Tamaam*. You think your passport will stand police scrutiny?'

'Almost certainly; our forgers are very good. But it won't have to. It'll be enough if it gets past the hotel reception, and it'll certainly do that. Even with *non*-diplomatic passports, once you're past Egyptian Immigration at the port of entry you have seven days in which to register with the police in the Mugamma Building in Midan el Tahrir. Normally the hotel does that for you in your first or second day, but I'll tell them I want to register myself; I've had complaints about the Mugamma service from Saudi visitors, and I want to check it

245

for myself. Even if the Borg won't buy any of this and insists on keeping my passport, I'm not arriving until nine-thirty in the evening, and no one in the hotel or the Magamma is going to do anything about my passport that night or early the next morning; this is Egypt. And after about ten past ten the next morning I'm not going to need that passport anyway. By that time I'll have killed the Abomination or I won't have. Either way I'd be wise to get out of that hotel fast.'

'What's our role on the day itself?' said Omar Masri.

'Let's start with October 5, the day before. I arrive at the Borg by taxi at 9.30 pm. You're driving, Omar; we can use the same taxi as with Talkhan. Ali Sarawi can be in front with you as driver's mate. Fuad's in the back with me, my old Egyptian friend. He comes into the Borg with me, to make sure everything's as comfortable for me as can be.

'But let me break a moment there. Omar, it's up to you and Ali to know the roads coming away from the Borg like the backs of your hands. You know that Sharia el Gezira itself is one-way past the Borg going north towards Zamalek. There is of course the turn left just after the Borg which goes past the Cairo Tower and the Anglo-American Hospital. That can take you to Hassan Pasha and back onto Tahrir Bridge and over into Dokki, but anywhere near the bridge is liable to be heavily patrolled by police. And explore all the routes out of Zamalek itself, over west into Muhandissin and east into Cairo city, using the 26th of July Bridge. Your quickest way out would certainly be the feeder road up onto the 6th of October Bridge, three or four hundred metres from the Borg, but the police or army may have that sealed. Look out for parking places for the morning of October 6 too. You can normally park right in front of the Borg in El Gezira, but the police may insist on clearing it that day.

'What I'll need from you two on the morning of October 6, the day itself, is the taxi, fully tanked up, parked as near as possible to the Borg, with you, Omar, in it, ready and waiting. And you, Ali, near to the steps of the Borg entrance, so you can guide us to the taxi. As for arms, nothing heavier than automatic pistols, and you'd better leave yours in the taxi, Ali, because there'll be searches at and near the hotel.'

'Abbas,' said the girl Zeinab, with pain in her voice.

'Yes?' he said courteously, turning to her.

'This is a most noble endeavour, a truly great blow for Islam and for God. But I think you give me no slightest part in it. Is it because I do not merit your trust? Yet I would do any service for you, for the Angels, for Islam. With my life . . .'

'I'm most sorry,' he said, 'I should have told you at once. Your duty is of grave responsibility: armed, to stay and guard this safe house. We *must* have a secure place to fall back on, win or fail. It's vital. In this I trust you fully.'

'Thank you,' she said. '*Taht amrak,* at your orders.'

Abbas turned to Fuad.

'Fuad, you will please be with me on the morning of October 6. You come in at eight in the morning, to have breakfast with me in my room. By now the hotel staff know you well. They love you. The evening before, after I have got myself and my big suitcase up to my room, with your and the hotel's help, you and I go and have a drink, or rather several drinks, in the hotel bar on the tenth floor. I'm wearing my fine white flowing Saudi robes. I have been throwing money about so far as though I personally have no time for the stuff. I give the front door porter ten Egyptian pounds as a tip – that's probably his normal week's wages – and fifteen to the reception clerk because he's of higher class, ten to the lift attendant and ten to the lad who carries my bag. Actually, he ought to have got more, because it contains not only my rifle and ammunition, but also a loaded sub-machinegun with two spare magazines for you. But the lad doesn't complain; for him that's perhaps ten days' basic salary. At the bar we drink nothing but Johnny Walker Black Label whisky, which in itself makes us practically as rare as visitors from outer space, and well-heeled ones at that. I throw the same sort of tips around at anyone who comes anywhere near us, and I throw in a Saudi riyal from time to time to add some convincing local colour. We follow this up with dinner in the restaurant on the same floor, and here we go for a couple of bottles of imported French wine and end up with Courvoisier brandy. The same order of tips, naturally. The staff can't take their eyes off us. By the time that night's through everyone who works for that hotel knows about us, and loves us dearly.

'So nobody stops Fuad when he comes into the Borg at eight next morning. Even if the police insist on searching him they find nothing. We're through our handsome breakfast by nine. Then we make ready.

'For me this eyrie is just about ideal. If I go out onto my balcony I can sit and shoot from it unseen. No one sees me from any other balcony, and no one sees me from in front, because in front of the Borg is nothing but some rather tall trees and then three hundred metres of the Nile. If I'm in Room 502 or near it, I have a beautifully clear view of Tahrir Bridge and the wide intersection where it meets Sharia el Gezira. In 502 I'm about 60 metres from ground level, say 70 at the most, and I'm some 70 metres away from the intersection. My trigonometry tells me that the square of the hypoteneuse is equal to the sum of the squares of the other two sides in a right-angled triangle. That means that I shall be shooting at a range of just under 100 metres. At that range,' said Abbas Sidki, his tone high in exaltation, 'with this small and beautiful gem of a rifle, I shall hit exactly what I aim at. We shall have cleansed a great Abomination from our beloved soil.'

After the silence, Fuad Wahbah said very quietly:

'And my role that morning, which I consider of great honour, will be to guard you from attack from the rear, while you carry out your execution of the Abomination?'

'Exactly. Please. To wait outside my door in the passage, your sub-machinegun under a raincoat, to guard against anyone coming from the lifts or stairs.'

'Then I have only one other question, Abbas,' said Fuad. 'Tell us, who will be our leader, our President, in our new Islamic Republic?'

Abbas Sidki gazed back at him, his bearded face set and serious, his powerful body still.

'I am not permitted to tell you his name,' he said, 'but it is a name you all know. Of a man great in politics and in honour. It is he who will lead us in our great Islamic State, and we may have all trust in him. He is a man giant in Islam.'

# 16

# Bearding the Lion

The second thing that Bridget O'Shaunessy noticed about Abbas Sidki was his beard. It was short and black and dense and it shone with health. It was as if a vigorous sap were about to burst forth from each curled hair. He had a full moustache too, and strong black eyebrows. The first thing she saw was of course his eyes, wide-set, black, very steady, and compelling, with their vibrant and mesmeric glitter, as if charged with black electricity. They were his signature.

The rest of him fell into focus as she stood before his small table in the Nile Hilton's Tavern Bar that early evening. The atmosphere was submarine. You came into the Tavern through a swing door from the hotel's entrails, and walked between a twin line of tables served with couchettes and armchairs. Through the expensive gloom over to the right was the main horseshoe bar, a scatter of small tables beyond it. To your left the tavern made an L, giving space for another cluster of small tables. Abbas Sidki sat at one of these, facing the swing door. Though she was there deliberately three or four minutes before their appointment, he was there before her. That made him a careful man; it is the one who waits in such meetings who holds the advantage. As he stood she noted the tall and powerful body, the commando camouflaged smock and supple parachutist boots, the black-and-silver Star of the Sinai at his throat, the paratrooper's badge on his left breast – no other medal there, as Daniel Gad had forecast; the major's eagles on his shoulders.

'Forgive me. I seem to be late.'

'No, no,' he said. 'It is I who am early. Please sit down.'

His English was accented, controlled, clear.

'It's extremely good of you to see me like this,' she said.

Abbas Sidki smiled slightly.

'When Daniel Gad rang me to ask me a favour,' he said, 'I was glad to do it. Daniel Gad is an important man in our country. You know what he does?'

'Not exactly, though I understand it's important.'

'Perhaps it's as well,' said Abbas Sidki. 'But I can tell you that any close friend of Daniel's is of particular interest to me.'

An Egyptian waiter was hovering. He was young, and seemed fascinated by Abbas's Star of the Sinai.

'What will you drink?' said Abbas.

She saw the almost full glass of orange-juice in front of him. Gad had mentioned to her that Abbas would not drink alcohol.

'I think vodka and orange,' she said. 'You don't mind?'

'*Vodka wa asiir burtu'aan lis-sitt,*' he said. '*Wi talq.*' The waiter departed at an impressive speed, as if seduced by the idea of promotion. Abbas went on: 'Of course I don't mind. We each have our customs.'

'Yes.'

'It's when one people apes the customs of another, perhaps, that things can go wrong.'

'Yes, perhaps,' said Bridget. 'Major Abbas Sidki, may I take notes as we're talking?'

'By all means.'

'Major, you wear the Star of the Sinai, a very high decoration for valour. My paper would be very interested to learn how you won it. Forgive me, I know you must have told this many times before –'

Abbas was very courteous. He showed no impatience. He told her quite graphically of his commando training, the intensive practice with the Sagger wire-guided anti-tank missile, fired from the shoulder, of his commando unit's penetration behind the Israeli Bar Lev Line, and its ambush of the Israeli armour as it was flung in disorderly mass into battle on that first war day of 6 October 1973.

'I had hit and burnt out my three Centurion tanks almost before I knew it,' he said. 'In a minute, a matter of minutes. My commanding officer saw me, and turned me into a hero. I was the one he happened to see. That medal's not mine. Many did braver things. It's for all our troops.'

He did not sound to her as if he were merely going through the motions of modesty. He seemed really to mean what he said. The medal might have been an embarrassment. Abbas Sidki, she thought, might really be a very honest man.

'It wasn't all just luck, though, was it?'

'You mean our victory during those first four days?' said Abbas. 'Certainly not. That was the fruit of two years very specific and thorough training, a very clear definition of our objectives, provision of the right arms and equipment, and a strong sense of dedication in our troops.'

'Which means you felt it a just war?'

Abbas looked at her levelly.

'Certainly. It was a just war. We were fighting to win back Arab lands taken from us by an enemy. To a Muslim, that is an absolute obligation. The Koran is categoric on it. A Muslim must fight to the maximum of his ability to win back occupied Arab land. He *may not* accept that such lands continue to be occupied by another if he could win them back. There are no exceptions.'

'So you cannot be too content with what still goes on on the West Bank and Gaza?'

Abbas looked at her again, heavily.

'How *could* we be? Here not only is an enemy not giving back Arab land it has occupied, but it is entrenching itself even more deeply every day on those lands.'

'Though technically Israel's no longer an enemy, because you still have a peace treaty with her. But from what you say you cannot be satisfied with that treaty. You must feel that your government is wrong to maintain it.'

Abbas sat impassive for some while. But he was too big or too astute wholly to evade that question. For then he said:

'As a military officer, I may not publicly criticize my government. I may not play politics. But if you ask me to confirm that the Sharia, Islamic law, requires Arabs to fight to their utmost to recover occupied Arab lands, I can only do so, referring you to that law itself.'

There was no doubt of his stature. Asked a straight question, he would answer the truth as he saw it, however unpopular it was politically.

'So things ought to be put right,' she said. 'By force, if necessary.'

He stared back at her heavily, approving her words by his silence.

'Well, it's only five days off now,' she said, 'isn't it?'

She saw his right hand, bringing the orange-juice down from his lips, lock abruptly in mid-air.

'Five days?'

'Till October 6, I mean.'

'October 6?'

He brought the orange-juice down onto the table slowly, and left it. He clasped his hands in front of him, still gazing intently at her. She saw him as suddenly absolutely concentrated, crouched. He was quite still. It was faintly alarming.

'The anniversary of the date when you *did* try to do something about it by force, I mean. The twelfth anniversary, isn't it?'

'Oh, *that!*' said Abbas Sidki. 'Yes, the twelfth.'

He took another, rather long, pull at his orange-juice.

Bridget, companionably, took a sip of her vodka and orange too.

'You quoted the Sharia, Islamic Law, as your authority. I understand that it, the Koran, with the Sunna and Hadith govern every single aspect of a Muslim's life?'

'That's correct,' said Abbas Sidki. 'Islam is a very *total* vision; what's your word for it? – holistic; it's a passionately *holistic* ideology. We don't divide life into the ecclesiastical and secular, as I think you tend to in the West.'

'I very much like that Hassan el Banna definition,' said Bridget. 'How does it go? Something like: "Islam's a faith and a ritual, nation and nationality, religion and state, spirit and deed, creed and a sword"?'

'You've been reading Hassan el Banna?' said Abbas. 'That is perceptive. Someone has been guiding you well!'

'I've read Mitchell and anything else I could find,' she said. 'And, yes, Daniel has been helping me a lot with books and advice.'

'*Ya Salaam!*' said Abbas. 'Daniel Gad? He's been helping you read up on Banna?'

'Yes. He seems to have read everything there is about him.'

'It's remarkable. Well, there are some very likeable things about him, for a pol– for a senior public servant.'

'He even checked my article about Banna before I sent it,' said Bridget. 'Here,' She pulled the folded clipping from the back of her notebook and passed it to him. He read it through very thoroughly.

'*Mumtáz!*' he said, giving it back to her. 'It's excellent! I wish we had more people from the West like you visiting and studying our country. So Daniel Gad –' He gazed at the wall opposite a few moments. 'What a pity!' he went on, as if to himself, 'I wonder –'

'A pity?'

Abbas looked back at her.

'What? Oh. That Gad's a Copt, I mean.'

'He spoke very highly of you.'

'He did?' said Abbas. 'Well. That's the way it goes. Well. So already you know something of the nature of Islam. That it is all-embracing. The highest good. So the true individual Muslim would do anything for it, for its wellbeing and progress. *Anything*. Even if that caused him great pain personally.'

'You put Islam first, then. All the time. The Islamic community? It seems always far above the individual . . .'

'Indeed,' said Abbas. 'For the *Umma,* the Islamic Community, is the vehicle – the only one – through which, under strict Islam with its very high regard for social justice, Allah can live out His glorious design in this world. That objective far transcends any which a mere individual might have. To assist the living out of that Divine Will, any individual Muslim must be ready to sacrifice everything, and certainly his life. Banna, you know, raised martyrdom for Islam to a key virtue. He noted that Allah granted the noble life only to the man who knew how to die a noble death. I think this a basic difference between us. You in the West start out with the individual and the individual soul, in your religion, your mythology, your literature, your culture. You move out from there to your community – if sometimes not very far, then you find egotism, materialism, crime. We, I think, tend to start with, *and stay with*, our Islamic Community. *That* is the end where we load the greatest importance, *not* the individual's. Perhaps that is why we have never allowed any representation of the human face or form in our art . . .'

'Yet Islam has always had its egotists, its godless, its criminals too!'

Abbas laughed.

'We'd just say they weren't true Muslims, but *Jahaliyya* pagans. No, they're an embarassment. But we'd strongly counter any accusation that, because we give so much greater weight to the welfare of the Islamic Community than we do to the individual's, Islam is therefore impersonal, heartless. No. I submit that Islam has through the ages had no worse a history than Christianity for tolerance and compassion. We may sometimes have been better – the Moorish rule in Spain, and Salah ed-Din, might be two cases . . .'

Bridget finished her drink, and Abbas promptly ordered her another, and an orange-juice for himself.

'You've given me many good points,' she said. 'Could we have something now about yourself? A few personal details?'

'Such as?' said Abbas cautiously.

'When and where you were born, how you grew up, your family, that sort of thing?'

'Oh, I was born in May 1955,' said Abbas. 'My village is called Beit Gibriel, The House of Gabriel. It's a Delta village about a hundred kilometres northeast of Cairo on the way to Port Said, but well off any main roads. It was a very poor village.'

'How poor was that?'

He glanced at her. His fine eyes seemed clouded.

'Very poor. We never had quite enough to eat. The arable land was almost entirely owned by absentee landlords, who took two-thirds of the crops' value as rent. The remaining third just wasn't enough. There was no electricity or proper sewage, no clinics, and no primary or secondary schools. Illiteracy was eighty per cent and life expectancy about forty years. It was a small village, four or five hundred fellahin, and somehow Nasser's agrarian reforms had passed it by.'

'And your family?'

'Oh, I was the eldest of nine children. Most of them, and my mother, are still there. I go to see them once or twice a year, and take them a bit of money. Though things are better now, of course. Not nearly good enough yet, all the same; we still have a bitterly long way to go. So many things are still deeply wrong in this country,' said Abbas Sidki, his voice troubled. 'We have so many terrible obstacles to remove —'

'But you must remember some pleasant things in the village?'

'Oh, yes,' said Abbas. 'Let's see. How strange, the Imam of our group of villages springs to mind! He was a great diversion, always with a red turban and a gold sash, and marvellous cedarwood worry-beads. He was so holy that he only spoke the purest classical Arabic, so none of us could understand a word he said. Oh, and other images – the village women coming to fill their jars with Nile water just after dawn and dusk, the marvellous grace afterwards when they walked away with them filled on their heads, their hips swaying. The feluccas in the Nile. For I worked then by the river, you see, when I wasn't studying at school, from when I was eleven till I joined the army at eighteen; I worked a shadoof by the Nile; it's a long counterweighted pole, used for stepping up irrigation water buckets from level to level into the final canals. But the thing I remember most warmly was my *kuttab*, my religious school, from when I was six till ten. It gave me the Koran and Islam. That was its best heritage.'

'You were never married?'

'No,' said Abbas, not elaborating.

'You've not mentioned your father.'

Abbas dropped his head forward suddenly, then raised it very slowly, so that Bridget said instinctively: 'I'm sorry!'

'It's all right,' said Abbas. 'He was a good man. A junior clerk at the post office in the nearest town. He only had primary schooling, and he forced me to go much further so I could work my way out of the village. Another thing – and I wouldn't have told you had you not talked like that about Banna – he was also a Muslim Brother. A very gentle one. But in 1966 someone betrayed my father falsely. He spent five years in Nasser's desert detention camps and he came out with lash-scars on his back and his spirit broken. He died a few years later, an old man before his time, sitting in the sun. Yet he had always only helped people. He had done no single act of violence in his life. A society which can do that,' said Abbas Sidki, a hard edge to his voice, 'has got to be changed.'

'Of course.'

He looked hard at her.

'I ask you on your honour not to print that information about my father. It might harm not merely me, but also my mother and brothers and sisters.'

'No, no, of course I'll not include it. I'm honoured that you told me about it.'

But he had sunk again into his reverie. He looked up once more at her.

'So you're a close friend of Daniel Gad. A very close friend?'

'Yes,' she said, 'I think I can say that.'

'Perhaps you can tell me where I can find you,' he said. 'In case I can think of anything more which may be of interest to you.'

'Certainly.' She gave him her street and flat number in Hassan Hegazi, and her telephone number there. He took out a diary from his camouflaged smock and wrote them down carefully, and put his small book away again. Then he stared at the wall opposite again, for a few long moments.

'A sad business,' he said finally and sombrely. 'One has got to correct things. At any cost. To oneself or others.'

257

'Yes,' said Bridget O'Shaunessy.

He looked straight at her.

'At any cost,' he repeated.

Outside at the back of the Hilton leading to the Egyptian Museum she, with his agreement, took two photos of him for her paper with her instantaneous Polaroid. She showed them to Daniel Gad in his flat that night, commenting most favourably on Abbas. Gad agreed with her assessment. The photos showed Abbas standing with his powerful trained body, his magnetic eyes set with deep purpose.

# 17
# *The Eve of the Strike*

'I had not thought to find so towering a figure,' said Avram Ben Yehuda. 'Though Wahid Hakki did warn me. You will make a great leader.'

Abdel Aziz Fawzi sat opposite him in a deep brown leather armchair, his broad hands steady on his knees. Two men were in Abdel Aziz's sober and spacious flat in Sharia Saleh Ayoub in Zamalek. It was half past four on the afternoon of Saturday, 5 October.

Abdel Aziz's head, massy as carved mahogany, seemed not at all turned by this awe, these compliments. Rather, his tone was sombre, deeply troubled.

'And I, for my part, had not thought to find myself allied in a most grave matter with one whom I can only see as an enemy of my country and my culture.'

'Certainly not your country. My party in Israel considers that we have only one committed Arab enemy, and that may hold true for the next ten, twenty years. And that is Syria. Never Egypt. We have a peace treaty with you that we shall respect to the letter. And remember that Syria has proved no great friend of yours in the last years, nor will she change in that.'

'Still, they are our fellow Arabs, fellow Muslims. They're part of our culture.'

'We in Israel have nothing against your culture either. Against Islam. Why should we have? We too, with the

Christians, are People of the Book as are you. As the Prophet Muhammed said. 'Didn't he?'

Abdel Aziz looked at him sharply with his light-grey eyes. They're not Arab, thought Ben Yehuda; this man has Turk in him.

'That may be so,' he said. 'But your behaviour in the last years to your fellow People of the Book, the Arabs, has been murderous. I speak of the West Bank, Gaza, the Lebanon, your bombing of the nuclear reactor in Iraq, your massacre of men, women, and children in the two refugee camps in Beirut. How can I in honesty and decency ally myself with an Israeli after that?'

'Most of those were things of war,' said Ben Yehuda, 'things of the past. Our strike against Iraq was preventive: from that reactor they would have built an atomic bomb and used it against us. But in what matters *now*, surely you must admit that we are honourable allies? We are most wholly with you in your present magnificent project. Haven't we backed you fully, exactly as we promised? When I say "we" I don't mean my political party in Israel, of course, but I and my very few colleagues. Can you honestly say that we have failed or cheated you? Can you not accept that my colleagues and I, however sharply different we may be from you, quite genuinely have a common objective with you in this noble thing, where you, with us, may change the whole racing course of the world, to the huge and lasting benefit of your people, and *perhaps of all Islam*? Can you truthfully say that you could have come this far forward without us? It was in immediate reply to your most urgent request via Athens which we got only yesterday morning that I am now here, in my own firm's aircraft, because neither – none of my colleagues in this could come with the lightning speed you asked. You told us that your arms suppliers were pressing for immediate payment. I have brought exactly what you asked, there on the table, which is twice what Wahid Hakki first brought you. Again, if Hakki, whom you will know as a most profoundly dedicated Muslim, can accept me, why cannot you?'

Abdel Aziz stared down at his two hands, set there like the

heads of small spades on his knees. The man in his powerful body, his dark-blue suit, was huge, monolithic. He would not be moved. This inflexible puritanical moral rectitude could ruin everything. Yet Ben Yehuda knew too that this weakness was also Abdel Aziz's great strength. With it he would move mountains, Egypt, the Middle East, the world a little. He was truly messianic because he calculated nothing for his own advantage. He truly served his God. People would believe him utterly because he meant exactly what he said, was just what he seemed. He could lead people over a precipice, and they, falling, would bless him for it.

'I could still reject it,' said Abdel Aziz heavily. 'I think I *should* reject it. And you. I should never have let you in, except that on the phone from the airport you mentioned the word Angels, and at the door you showed me the note in Hakki's handwriting. I was very wrong. I should have insisted at the start on knowing full details of who was backing me. I was weak and allowed Hakki to seduce me with his arguments for secrecy. Because it suited me. It gave me the opportunity for this great and noble action for Islam. I should have insisted. There are no short-cuts, and it is too late to cancel so many orders. This means that I shall have to announce publicly what we intended. I shall have to go honestly to the authorities. It means springing the trap beneath some men's feet, hanging them. This is a terrible business.'

'You cannot do that!' said Ben Yehuda in monstrous alarm, knowing that the other could indeed do precisely that. 'You cannot let good men, good Muslims, die helplessly and no doubt most painfully for what is not their fault. For what may be *my* fault!'

Abdel Aziz turned his great head upon him, studying him. Then he said:

'Then, at least, I must know everything about my backing. I must know exactly who the others are. Then I can judge. If I do not have that, and feel satisfied with it, then I must go *now* to the police, and stop this thing.'

'Even at this late stage?'

'Oh, yes,' said Abdel Aziz. 'Even now.'

His English, which was the language in which they spoke, was a little heavy and measured, but very straightforward, and unadorned and competent, rather like himself.

Avram Ben Yehuda, at this crossroads, felt his heart plummet, his throat dry. But, if they were not to lose everything, he had no choice.

'Sir John Mainstree,' he said, 'MC, MM and chairman of Mainstree Oil International Limited, UK-based, but trading internationally. It's on the small side, as oil companies go; about a quarter of a million barrels a day, say a third of what Egypt produces.'

'Ah. And what incentive has Sir John Mainstree to risk himself in this grave endeavour?'

'His first argument to us was economic. Mainstree Oil gets all its crude oil from the British North Sea fields and other non-Arabian Gulf sources. He says that if we can destabilize the Arab Middle East countries that must force up the costs of Middle East and other OPEC crudes, and thus their price levels, and, consequently, *all* crude oil price levels. Companies like Mainstree's would make a financial killing, because they'd benefit from the new higher world oil product prices, while their production costs wouldn't have gone up at all – by one red cent, in his words.'

'You don't believe him?'

'Neither Hakki nor I believe that's the main motive. We think that his main motive is his passion for the Middle East, deserts and Arabs. As you know, it's quite a common form of English romanticism, particularly among their upper and middle classes. Well, Mainstree's father was a liaison officer in World War One between General Storrs here in Cairo and Colonel T. E. Lawrence in Arabia, supporting him in his mission of inciting the Arabs of the Peninsula to wage their war of attrition against the Turks –'

'Which the British government then recognized,' observed Abdel Aziz drily, 'by declaring Palestine a National Home for the Jews.'

Ben Yehuda shrugged and smiled.

'In any event, Mainstree's father, a baronet, evidently

developed a powerful mystique about Lawrence and desert wars. After World War One, instead of coming back to Britain, he joined the British Palestine Police and served with them for years. His two sons were born there. The present Sir John inherited his father's mystique. In World War Two he joined a specialized British-Rhodesian desert reconnaissance group, and spent most of his war running around behind the German lines in the Western and Libyan Deserts. After the war he was with airborne troops in Palestine. He became chairman of Mainstree Oil only because his brother, who created it, fell dead. But his heart has stayed in the Middle East. In the deserts and, I fear, with the Arabs. He's fascinated to have something active to do with them again. He's very pro-Islam. Also, I think, he would like to help change the face of history a little.'

'You speak very fairly about him, Mr Ben Yehuda,' said Abdel Aziz.

'I'm always fair to a good enemy. Besides, I've spent so much of my life in this area now that I find I'm even getting partial to its deserts myself.'

Abdel Aziz gazed at him for a moment or two, then gave a curious loud wuff of laughter.

'Where can I learn more about this Sir John Mainstree?' he said.

'From a *Who's Who* in your library. Or at the British Embassy.'

'He sounds a good man.'

'Yes. An original man, anyway.'

Abdel Aziz sat absolutely motionless for a full minute, staring straight ahead of him. Then he gave a tremendous sigh. It shook all his body. He could have been a tall and bulky building mined at its base. He stabilized, and looked back at Ben Yehuda.

'All right,' he said.

'All right?'

'I accept your explanation. Your participation in this great venture.'

Ben Yehuda's soul leapt like a young lamb.

'Excellent. I'm very glad. Then may I ask you a favour?'

'Certainly.'

'I wonder, could you bring us up to date a little on what's happening on the ground?'

Abdel Aziz looked at him steadily.

'Everything is going exactly as planned.'

'I see. That's excellent. Could you give a little detail, perhaps?'

Abdel Aziz gave an odd circular turn to his head, looking round his sitting room.

'Why don't we go for a walk?' he said. 'It's a fine afternoon.'

'Of course.'

'I haven't liked the feel of it in here for the last couple of weeks. I suppose it's that I haven't been getting out enough.'

They went down in the lift to the street, then round the corner into Baha el Din Qaraqosh, and to Sharia el Gezira, curving then round to the right with it until, parallel with the Nile, they reached the entrance of the Gezira Sporting Club. The men on duty at the gates knew Abdel Aziz at once. Their voices dropped and they bowed at him; there was no doubt of their respect, even awe. Ben Yehuda, half a head the taller, felt that he walked with a prophet, a guru. In the open, Abdel Aziz seemed more at ease, suddenly living fully and vividly, like a boy out of class. He led Ben Yehuda ahead, pointing out where the clubhouse and the swimming pools lay. He seemed quietly pleased and proud, like a host showing a friend round his garden. He led then to the right, then left, and onto the grass racecourse. They had it to themselves; there were no races that day.

Abdel Aziz answered all Ben Yehuda's questions fully, almost gaily, as if seeking to make up for his earlier suspicion. Yes, the strike against the Abomination was for the morrow. No, he did not know exactly from where the Angels of the Sword execution team would strike: that secret was their right and their privilege. No, that would not be the only strike tomorrow. All he was prepared to say was that the Angels planned simultaneous attacks on key points not only in Cairo but in every main city and town in Egypt. The Islamic State of Egypt was one day away.

The special rifle in its hard suitcase had arrived safely. Concerned that his pervading sense of malaise might be warning him that he was being watched, Abdel Aziz had taken great care in delivering it. He had brought it half an hour before the agreed time in his car to Khan el Khalili and left the car in the park by the Mosque of Sayyidna el Hussein. He had taken the hard suitcase then and walked quickly, twisting and doubling back many times on his tracks, finally coming out swiftly onto and crossing the light-blue-painted pedestrian bridge to the other side, where he had caught a taxi immediately. He had taken it to the address given him in Sharia el Mansuriya. A big man with a short black beard and piercing gaze had taken it from him at the front door of the ground-floor flat. He had been dressed in the flowing white galabiah and loose cowl, colour of purity, of the militant Islamic groups. No, Abdel Aziz thought that the two million dollars Ben Yehuda had brought that day would be enough; after all he, Abdel Aziz, would with luck have control of all of the government, including the Treasury, by the morrow, and the country would have to learn rapidly to run itself efficiently with the funds it generated itself, without running up huge foreign debts. Ben Yehuda left him at the Sporting Club entrance, well pleased, and caught a taxi for the airport.

Daniel Gad and Khalil were waiting for him there. Gad had found where Ben Yehuda's twin-jet Hawker-Siddeley executive aircraft was parked, away from the main commercial lines' aprons, and he and Khalil were sitting with the driver in the cab of an airport service van stationed near it. Both were armed with their pistols. Gad had heard every word of that afternoon's conversation in Abdel Aziz Fawzi's flat between him and Ben Yehuda, faithfully recorded on the sophisticated electronic listening devices which the Russians had so kindly provided for Egyptian Intelligence. Sadly, they had not had the equipment to hear what the two men said on their walk outside to the Gezira Club. Still, Gad had the full talk in the flat. It was crystal-clear from that recording – for the first time – that Ben Yehuda, Wahid Hakki and Sir John Mainstree were allied to provide support for Abdel Aziz to build up a powerful party to take over government in Egypt, whether constitutionally or not, but probably not – Abdel Aziz had talked of causing the death of some of his men if he went to the police about what Ben Yehuda had called the other's magnificent project. There was almost certainly an Islamic Fundamentalist slant to it, possibly a pan-Islamic slant; Ben Yehuda had also talked of Abdel Aziz changing the world to the benefit of all his people, and perhaps of all Islam.

There was nothing at all about how they proposed to do this, to whom, where or when. But it could be any time. There was an ugly feeling in the city these days. In the Shubra area, and elsewhere, there had been killings between Muslims and Copts which never reached the newspapers, a few churches and mosques burned down. It could just be self-generating, or somebody could be moving it, very deliberately. There was anyway certainly enough in that recorded conversation to justify Gad arresting Ben Yehuda at once and holding him until Mossad could pick him up. They would be happy to get their hands on him after Uri Allon's grim death. Gad could never get Hakki, so close to Ghaddafi, who was no friend of Egypt, but he might be able to get something done about Sir John Mainstree, through British Intelligence and the British police.

Daniel Gad had been in his office on the tenth floor in Kasr el Nil when his electronic ears started recording this memorable dialogue that afternoon. The sound engineers tipped him off and he listened in live while they recorded it. Mossad's telex from Jerusalem that Ben Yehuda was on his way to Cairo by his private jet, and Cairo Immigration's advice that they had just processed him through, arrived in fact after he had started listening to the dialogue. The airport advised him that Ben Yehuda's jet had booked a 6.30 pm ETD with the control tower, so Gad and Khalil took a helicopter out there the moment the recording ended, from one of the police pads in the city, so that they could set up a worthy reception before Ben Yehuda arrived. Gad intended to give himself the pleasure of a fairly tough interrogation before Mossad arrived to take him off; he too had not forgotten Uri Allon.

Avram Ben Yehuda was clearly a disciplined man. He appeared walking out from the terminal buildings just before six-thirty. He looked very happy, his tall slim body striding merrily along, his reverse horse-shoe of iron-grey curls riding on his brown head like a victor's laurels, and a wise smile on his face. That complacent delight must have come from what he had heard from Abdel Aziz in the Sporting Club. Gad would do what he could to winkle that out.

Ben Yehuda's smile faded as he saw the two men slip out of the cab and stand in his way.

'Mr Avram Ben Yehuda?'

'Yes?'

'We're police officers. Here are our cards. Will you please come with us?'

He stood a metre from them.

'But my passport's perfectly in order! Take a look!'

He put his right hand towards his inside breast pocket, but diverted it suddenly to his left wrist. He swung in low towards the nearest man, Gad. Then he was running like lightning for the jet.

Daniel Gad felt the rip in his left side, looked swiftly and saw the blood seeping out. He and Khalil swung their bodies towards the running man, their pistols out, arms straight ahead in the double-handed grip.

'Stop, or we fire!'

Ben Yehuda kept running. He was now ten metres from the jet. That jet would have its twin engines going within seconds. Once it was taxiing they could never stop it. Gad could try to get the Egyptian jets to scramble, but he could almost certainly never get that across in time for them to stop the Hawker-Siddeley — for which the Israeli border, 300 kilometres away, was only some twenty minutes' flying time. And, if they caught it, and shot it down, that would cause a much greater international furore than shooting just one Israeli here.

So Daniel Gad shot him. He heard Khalil's Colt .45 go off just after beside him. Ben Yehuda was down, a metre from the jet. The jet's two pilots jumped down from the door and stood transfixed. Gad and Khalil ran to the lying man.

Ben Yehuda was on his face. Gad saw that one shot had taken him behind his right knee, to bring him down. The other had hit him between the shoulders. Gad turned him over gently, and Ben Yehuda moaned. There was not much left of the area about his solar plexus. It was a bloody and spongy mess. Gad could see that the heart was still beating. The man would be dead in thirty seconds. His eyes came open.

'We'll get you to a hospital,' said Gad to the killer of Uri Allon.

Ben Yehuda looked at his chest.

'No hospital,' he said succinctly. He looked up at Daniel Gad, who was stemming his own cut with a handkerchief; his rib cage had saved his lung.

'Too late!' he said, ambiguously. 'And just think, anniversary of an anniversary!'

He died, literally, laughing.

# 18

# *The Lion Goes Hunting*

'Is that Miss Bridget O'Shaunessy's flat-mate, please?'

The voice on the phone was male, Egyptian, careful, and courteous. Bridget had heard it before somewhere.

'I'm sorry,' she said, 'she's just gone out for the evening. I doubt that she'll be back before eleven-thirty. Can I take a message?'

'I beg your pardon,' he said, 'I just didn't recognize your voice, Miss O'Shaunessy. It's Muhammed Abbas Sidki.'

'Hello, Major!' she said. 'It's good to hear from you! I sent off that article on you, you know. I didn't say anything about your father.'

'Thank you,' he said. 'So your flat-mate is out?'

'Yes,' said Bridget. 'Till late.'

'I'm not disturbing you? Perhaps you have friends with you?'

'No, I'm alone. Just studying my Arabic.'

'But you'll be going out, of course,' he said. 'It's a Saturday evening.'

'No, no,' she said. 'Daniel's busy this evening.'

'Of course,' said Abbas. 'Quite a few senior government officers are working tonight, on the arrival of your President here tomorrow. And some others,' he added ambiguously. 'It's going to be a big day.'

'Yes.'

'A day people won't forget,' said Abbas.

269

'Indeed,' said Bridget.

'It's in relation to that that I'm calling, in fact,' said Abbas Sidki. 'I can show you part of something which should make very big news indeed tomorrow.'

'Relating to the US President's arrival?'

'Yes. And to the following ceremony. In a sense, you'd be in a ringside seat. You'd have been made part of it.'

'Terrific!' said Bridget.

'It's a story that, if you could get it out right, would I think be what you'd call a world scoop.'

'Thank you!' said Bridget, her reporter's blood racing. 'It's incredibly kind of you!'

'You wrote very sympathetically about Hassan el Banna,' said Abbas. 'I owe you a debt for that. We pay back our friends the way we can.'

'Can you give me anything more of an idea about it?'

'Not like this,' said Abbas. 'But I can assure you it will be a great thing for Egypt. Of that I'm profoundly convinced. Now, can you be ready in say ten minutes? I'll come and get you and take you to a scene of action.'

'Ten minutes? Of course.'

'And please tell no one of this. Or we risk losing that world scoop.'

'No one? Not even Daniel Gad? I could leave a message at his flat —'

Abbas hesitated a moment.

'No one,' he said then. 'I think it better.'

'Fine,' she said. After all, it was Daniel who had introduced her to Abbas. It was Daniel who had talked so highly of him.

'I'll be there,' said Abbas.

'Do I need any special clothes at all?'

'No,' said Abbas, 'not where we're going.'

Promptly ten minutes later, at 8.15 pm, Bridget heard her front door bell ring. When she went to it and opened it, her notebook and her instantaneous Polaroid camera diligently in her handbag, she was oddly startled. For Abbas was not in his commando uniform, and that was the only way she had

270

known him. Now he wore a long flowing white robe and a white cowl over his head. The vigorous black curls of his short beard and his burning black eyes crackled against this sharp white background, even in the pale light of the landing. He was a suddenly new character, priest-like, uncanny, unknown, obscurely menacing.

'Abbas!' she called out. Instinct tugged at her mind to go back on any pretext to her bedroom, there to leave a note for Gad that she was going out with Abbas, with the date and time; a kind of desperate last-minute lifeline flung out blindly into a fog. But Abbas just smiled and said: 'You're not used to me like this.'

'No.'

'But I'm not always a soldier. I'm other things too.'

She smiled back. The moment of flight was past. Her panic had been groundless.

'Ah!' she said. 'Such as?'

'Oh, a man seeking meaning in things, I suppose. Love. Justice. What all men seek.'

They walked down the stairs and Abbas led her across the pavement to his Fiat 127, and opened the front right door for her. He drove them steadily down Hassan Hegazi, to the right into Kasr el Aini, past Sheikh Rihan and the American University and into Midan el Tahrir, Independence Square. They hesitated before entering Talaat Harb, poised five metres below the 150-metre-diameter circular pedestrian bridge, packed with its seething humanity. In front, at the murderous level of the street, the long steel cylinder of a tram, stuffed to the brim with passengers, ground ruthlessly across from left to right towards the Sharia Tahrir, transfixing all other traffic. They moved forward again. Abbas turned his Fiat 127 right at Suleiman Pasha Square into Kasr el Nil, then east up it to Sharia el Gumhuria and Opera Square. Here he turned right past the General Post Office and a police station, and into Sharia el Azhar. Because Abbas had been driving so seriously, she had pardoned him his silence, and had not interrupted him. He seemed locked too in deep thoughts of his own. But now she said:

'This way we go to Khan el Khalili, El Azhar Mosque and University.'

He glanced to the right at her from above the wheel.

'You know your Cairo well.'

'Not so well,' she said, 'but I love this old part. Islamic Cairo. Particularly the area beyond El Azhar and the line of the Old Wall of Cairo – the Northern Cemetery, say, and the Mosque and Tomb of Qaitbai –'

She stopped, for he had looked at her again, this time very suddenly indeed. With an apparent effort, he turned back to the road.

'Qaitbai?' he said. 'How on earth did you know that? What made you say that?'

'I've been there twice with Daniel Gad,' she said. 'It's a place we both love.'

'It's a strange business,' he said. 'Yet he is a Copt, you are a Western Christian.'

After a moment she said: 'Do we still go a long way?'

'No,' said Abbas, 'no, yours is not a long journey.'

Then she said: 'Do you remember the article I wrote on Hassan el Banna, the one I showed you?'

'Of course,' said Abbas.

'Perhaps I should have made it clearer that, even if it was the police who shot and killed him, it was really Banna himself who, by his own will, gave his life for his community.'

'Perhaps,' said Abbas. 'Though every true Muslim should be ready to give his life for his community, you know. Perhaps even to make others give theirs. No individual Muslim's life could have a shadow of the importance of that.'

'Isn't it a little sad,' she said, 'that one should have to die for it?'

Abbas looked at her again. He seemed genuinely surprised.

'No, no,' he said. 'To die for the community? I think it's the greatest good fortune that one could have. A step straight to the noble life, you see. In honour.'

He seemed to have been accurate about the voyage, for he turned the Fiat 127 left now, into the last street before the line of the Old City Wall. There was a traffic policeman at the crossroads. Abbas drove on another hundred metres and stopped. She saw a huge illuminated Pepsi-Cola sign facing her on the other side of the road. Abbas opened the door for her, and they walked into the building. It seemed like a block of flats. She saw no *bawwab*. Abbas stopped at the first door on the left on the ground floor. He pressed the bell. Within seconds a female voice came from within:

'*Min?*'

'Abbas,' said Abbas, then immediately added a few words in Arabic. Bridget caught only the last one; she had learnt it that week. It was *Sayf*, Sword. The door had opened now, but only to the short length of a thick chain. A girl's eye peered at them from the crack. '*Bilzabt!*' said the girl. The door opened fully, the girl behind it. With the slight pressure of Abbas's hand in the small of her back, Bridget was inside the flat's small hall at once. The door was closed and locked behind her with admirable despatch. Bridget turned to look at the girl.

She was more woman than girl. This was true though her clothes covered her totally, even her hair, leaving only her face and her long slim hands bare. Her basic curves still muttered within. She held her sex in there like a loaded gun with the safety on, potentially lethal but controlled for the moment. She was tall. Her face was arresting, with high cheekbones and a fine brow, and features as classically chiselled as a Florentine cameo's. She had splendid dark-brown eyes, warm and widely set.

Also, as Bridget noticed, what appeared to be an automatic pistol in her right hand.

Bridget turned at once to Abbas.

'What is this comedy?'

'It's not a comedy,' said Abbas.

She saw that Abbas, as if thoughtfully to underline his words to her for greater clarity, was also now carrying a pistol in his right hand.

'But this is *farcical!*' shouted Bridget. 'You mean you've *tricked* me to bring me here like this? Why, I'll scream my head off!'

And opened her mouth wide to do so. Abbas was across the

two paces that separated them in a flash. He hit her with his open left hand. The impact was terrific. It flung her heavily to her left. She ended up right out of the hall in the adjoining main room, on the floor against a heavy black wooden chair. She tasted blood inside her right cheek; her teeth had lacerated it badly. Bridget spat blood. The blow had also dazed her. She was not going to do any screaming for the moment.

'I don't like to do it,' said Abbas, 'but, force me, and I shall most certainly do it again!'

Bridget, now, had no doubt of that.

'It would do the little yankee bitch good to get a few more,' said the statuesque girl in her severe Islamic dress, in perfect American. Bridget looked at her. The tall girl's warm brown eyes were fixed adoringly on Abbas. If he just said the word, she would happily beat Bridget to death. All her sexual guns were trained on Abbas. He could walk all over her for thrills. But Abbas just looked completely aloof. The tall girl seemed to absolutely love that too. She just could not get enough of him. Funny how that vicious circle never fails, thought Bridget.

'What's it all about *anyway*?' said Bridget helplessly.

Abbas looked down at her.

'You'll find out tomorrow,' he said. 'Till then I want you to stay here. That chair next to you – please get up and sit in it.'

Bridget spat some more blood and did what she was told.

'What happens to me?' she asked.

'Nothing,' said Abbas. 'Provided you give us no trouble. Provided your friend Daniel Gad does what we want. Which is nothing.'

'We really ought to beat her up thoroughly anyway,' said the statuesque girl, in her faultless American. 'On principle. As fair return for the rotten values of her goddamned godless culture, as exported to us here for free. For the corruption too. And for Palestine.'

She liked talking American. She liked Bridget to know how she felt.

'I don't want that,' said Abbas.

'Maybe a little judicious use of the cigarette?'

'None of that!'

'Oh,' said the tall girl. 'Not even if she gives trouble?'

'That's different,' said Abbas. 'If she gives trouble, serious trouble, you shoot her.' He looked down at Bridget. 'See these bell-like snouts on our pistols? That means that my friend here can shoot you and no one outside will ever know a thing about it. And if you give her trouble she may not make it quick. It can be painful in the stomach, you know.'

'I believe you,' said Bridget. 'You won't be here?'

'No,' said Abbas.

Oh, God, thought Bridget.

'And if they try to rescue her?' said the tall girl.

'The same thing,' said Abbas. 'Shoot her first. Then them.' He looked at Bridget. 'You must know that. And the same if you yourself try to escape. Just stay quiet.'

'I'll stay quiet.'

'Good. Now we're going to tie you. Sit still.'

'Oh, God, no! At least then let me go to the bathroom first!'

Abbas sighed and straightened and looked at his watch.

'All right. But quickly. Zeinab, go with her. Go inside too. Shoot her if she tries anything.'

'With pleasure,' said Zeinab, meaning it.

Indeed she went inside with Bridget in the lavatory at the back and watched her balefully throughout, her pistol always ready. Afterwards they came out and she and Abbas tied Bridget to the throne-like black wooden chair, round her wrists and elbows, her waist, round her knees and ankles. While they tied her Abbas said, in English: 'She's from Boston too.'

'Oh, she is?' said Zeinab, eyeing Bridget. 'Well, then I've two reasons to love her.'

At the end they slapped a length of sticking-plaster horizontally over her lips. Now she could not even talk. They left her chair so that she could see to the front door to her right and to the bathroom exit to her left. She saw Abbas go there. He came back in five or ten minutes. At first she did not know him. There was something shockingly naked about him. Then she understood; he had shaved off his beard and moustache. It seemed almost immoral to look at him now. As he passed in front of her he looked down cursorily at her, a pawn in his grand design. She heard him say to Zeinab: '*Ana rayeh el fundook.*' I'm going to the hotel. That was easy enough, even for her. But which hotel? Why? Her soul clamoured for Daniel Gad.

Now she was alone with this monstrous girl. Bridget's stomach dropped hideously away from her in terror, down through vaulting infinities. The monstrous girl registered in front of her. She wore leather shoes. Zeinab drew back her right foot then kicked Bridget savagely in the left shin. The impact shifted the heavy wooden chair a centimetre. Physical agony burst over Bridget, crimson reds upon whites upon blacks. Perhaps the bone was splintered. She could not even move her leg. Zeinab said, in her fluent American:

'That's as a start. For Boston.'

It looked like a great evening.

# 19

## The Night of the Strike

Daniel Gad had a great evening.

After their killing of Avram Ben Yehuda at Cairo Airport at six-thirty, Gad and Khalil had got the regular police to hold the two Israeli pilots, whose evidence they might need, and to send Ben Yehuda's corpse to the police morgue. Gad himself had taken charge of Ben Yehuda's finely honed stiletto, with its wicked twin-edged five-inch blade, its beautiful small silver guard, and intricately scrolled round silver top; wrapping it carefully in a silk handkerchief to preserve the fingerprints. This could be the weapon that had murdered Uri Allon in Berkeley Square; Dan Abromowitz of Mossad had told him that Allon had died from the stab of an icepick-like weapon in the heart. Gad took some mild first-aid at the airport, several rolls of bandage round his rib-cage. The cut was in fact light, but still bleeding helpfully – for Gad guessed that the melodrama of a few blood-soaked bandages would not come amiss in Cairo. He had rung General Abd el Nour to tell him the news. The Servant of Light had not sounded pleased. Gad and Khalil had then helicoptered back to their fate.

Their fate had received them in his tenth-floor office in Kasr el Nil. The Servant of Light sat immaculately behind his glass-topped football field of a desk, innocent of anything except the little silver-masted Egyptian national flag, horizontal red, white, and black, with the gold Egyptian eagle in the centre of the white. Not a hair of Abd el Nour's elegant silver coiffure looked out of place.

'What!' he thundered. 'You've killed yet *another*? Without even giving him half a chance to open his mouth?'

'He did open his mouth,' said Gad. 'He said: 'Too late. Anniversary of an anniversary.' Or some such.'

'Doesn't make sense,' said the Servant of Light. 'Can't you ever take any of these characters *alive*?'

'We did our best,' said Gad, 'but it was a matter of life and death. See!'

He pulled up the left side of his bush-shirt, like a coy stripper. The Servant of Light eyed with him distaste.

'Put it away!' he said. 'Who on earth could ever hope to kill *you*? They'd never stand a chance. If they blow one head off you'd probably grow another.'

He stared at Gad gloomily. From his left, up on the wall, President Hosni Mubarak, man of destiny, also frowned punitively down upon Gad. The two of them made quite a battery. Despite their clout Gad still had, just, enough sporting instinct not to tell Abd el Nour that it must in fact have been Khalil who killed Ben Yehuda. Khalil used a Colt .45. It was that heavier slug that had hit Ben Yehudu right between his shoulder blades. Instead Gad said:

'Well, we still have Abdel Aziz Fawzi. That recording of his first talk with Ben Yehuda this afternoon is conclusive. It's absolutely certain that he, Ben Yehuda, Wahid Hakki from Libya, and this Sir John Mainstree from Britain, are in some conspiracy against our present government, to replace it by one led by Abdel Aziz. How, where, when, we don't know. But Abdel Aziz must. It's probably Fundamentalists; Ben Yehuda talked of the lasting benefit to all Islam, Abdel Aziz of a great and noble action for Islam. And Mainstree's supposed to want to destabilize the Arab Middle East to force up the price levels of crude oil. There's enough there and to spare for us to take in Abdel Aziz.'

'Yes, but how am I to know that you won't knock him off neatly too, push him under a bus or something? Maybe,' added the Servant of Light snidely, 'we should get the regular civil police to lift him for us. Don't you think that would be safer?'

Gad sighed.

'Abdel Aziz is not a violent man,' he said. 'He won't resist.'

'On your head be it,' said the Servant of Light. 'I mean that. Oh, and it can be *you* who tells Mossad about your, ah, *elimination* of Ben Yehuda.'

Gad did, by phone from his own office, in guarded terms. But Dan Abromowitz, whom he found at home, got the message all right. He did not take the news of Ben Yehuda's demise too tragically, particularly when Gad described the stiletto Ben Yehuda had used. Instead, he sounded rather pleased.

Then began the happy hours of Gad's evening. He had his ambush in place outside Abdel Aziz's flat building in Sharia Saleh Ayoub by eight-fifteen. The Russian electronic devices had recorded Abdel Aziz saying goodbye to his *khadama* at seven-thirty and the sound of his front door shutting after that, but he had *not* said when he would be back. Gad had brought two cars for the job. He was in the first, the shiny black Fiat 2000, with Khalil, and there were two other men from his unit in the car behind. The cars were parked quite naturally. There was a wall, and a gateway in it leading through a garden to the entrance to the building. They could pick up their quarry anywhere from the gate to there, get him into Gad's car at the back, with one of the police from behind in with him, and they would then drive him to a certain soundproofed basement in a building not far from the entrance to the Gezira Sporting Club.

That was the theory. Abdel Aziz's building had no *bawwab*, or he was asleep. There was no problem. But for things to work they needed Abdel Aziz, and Abdel Aziz did not come home. Not at nine o'clock. Ten. Eleven. Twelve. One am. Two. Three. But no Abdel Aziz. This meticulous waiting, key to so much police work, was what Daniel Gad was least good at. His impatience tore him to pieces. To stay sane and awake, he talked all he could, quietly, with Raafat Khalil. He even told Khalil a fair amount about Bridget O'Shaunessy, in general terms, with whom he would dearly have preferred to be at the moment. But Gad did not dare to move. He was sick with disappointment that they had not yet got Abdel Aziz. Perhaps he had somehow heard what had happened to Ben Yehuda, and fled the country . . .

Abdel Aziz Fawzi arrived home in a taxi at 3.15 am. The taxi had left, and they had surrounded him before he had taken four paces past his gateway. They showed him their police cards. Abdel Aziz stood massively, his powerful shoulders immobile, his great square hands hanging at his sides like small spades. His mahogany-smooth face was impassive. He might have been expecting something like this to happen all the time. Abdel Aziz stared steadily out at them from his dark-blue suit.

'Could I then at least tell my wife that you are taking me away?'

'I'm afraid that won't be possible.'

Abdel Aziz shrugged and turned and walked between them to the front police car.

Up till 6 am, directing a pitiless high-powered white spotlight ceaselessly upon him, Daniel Gad interrogated Abdel Aziz in the soundproofed basement room, battering him with questions. The police had absolute proof that he, Ben Yehuda, Wahid Hakki and Mainstree were conspiring to bring down the present Egyptian government and replace it with one headed by Abdel Aziz. The police already held Ben Yehuda in Cairo (Gad omitted to add in frozen form in the morgue) after his talk late that afternoon in Abdel Aziz's flat, and Ben Yehuda had told them things. Abdel Aziz had better talk too. Was the attack on the government to be by force? In what form? Using what men? What weapons? Where? When? What fuelled the conspiracy? What were the conspirators' motives? Their objectives? Mainstree had talked of destabilizing the whole of the Arab Middle East. How? Ben Yehuda had talked of creating a lasting benefit to all Islam. How? Abdel Aziz had spoken of a great and noble action for Islam. In what sense? The movement was obviously Islamic Fundamentalist, wasn't it? What was their organization? Its name? Who were their troops? How well trained? What arms and explosives did they have? How did they plan to strike? Against whom? Where? When?

Gad watched the merciless white light beating down on

Abdel Aziz, in brassy counterpoint to the endless hammering rain of questions. He could almost see the twin effect eroding Abdel Aziz's resolve, for the other was sweating heavily now. But not enough. Abdel Aziz still stared back at him monolithically and in total silence. His big smooth face still had its characteristic sheen of almost impenetrable hardwood. It would take crueller measures than these to break the contours of this man's giant stature, to shatter this iron will. Gad got up from his chair and left that to the specialists. Most police forces in the world had them, and used them if the stakes were high enough. Gad was fairly convinced now that the stakes were high enough. But he was not staying for the party. The specialists would know where to find him. For one thing, he was completely exhausted; for another, he got no pleasure out of watching the infliction of physical pain.

It was thus in a fairly morbid frame of mind that Gad got back to his flat in the Corniche el Nil, there to learn from Sergeant Adel Badawi, on shift in his kitchen, that at some time during the night somebody had noiselessly pushed a note under Gad's front door. It was in English, so the sergeant had not been able to read it. He gave it to Gad. It was curt, but to the point. It said:

'We have Bridget. If you want her back, do nothing.'

Gad's entrails plummeted through the floor in shock and horror. He ran to his phone. After a minute a drowsy Deborah answered him.

'I'm sorry,' said Gad, 'Bridget may be in trouble. Could you please check her room?'

'Oh, dear!' said Deborah. 'I thought she was with you. I don't think she's back.'

'While you're there, look out for any signs of a struggle. Anything out of the ordinary. Any sort of signal. Her clothes left in an unusual way. A note.'

'I'll go at once.'

Gad passed his two minutes of waiting in agony. Who the hell was his enemy? He had no doubt it was the same group that had tried to kill him in his flat. Gad had passed these many days since then always half-expecting the grenade under his car in the street, the plastic bomb stuck under his engine, the sniper's shot anywhere, but he understood now that the murder group must simply have calculated coldly that, with Gad forewarned, it just did not pay to try to take him out again by the standard methods, and that they could neutralize him far more effectively by kidnapping Bridget. But who *knows* about me and Bridget? he thought. The answer was almost anyone who had watched him at all consistently. Gad could not think very straight. He felt very tired and confused.

'Nothing,' said Deborah. 'I've looked carefuly. There's nothing unusual. No note.'

'I'd better come over,' said Gad. 'I'll be there in ten minutes.'

His search found nothing unusual in the flat. Deborah said: 'I suppose we have to notify the US Embassy. Call the police.'

'I wouldn't do that yet,' said Gad.

'I think we should,' said Deborah, tall, erect, fair, Scottish and decided.

'I *am* the police,' said Gad, seeing no other way out, and showing her his card.

'Oh my God!' said Deborah.

'Give me time,' said Gad. 'It's me they're after. So I'm probably the only one who can get her back.'

He wished he could believe that himself.

Back in his flat, he sat. He could see nothing that he could do, except wait. He slept fitfully and horribly, on his chair by the phone.

## 20

# *A University Girl's Last Lesson*

That phone woke Gad at 9.20 the next morning, 6 October. He struggled up to it out of his painful unconsciousness.

'Abdel Aziz has just cracked,' said one of the specialists from the soundproofed basement. 'D'you want it over the phone?'

'No, I'll be right there,' said Gad. But first he rang Khalil, already at his Kasr el Nil office.

'They've broken Abdel Aziz,' he said. 'I'm getting there at once. Can you stand by? I'll brief you by phone from there.'

'*Hader*,' said Khalil.

'Also they've kidnapped Bridget,' said Gad.

'Bridget?' said Khalil. '*Ya khassara!*'

In the soundproofed basement the specialist said:

'Abdel Aziz doesn't remember the man's name. Because he never knew it. That's a privilege and a protection which the Angels of the Sword give to those in their activist cells.'

'So it's the Angels of the Sword,' said Gad.

He looked down at Abdel Aziz Fawzi, on his back on the broad bench with its manacles for hands and feet. Abdel Aziz was not manacled because he was unconscious. His eyes, in his bloody mask of a face, were shut. Gad preferred them like that. He preferred that those eyes should not see him. He had admired Abdel Aziz for too many years, from a distance, as a politician of towering moral stature and granite principles, even if these were far from his own.

'But he did admit,' said Gad, 'to taking this special rifle with its telescopic sight to this address in Sharia Mansuriya, just beyond Khan el Khalili, and giving it to the man he described?'

'Yes. That number's a ground-floor flat on the left. The man was thirty or so and *big*. One metre 85 to 90 tall and weighing say 85 to 90 kilos. Dressed in Islamic Fundamentalist white, with white cowl. Most striking feature was his glittering black eyes. Short black beard. But the eyes were hypnotic, he said.'

*Christ!* thought Gad. That, except for the Islamic white, was exactly how, one week ago, the landlord of the trisected chemist Abdallah Hassan had described to Gad by phone a man he now remembered twice having seen near Bab el Louk Station with Fuad, the big-shouldered man who had cleared out Abdallah's room with such lightning speed after his suicide. The links of this Angels of the Sword cell were crystallizing out.

'Couldn't you have got this to me before?' he cried, with rasping urgency.

'He only broke five or ten minutes ago,' said the specialist. 'I called you at once. You wanted nothing on the phone.'

*Broke*, thought Daniel Gad, looking down at the fingers of Abdel Aziz's broad and once powerful hands. He took his eyes away quickly. He looked at his watch: just past quarter to ten. The Presidents' cavalcade in the city's centre had all but started. It would be almost impossible to get messages out now to stop or deflect it without hideous confusion, but he had better try it. As he half-ran to the phone in the corner the specialist called out rapidly:

'And I've told you he said the assassination's for today, the target Mubarak. Somewhere between the fly-off at the Ramses Hilton and the Sheraton on the other side of the Nile. He didn't know where. Then riots.'

'I know!' said Gad, who now did. This was what Ben Yehuda's dying mockery of the anniversary of an anniversary meant. Today was the anniversary of the killing of Sadat, on the anniversary of his nearly successful 6 October 1973 war.

'Don't forget their password for the day!' called the specialist. ' "Holy text and a Sword." '

' "Holy text and a Sword",' said Gad.

As he reached the phone it rung at him. It was Khalil.

'They should have rushed it to us before, *Yafendim*. You recall your Identikit of the big-shouldered Fuad who cleaned out the dead chemist's room? The civil police saw him last night in the Borg Hotel drinking and having a wild dinner with a big man, supposedly Saudi, height say 1 metre 85, weight 85 kilos, very compelling black eyes, clean-shaven. The police saw Fuad there this morning too, gone up to the big man's room, No. 502.'

'*That's it!*' shouted Gad. 'Compelling black eyes! Glittering black eyes! That height and weight! It's Muhammed Abbas Sidki! The 1973 Sagger hero! Of *course* I knew I'd seen his eyes before when I met him in the El Salam reception last month. The big man of the hit team in my bedroom the night before to kill me! And *he* has Bridget – I introduced her to him, he knows he can get to me through her! Khalil, it all ties – Abdel Aziz has cracked. It's Islamic Fundamentalist, called the Angels of the Sword. A repeat of the Sadat killing. They go for Mubarak today in the cavalcade. Sniping. Somewhere between the Ramses Hilton fly-off and the Sheraton – while they're standing. We know now the Borg, Fuad and Abbas Sidki. Look, take this address down. It's 3768 Sharia el Mansuriya, just after Khan el Khalili. Abdel Aziz took a sniper's rifle with telescopic sights there, to a man who must have been Abbas Sidki. It's ground floor first left. It must be their safe house. Khalil, get this all to Abd el Nour at once, and to civil police headquarters. They must get all patrol cars in the area at once to the Borg. I'm there immediately now too – and Khalil!'

'*Effendim?*'

'Would you have a go at their safe house? If they have Bridget anywhere it's there. You're nearer to it. Remember, it's the Angels of the Sword. I'd call yourself Fuad – we know their cell has one. And the password is "Holy text and a Sword".'

'I'll go,' said Khalil. ' "Holy text and a Sword." '

Zeinab had had a pretty good night, all things considered. She had hacked the little American bitch from Boston several times more on each shin with her hard leather shoes just for the sake of good order and discipline, but she had then desisted. For one thing it had been quite hard work. The helpless girl had shown astonishing resistance for a soft American. She had only broken down late; quietly, for she was of course unable to open her mouth. The sight had given Zeinab a distinctly pleasurable warm thrill. Nonetheless it would not be bright to kill the girl by mere physical brutality. Abbas Sidki had made it clear that he would not like that. Zeinab could think of no more powerful an argument for mercy. Mind you, Abbas had *not* said that Zeinab might not shoot the wretched child should there be a rescue attempt or should she herself try to escape. The contrary was true; he had even *ordered* Zeinab to shoot in such circumstances.

Or if she *thought* she was in such circumstances –

But that could wait. Not yet. That could be spun deliciously out. Power over a known enemy was an infinitely pleasant state. Arabs could be magnanimous and deeply compassionate people. They could also have as exquisitely subtle a sense of vengeance as any race in the world. Humiliation, particularly racial humiliation, was a great teacher.

The child was not looking too frisky this fine morning, however, this great historic morning of 6 October. Her eyes were shut from suffering; she was trying to keep it to herself, but being valiant was getting her nowhere. What hope would she have now? Her face was puffed, the right cheek notably swollen, probably from the blow Abbas had so justifiably given her the evening before. All of her jeans from the crotch down was stained black. Their enemy's whore had made noises for minutes on end behind her sticking-plaster gag early that morning, evidently to be allowed to go to the lavatory, but Zeinab had affected steadily not to hear her, until at last the waters had broken. Zeinab, going then herself casually through to the bathroom, had returned to simulate horror and disgust before this infantile sight. There were more ways of degrading a person than by physical blows, though Zeinab added one of those too; a sharp kick to the left kneecap. Now, standing again before this helpless child, she sent a sister kick under the child's right knee; for balance, as it were. The child's eyes came open again in shock, beyond pain now, blank as a blind beggar's.

It amused Zeinab to recognize her need to see the little American bitch as a child, against whom she herself was infinitely mature. She could not in fact have been more than a year or two older than her charge. Still, the vision was deeply accurate. The Americans were a godless and childish race, of no spiritual profundity. Yet they had dared to reject her, Zeinab, of a great and ancient Egyptian civilization. Her Arab ancestors in the thirteenth and fourteenth centuries were creating marvellous heights of culture in Cairo in philosophy, mathematics, sculpture, medicine, science, literature, while this child's forefathers were still rooting about like beasts in muddy and unsanitary hovels in Britain. Yet this same philistine race had scorned and mocked her blood and colour in America, and laughed up its sleeve when her husband betrayed her. All her hatred of that bitter and lasting humiliation concentrated now upon the bound and reeking girl.

This splendid vengeance apart, Zeinab had enjoyed herself in other ways too. The kitchen refrigerator was well stocked with cold chicken, salads, eggs, pineapples, oranges, fruit juices and milk. There were *taamiya* fava beans, and round flat cherubic *khubs* bread. She had a royal chicken and salad feast followed by pineapples that night, taking the laden plates back to the main room where she would see her prisoner, and her prisoner could see her. Afterwards she settled down by the radio with the Umm Kulthum tapes. She played them over and over again:

'The first thing they do is entangle you in love,
Then they demand patience, obedience . . .
And then, with no warning, they leave you . . .

'The Guide was born and all Creation was radiant,
And the faces of the ages smiled and glowed,
Gabriel, the angels round him, brought the
Glad tidings for religion and the world . . .

'  . . . The throne of God and the court bloomed with pride,
And everything near him was excellent . . .

'I do not come to your gate to praise you only,
But, by my praise, to beg you and implore you,
Not for myself alone, but for my poor nation, Egypt . . . '

She revelled in the rounded golden voice, the sense of her
regained identity. She found it hard to believe that she had ever
been so shallow as to trade herself into a materialistic, ruthless,
corrupt and graceless American culture, and, even more
incredibly, marry into it. After that act of personal treason her
Islamic rebirth seemed all the more poignant. Now indeed she
would work without limit for her poor nation, Egypt, and for
all Islam. She would make any sacrifice. She found a superb,
almost sensual glow now to her Islamic faith. It was as if its
very exigencies themselves, its gaunt austerities, its fervent and
selfless devotions to Allah and the *Umma*, were sexually
charged in the sublimest and most rarefied form. Zeinab
vibrated with the desire to serve. She was supremely content.
She could think of no more ideal an Islamic man to serve, or to
serve with, than Abbas.

Zeinab attended sensibly to her material needs too. She slept
well, on one of the main room's two beds, fully dressed, her
pistol at her fingertips, after first thoroughly checking her
captive's bonds, and tightening a few judiciously. She also
fried herself a hearty breakfast of *taamiya* cakes and eggs, and
again took them and an ample pot of coffee back to consume
in the main room. Her prisoner looked at the food hungrily,
and Zeinab, sitting and eating, went through a full debate in
her mind as to whether she should prepare her something. She
decided scrupulously in the end against it; she would have to
take the child's sticking-plaster gag off to let her eat, and
Bridget might always scream.

After her breakfast Zeinab diverted herself with the radio
coverage of the American President's arrival at Cairo Airport
and Mubarak's reception of him, then their cavalcade into the
city. And soon we shall have corrected *that* Abomination with
our hands! thought Zeinab in exaltation.

It was just on ten, and the cavalcade was already passing through the Midan el Tahrir, with the two Presidents standing side by side to take their applause, when she heard the doorbell. She turned down the radio at once and went into the hall, her pistol in her right hand.

'Who is it?'

'Fuad. I've come for the girl.'

'And?'

'Ah. "Holy text and a Sword." '

She opened the door, to the limit of the chain. The hinges were on her right, so it was the left of the door that opened. She looked through the crack. Right-handed, she had not brought her pistol into play. She saw a good-looking Arab of youngish age, in civilian clothes.

'You're not the Fuad I know!'

'Another cell,' said the Arab crisply. 'Here!'

And he dived his right hand, though not to his shirt pocket, but to his waistband. The Colt .45 came out like lightning and the two shots followed immediately, like claps of thunder. She saw the door-chain swing down and loose. The door kicked in on her, and she fell back. As Raafat Khalil came through the doorway she shot him.

Raafat Khalil spun left and down onto the floor. Left shoulder high, he thought crisply, bad but not fatal. The statuesque girl with the noble brow in the Islamic clothes had already turned from him to start to run back towards the main room, doubtless to kill her prisoner, standard procedure, thought Khalil. Learn a last lesson, girl, he thought. Until you're sure he's really dead, *don't* turn your back on an enemy. And, to mark his words, he shot her in it twice.

## 21

# *Flight of an Angel*

It was just on ten. They could not see the cavalcade yet, but they could hear the voice of the crowd, like the sound of a heavy sea breaking and ebbing. The day was fine, a strong sun, no wind, a light-blue sky like spun glass. The crowds massed on the pavements at both sides of Tahrir Bridge. Inside them, standing at the edge of the road itself, were the two long lines of police, neat in their white uniforms, black berets, and black boots. Each carried a Kalashnikov Ak–47 automatic rifle. There was about a metre between each policeman. Each long line of police faced outwards. There was logic to that. It might mean that the Presidents, the guests of honour, would see only the policemen's backs. Nonetheless it was sensible that they faced the people. That, after all, was where any threat was expected to come from.

The two men sat on the balcony of Room 502, their arms across their knees, the Sako Finnbear .30–06 with its high-mounted telescopic sight, and the 9 mm sub-machinegun. No one from any other balcony could see into theirs, nor could anyone from the roads outside. Their breakfasts had long since been eaten, and the trays removed. Abbas Sidki had had his bed made up early. Though they should now be safe from incursions by the staff, they had locked their door.

'When we hear the cavalcade come onto Tahrir Bridge,' said Abbas, 'and that must be within a few minutes now, then, my brother, I think that you should go out into the corridor, with your *bundukiya* hidden under your raincoat. And, my brother Fuad, you must have no mercy against any who come against us. For you and I are bound in the most sacred of all duties, to defend the purity of Islam, our creed.'

Fuad Wahbah, the civil engineer, the heavy-shouldered boxer, had been staring at the cheerful light-blue paint of the inside of the balcony. He shivered suddenly, and looked at Abbas Sidki.

'I shall have no mercy against any enemy of Islam who may come against us.'

Abbas's abruptly beardless face still unnerved him, almost morally; an astonishing nudity. But the tall and powerful body was unchanged, his shining black mesmeric eyes, the majestic certainty of his leadership.

'Whatever happens, Abbas,' he said, 'this has been a great comradeship. A company of good men, brave men, wanting clean aims. It has justified all my life. You have given me that.'

'You have given yourself that,' said Abbas. 'The good and the bravery is from within yourself. The greatness of man's spirit is within him, if he can only find it. It is his personal piece of God. It has been my great fortune to have had men of your quality with me, for a good and just world. Perhaps through this,' he went on a little painfully, touching his rifle, 'we shall come nearer to that good world.'

'*Insha Allah*,' said Fuad. 'If God wills.'

Abbas looked down at the world, at Midan el Tahrir.

'We're near to our great moment now,' he said heavily. 'This is the spear-point stemming from so much pain, and fear, and humiliation, and long and arduous preparation. In a few minutes all that, and we, should be most richly justified.'

'Yes.'

Abbas looked at him.

'It's not why we do it, but Islam will always call us noble,' said Abbas Sidki, almost in a tone of consolation. 'Our people will always remember our names.'

Abbas Sidki heard the police sirens screaming in from the left along Sharia el Gezira below him. All other traffic had been stopped now. At that moment he saw the cavalcade coming onto Tahrir Bridge between the Ministry of Foreign Affairs and the (through Egypt's criminal fault) sadly disused Arab League building. Fuad Wahbah had gone out into the corridor one minute before to protect Abbas's rear. Abbas was probably going to need him. The police cars slammed to a halt below him and police tumbled out of them and ran down the steps into the hotel lobby.

Abbas was curiously unmoved. It was as if he had known all along that this was how it must turn out. It was Allah's will. You had to pay high, even with your life, for great and noble actions. He looked through his telescope at the leading open car. He could see the two Presidents standing in it very clearly, side by side. Now they were no more than a hundred and fifty metres from him. He could shoot at any moment. It gave him a glorious sense of freedom. Whatever they did to him afterwards was unimportant. They could not touch what he already had within his power. *This* was what mattered! In a minute or two, his great mission completed, he would see the Face of God.

The police were up to this landing now. He heard Fuad's sub-machinegun repelling them. Pistols and four or five sub-machineguns replied. He heard Fuad's sub-machinegun suddenly trail away aimlessly. So he heard Fuad die.

Now Abbas's telescopic sight was dead on Mubarak. It was a hundred metres. He could not miss. From Abbas's view-point, Mubarak was on the left, the American President on the right.

'Whosoever amongst you sees an abomination, he must correct it with his hands –'

Abbas Sidki took up the pressure on the trigger.

But if there were two Abominations, should he not first take out the greater?

And did not the greatest evil unquestionably come from this American leader, whose face all the world knew? His was the imperialism of power, the godless materialism, the sexual licence, the corruption, the support to Israel –

Abbas moved the tip of his rifle fractionally to the right and squeezed gently on the trigger as he focused on the face on the right. The beautiful precise rifle in his hands fired itself. He saw the face in his telescopic sight explode red.

As he was about to move the rifle back, the door burst open behind him, and he spun round. A blue-eyed fair man in civilian clothes fired a pistol very fast at him and he took the shots in his chest like blessings. Tarek Daniel Gad, of course, he thought amiably, without a hint of enmity; I've done my task here, nobody can take that away from me, and the best of luck to you –

Other men in uniforms slammed bursts of sub-machinegun fire at him. They hurled him against the balcony wall and over it. He spun down, the black rings of his Saudi *ogals* whirled away, his white head-dress awry, his arms outstretched and his long white robes flapping. The beautiful small gem of a rifle spun companionably down with him. So Muhammed Abbas Sidki, fulfilled and without a shadow of rancour, flew down to meet his God.